THIEF OF SOULS

THIEF
OF
SOULS

BRIAN
KLINGBORG

MINOTAUR
BOOKS
NEW YORK

Published in the United States by Minotaur Books, an imprint of St. Martin's Publishing Group

THIEF OF SOULS. Copyright © 2021 by Brian Klingborg. All rights reserved. Printed in the United States of America. For information, address St. Martin's Publishing Group, 120 Broadway, New York, NY 10271.

www.minotaurbooks.com

Designed by Omar Chapa

The quotation from Zhaungzhi is from *Chuang Tzu: Basic Writings*, translated by Burton Watson (Columbia University Press); the quotes from Chairman Mao are adapted from *Quotations from Chairman Mao Tse-tung* (Peking Foreign Language Press); all other translations are rendered by the author.

The Library of Congress has cataloged the hardcover edition as follows:

Names: Klingborg, Brian, 1967– author.
Title: Thief of souls / Brian Klingborg.
Description: First edition. | New York : Minotaur Books, 2021. | Series: Inspector Lu Fei mystery; 1
Identifiers: LCCN 2020053268 | ISBN 9781250779052 (hardcover) | ISBN 9781250779069 (ebook)
Subjects: LCSH: China—Fiction. | GSAFD: Mystery fiction.
Classification: LCC PS3611.L5629 T48 2021 | DDC 813/.6—dc23
LC record available at https://lccn.loc.gov/2020053268

ISBN 978-1-250-84816-1 (trade paperback)

Our books may be purchased in bulk for promotional, educational, or business use. Please contact your local bookseller or the Macmillan Corporate and Premium Sales Department at 1-800-221-7945, extension 5442, or by email at MacmillanSpecialMarkets@macmillan.com.

First Minotaur Books Trade Paperback Edition: 2022

10 9 8 7 6 5 4 3 2 1

For Lanchi, without whom this book would have never been written

SATURDAY

> Apart from their other characteristics, the outstanding thing about China's 600 million people is that they are "poor and blank." This may seem a bad thing, but in reality it is a good thing. Poverty gives rise to the desire for changes, the desire for action, and the desire for revolution. On a blank sheet of paper free from any mark, the freshest and most beautiful characters can be written; the freshest and most beautiful pictures can be painted.
>
> —*Quotations from Chairman Mao Zedong*

On the night the young woman's corpse is discovered, hollowed out like a birchbark canoe, Inspector Lu Fei sits alone in the Red Lotus bar, determined to get gloriously drunk.

In keeping with the season, Lu's beverage of choice is Shaoxing wine, served in a red earthenware jar and drunk from a rice bowl. It is twenty below outside, and Shaoxing is renowned for "revitalizing the blood" and warming the qi.

But never mind the health benefits—Lu just loves the taste. Sweet, bitter, sour, and spicy, all at once. An apt metaphor for life, fermented and distilled.

The plaintive strains of a Chinese fiddle warble through the bar's cheap sound system. The melody plucks at the frayed filaments of Lu's soul. He closes his eyes and pictures the moon reflecting off the rippling waters of the West Lake. Pink peony blossoms, fluttering in a summer breeze. A naked woman, her smooth skin burnished to a golden glow by candlelight.

"*Yi! Er! San!*" Four men in their early twenties sit at another table, the only other patrons in the bar. Lu has seen them around town but doesn't know their names. They shout and gesticulate wildly as they play a traditional drinking game, the goal of which is to guess how many fingers your opponent will hold out at the count of three. "Drink!" one of the men demands. The loser drinks. The faces of all four are flushed bright red.

Lu sighs. There will be no peace in the Red Lotus tonight, not with these youths guzzling *mao tai* liquor and smoking pack after pack of Zhongnanhai cigarettes. If he were inclined to throw his weight around, he might tell them to keep it down, but it *is* Saturday night, and they have every right to blow off some steam.

Besides—Yanyan needs the business.

Speaking of Yanyan, she approaches, bearing a dish of boiled peanuts and a mild look of disapproval.

"Every weekend, the same thing." She takes a seat and slides the dish over. "Drinking by yourself until you can barely see straight."

Lu pops a peanut into his mouth. "Lacking a companion, I drink alone. I raise my cup and toast the moon. Together, the moon, my shadow, and I make three."

Yanyan takes a peanut for herself. "Who's that? Li Bai?"

"Correct. I'm pleased we can enjoy a mutually beneficial relationship. You supply the drinks, and I provide the poetry."

"You're getting the better end of the deal."

"For sure. In any case, there's no need for me to drink with just the moon and my shadow. Bring a cup over."

"I can't. I'm working."

"Call it customer service, if that makes you feel better."

"Hey, pretty lady!" One of the young men at the other table waves his cigarette. "We need some beers."

Yanyan gives Lu a wan smile and gets up to fetch the drinks. Lu shoots the kid a baleful stare, then pours himself another bowl of wine. He watches Yanyan collect four bottles of Harbin Premium lager from the chiller.

She is tall and long-limbed, with thick black hair, a high forehead, and large, expressive eyes. Full lips and cheeks that are always a charming shade of pink, as if kissed by the cold.

Lu has never asked her age, but he believes Yanyan is in her midthirties, a few years younger than himself. He knows she is a widow. Her husband died a few years back of some illness or another, leaving her to run the Red Lotus by herself. It is a tiny place, just four tables, serving drinks and basic snacks, nothing special. Most nights, it brings in only a handful of customers. It's not an easy way to make a living. But for a country girl like Yanyan, it's better than working in the fields or at some other menial, dead-end job.

Lu is secretly smitten with her. So, he suspects, are the four men playing drinking games.

And a sizable percentage of the male population in Raven Valley Township.

Yanyan carries the bottles over. One of the young men plucks at her sleeve and asks her to join them. She brushes him off, same as she did Lu. All four of them stare at her wolfishly as she walks away.

Lu finds this irritating, but understandable. He, too, cannot help but stare wolfishly at Yanyan.

His cell phone rings. It's the *paichusuo*—the local Public Security Bureau station.

The PSB, in the People's Republic, is analogous to a Western police department, with branches at the provincial, county, municipal, and local levels. PSB officers are responsible for crime prevention and investigation, traffic and fire control, public safety, household registration, and keeping tabs on foreigners and visitors.

In Raven Valley, a modestly sized township about seventy kilometers from Harbin City, the station is staffed by a chief, a deputy chief—that's Lu's official role—a sergeant, and a handful of constables.

But Lu is not on duty tonight. So why is the *paichusuo* calling him?

He answers. "Lu Fei."

"Inspector!" Lu recognizes the voice on the end of the line. Constable Huang, aged twenty-one, excitable disposition, dumb as a wheelbarrow full of pig shit.

"What is it, Constable? It's my night off."

"I know, Inspector, but there's been a . . . a . . ."

"Go on," Lu says.

Huang whispers. "A *murder*."

Lu sits up a little straighter. "Why are you whispering?"

"I don't know."

"Did you call the chief?"

Lu means Chief Liang, his direct superior.

"He didn't answer his phone," Huang says.

Lu looks at his watch. It's a little past nine. A bit early for the chief to be in his cups, but not inconceivable.

"Where?" Lu says.

"Where didn't he answer?" Huang asks.

"No, Constable. Where is the scene of the . . ." He is suddenly aware of the men at the other table listening in. "Incident?"

"Oh. Yang residence. Kangjian Lane."

That is on the outskirts of town. Lu is familiar with the area but doesn't personally know any Yangs who live there. "Is there a suspect in custody?"

"No suspects yet."

"Okay. I'm at the Red Lotus bar. Have someone come get me."

He hangs up. The young men are looking at him. "What's going on?" one of them asks. "Something exciting?"

"No," Lu says. He does not elaborate. He swallows the last of the wine and considers pouring another round, but decides against it. He puts money on the table and stoppers the earthenware jar. "Sister Yan, please keep this jar safe until such time I am free to renew its acquaintance."

"Of course, Inspector."

Lu shrugs into his coat and pulls a hat over his ears. He goes to the front door and slips on a pair of gloves while he waits. When the patrol car arrives, he gives Yanyan a quick wave and heads out into the cold.

There are five police officers in the car. And it is not a large car. But the *paichusuo* possesses only two patrol vehicles, as well as a small fleet of scooters, bicycles, and one riot van that always reeks of boiled cabbage, although no one seems to know why.

Behind the wheel is Sergeant First Class Bing. Bing is in his early fifties, short, squat, and tough as old rhinoceros hide. Lu likes and respects him very much.

Crammed into the back seat are constables Sun, Li, Wang, and Wang. Of course, there are two Wangs. It is the second-most common surname in China.

Constable Sun is female, midtwenties, generally cheerful and competent. She scored well enough on her national exams to attend a top university in Heilongjiang Province. Lu is mystified as to why she elected to join the Public Security Bureau. Better she had majored in accounting or business and gotten moderately wealthy. Now she is doomed to a life of high risk and low reward in a profession dominated by men who crack crude jokes and compulsively scratch at their balls as if they were lottery tickets.

Constable Li is thirty, cadaverously thin, and never speaks unless spoken to. His colleagues call him *Li Yaba*—"Li the Mute."

Wang number one's given name is Ming, but as he's a few kilos over his ideal weight, he is known to most folks as *Wang Pang Zi*—"Fatty Wang." He takes no offense to this. On the contrary, it's considered an affectionate nickname in the People's Republic.

The second Wang's given name is Guangrong. He is the kind of man who became a police officer out of some deep-seated insecurity, believing the uniform would provide him with the deference and respect he so desperately craves.

Sadly, after a thousand-plus years of corruption, abuse, and incompetence, many Chinese citizens regard the institution of law enforcement as equivalent to a pit of quicksand. A hazard that is largely avoidable—but if you are careless enough to step in it, you're probably screwed.

At 185 centimeters and 83 kilos, Wang Guangrong is a big man, even for a northern boy raised on wheat, mutton, and pork. As a consequence, everyone calls him "Big Wang."

"Are you drunk?" Sergeant Bing says by way of greeting when Lu climbs into the passenger seat.

"When presented with wine, one should sing," Lu quotes. "For who knows how long you might live?"

"Is that a yes?"

"I'm sober. Ish."

"Sorry to call you on your night off. We tried to raise the chief, but you know how that goes."

"No problem. It's my duty."

On the drive to Kangjian Lane, Sergeant Bing brings Lu up to speed.

"The neighbor—a Mrs. Chen—claims the Yangs' dog has been barking incessantly since last night. She finally got fed up and went over to complain and found the dog shivering in the yard. She knocked on the front door, but no one answered, so she went inside. She found the victim in the bathroom."

"What do we know about her? The victim?"

Sun leans forward and reads from a notepad. "Ms. Yang Fenfang. Aged twenty-three. Single. High school graduate. Born and raised on Kangjian Lane. For the past three years, residing in Harbin City. Her father died eight years ago and her mother just recently. A week ago, in fact. No criminal record."

Lu nods. Already, his mind is swirling with possible motives and potential suspects, but for now he prefers to ignore such thoughts and evaluate the crime scene without any preconceived notions.

Kangjian Lane is one of the last residential streets before Raven Valley proper yields to expansive grain fields leased by huge corporate agricultural conglomerates. The houses here are old and ramshackle, with sizable yards where the locals keep small vegetable gardens and perhaps a few pigs or a handful of chickens.

The *paichusuo*'s other patrol car is parked in front of the Yangs' property, and a constable sits inside it, with the engine running, smoking a cigarette. His surname is Chu. Like Big Wang, Chu is a bully. Lu has taken to calling him *Yuehan Weien,* after the American actor with the round belly who made cowboy movies and always played a heroic tough guy. Chu does not like this nickname, but given Lu's seniority, there isn't much he can do about it.

Sergeant Bing parks the car, and everyone disembarks. Lu glances up at the row of telephone posts arranged along the lane. The People's Republic has embarked upon an ambitious plan to blanket much of the country with an extensive network of surveillance cameras. Already, major cities like Beijing and Shanghai are nearly 100 percent covered. But in Raven Valley, this technology is available only in the center of town.

While Lu has mixed feelings about the surveillance program, he cannot help but admit it would make his job easier if there were one or two cameras here to capture the events that have recently transpired.

He takes a minute to get his bearings, then starts issuing orders. He posts Sun at the entrance to the front yard. He dispatches Yuehan Chu and Fatty Wang to canvass the neighborhood to the east, Big Wang and Li the Mute to canvass to the west. He opens the trunk of the patrol car and roots around for a box of latex gloves. He and Sergeant Bing each slip on a pair.

They enter the yard and make their way toward the house, Lu motioning for Sergeant Bing to watch where he puts his feet. The ground is covered with a layer of dirty iced-over snow, and Lu wants to avoid trampling on any tracks the suspect may have left.

There is a white banner draped over the front door, signifying a recent death in the family.

Two deaths, Lu amends silently.

Lu opens the door and they enter. It is nearly as cold inside the house as it is outside. Traditional northern homes like this one lack central heating—they are warmed by means of a *kang*—a brick-and-clay platform used as a bed or sitting area with a hollow space beneath where a fire is lit. But no fire has been kindled at the Yang residence today.

Despite the chill, Lu picks up the scent of a dead body immediately. An odor reminiscent of raw pork. Sergeant Bing takes a cotton face mask out of his coat pocket and strings it over his mouth and nose.

"Did you bring one for me?" Lu says.

"We can take turns."

They are standing in a short hallway. To the right is a living room, and to the left, a bedroom. Straight ahead, the open mouth of what Lu assumes is the kitchen.

Lu and Sergeant Bing make an initial sweep.

In the living room, Lu notes the *kang,* heaped with padded quilts and cushions, a large cabinet, two wooden chairs, a low stand draped with a tattered quilt, a space heater, and, brightening the drab plaster wall, a New Year's couplet on red paper and a giveaway calendar printed by Raven Valley's largest corporate agricultural enterprise, Abundant Harvest Industries.

The cabinet looks to be an antique, its dark varnish cracked and peeling. The bottom half is a closed compartment decorated with chipped mother-of-pearl inlay and a painting of flowers and butterflies. Above this is a shelf where a black-and-white funeral portrait of a middle-aged lady and her ancestral tablet have been placed, along with an urn for incense and a few offerings of food and drink. Lu leans in to read the tablet—it is inscribed with the name Yang Hong. He assumes this is the recently deceased mother of Yang Fenfang.

Behind the shelf are irregularly sized niches stuffed with little treasures—carved figurines, a cloisonné jar, a porcelain flower vase, a lacquered wooden box shaped like a peach, and so on.

The bedroom is tidy but cramped, with a bed, a cheap wooden vanity (its mirror covered with red cloth), a chest of drawers, a plastic zip-up wardrobe, a floor fan, another space heater, and other furnishings.

Heading down the hallway to the kitchen, Lu and Sergeant Bing pass the bathroom door, slightly ajar. By unspoken agreement, they do not look inside.

Not yet.

The kitchen is large and serves as a combination food preparation area, dining room, and all-purpose storage space. There is an ancient wood-burning stove, the walls above it blackened by the smoke of a thousand home-cooked meals. Cabinets and racks are stuffed with crockery, cooking ingredients, tins of biscuits, and so on. Rice sacks and plastic water jugs sit on the floor. Lu sees a few appliances of recent manufacture on the counter—a rice cooker, a deep fryer, an electric teakettle. A dining table dominates the center of the room. An electric scooter leans against one wall. A dog's sheepskin-lined bed lies underfoot. The atmosphere is one of organized chaos.

Sergeant Bing tries the door leading to the backyard. "Still locked."

They return to the living room and search it more thoroughly, kneeling to peek under the furniture and inspecting any stains or markings on the floor and walls. There are no obvious signs of a struggle. No blood, no mess. But some of the objects in the cabinet are slightly askew—as if they've been jumbled or knocked over, then set back in place.

"The suspect and victim fought and knocked up against the cabinet?" Sergeant Bing suggests.

"Could be."

They return to the bedroom. Lu unzips the plastic wardrobe. He finds a bipolar assortment of apparel—half somber working clothes and half chic outfits. Lu guesses the former belonged to the deceased mother and the latter to the deceased daughter.

"How did Mother Yang die?" Lu asks.

"Don't know, but must have been natural causes or there'd be an incident report. Why? Think it's related to this?"

"Let's just remember to check the death certificate."

While Sergeant Bing roots through the chest of drawers, Lu inspects the vanity. He removes the cloth covering the mirror and finds a strip of photo booth prints showing a young woman striking different poses. It's hard to tell if she's pretty, because the prints are overlaid with fuzzy filters and flourishes—a cartoon cat nose, whiskers, artificially enlarged eyes. But Lu figures this must be Yang Fenfang.

Sitting on top of the vanity are a supply of cosmetics, a hairbrush, two cell phones, one newish and one an older model, and a jewelry box. Lu opens the box. He finds earrings, necklaces, rings. Some of them might be of value, but Lu doesn't have an eye for such things.

He picks up the newer cell phone. It is charged but requires a pass code. The screensaver displays another photo, likewise highly filtered, of Yang Fenfang. The older cell phone is out of power.

Beneath the vanity, resting on the floor, is a purse. Lu tugs it out. He searches for a wallet and finds one. He opens it and removes Yang Fenfang's identity card. He shows it to Sergeant Bing.

"She looks just like Fan Bingbing," is Sergeant Bing's generous assessment.

"Really?" Lu holds the ID card up to the ceiling light and takes a closer look.

Fan Bingbing is famous not only for her beauty and her status as the highest-paid actress in the Chinese film industry but also for mysteriously disappearing from public view after being accused by the government of tax evasion. Rumors spread that she was under house arrest or even that she'd fled to the United States. When she did resurface, ten months later, she issued an apology in typical Chinese fashion: "I failed the country which nurtured me. I failed the society which trusted me. I failed the fans who loved me. I beg everyone's forgiveness!"

Lu half laughs to think about it. Less than a decade ago, Hollywood was the undisputed king of the international box office. Now China is the fastest-growing film industry in the world, with annual revenues and audience numbers that far exceed North America.

And with first-world status comes first-world problems. As the People's Republic is discovering on a daily basis.

While Lu doesn't see the resemblance to Fan Bingbing, he can't deny Yang Fenfang is—*was*—an attractive young woman. He slips the card into his pocket.

In the chest of drawers, Sergeant Bing finds clothes, folded and mothballed. Papers, receipts. Jewelry and personal items that likely belonged to Mother Yang. And her identity card, which he hands to Lu. Lu is struck by how young she looks in the photo, but then realizes if Yang Fenfang was only twenty-three, her mother was probably still in her forties when she died.

"Hard to tell if anything is missing," Sergeant Bing says. "Want to keep searching?"

"We should probably . . . you know."

Sergeant Bing nods toward the door. "After you, boss."

In the hallway, Lu takes a breath, holds it, then pushes open the bathroom door.

The room is small and rudimentary, with cement walls, a squat toilet, a shallow water basin fed by a rubber hose, and a sink with a mirror hanging over it.

Yang Fenfang's body lies on the floor. She wears a yellow silk dress. Her hair is coiled into a neat bun. Her face is fully made-up. Powder, lipstick, eye shadow.

She looks, truly, like a porcelain doll. Even down to the cold, dead eyes.

The translucent white of her skin contrasts with angry red welts encircling her neck and wrists.

Lu doesn't step into the room. He peers at the floor, walls, and ceiling, searching for any visible evidence. There is nothing.

"Looks like she was dressed for a date," Sergeant Bing says.

"Don't say it," Lu warns.

"What?"

"A date with *death.*"

"I would never," Sergeant Bing says. "Only a sick mind would even think of such a joke."

Guilty as charged, Lu thinks. "Seen enough?"

"More than enough."

"Okay, let's go."

Lu and Sergeant Bing walk down the lane to interview the neighbor, Mrs. Chen. She lives with her elderly mother, adult son, daughter-in-law, and grandson. The entire family is present for the interview. Lu suggests that perhaps the grandson be taken into the bedroom or kitchen, to no avail.

Mrs. Chen's daughter-in-law serves them tea. Her son smokes and fidgets. Her mother watches a large television with the sound cranked up. The grandson runs around the room like a dervish on amphetamines.

Yang Fenfang's dog cowers under a table. Lu is generally fond of dogs, but this one is extraordinarily ugly. Small, pig-faced, rat-tailed, with a rhinestone-studded collar. A city dog, for sure.

Mrs. Chen is a frumpy woman of about sixty. Lu asks where her husband is.

"Working, in the city," Mrs. Chen says. She tells Lu what he already knows. The dog was barking most of Friday night, today, and this evening. Finally, she could stand it no longer and went over to complain.

"Yang Fenfang doted on that dog," she says. "He ate better than most humans. He was always a yapper, but it wasn't like her to not pay the little beast any attention." She goes on to relate the discovery of the dog shivering outside and then Yang's body in the bathroom, pausing to weep for effect. The dog, right on cue, begins to bark at the grandson. The grandson screeches like a barn owl. The TV blares.

"Have you seen any strangers around recently?" Lu asks.

"Not really, but I'm usually in bed by nine. If strangers are prowling around in the middle of the night, I wouldn't know."

"Any idea who might do this to Yang Fenfang?"

Mrs. Chen blows her nose and shakes her head.

"What can you tell me about her?"

"She wasn't too smart, but she was pretty. A couple of years after graduating from high school, she moved to the city to find work. The younger generation—none of them want to live in the country anymore. Make an honest living. Get dirt under their fingernails. They think if they move to Harbin, grains of rice and gold coins will drop from the sky into their pockets." She gives her son a sidelong glare. He picks at his nose and holds the cigarette in front of his face like a shield.

"What kind of work?" Sergeant Bing says. He is taking notes in neat block characters.

"I don't know, but I can guess. When she returned to visit her mother—which was almost never—she wore these skirts up to here and these shirts down to there." She demonstrates with a hand that shifts from crotch to navel. "Slathered makeup all over her face. And high *heels*! Who in their right mind would wear high heels in our little neighborhood?"

Lu declines to speculate. "But she recently moved back home?"

"A couple of months ago, when Sister Yang's condition started to get worse."

"What was the nature of Mrs. Yang's illness?"

Mrs. Chen shrugs. "Who knows? The doctors sure didn't. Better you light incense at a temple than go to a hospital."

"I'm inclined to agree, Mrs. Chen," Lu says. "So . . . Yang Fenfang returned to care for her mother."

"Yes, and Sister Yang died a week ago. I'm surprised Fenfang isn't—wasn't—already back in the city. I expected her to run off the second her mother was cremated."

"Perhaps she was observing a period of mourning."

Mrs. Chen dabs at her eyes. "Better she was here to care for her mother when she was alive than sitting alone in an empty house when she's dead."

Mrs. Chen's evaluation of the victim strikes Lu as ungenerous. Yang Fenfang had obviously forged a life for herself in Harbin. One that probably afforded her a standard of living she could never hope to achieve in a township like Raven Valley. Yet when her mother had grown ill, she'd immediately returned, as a filial daughter should.

"While your parents are alive, comply with the rites in serving them," Lu quotes. "When they die, comply with the rites in burying them."

"What?" Mrs. Chen says.

"Master Kong."

"Oh." Mrs. Chen dismisses Confucius, the most influential philosopher China has produced in over four thousand years of continuous civilization, with an indifferent wave of her hand.

Lu grows anxious to wrap up the questioning. The grandson, dog, and TV are conspiring to give him a migraine. "Did Yang Fenfang have a boyfriend that you know of?"

"Well, I don't really know what she was getting up to in the city. Perhaps she had *lots* of boyfriends."

"I mean locally."

"Oh. In high school, I think she had one. His surname was Zhang. He lived over on Yongzheng Road. I don't know the family personally; I just remember Sister Yang talking about how he was always following Fenfang around like a lost little puppy."

"Thank you, Mrs. Chen. You've been helpful. We'll probably be back to ask more questions, but that will do for now. I'm very sorry for the shock you experienced this evening."

This elicits a fresh bout of weeping. Lu and Sergeant Bing hastily take their leave.

Outside, Lu rubs his temples. "Good thing I don't carry a gun or I might have started spraying bullets."

"Did you see the son? He was bouncing around like there was a fistful of hot chestnuts stuffed up his ass."

"A vivid description, Sergeant, but yes, I agree—he seemed nervous. Perhaps it was our uniforms. Anyway, I'm curious about the boyfriend Mrs. Chen mentioned."

"I'll have Constable Huang check the *hukou* records, see if we can pin him down."

The *hukou* is a mandatory household registration system that categorizes citizens, according to birthplace, as either urban or rural residents and tracks all births, deaths, marriages, divorces, and relocations. Its lawful purpose is to "maintain social order and be of service to the establishment of socialism." In practice, it is very much a means to keep tabs on China's huge populace.

As they make their way back up toward the Yang residence, Sergeant Bing places a call to Constable Huang and tells him to run a search for a Mr. Zhang, approximate age twenty-three, who lives on Yongzheng Road.

After the chaos of the Chen household, Lu enjoys the soft crunch of his shoes on the frozen ground and the scent of woodsmoke in the frosty air. The neighborhood is still and silent, and the windows of most residences are dark, apart from the occasional soft blue glow of a television set. It's early to bed and early to rise this far north.

Lu considers the boyfriend a viable lead. More than half the murders committed in rural China are the result of a love affair gone wrong. Perhaps Yang Fenfang dumped this Zhang kid soon after moving to Harbin. That sort of thing isn't at all unusual. A country girl finds herself in the big city, and suddenly her paramour back home seems unspeakably bumpkinish in comparison to the more worldly—and well-heeled—men she encounters.

By now, the constables dispatched to canvass the lane have returned and are sitting in one of the patrol cars, smoking cigarettes with the windows up and the engine on, sheltered from the bitter cold. Lu inquires if the neighbors saw or heard anything suspicious.

The neighbors did not.

Lu assigns Li the Mute and Big Wang to keep watch over the house. "Get some crime scene tape out of the trunk and cordon off the front and backyards."

"How long do we have to stay here?" Big Wang asks.

"Until further notice."

"What's that mean?"

"Just what I said."

"Are you going to at least leave us one of the cars?"

"No."

"We'll freeze to death!"

"Don't be so dramatic, Constable Wang. You can stay in the living room of the house. But make sure you don't touch anything, and do not, under any circumstances, enter the bathroom. If you have to take a piss, do it outside. And don't trample around the yard. The suspect might have left footprints or some trace evidence behind."

Lu starts to walk away, then turns back.

"Oh, and keep your eyes and ears pricked for anyone skulking around," he says. "Sometimes, as they say, the murderer returns to the scene of the crime."

Li the Mute gulps audibly. It is the first vocalization Lu has heard him make in over a week.

Lu tells Yuehan Chu and Fatty Wang to take one of the patrol cars and go home. "Keep your phones handy, though. You're on call if anything else happens tonight."

"I'm not supposed to be working this weekend," Chu grumbles.

"That makes two of us."

Sergeant Bing finishes speaking to Constable Huang. "Only one family on Yongzheng Road with an individual surnamed Zhang who is of the right age."

"What's the kid's full name?" Lu asks.

"Zhang Zhaoxing."

"Criminal record?"

"None."

"All right, let's go over there now," Lu says.

He, Sergeant Bing, and Constable Sun pile into the remaining patrol car and drive to Yongzheng Road.

Zhang lives in a broken-down house on a modest patch of land enclosed by a crumbling brick wall. Lu searches for surveillance cameras mounted on the telephone wire posts outside, and as he expects, there are none.

He turns to Sergeant Bing. "Why don't you head around back?"

Sergeant Bing nods and wordlessly slips off into the darkness. Lu walks through the front gate and motions Constable Sun to follow.

The yard is cluttered and unkempt. A dormant Harbin pear tree rises out of the earth like a skeletal hand emerging from a grave. Piles of old bricks, broken farm tools, empty feed sacks, scraps of rotten vegetables, and broken plant urns litter the ground. Along one part of the wall, someone has erected a do-it-yourself outbuilding that defies the laws of physics. Lu can hear the soft cluck of chickens coming from inside it.

The house is very old—brick walls, waxed paper windows, and a timber-and-tile roof supported by heavy wooden posts.

Lu sees weak light bleeding through the paper windows, flickering and pulsating. He waits a few moments, giving Sergeant Bing time to get into position. Then he extends a hand to Sun. "Give me your baton." She does so. "Wait outside until I call you," he says.

"I'm not a delicate flower, Inspector," Sun protests. "Please don't feel obligated to protect me."

Lu stops to consider her words. Although firearms are exceedingly hard to come by in the People's Republic—even Lu does not routinely carry one in his capacity as a police officer—every Chinese home maintains a collection of kitchen knives and cleavers. Most rural households also have access to a range of potentially lethal farm implements—machetes, sickles, and the like.

Who knows what awaits them inside Zhang's house? A madman wielding an ax?

But as Chairman Mao Zedong once said, "Women hold up half the sky."

"Fine," Lu says. "But since I have the baton, stay behind me."

Lu doesn't bother to knock. In the People's Republic, private property remains a loosely interpreted concept. He opens the door and yells, "Public Security Bureau!"

He finds himself in a filthy room with cracked plaster walls, a tiled floor, and exposed beams overhead. A huge *kang,* large enough to sleep a family of four, is built into one wall. A fire must be lit under it, because the room is stiflingly hot. A TV sits opposite the *kang.*

The TV is on, with the sound off. It's showing a hoary old classic: *The East Is Red.* A 1960s song-and-dance extravaganza that is something of a cross between Beijing Opera and a classic American musical—*West Side Story* or perhaps *Oklahoma!*—dished up with a generous serving of Maoist propaganda.

The film is just now reaching its climax—dozens of apple-cheeked agricultural workers, proletariats, and People's Liberation Army soldiers cavort in front of a backdrop depicting an enormous portrait of Chairman Mao hanging over the front gate of the Imperial City.

As a schoolchild, Lu was subjected to multiple viewings of *The East*

Is Red in his political and moral education classes. It was on constant repeat in waiting rooms at doctors' offices and the lobbies of government buildings, anywhere that required ideologically innocuous entertainment. During public holidays, it frequently preempted the cartoons that Lu preferred, such as *Black Cat Detective* or *The Gourd Brothers.*

As a consequence, Lu hates the film.

"Inspector," Sun says. She points.

There is a man lying on the *kang*. Lu didn't notice him at first because he is nearly hidden beneath a heap of blankets. The man has not reacted to Lu's intrusion. Not a peep. Not a twitch.

Lu takes a step closer.

The man looks to be about eighty. His eyes are half-closed. The action on the TV screen is mirrored in the tiny slivers of cornea that are visible between his wrinkled and sagging eyelids.

"*Ta ma de,*" Lu says. Literally, this means "his mother," but in this context, it is like saying, "Oh shit!"

Lu's first thought is that, despite his age, the man is Zhang Zhaoxing's father, and Zhang has murdered him in addition to the Yang girl. He feels a shiver of dread. Dead things are unclean. Dead things bring bad luck.

He knows, logically, that this isn't true—he's studied biology in university, he's aware that death is simply the cessation of bodily functions. As his favorite Daoist philosopher Zhuangzi once said, "Life and death are like day and night. Death and life have the same root, like twins."

Simple as that. Part of nature.

But despite his thoroughly modern education, come the seventh month of the lunar calendar, when tradition holds that the gates of heaven and hell open and spirits are free to roam the earth, Lu is hard-pressed to ignore the creeping suspicion that invisible entities stalk the night, prowling for offerings of rice and incense.

E gui. Hungry ghosts. Those unfortunate souls who died without descendants to provide for them in the afterlife.

The man suddenly shocks Lu with a sharp cough, then begins snoring.

"*Cao!*" Lu mutters.

So not dead, after all. Apparently, the old geezer just sleeps with his eyes open.

Lu spies a doorway leading to the back of the house, with a thread-bare blanket acting as a partition. He uses the tip of the baton to pull it aside cautiously. He slips through, into the kitchen.

Lu sees an old-fashioned wood-burning stove, and next to it, a bam-boo rack holding an assortment of cooking oils and condiments and a motley collection of bowls, dishes, and utensils. A small round table and three stools sit in the center of the room. Directly ahead is a door leading to the backyard. Pushed up against the side wall is a cot.

A young man lies sideways on the cot, his back to Lu. He is looking down at something.

Lu motions for Sun to be quiet as she comes in behind him.

"Zhang Zhaoxing," Lu says.

Zhang—if that is indeed he—does not respond.

"He's wearing earphones," Sun remarks.

Lu steps over and taps Zhang's shoulder with the baton. Zhang looks up at Lu, his eyes go wide with surprise, and he springs off the cot. The phone in his hand goes flying.

"Easy!" Lu says, holding out a hand. "Public Security Bureau. Are you Zhang Zhaoxing?"

Zhang stares at Lu in abject terror.

"Are you Zhang Zhaoxing?" Lu repeats.

"What?"

"I'm looking for Zhang Zhaoxing. Are you him?"

"Who are you?"

"Inspector Lu. Public Security Bureau."

"I didn't do anything."

"So you *are* Zhang Zhaoxing?"

"Yes."

"Are you carrying a weapon?"

"A what?"

"A weapon."

Zhang's eyes skitter wildly in their sockets.

"Are you carrying a weapon?" Lu says again. "A knife?"

"I . . . No."

"Get down on your knees."

Zhang doesn't.

"On your *knees*!"

Zhang sinks to the floor, his joints cracking.

"Open the back door for Sergeant Bing," Lu says.

Constable Sun opens it, and Bing comes in, baton in hand.

"Search him, please," Lu says.

Sergeant Bing holsters his baton and frisks Zhang.

"Constable Sun, check the bed," Lu says.

Sun runs her hands across the blankets, over the pillow, and under the thin mattress.

Neither Sergeant Bing nor Sun find anything of note.

Lu points to the cot with the baton. "Sit down."

Zhang reaches for his phone.

"Leave it!" Lu says.

Zhang reluctantly sits on the cot. He shakes and trembles like a cold, wet dog. Constable Sun retrieves the phone and hands it to Lu.

"I didn't do anything," Zhang says.

Lu gives him the once-over. Zhang is large for a Chinese country boy. Not as tall but perhaps heavier than Big Wang. His hair is cut short and amateurishly so—there are big bald patches where the electric razor has followed a scorched earth policy. He has a round face, flat nose, thick lips. A scatter of acne across his cheeks and chin. His eyes are the color of mud.

It is the face of an ox. Slow. Vacant.

"Who is that in the other room?" Lu says. "The elderly man?"

"My grandfather."

"Is he all right?"

"Isn't he?"

"When we came in, he didn't move or say anything. Is he sick?"

"No." Zhang says. "Just old. And deaf."

"Where's your mother and father?"

"Gone."

"Gone where?"

Zhang gives Lu a quizzical look. "Dead."

"Both?"

"Yes."

"How did they die?"

"They got sick."

"At the same time?"

"No."

"When, then, Zhang Zhaoxing?"

"My mother, when I was a boy. My father, when I was in high school."

"What kind of sickness?"

Zhang shrugs.

"Where's your identity card?" Lu asks.

"There." Zhang points to the round table. Lu sees an ID card, an empty bottle of lemon-flavored soda, some crumpled yuan, a set of keys. Lu picks up the card, looks at the picture. It's Zhang, all right. He puts it in his pocket.

"So it's just you and your grandfather, then?" Lu asks.

"Yes."

"You're not married?"

"Not yet."

"What's that mean?"

Zhang shrugs.

"I asked you a question. What do you mean, 'not yet'?"

Zhang covers his mouth. It seems to Lu that he's stifling a grin.

"Answer me."

"I have a girlfriend," Zhang says.

"What girlfriend?"

"I can't say."

"Why?"

Zhang shrugs.

Lu isn't sure if Zhang is being purposely evasive or if he suffers from some kind of *mao bing*—mental defect.

"I'm Public Security Bureau," Lu says. "You have to answer my questions."

"She told me not to tell anyone."

"I'm not in the mood for games. Answer me or I'll take you down to the station and let the sergeant here pry off a few toenails."

Zhang's eyes nearly pop out of his skull. "Her name's Fenfen."

"What's her full name?"

"Yang Fenfang."

Lu and Sergeant Bing exchange a look.

"When's the last time you saw this Yang Fenfang?" Lu says.

"I'm not sure."

"Well, I need you to be sure. When?"

"The funeral."

"What funeral?"

"Her mom's funeral."

"When was that?"

"A week ago."

"Where?"

"Where what?"

"*Ta ma de,*" Lu says. "Where was the funeral held?"

"The funeral home. Outside of town. There's only one."

"When was the last time you were at the Yang residence?"

"I don't know. Can I have my phone back?"

"No. How long since you were at the Yang residence?"

"I can't remember." Zhang digs a finger into his ear.

"A month? A year?"

"Maybe . . . maybe a few months."

"Where do you work, Zhaoxing?"

"The pork processing plant."

"And what is your job there?"

"I work on the separation station."

"What's the separation station?"

"It's where we cut the meat into different parts for packaging."

"Describe exactly what you do there."

"Why?" Zhang says.

Sergeant Bing leans over and whaps Zhang across the top of his head. "Just answer the inspector's questions!"

"That won't be necessary, Sergeant Bing."

"Yes, Inspector. Sorry."

"Why don't you search the next room? Don't bother the elder Zhang if you can avoid it."

Chastened, Sergeant Bing slides through the curtained doorway.

Lu pulls a stool out from under the table and sits down. "Go on. Tell me about your job."

Zhang rubs his head and shrugs. "The pigs come down on a conveyer belt. We cut them into pieces. The shoulder, the hock, trotter, loin, ribs. Then they get packaged."

"How long have you worked there?"

"Since high school. I started out cleaning up pig shit. Then I moved to the bloodletting station. I've only been on the separation station for eight months."

"Bloodletting?"

"Yes."

"Explain."

Zhang rolls his eyes. "After the pigs are stunned, we cut their throats and drain the blood out."

"You use a knife for that?"

"What else would we use?"

"Answer the question," Lu growls.

"Yes. A knife."

"Did you work this Friday?"

"I work every Friday, except Lunar New Year."

"And what did you do after work? This past Friday?"

"Came home."

"And then what?"

"And then nothing. That was it."

"You didn't go out?"

"Where would I go?"

"How about to see your girlfriend?"

Zhang shrugs, his go-to response.

"Yes or no, Zhang Zhaoxing?"

"No. I just came home."

"This is where you sleep? In the kitchen?"

"Yes," Zhang says. "My grandfather snores. And sometimes he pisses himself."

"And he's deaf, you said?"

"He can't hear a single thing."

If what Zhang says is true, he could easily come and go at night through the back door with his grandfather none the wiser. "We're going to have a look around. You will sit right there on the bed. Do not get up. Understand?"

"I didn't do anything."

"Just sit still." Lu returns the baton to Constable Sun. "If he misbehaves, give him a thump."

Lu goes into the front room. Sergeant Bing has found nothing in his search. Grandpa Zhang remains sound asleep.

"Let's look around the property," Lu says.

"Do you think it's safe to leave Constable Sun alone with him?" Sergeant Bing says.

"We shouldn't treat her any differently from how we would one of the other constables."

"I wouldn't trust most of them to be alone with him, either."

"True, but the kid doesn't strike me as dangerous."

"That's who you have to watch out for. The ones who don't strike you as being dangerous—until they actually strike you."

"You're on a roll tonight, Sergeant Bing. I think she's fine. Come on."

They sniff around the yard, then enter the jury-rigged outbuilding. Inside is a chicken coop, some gardening tools, a bicycle, assorted junk. And, hanging from the rafters, a set of white plastic coveralls.

Lu borrows Sergeant Bing's flashlight and closely inspects the coveralls. There are small discolorations and smears that might possibly be blood around the snaps and cuffs, places where it would be hard to clean them thoroughly.

"Can you get a bag out of the car and put these coveralls in it?" Lu asks. "Make sure to wear gloves."

"Yes. What are we going to do about the kid?"

"I'm not sure yet."

Lu returns to the kitchen. Zhang is quietly sitting on his cot.

"Any trouble?" Lu asks Sun.

"No, Inspector."

"We found a set of coveralls where you keep the chickens," Lu tells Zhang.

"Those aren't mine."

"Those coveralls aren't yours?"

"No."

"So . . . someone snuck in there and hung up a set of coveralls?"

"I don't know."

Lu eyes his watch. It's getting late. He takes a seat on the stool and looks down at Zhang's phone. "What's your pass code?"

"Why?"

"So I can look at your phone. Why do you think?"

"Are you allowed to do that?"

"Don't be difficult."

"But—"

"Pass code. Now."

Zhang resists. They have a brief staring contest. Zhang loses. He gives Lu the pass code. The screen opens to show a webcam site. The kind where pretty women flirt with customers and sometimes take off articles of clothing in exchange for digital money.

Lu looks at Zhang. Zhang keeps his eyes on the floor. Beads of sweat have broken out on his pimply upper lip.

Lu quickly reviews Zhang's phone log. It is devoid of calls, made or received. Zhang has either erased them or he has no friends with whom he corresponds. Either is a distinct possibility. Lu opens Zhang's camera app.

He is shocked to find a dozen or so photos of nude women—legs apart, openly displaying their most private anatomy for the camera. The photographs are high quality, airbrushed, professional. Lu suspects they have been downloaded from the internet.

Pornography is forbidden in China, but enterprising web users have discovered a variety of ways to get around restrictions. Videos and pictures are shared through online forums or gaming platforms. Live-streaming apps have become popular. Young women, called *anchors,* film themselves doing mundane tasks, such as eating, painting their nails, applying makeup, changing their clothes—but also perform special acts for viewers who pay them through virtual coins.

Lu has mixed feelings regarding such technology. Pornography is misogynist, exploitative, and antithetical to socialist values. But in a country where men outnumber women by thirty-four million, and a poorly educated, poorly paid, and socially awkward country boy like Zhang will find it nearly impossible to find a suitable mate, any means to lighten the burden of loneliness and vent a little pent-up tension isn't necessarily a bad thing.

Better porn than drinking and fighting.

But perhaps that's just the cop in him talking.

Besides the nude pics, the cell phone also contains photos of a young woman in a setting that looks very much like Kangjian Lane. The photos are not of the best quality—Lu assumes they were taken by Zhang using the digital zoom feature on his phone.

But there is no doubt. The woman is Yang Fenfang.

That means two things. First, Zhang has been taking candid snaps of Yang, probably without her knowledge. And two, while he may be telling the truth in a literal sense when he says he hasn't visited the Yang household in several months, he has certainly been to Kangjian Lane more recently than that.

Zhang suddenly bolts up from the bed, shoves Constable Sun— she goes flying into a wall—and knocks Lu off the stool. Before Lu can scramble to his feet, Zhang has yanked open the back door and fled into the night.

Zhang moves fast for a big man. Lu has to chase him fifty yards into a field of winter wheat. But Zhang is dressed only in socks and a ratty sweat suit, and he soon grows tired and cold. He slows, stumbles, and drops into a furrow. Lu finds him curled into a ball.

When Constable Sun and Sergeant Bing arrive, the three of them get Zhang up and back to the house. Zhang does not resist. He staggers along submissively, quietly blubbering.

They put Zhang in the back of the patrol car and wake up his grandfather to tell him they are taking Zhang to the *paichusuo*. The old man does not seem to comprehend their message.

Sergeant Bing whispers in Lu's ear, "Perhaps he has dementia."

"Runs in the family," Lu says, then immediately regrets making the comment.

They run Zhang in, process him, and stick him in a holding cell. Lu is obligated to inform Zhang that Yang Fenfang has been murdered and he is a suspect.

Zhang bursts into tears. "Fenfen? Dead?"

"Calm down, Zhaoxing," Lu says. "Is there anyone we should call? Family members? Perhaps someone to come stay with your grandfather?"

It is some time before Zhang is collected enough to give Lu the name of a relative. Lu sends Constable Sun off to phone her.

Lu hands Zhang a packet of tissues. "Wipe the snot off your face, Zhaoxing."

Zhang blows his nose, leaving bits of soggy paper ringing his nostrils. "I didn't do it, I swear."

"Then don't worry."

"But what will happen to me?"

"You will be detained while we carry out our investigation. At a later time, you'll have an opportunity to speak to a lawyer. Is there anything you'd like to tell me now?"

"I didn't do it!" Zhang wails.

Lu leaves Zhang sobbing in his cell and checks in with Constable

Huang. Besides the discovery of Yang Fenfang's body, it has been an uneventful night. Lu stops by the canteen to add hot water to his thermos, then goes into his office and makes himself a cup of instant coffee.

Lu looks up Yang Fenfang's biographical data. Her date of birth, marital status (single), reproductive status (no children), educational background (high school graduate). The house on Kangjian Lane is still listed as her official place of residence.

He sees that she is employed at a place called the Hei Mao—"Black Cat." Sounds like a bar to Lu. Not the kind of job that requires any particular qualifications beyond a pretty face and a sociable nature.

Lu makes a note of the bar's address in his cell phone.

He pulls up Zhang Zhaoxing's information. Again, nothing of note. High school. Place of employment. The house on Yongzheng Road.

For good measure, he runs a quick check on Mother Yang. No criminal record there, either. Cause of death is listed as kidney disease. No obvious connection to her daughter's murder.

Lu calls the Ministry of Public Security headquarters in Beijing. When the operator answers, he gives his name, rank, and ID number and asks to be connected to the Criminal Investigation Bureau. The operator transfers him, and a CIB duty officer picks up. Lu explains the situation. The officer says someone will call him back.

Thirty minutes pass. Lu considers going home to bed, but then the phone rings.

"I'm looking for Inspector Lu," a man says.

"I'm Inspector Lu."

"This is Superintendent Song, deputy director of the Criminal Investigation Bureau."

"Thank you for calling me back."

"I understand you have a homicide case."

"Yes." Lu gives Song a quick rundown.

"Right," Song says. "This suspect—you haven't officially questioned him yet, is that correct?"

"Not officially, no."

"You canvassed the neighbors?"

"Nobody saw anything."

"Any camera feeds in the area?"

"Unfortunately not."

"All right. I'll gather my team, and we'll fly up in the morning. Probably be there around noon. For the time being, just sit tight. Don't question the suspect any further. Don't search the house. Just seal it off and wait. I don't want your people compromising evidence."

Lu gets the sentiment but is annoyed by Song's tone. "Yes, Deputy Director."

Song abruptly hangs up without saying goodbye. Lu stares at the receiver for a moment, shocked at Song's rudeness, then places it back in the cradle.

Two minutes later, Lu's cell phone rings. It is Chief Liang.

"Hello, Chief."

"What's this about a murder?" Liang's speech is slurred and guttural. Loud music plays in the background. Lu pictures the chief at a seedy karaoke joint, a microphone in hand, singing sad country tunes with his cronies, drunk on Johnnie Walker. Perhaps with a plump bar girl in a short skirt sitting beside him, her hand resting on his thigh.

"A young woman on Kangjian Lane. Yang Fenfang."

"Don't know her. What's the family's background?"

By this, the chief means, "Was the family connected in local business or politics?"

"Average citizens. Mother and father are deceased. Mother just died, actually."

"Any suspects yet?"

"We have a suspect, but he's iffy."

"Did you alert Magistrate Lin or Party Secretary Mao?"

Lin and Mao are the two most senior government officials in Raven Valley Township.

"Not yet. No reason to bother them on a Saturday night. We can call first thing in the morning. I did contact the Crime Investigation Bureau, though. A team arrives tomorrow."

"Why'd you do that?"

"Because we lack the tools and expertise for a case like this, Chief."

"Those bastards will come up here with their noses in the air and lord over us like little emperors."

"We need their help. Wouldn't you agree?"

Chief Liang belches into the phone. "It was probably some sex-crazed farmer who saw the girl on the street and followed her home."

Lu's gut tells him it wasn't just a libidinous farmer. "We'll see about that, Chief. In the meantime, enjoy the rest of your evening."

"My evening is already ruined." Liang hangs up.

Lu hopes the chief is nearly done drinking for the night. It will be a huge loss of face for the Raven Valley PSB if he shows up to greet the CIB reeking of booze and cheap perfume.

Lu finishes his coffee and briefly considers going home. Instead, he takes one of the patrol cars and drives to Kangjian Lane. He sits outside the Yang residence for a few minutes, listening to the engine tick, watching the neighborhood sleep. Then he gets out, opens the trunk, collects a pair of latex gloves, ducks under police tape, and approaches the front door of the house.

"It's me," he calls out. He doesn't want to give Big Wang and Li the Mute a heart attack by just barging in. He opens the front door and enters.

Wang and Li stand at attention. Li runs a hand across his tousled hair. Clearly, both have been sleeping, despite the cold and their initial fear of being left alone in the house.

"What did I miss?" Lu asks.

"Some nosy neighbors came by," Big Wang says. "Asking questions and so on. I had to shoo them away."

"Okay, you two can go home," Lu says. "But first, return the patrol car parked out front to the station, and be in before noon tomorrow. We have a team arriving from Beijing, and I need all hands on deck."

"I've been on duty since eight this morning," Big Wang says. "That's sixteen hours, and you want me to work tomorrow too?"

"Your commitment to the citizens of Raven Valley is noted, Constable Wang," Lu says dryly. "See you tomorrow before noon."

Big Wang and Li the Mute take their leave, the former grumbling under his breath on the way out.

Lu sits on the *kang* and takes a moment to attune himself to his surroundings. A dog, possibly Yang Fenfang's, barks in the distance. Outside, the patrol car starts up and drives away. The house creaks as its old bones shift.

Is it his imagination, or is the corpse stench growing stronger?

Truth be told, Lu resents the brusque, dismissive manner in which Deputy Director Song addressed him on the phone. Raven Valley Township is *his* jurisdiction, and Yang Fenfang's murder is *his* responsibility. Lu isn't about to just cool his heels and wait for Song to show up, discover crucial evidence, and wave it under Lu's nose as proof of his investigative incompetence.

He slips on the latex gloves and conducts a thorougher search of the living room. He finds nothing.

He returns to the bedroom. In a moldering box under the bed, he discovers a collection of old photographs. None of them date to before the early '70s. That is not surprising—during the Cultural Revolution, photography was approved only for propaganda purposes, and very few citizens had access to cameras or film. Besides, most people were too busy not starving to death to worry about something as frivolous as posing for snapshots.

The first photo in the stack is a faded formal portrait of a young girl and her parents. The girl is perhaps eight. She sits on her mother's lap, wearing a sweater, her hair in pigtails. Her parents are both dressed in dark tunics and cheap Mao caps with red stars above the brim.

Lu assumes the girl is Yang Hong, Yang Fenfang's mother.

Next is a class photo, eighteen female middle school students posed in three rows of six each. They wear a motley assortment of tunics, some with pins featuring Chairman Mao over their left breasts. None of them are smiling. Yang Hong is in the front row, on the right. Sans Mao pin.

Following this is another family portrait, with Yang Hong in her late teens now, her parents looking thin and gray.

And then, magically, the sullen schoolgirl has blossomed into a happy bride. Yang Hong and her husband pose in street clothes in front of a wall of silk roses, displaying their identification cards for the camera. They are a handsome couple. No wonder Fenfang was such a looker.

This is followed by a new family portrait—baby Yang Fenfang and her parents. Gone are the tunics and Mao caps of yesteryear. Fenfang appears happy and healthy. Fat cheeks and a toothless grin.

But a lean, hungry look lingers in the faces of Mother and Father Yang.

Lu shuffles through the rest of the stack. Yang Fenfang slowly grows up before his eyes.

There are photos of her in middle school, wearing a white shirt with a blue collar. In high school, posing with her mother beside a portrait of Fenfang's father. A pair of white flower wreaths, probably plastic, bookend the portrait. Fenfang's eyes are red and swollen. Mother Yang is stone-faced.

The occasion is obviously Father Yang's funeral.

The final series of photographs are ones that Fenfang must have taken herself and sent to her mother. In them, she has already moved to Harbin and appears to be enjoying city life. Eating garlic oysters. Posing in front of the Saint Sophia Cathedral, lovely in the yellow dress—the same one her corpse wears now—coltish on six-inch stiletto shoes. Wearing a red skirt and white faux fur coat, and the same shoes again, standing in the public square in front of Harbin's Dragon Tower.

Lu pockets a few recent pictures of Fenfang and puts the others back in the box.

He returns to the wardrobe, runs his fingers through the pockets and along the seams of Fenfang's clothes. She seems to have spent a great deal of money on her outfits—or perhaps someone, a boyfriend or suitor, bought some of them for her? He sees the faux fur coat and red skirt from the photographs. Western jeans, silk tops, more dresses and skirts, boots, sneakers, and high-heeled shoes.

Lu pulls Fenfang's purse out from beneath the vanity, removes her wallet, and spreads its contents across the bed. There is a subway pass, a Chinese UnionPay bank card, and a smart card for something called

Harbin Good Fortune Terrace, which Lu assumes to be an apartment building. He photographs the card with his phone and puts it back into the wallet.

Lu inspects the kitchen. As previously noted, the rice cooker, deep fryer, and electric teakettle are new. Lu assumes Fenfang's work in the city provided the money for them.

It occurs to him that there is one item he might have expected to find, even in a rural home like this one, but hasn't—namely, a television.

Nearly 90 percent of Chinese households have electricity—and of those, almost all have a television. A TV is usually the first modern appliance a family will buy.

Lu returns to the living room. There is a low table facing the *kang* that might have served as a TV stand. Behind it, Lu finds disconnected electrical and cable wires.

Curious.

He spends another twenty minutes searching, but finds no smoking guns, no bloodstained murder weapons. He decides to leave the bathroom and Yang Fenfang's body for the CIB forensic experts. He knows he is not qualified to process a murder scene.

Lu lies down on the *kang* and closes his eyes. Eventually, he nods off, only to have a vision of Yang Fenfang hovering in the mouth of the hallway, her porcelain skin smeared with blood, her head dangling by its long hair from her hand like a grotesque parody of a child's paper lantern.

Lu sits up with a start. He walks through the house. It is empty. He does not look inside the bathroom.

At 5:00 a.m., he calls Yuehan Chu and Fatty Wang and tells them to be at the house in one hour. They arrive, tired and cranky, at 6:15. Lu appropriates their patrol car and drives to his apartment.

He sets his alarm for 8:30, strips, and climbs into bed. He dreams of Yang Fenfang as a little girl, in pigtails and a yellow dress, rolling down a conveyor belt to where Zhang Zhaoxing waits to dismember her with a butcher knife.

Not far from where Lu Fei sleeps uneasily, there is an oddly shaped room, slope-roofed, windowless, lit by a single naked, flickering bulb, devoid of furniture apart from a makeshift wooden altar. The altar is painted red—a color that traditionally symbolizes good fortune, happiness, youth. This is rather ironic, given the objects presently arrayed on its surface: dishes of fruit; bowls of rice with chopsticks planted vertically in them like tiny flagpoles; cups of sweet tea.

Offerings to the dead.

The room is cold and smells strongly of incense, but underneath this sweet perfume, there is another odor. A pungent, unpleasant, chemical tang that leaks from a row of big-bellied glass jars that rest on the altar behind the rice and fruit. Shapeless lumps of gray matter float in these jars.

A man kneels in the center of the room. He has prepared a metal brazier, stacks of joss money, and paper funeral goods, including a tiny house, clothes, jewelry, even a replica of a BMW. He lights these objects on fire, one by one, and tosses them into the brazier. As he does so, he mutters a benediction. A promise. A warning. A mea culpa.

"I pray for your swift and smooth journey to the underworld. I solemnly swear to provide for your every need and comfort in the afterlife. I adjure you with the power I wield over your immortal soul to do me no harm. And"—here the man bows down and knocks his forehead on the floor—"I beg you to forgive me. Forgive me. Forgive me."

SUNDAY

> You can't solve a problem? Well, get down and investigate the present facts and its past history! When you have investigated the problem thoroughly, you will know how to solve it. Conclusions invariably come after investigation, and not before. Only a blockhead cudgels his brains on his own, or together with a group, to "find a solution" or "evolve an idea" without making any investigation. It must be stressed that this cannot possibly lead to any effective solution or any good idea.
>
> —*Quotations from Chairman Mao Zedong*

The alarm shrills much too soon, and Lu pries himself out of bed. He takes a shower and shaves. In general, he shaves only twice a week—his facial hair grows sparsely, and Chief Liang is not a stickler when it comes to personal hygiene. But in spite of his unfavorable first impression of Deputy Director Song, Lu wants to start off on the right foot.

He lives about ten minutes from the *paichusuo* in a relatively new residential building. His apartment is tiny by Western standards. The front door leads directly into a narrow kitchen area with a sink, a small counter, a two-burner stove, and a half-size refrigerator. Just off the kitchen is a bathroom with a Western-style toilet and sink. There is no bathtub or shower stall—just a showerhead poking out of the wall. The bathroom also holds a tiny clothes washer.

Through the kitchen is a larger room that serves as the combined sleeping, eating, working, and living area. Beyond it is an enclosed balcony, where Lu hangs his wet laundry.

The apartment is comfortable, if cramped. For now, it suits his needs. If he were ever to get married and start a family, he would definitely need a larger space.

Lu is in no particular hurry to get married—and neither is he opposed to the idea. Given his university degree, decent salary, and position in the PSB, he might be considered a good catch. If he joined a dating service, no doubt he would encounter many young women willing to be his wife.

But Lu wants something more than just a warm body and an incubator for his offspring.

What he desires is more along the lines of the sentiment expressed in the ancient poem "Oh, Heaven":

> *My wish to be close to you*
> *Will never wane, though my life be long*
> *Only when the mountain peaks have worn away*
> *Rivers have dried up*
> *It thunders in the winter*
> *Snows in the summer*
> *And Heaven and Earth collide*
> *Would I ever dare to say goodbye*

After showering, Lu changes into a formal uniform. Dark trousers, a sky-blue shirt and dark tie, a blue jacket with shoulder boards featuring three pips and two silver bars, denoting his rank.

Over this goes his winter coat and a fur-lined hat with the Bureau of Public Safety insignia on the front.

He drives the patrol car to the *paichusuo*. Along the way, he stops by a food cart to buy breakfast: a couple of fried *shaobing* cakes filled with red bean paste, and a cup of *doujiang*—hot soy milk.

The *paichusuo* is a drab two-story building with metal doors and barred windows. On the ground floor is a waiting room with plastic seats and glassed-in reception desk, and behind that, through a locked door, the administrative section, squad room, private offices for Lu and Chief Liang, an interview room, a canteen, and a temporary detention center with two small cells.

On the second floor are dormitories for unmarried male and female staff, locker rooms with showers, an armory, and a property room where evidence and confiscated possessions are stored.

Lu parks in the lot at the rear of the *paichusuo* and enters through the back door. He first stops into the detention center. Zhang is asleep in his cell, covered in a thin cotton blanket. Lu does not wake him. He goes to his office and drops off his breakfast, then grabs his thermos and walks down to the reception desk, where Constable Huang is just about to go off duty. The constable looks fairly chipper for someone who has been up all night. Probably, Lu suspects, because he spent most of it sleeping on the floor with his jacket for a pillow.

"Morning, Constable."

"Morning, Inspector."

Lu checks the night log. Then he carries his thermos down to the canteen and fills it with hot water. He goes to his office, makes tea, and eats his breakfast.

Sergeant Bing rolls in around 9:30. Chief Liang arrives at 10:00. Lu is relieved to see that he looks presentable. The chief comes into Lu's office, takes a seat in front of Lu's desk, and lights a cigarette, although he's well aware that Lu doesn't smoke.

"All right," Liang says. "Let's hear it."

Lu turns and cracks a window. He tells the chief what he knows so far. There is no ashtray on Lu's desk, so Liang taps his cigarette ashes into the wastebasket.

"This kid, Zhang, sounds like a pervert and a creeper."

"Pretty much," Lu says. "But that doesn't necessarily make him a killer."

"I guess you didn't find a potentially purloined TV at his house?"

"There was a TV, but not a new one."

"Maybe Zhang sold it already?"

"Shouldn't be too hard to find out. I'll send some of the constables around the neighborhood to ask."

"What about interviewing his employer?"

"It's Sunday. The plant's closed. We'll have to wait until tomorrow."

"Who's coming from the CIB?"

"Deputy Director Song."

Liang makes a face.

"Do you know him?" Lu asks.

"Only by reputation. He's a rising star. A police captain in Nanjing before he started clawing his way up the ranks of the ministry. Ambitious and power hungry, like most southerners."

Lu was born in Shanghai, and Liang never bypasses an opportunity to make a snarky comment referencing this fact. To the chief's way of thinking, northern China is the true cradle of civilization, while all Chinese born south of the Yangtze River are little more than jungle savages.

"When meeting a superior person, think of how to become his equal," Lu quotes. "When meeting an inferior person, look inside and examine your own faults."

"Master Kong?"

"The same."

"You were born two thousand years too late, kid."

"Better too late than not at all," Lu says.

"Really," Liang says. "Just wait until Prince Song shows up to make your life miserable, and then tell me if you feel the same." He stubs his cigarette out on the sole of his shoe. "Are you driving out to the airport to meet him?"

"He seems to have arranged his own transportation."

"Just make sure the constables look sharp before he gets here. I don't want to lose face with His Imperial Highness."

"Understood."

"And you'd better make a reservation for lunch somewhere. Maybe Nine Dragons restaurant."

"I'll take care of it, Chief."

Liang yawns and stands up. "I'm going to go have a look at this suspect of yours and then call Magistrate Lin and Party Secretary Mao. They might want to join us for lunch. You know what suck-ups they are."

"What about the procurator?"

In the People's Republic, the Procuratorate is the government department in charge of investigation and prosecution, akin to the public prosecutor's office in the U.S. justice system. Criminal procedure requires a formal arrest request to be approved by the local procurator, after which an investigation is conducted. If the investigation proves conclusive (they usually do), the procurator issues an indictment and represents the government in the subsequent trial.

The county procurator's surname is Gao. He is a rather humorless, by-the-book sort.

The chief rolls his eyes. "That dull dog's dick. I'm not asking him to lunch."

"I mean, we should inform him of the case," Lu says.

"Fine, I'll call him." Liang goes to the door, then turns around. "Can you tell I'm not looking forward to having a bunch of snotty CIB investigators poking around?"

"We must 'seek truth from the facts,'" Lu says. This is an old slogan that really has no meaning, apart from whatever the current leadership ascribes to it.

Liang shakes his head and walks out, taking his cigarette butt with him.

Deputy Director Song and his entourage arrive just after 1:00 p.m.

Song is tall and lean and rather handsome. He looks to be in his early fifties. He wears a uniform with two pips and olive leaves on his shoulder boards. Given his relative youth, Lu figures Song will likely be promoted to the rank of deputy commissioner and given a leadership role at the Ministry of Public Security before his career comes to an end.

That makes him a good person to have as a friend and an exceedingly bad one to have as an enemy.

Song has brought with him three colleagues from the CIB. Two are crime scene technicians. Their surnames are Hu and Jin.

The third is Dr. Ma Xiulan. She is around forty, and something of a minor celebrity in law enforcement circles—one of the few women to achieve a high position in the country's rapidly developing forensic field and the author of a book that caused quite a sensation when it was published: *Death Is My Trade: True Tales from a Female Medical Examiner.*

The book is notable not only for Dr. Ma's rebellious and highly controversial criticism of the current state of forensics in China, which she believes to be slipshod and subject to political tampering, but also the somewhat risqué author photo on the back cover. It shows Ma in full glamour makeup, wearing a low-cut blouse that displays a good four inches of cleavage, her hair streaming back from her forehead as if she's seated behind the wheel of a fast-moving convertible sports car.

In person, Ma wears less eye shadow and dresses more conservatively, although that may just be due to the frigid Heilongjiang weather. But even with her hair pinned up and wearing long pants and sensible shoes, she is intimidatingly attractive.

Introductions are made. Chief Liang is obsequiously charming. One does not rise to police chief in the People's Republic, no matter how small the jurisdiction, without knowing how to, as they say, *pai ma pi*— "slap the horse's butt."

"Would you care for some lunch?" Chief Liang says. "We have an excellent hot pot restaurant in town."

"I'd like to see the crime scene right away," Deputy Director Song says. "Every passing minute is crucial in a homicide investigation."

"Yes, of course," Liang replies, a hint of disappointment in his voice. He was looking forward to some hot pot.

Liang manages to wrangle a seat for himself in Song's vehicle, a Great Wall Haval SUV. Lu and Sergeant Bing take one of the patrol cars. Lu asks Sergeant Bing to call ahead to Yuehan Chu and Fatty Wang. The two constables don't answer their phones. Lu gooses the patrol car to Kangjian Lane, worried that something has gone awry with the scene during his absence.

When he gets to the house, he opens the front door only to find Yuehan Chu and Fatty Wang napping on the *kang.*

"Get up, you lazy bastards!" Lu shouts. "CIB will be here any second!"

By the time Song and party arrive, Chu and Wang are standing at attention in the front yard.

Hu and Jin unload metal boxes of equipment from the back of the Haval. They suit up in coveralls, booties, and gloves. Dr. Ma removes her coat and pulls on her own set of coveralls and booties. She and the two technicians carry their equipment inside.

Fatty Wang and Yuehan Chu are dispatched to the lane to run interference for a crowd of curious neighbors slowly assembling in front of the house, with Sergeant Bing watching over them.

Chief Liang, Deputy Director Song, and Lu remain huddled in the lee of the SUV. Liang offers Song a Zhongnanhai cigarette. Song declines and takes out a soft pack of Chunghwas, thereby cementing, if there was ever any question, his status as Chief Liang's social superior.

Because, as everyone knows in the People's Republic, a cigarette is never just a cigarette. It is also a means to express rank, power, wealth, and even regional loyalty.

Good Cats are favored by natives of Xian Province. Sichuanese smoke Prides. Zhongnanhai cigarettes, named after the Communist Party's headquarters in Beijing, are a patriotic, if somewhat pedestrian, choice.

Meanwhile, a pack of Chunghwa cigarettes costs five times as much as the other brands and, as a consequence, are preferred by upwardly mobile businessmen, ambitious politicians, and senior Communist Party members. When offering a thank-you gift or a bribe to your local government official, you can't go wrong with a carton of Chunghwas.

Deputy Director Song puts a cigarette into his mouth and, after a slight hesitation, offers the pack to Chief Liang.

"I don't dare take one," Liang says. Then he takes one. Song grudgingly proffers the pack to Lu.

"No, thanks," Lu says.

"You don't smoke?" Song asks.

"No," Lu says.

"He makes up for it by drinking heavily," Liang says.

Lu scowls at the chief. Liang ignores him and hastens to light Song's cigarette.

Song inhales deeply. "Tell me everything from the time you received the initial call alerting you to the homicide."

Lu reviews the events surrounding the discovery of Yang's body, the initial search of the house, the subsequent interviews with Mrs. Chen and Zhang Zhaoxing, and the evidence, or lack thereof, turned up so far.

"This Zhang Zhaoxing ticks a lot of boxes," Song says. "Physically strong. A consumer of pornography. No mother or father. Socially awkward. A Peeping Tom. Experience with butchering animals."

"At first glance, yes," Lu says, "but we've just begun the investigation, so perhaps it's best to take it one step at a time."

"That goes without saying," Song says rather sharply. He finishes his cigarette and pinches the end, then slips it back into the pack. "When you're done, dispose of the butt properly," he tells Chief Liang. "The property around the house should also be considered part of the crime scene."

"Of course," Liang says. He was, in fact, about ten seconds away from tossing the butt on the ground.

Song turns to Lu. "Let's take a look inside."

He goes to the back of the SUV, removes a pair of plastic booties from a box, and hands them to Lu. He takes another pair of booties for himself and also pulls out two pairs of latex gloves and two sets of plastic coveralls. Chief Liang stands there watching. Song says, "Did you want to join us for the walkthrough?"

"Ah, no," Chief Liang says. "We don't want any more feet tromping around in there than necessary, do we?" The truth is, he has no desire to see a dead girl.

"Quite right," Song says.

Technician Hu is photographing the bedroom when Lu and Song enter. Technician Jin is busy setting up lights for the bathroom.

Lu takes the deputy director on a quick tour. He points out the new appliances and the unattached TV cables.

Song agrees that the absence of a television is conspicuous.

When the lights are ready, Hu carefully photographs Yang Fenfang's corpse from every conceivable angle. Then Dr. Ma enters the bathroom and squats on a tarp laid beside the body.

She gives her first impressions. "Extensive bruising on the neck. Perhaps she was choked manually first, then strangled to death with a strap or belt. Her wrists were bound, probably with tape." She caresses Yang Fenfang's cheek with a gloved finger. "I'm going to assume the suspect applied this makeup postmortem. Otherwise, it would be mussed." She looks up at Lu. "Any idea if he used the victim's cosmetics or brought his own?"

"No, sorry. But she's got plenty of beauty products on the vanity in the bedroom."

"Easy enough to take samples and confirm either way." Dr. Ma manipulates Yang's arm. "Body is moderately rigid. Can't be sure if it's rigor mortis or she's just half-frozen. It's like an icebox in here. Hm? What's this?" Dr. Ma peers down the front of Yang's dress.

"What?" Song asks.

The yellow dress is of the sort that has buttons running all the way down its front. Dr. Ma unfastens it and exposes Yang's body. Yang is not wearing a bra or panties. Lu quickly averts his eyes. Then forces himself to look back.

Grotesquely puckered lines of stitching run in a Y pattern from Yang's shoulders, across her breasts, and then down to the neat triangle of dark hair on her mons pubis.

"It looks like she's been autopsied," Song observes.

"It certainly does." Dr. Ma leans in. "The edges of the cut are clean. Something sharp was used. Not a kitchen knife. A scalpel or something similar."

"A butcher knife?" Song suggests.

"Perhaps. One with a very, very keen edge."

"What can you tell me about the stitching?" Song says.

"It's not aesthetically pleasing, but it's not the work of a rank amateur, either."

"A lot of locals sew their own clothes, quilts, embroidery, stuff like that," Lu says. "Is it your opinion that someone with such skills could have done this, or would it require medical training?"

"Suturing skin is not like darning your socks. So probably not. But I would say any country doctor or physician's assistant could have done it."

"Maybe your suspect brought a pig trotter home from work and practiced," Song says.

Lu doesn't respond. The sight of Yang's mutilated body perversely calls to mind a snippet from his favorite Daoist classic, the *Zhuangzi:*

Butcher Ting was cutting up an ox for Lord Wen-hui. Zip! Zoop! He slithered his knife along with a zing and all was in perfect rhythm, as though he were performing the dance of the Mulberry Grove.

"This is marvelous," said Lord Wen-hui. "Imagine skill reaching such heights!"

Butcher Ting laid down his knife and replied: "When I first began cutting up oxen, all I could see was the ox itself. After three years I no longer saw the ox. Now I use my spirit and don't even look at it with my eyes. I go with the natural form, strike in the big hollows, guide the knife through openings, and never touch a ligament or joint."

Lu excuses himself and goes out to the front yard, where he breathes in deep lungfuls of painfully cold air.

Processing the crime scene proceeds for another couple of hours. Song's team is meticulous and efficient. They measure and graph, photograph and document, dust for fingerprints and collect every scrap of potential evidence.

In due course, Dr. Ma requests Lu to call an ambulance. When it arrives, she and Technician Jin take two cases of equipment and ride with Yang's body to the county hospital, where they will carry out the postmortem examination.

Chief Liang has long since grown bored standing around and left, perhaps in search of hot pot.

By this juncture, despite the chill, a sizable crowd of neighbors has gathered outside the front gate. Lu goes out to speak to them. He informs them of the homicide (they already know, including many of the gory details, thanks to Mrs. Chen) and asks anyone who has information that might help with the investigation to come forward. He receives an earful about strange lights in the sky and animals acting bizarrely in the night. Ill omens in the weeks leading up to the murder. A lot of chaff and no wheat. Nevertheless, Lu assigns constables Fatty Wang and Yuehan Chu to take down statements.

While Technician Hu wraps things up inside the house, Lu takes Deputy Director Song to Mrs. Chen's residence so he can question her firsthand.

As before, the daughter-in-law serves tea; Mrs. Chen's son sits on the *kang,* smoking. The elderly mother watches TV with the sound blasting. The grandson is obnoxiously underfoot.

Song, however, lacks Lu's patience. After thirty seconds of this cacophony, he asks Mrs. Chen to turn down the volume on the television.

"Ah Ma can't hear very well," Mrs. Chen says.

"Neither can I with all this racket!" Song snaps. "And take that child outside."

"He's got the sniffles," the daughter-in-law says. "The damp will creep into his bones and give him pneumonia."

"Then let's go into the bedroom to talk," Song suggests.

Mrs. Chen's son stands up. "No, don't trouble yourself." He brushes ash off his lap and waves at his wife. "Take Yongyong into the bedroom."

"He won't like that," she says.

"Just do it!" the son barks.

The daughter-in-law snatches up the child and carries him away, squealing and protesting. She slams the door behind her. The boy's muffled wailing is drowned out by the soap opera Mrs. Chen's mother is watching.

Song rubs his eyes. "The TV, if you please."

"But Ah Ma . . ." Mrs. Chen starts.

"I'll do it," the son says, his face darkening. He takes the remote and fiddles with it, but manages only to switch the channel. Mrs. Chen's mother protests in a croaking voice.

"Wait just a minute!" the son growls.

"Don't take that tone of voice with your grandmother!" Mrs. Chen says.

"Sorry." The son turns the channel back to where it was and lowers the volume. Mrs. Chen's mother complains that she can't hear, but everyone ignores her.

"Now I'm sorry to have to ask you to go through this again," Song continues. "But please tell me everything you remember. No detail is too insignificant."

The waterworks resume as Mrs. Chen recalls the events of Saturday night. Song captures her statement on a handheld recorder. He asks for clarifications on a few points, then wraps up the interview.

"Oh, by the way," Lu says. "Where's Yang Fenfang's dog?"

"Ah . . ." Mrs. Chen shifts uncomfortably on the *kang*. "We gave it to some relatives."

Lu considers inquiring further, but then decides he really doesn't want to know whether or not she's telling the truth.

Once outside, Song lights a cigarette and exhales smoke through his teeth. "What an irritating family."

They return to the Yangs' house to pick up Technician Hu and then drive to Yongzheng Road.

They park and approach the front door of Zhang's house. Lu knocks. No one answers. He shouts, "Public Security Bureau!" They are met with silence.

Song reaches past Lu and opens the door, then walks inside. Lu has little choice but to follow. Technician Hu veers off to look in the chicken shed.

As before, the old man—Zhang Zhaoxing's grandfather—takes his ease on the *kang*. He's eating a bowl of instant noodles, watching TV. He does not seem surprised to see Lu.

"Good afternoon, Uncle," Lu says. "I'm Inspector Lu with the Public Security Bureau. Do you remember me?"

The old man mumbles. Lu sees that he only has one or two teeth in his mouth.

"What's that?" Lu says.

"I shit in the pot."

"You . . . what?"

"Shit in the pot," the old man says.

"What did he say?" Song asks.

"Something about shitting in a pot."

"Hello, Uncle," Song says. "I am Deputy Director Song of the Criminal Investigation Bureau."

The old man turns back to his TV program.

"He's deaf," Lu says. Now that he has been standing inside for a moment, he is beginning to catch the old man's meaning. There is a clay pot sitting beside the *kang*. It is white with the Chinese character for double happiness painted on the side. Lu walks over and, against his better judgment, opens the lid. Sure enough.

"Mystery solved," he says.

"Can you hear me, Uncle?" Song says, louder than before.

The old man waves for Lu to take the pot away. This must be a service his grandson provides. Waste disposal.

"Hallo, Uncle!" Song says, louder still.

"He can't hear you," Lu says, "but I don't think he cares if you have a look around. Or will even notice." He picks up the pot and walks through the kitchen, out the door, and dumps its contents into the squat toilet of an outhouse connected to the back of the house. He uses a water hose to rinse out the pot.

Lu walks back into the kitchen, where Song is looking through cupboards, and then into the front room. He sets the clean pot beside the *kang*. "There you are, Uncle."

The old man looks at him as if he's never seen him before. "I shit in the pot," he says.

"Congratulations," Lu says.

When Song is finished snooping, they say goodbye to the old man, who shrugs at them, and then go outside to the chicken shed.

"Find anything?" Song asks Technician Hu.

"Yes," Hu says. "Three eggs and a lot of chicken shit."

"We'll have to come back and conduct a thorougher search," Song says. He looks at his watch. "But for now, we'd better get over to the hospital for the autopsy."

"I'd like to head over to the station," Technician Hu says, "and get started on processing evidence from the crime scene."

"While you're at it, draw up a search warrant for this property," Song says.

"Will do, but it won't be considered until Monday."

"That's fine," Song says. "The chicken shit's not going anywhere."

In the People's Republic, health services are administered by means of a three-tier system. At the lowest level are what in Mao's time were known as "barefoot doctors"—minimally trained practitioners, operating out of local makeshift facilities, qualified to do little more than offer preventative care and treat common illnesses and minor injuries. Next are the township clinics, with a capacity of twenty or thirty beds, staffed by assistant doctors and functioning mainly on an outpatient basis. Finally, there are the county, urban, and provincial hospitals, where more serious cases are treated by fully trained physicians and specialists.

The Raven Valley Township clinic is small, antiquated, and lacking in the necessary amenities for Dr. Ma to conduct her postmortem, so Yang Fenfang's body has been transported to the nearest county hospital, a thirty-minute drive away. When they arrive, Lu parks, and they enter the crowded waiting room (hospital waiting rooms are always crowded in the People's Republic) and inquire from the receptionist as to the location of the morgue.

"Down," she says, jerking her head toward a stairwell door.

Lu and Song descend to the basement and emerge into a green-tiled corridor. There are doors on either side with small windows set at eye level. Most of the windows are dark. Lu walks down the corridor until he spies Dr. Ma and Technician Jin inside one of the rooms, wearing scrubs and face masks, huddling over the remains of Yang Fenfang.

Song and Lu enter. Once inside, Lu is assaulted by a scrum of odors, each jockeying for dominance. Bleach and rubbing alcohol. Intestinal gas. Feces. Rotten garlic. Spoiled meat. Formaldehyde.

Yang Fenfang is naked, a rubber brick propped under her shoulders, her neck flexed and breasts arched toward the examination lamp. It pains Lu to see her posed in such an awkward and immodest posture.

Dr. Ma shows Song and Lu a square of wet paper gripped in the teeth of her forceps.

"What's that?" Song asks.

"Hell money."

In the murky cosmology of Chinese folk religion, life after death is not so different from existence on the earthly plane. Just because you now lack a corporeal body doesn't mean you don't have *needs*—food, shelter, clothing, perhaps a servant or two, a reliable car, a smartphone, a flat-screen television, and all the rest. Hell money—a.k.a. joss paper, spirit money, dark paper, ghost money—is legal tender in the underworld and the means to pay for such items. When a loved one dies, relatives and friends burn mounds of the stuff as an offering—not unlike transferring funds through a spiritual bank wire or paying into someone's spectral Venmo account.

These paper notes generally feature an illustration of the Jade Emperor on one side, and the Bank of Hell on the other, and are cosigned by both the Jade Emperor and Yan Wang, the god of death and ruler of the netherworld. In the old days, denominations of five or ten yuan were sufficient—but with inflationary pressures and the rise of consumerism, nothing less than ten-thousand-yuan notes are now considered respectable.

"How much?" Lu asks. He doesn't think this is significant to the case—he's just curious.

"One billion," Dr. Ma says.

"A single note?" Song asks.

"Yes. In her mouth."

"Odd," Song says. "What else?"

"We've just completed the exterior exam. In addition to the previously noted ligature marks on the wrists and neck, I see a significant contusion on the right rear quadrant of the skull, consistent with a hammer or similar weapon. Vaginal trauma as well."

"Raped?" Song asks.

"Judging from extensive tears in the tissue of the vaginal wall, I'm thinking it was a foreign object."

"Foreign object?" Lu says.

"Such as the handle of a hammer."

"*Kao,*" Lu mutters.

"We took swabs, so we'll know for sure when the results come back. Now we're proceeding to the internal examination."

Wonderful, Lu thinks.

Dr. Ma snips the sutures crisscrossing Yang Fenfang's torso. As she works, she narrates into a portable recorder.

"Torso incision closed by means of a deep continuous suture pattern using thick nylon thread. Incision runs from the acromial end of each clavicle and extends above each nipple to meet at the xiphoid process, and then down the midline to the pubic symphysis."

When the thread has been removed and placed in an evidence bag, Dr. Ma and Technician Jin peel Yang's skin away from her torso.

"See that?" Technician Jin says.

"I see it," Dr. Ma says.

"What?" Song asks.

Dr. Ma pops out a large section of Yang Fenfang's rib cage and holds it up. "The suspect cut through her sternum."

Technician Jin points into the gaping hole in Yang Fenfang's chest. "Look, there."

Dr. Ma pokes a finger into the cavity. "Hm."

"What?" Song says.

"Her heart is missing."

"What do you mean, missing?"

"It's been excised."

"*Gao shenma gui,*" Song says. *What in the hell?*

Dr. Ma shrugs. "Let's see what else we can find."

They inspect Yang's chest and abdomen. Lu covers his mouth and nose with his hand. The smell before was bad—but now it's exponentially worse.

After a few minutes, Dr. Ma soon issues a verdict: "Lungs and liver are also excised."

"Organ theft?" Song says.

"Possibly," Dr. Ma says, "but the demand for kidneys outweighs the demand for all the other organs by a huge margin. It doesn't make sense that the perpetrator would leave them behind."

"Maybe when he cut her open, he saw there was something wrong with them?" Song suggests.

"Let's have a look." Dr. Ma removes a kidney and sets it in a stainless steel pan. "No outward signs of abnormality." She cross-sections it. "Seems perfectly good to me."

"Perhaps the killer had a specific contract to fulfill," Song suggests. "Heart, lungs, and liver only."

"Perhaps," Dr. Ma says.

She and Technician Jin remove what remains of Fenfang's innards and take samples of tissue, blood, urine, and bile. Dr. Ma slices open Yang's stomach and pronounces her last meal to be one of "rice and vegetables—possibly cabbage." She extracts a sample for further testing.

Next, she picks up a scalpel and cuts across the top of Fenfang's head from ear to ear. Lu stares at the scuffed linoleum floor and plays a silent guessing game regarding the origin of certain discolorations and dark spots while Dr. Ma peels Fenfang's skin over her face and then uses an electric saw to remove the top of her skullcap.

Dr. Ma narrates: "Right temporoparietal region of skull and cerebrum display trauma consistent with a sharp blow from a hammer-like weapon. Otherwise, no sign of contusions, hematoma, or lacerations."

The brain is removed and placed in a basin. Technician Jin deftly carves off a few slivers and slides them into a fixative solution.

Eventually, the examination mercifully concludes. Dr. Ma and Technician Jin begin to reassemble Yang Fenfang's twice-butchered body.

"I'll be waiting in the corridor," Lu says.

Song joins him a few moments later. "Let's get some air."

They go out to the parking lot. It's freezing—but compared to the oppressive atmosphere of the autopsy room, Lu finds the cold refreshing.

Song lights a cigarette. "Attend many autopsies?"

"Enough. Generally not quite so exciting as that one, though."

"How long have you been a cop?"

"About seventeen years."

"Always here? In Raven Valley Township?"

"No." Lu doesn't elaborate.

"Where did you go to college?"

Lu wonders why Song cares. "People's Public Security University."

"Hah?" Song is astonished. The People's Public Security University, based in Beijing, is the undisputed number-one police academy in China. Many of its graduates rise to high positions in provincial police departments and the Ministry of Public Safety. "But you're from here, right? Heilongjiang Province?"

"Yes."

Song draws on his cigarette. "Go on."

Lu hesitates. Song watches him expectantly. "My father was born in Shanghai, but he was sent to Heilongjiang in '68 as an 'educated youth.'"

"Ah," Song says knowingly.

Educated youth is a loaded term. When Mao Zedong defeated the Chinese Nationalist forces in 1949, he inherited a country ravaged by war and neglect. Inspired by the Soviets, he quickly embarked upon a series of social and economic development initiatives known as Five-Year Plans. But he soon grew impatient with a lack of progress, and in 1958, he launched a radical new campaign that he believed would quickly transform the People's Republic from a poor agrarian economy into a prosperous socialist society through mass industrialization and collectivization.

He called it the Great Leap Forward.

Sadly, Mao's Great Leap turned out to be a massive step backward. Instead of prosperity, it produced widespread famine.

Tens of millions died.

Mao's political stock dipped precipitously. Old friends suddenly became dangerous rivals.

In a bid to reassert his authority, Mao declared that the government and military had been infiltrated by bourgeois elements seeking to restore an oppressive capitalist system. He called for renewed class struggle and the destruction of the "four olds"—old ideas, old habits, old customs, and old culture. In 1966, a massive social revolution erupted across the nation as hordes of Chinese students adopted Mao's cause and formed themselves into paramilitary units known as the Red Guards.

These young activists—later joined by urban laborers and various other disaffected mobs—took Mao's directive to "destroy" quite literally. They roamed the city streets in gangs, looting, smashing, and beating up anyone whose clothing or haircut marked them as being under the influence of Western culture. Precious historical sites were burned to the ground. Temples, churches, ancient tombs, cemeteries—the holier, the more sacred, the greater the desecration.

Intellectuals, artists, teachers, landowners, merchants—anyone who wasn't of pure proletariat stock—were targeted. Tortured, imprisoned, forced to endure self-criticism sessions, denounced by their loved ones, sent off to labor camps. Many died.

By 1968, Mao decided that the Red Guards had achieved their purpose—purging the government of his ideological enemies—and were beginning to spiral out of control. He marched the People's Liberation Army into cities, forcibly dismantled the Red Guards, and—in a stroke of particular genius—launched a new drive known as Down to the Countryside.

The idea behind Down to the Countryside was for so-called educated youth—mainly teenagers with undesirable bourgeois family backgrounds, but also ex–Red Guards—to be exiled to remote villages, ostensibly to learn socialist values and the importance of good honest toil among rural farmers and laborers.

The reality was that seventeen million kids were forcibly relocated, some as young as fifteen years old.

As the offspring of a university professor and an artist mother, two fundamentally bourgeois occupations, it was a forgone conclusion that Lu's father would be shipped two thousand kilometers from his home in Shanghai to remote Heilongjiang Province, where he spent a decade raising pigs and growing wheat.

Like many young people of the time, in need of comfort and solace, Lu's father eventually met a local girl, and a relationship flowered. Later, after the chaos of the Cultural Revolution slowly began to recede, they married. Lu's grandfather was dead by this point—he never made it home from a reeducation camp—but his grandmother was still alive and living in Shanghai. Because she was elderly and sickly, Lu's father and mother were allowed to move there from Heilongjiang, and in due course, that's where Lu was born.

But Lu's mother hated the heat and noise and chaos of Shanghai, and when the grandmother died, she begged Lu's father to move back north. The little family returned to Heilongjiang in time for Lu to attend secondary school in Harbin City. After graduation, his college entrance exam scores were good enough for a top-tier college, and having already set his mind upon a career as a police officer, he applied to the People's Public Security University.

Four years later, Lu joined the Harbin metro police department as a sergeant second class (the starting rank for university graduates) and spent the next ten years working his way up in various divisions, eventually receiving a promotion to inspector second class.

Lu relates all this to Song, but not in so many words.

"So how is it you went from being a cop in Harbin to deputy chief of a county township?" Song asks.

"It's complicated."

Song finishes his cigarette and lights another. "Finally, we're getting to the interesting part."

"Why is my background of interest to you?"

"I like to know who I'm working with."

"I'm not sure what you mean."

"Simple. My job requires me to crisscross the country investigating various crimes that local police don't have the resources or expertise to tackle. One week, I'm in Heilongjiang; the next, Gansu Province; the week after that, Zhejiang. This leaves me perennially a fish out of water. Every time I step off a plane, I find myself at an immediate disadvantage. I don't know who the local players are, who's got clout, who's bribing who, who's screwing who, whether the local cops are corrupt or just incompetent. Who I can trust and who I can't." He blows smoke out of the corner of his mouth. "A homicide investigation is rarely just about the homicide itself. There's always some degree of politics involved. The cops, the local party representatives and government officials, the prosecutors—everyone has an agenda. A desire to advance one's career. Often at the expense of others. Sometimes at the expense of the truth. So it helps to have a local guide, and if that's going to be you, I need to know—what's *your* angle?"

Lu is surprised by Song's directness. In the People's Republic, bureaucrats are rarely so straightforward and plainspoken. They generally prefer an indirect approach, like a cat circling a dead mouse.

"Apart from wanting to arrest the guilty party, I don't have an angle," Lu says.

"Everyone has an angle, Inspector."

"What's *your* angle?" Lu asks.

Song smiles. "I want to be a provincial governor within ten years or perhaps finish my career as the head of the Ministry of Public Security. For that, I need a record of closing big cases."

"A lofty goal, Deputy Director."

Song quotes an old saying: "Don't be afraid if the road is long. Only be afraid that you are not aiming high enough."

Lu quotes another: "Wealth and treasures are but illusions that one can never possess."

"Oh, really?" Song says. "They seem pretty possessable to me. At least, judging from the houses high-ranking officials live in and the cars they drive. With an attitude like that, Inspector, you'll end up retiring to

a sixty-square-meter apartment and be forced to subsist on instant noodles."

"Quite likely," Lu allows.

"So go on, then. Tell me how you came to be deputy chief in Raven
Valley Township. I'm sure it will provide some insight into your character."

Lu does not wish to share the intimate details of his life with Song,
but he can't very well refuse a direct order, even one couched as a casual
request. "I had some conflicts with my supervisor. We decided that we
didn't want to work together anymore, so he arranged for a transfer and
a promotion."

Song is about to dig more deeply, but at that moment, Dr. Ma exits
the hospital. She winds a red scarf around her neck as she walks over. "It's
positively glacial out here."

"Welcome to Heilongjiang in January," Lu says.

"All done?" Song asks.

"Technician Jin is just finishing up a few things." Dr. Ma smells
heavily of disinfectant. "I could use a shower. And a drink."

"You must be hungry, too," Lu says. He turns to Song. "If you like, I
can take your team to a restaurant for dinner."

"Dinner can wait," Song says. "I want to talk to this Zhang kid."

The best hotel in Raven Valley Township—the *only* hotel in Raven Valley Township—is the Raven Valley Friendship Guesthouse. After drop-
ping off Technician Jin and Dr. Ma, Lu and Song continue on to the
paichusuo.

Song orders Zhang Zhaoxing brought into the interview room.
He offers him tea and a cigarette, both of which Zhang accepts. Zhang
drinks the tea but just holds the cigarette curled into the palm of his
hand, like a captured insect. Lu doesn't recall ever having seen Zhang
smoke.

The interview room lacks a two-way observation window, as one
might find in foreign police stations. Instead, Li the Mute carries in a
camera on a tripod, presses Record, and then makes himself scarce.

In the People's Republic, there is no legal "right to remain silent" and no law that requires a lawyer to be present during initial police questioning, so Song launches right in.

"Do you know why you're here, Mr. Zhang?"

"He . . ." Zhang points at Lu. "He told me Fenfen's been . . . been . . ." Tears well in his eyes.

"That's right," Song says. "Murdered. And you're the primary suspect."

"Why me?"

"Why do you think?"

"I don't know."

"How were you acquainted with the victim?"

"Huh?"

"How did you know Yang Fenfang?"

"We went to high school together."

"And what was the nature of your relationship?"

Zhang shrugs.

"Use words, Mr. Zhang. You were what? Friends?"

"She was my girlfriend."

"Oh, really?" Song's voice is acid. "She was your girlfriend? Can you prove that?"

Zhang shrugs.

"You are shrugging, Mr. Zhang, but you are not answering the question."

Zhang shrugs.

"Stop shrugging, damn your mother!"

Zhang blanches at Song's tone. Zhang looks to Lu for support.

"Go on, Zhaoxing," Lu says. "Answer honestly. If you're innocent, you have nothing to fear."

Zhang wipes his nose with the heel of his hand. "She was my girlfriend in high school, but I hadn't seen her for a while. Before . . . Before . . ." He chokes up.

"Then why do you have recent pictures of her on your phone?" Song presses. "You were following her around! Stalking her! Weren't you?"

"No!" Zhang cries. "She was my *girlfriend*!"

Song snorts. "A pretty girl like her with a stupid, ugly boy like you? The very idea is ridiculous beyond words."

Lu does not care for Song's interrogative approach, but he knows better than to interfere.

"The truth is," Song nearly shouts, "she rejected your advances. Isn't that right?"

"No!"

"But you kept after her. Watching her. Photographing her. And when the lust and rage got to be too much, you attacked her!"

"I didn't!"

"Don't lie to me!"

"I'm not lying."

"You raped and murdered that poor girl!"

"No, I swear!"

"*Liar!*" Song pounds the table.

Zhang lurches up, his hands curled into fists the size of bricks. Song backs away, his chair tipping over.

Lu moves forward. "Zhang Zhaoxing! Sit down!"

Zhang has a crazed look in his eyes. There's no telling what he might do. Make a break for it, like he did Saturday night? If so, Lu wouldn't want to be the person standing between him and the door. "Zhaoxing," he says again, more gently. "Sit down. Please."

Zhang slowly uncurls his fists and slumps into his seat. The cigarette in his hand has been crushed to bits. Flecks of paper and tobacco litter the front of his shirt.

"Put some damn handcuffs on him, why don't you?" Song snaps.

"I don't think that's necessary," Lu says. "Is it, Zhaoxing?"

Zhang looks down at the table and shakes his head.

After a moment, Song smooths his hair, rights his chair, and sits back down. "I'm sorry, Mr. Zhang. I didn't mean to yell at you." He takes a handkerchief out of his pocket and hands it over. "Wipe your nose."

Zhang honks into the cloth. Song watches him with distaste.

"Now, *Xiao* Zhang, let's speak honestly." Song uses the diminutive "little," as a friend might. "I'm quite sure the whole thing was an accident. You didn't mean for it to happen."

"No . . . I didn't . . . I didn't *do* that."

"If you tell me the truth, I'll promise I'll do everything in my power to help you."

"I *didn't*."

"You know what will happen if you don't confess, right?" Song says. "There will be a trial. A quick one. We have plenty of evidence."

"What evidence?"

"I can't tell you that. But believe me, we have all we need."

This is a lie, of course. Still, Lu says nothing. Song is his senior, and to interrupt would cause grave offense.

Song continues, "After the trial, Xiao Zhang, and I mean *immediately* after the judge hands down the sentence, you will be taken out through the back door, put in a car, driven to a desolate field in the middle of nowhere, and executed by means of a bullet to the back of your head. Then your organs will be harvested, if they're at all worth keeping, and you'll be dumped into an unmarked grave with various other moral degenerates and enemies of the people."

Lu knows this is also not true. If Zhang is found guilty, he will have a chance to appeal. When *that* trial ends in a guilty verdict, *then* he'll be executed. Lu is not sure about the organ harvesting part of it.

"So tell me," Song says. "Tell me what really happened. Tell me, and I'll make sure you get a fair trial."

"I took pictures," Zhang says, "but I didn't kill her!"

"You're a pervert and a liar," Song says, "and a rapist and a murderer."

"No!"

"Admit what you did to that girl or you'll be shot, and for a thousand years, every citizen in Raven Valley will spit on the ground when they hear your name!"

"No!" Zhang wails.

"You sick, disgusting animal. Confess!"

Lu can take no more. "Deputy Director!"

Song's face darkens. "What?"

"Apologies," Lu says, "but I don't think you'll get anything useful out of him this way."

"Are you experienced in conducting interviews with homicide suspects, Inspector?"

"Not exactly."

"Then how dare you tell me my business."

"Yes, but—"

Song abruptly stands. "Since you know best, by all means, carry on." He wrenches open the door and leaves, slamming it shut behind him.

Ta ma de. Lu switches off the camera and sits down across from a weeping Zhang. "Stop crying."

"I want to go home!"

"I'm sure you do," Lu says, "but I'm afraid it's not possible just yet."

"*Why?*"

"You *do* understand what's going on here, Zhaoxing?"

"I want to go hooome!"

Lu cannot reconcile the sight of Yang Fenfang's violated corpse with this sad, idiotic, hapless boy.

"Come on," Lu says. "I'll take you back to your cell and bring you some tea and biscuits."

After Zhang is settled, Lu goes looking for Deputy Director Song to make his peace, but notices the door to Chief Liang's office is closed. He can hear the sound of voices and smell cigarette smoke coming from behind it.

Lu figures Song is probably giving Liang an earful—and Liang is happy to listen and nod along, provided he can bum one of Song's Chunghwas.

Lu returns to his office. Five minutes later, Chief Liang comes in and shuts the door.

"The deputy director says you butted into his questioning of the suspect."

"He was being overly aggressive," Lu says.

"You mean he hit Zhang? With what? His fists? A shoe? A teakettle?"

"No, he didn't hit him."

"So he raised his voice, then? Perhaps yelled? Used a bit of rough language, even? Is that it?"

Lu shuffles papers.

"How is that you've been a cop for nearly twenty years and you're as sensitive as a royal consort?" Liang says.

"I'm not sensitive. I just don't think threatening Zhang with bullets and unmarked graves is the right approach."

"Don't be such a pain in the ass, kid. If you don't care about your own career, at least don't take a dump on mine. I've managed to do this thankless job for thirty years without Beijing taking the least bit of notice about me, and I'll not have you mess that up when I'm within pissing distance of retirement."

"Well, I'm not going to let Song mistreat our suspect," Lu says, "*or railroad him.*"

"Zhang's not *our* suspect anymore. He's property of the CIB. And as far as you're concerned, Song *is* the CIB. Get it? So play nice. Otherwise, I'll assign Sergeant Bing to work with Song, and you can spend the next few days helping old ladies search for their missing cats."

"All right, Chief. I hear you."

"You sure?"

"Yes."

"Good. Now first thing tomorrow, there's going to be a briefing attended by Procurator Gao, Magistrate Lin, and Party Secretary Mao."

"Fine."

"You will strive to be diplomatic."

"All right."

Liang looks at his watch. "It's late. Why don't you go home?"

"Do you need someone to drive Song to the guesthouse?"

"I'll do it."

"Ah."

"What's that mean?" Liang says. "Ah?"

"An opportunity for another Chunghwa cigarette."

"That tight bastard hasn't offered me a single one since this afternoon. On his salary, I'm sure he can afford to smoke two packs a day."

"Your sixtieth birthday is coming up. I'll buy you a carton as a gift."

"*Cao ni de ma.* I'm only fifty-four."

"The stress of your job has prematurely aged you."

"Idiot." Liang opens the office door. "You're a good cop, Lu Fei. Unfortunately, that's not enough. You need to play the game, or you're going to end up in Raven Valley for the rest of your life."

"Raven Valley's not so bad."

"Is that the extent of your ambition? To ascend to the lofty position of Raven Valley PSB chief?"

"It's good enough for you."

"My goals are modest: a full belly and a full glass."

"You are like the Daoist sages of old."

"Those fools lived in grass huts, retained their semen, and ate nothing but uncooked grains. Pretty dumb, if you ask me."

Lu takes the bus home, changes into civilian clothes, and eats at a nearby noodle shop.

Then he walks to the Red Lotus, which is located about a kilometer from his apartment.

Yanyan gives him her customary smile when he enters, the one he imagines is for him and him alone. She is wearing a red sweater that brings out the color in her cheeks and matches the lacquered cinnabar bracelet she never seems to be without. Her hair is wound into a messy bun on top of her head and pinned in place with an old chopstick.

One of the tables is occupied by two middle-aged men drinking warm Shaoxing wine served with slivers of ginger. When they see Lu, they lean forward, speak in whispers.

Lu takes a seat at the table farthest from them.

"Will it be wine tonight, Inspector?" Yanyan says.

Lu has asked her many times to address him more informally as *Brother Lu,* but she steadfastly refuses. "I think beer."

Yanyan takes a bottle from the chiller and brings it over along with a glass. She pops the cap and pours.

"Cheers." Lu takes a long pull. "Ahh. The elixir of life."

Yanyan sits and folds her arms on the table. "The rumors are flying," she says, sotto voce. Her eyes flicker toward the two old men, who are likewise watching Yanyan and Lu. Lu gives them a sharp look. They turn away.

"What rumors?" Lu asks.

"Lots of crazy things. That the poor girl was butchered like a pig."

"Hm," Lu says. He gulps the beer in his glass.

"Slow down." Yanyan pours another round. "Also, that she was partially eaten by her dog."

"I can confirm that is *not* true," Lu says. "Anyone have a theory as to who did it or why?"

"Everyone knows you've arrested some young man. Zhang something or other."

"We haven't arrested him. He's just been taken in for questioning. What do people think about him as a suspect?"

"Nobody seems to know him personally, but the guy who delivers my liquor says he heard the girl was a prostitute and Zhang murdered her because he didn't want to pay her exorbitant fee."

Lu shakes his head. "Why is it human nature to always assume the worst of people?"

"The lady who runs the food cart down the street said she thinks the girl's dead mother's ghost killed her."

"Why?"

"The girl didn't burn enough joss paper or send her a paper microwave or whatever."

"Perhaps I should bring the ghost in for questioning." Lu drains his glass.

Yanyan pours. "I've always thought I would make a good detective. Did you ever read Qiu Xiaolong's books? Or Ah Yi—I think he used to be a police officer?"

"I'm more partial to Judge Bao." Judge Bao was a government official who lived during the Song Dynasty and was famously incorruptible at a time when bureaucrats routinely took bribes and flouted justice. Over the centuries, he became a folk hero and the epitome of an honest civil servant, of which the People's Republic generally appears to be in short supply.

Yanyan scrunches her nose. "I think I saw a movie about him once. A Hong Kong comedy."

"Sacrilege," Lu says.

One of the old men at the neighboring table, no longer able to contain himself, calls out, "Hey, Inspector!"

"Yes?"

"People are saying there's a murderer on the loose who eats the livers of young women. Now my wife won't let my daughter-in-law out of the house."

"Heavens," Lu says. "Someone's been watching too many American movies."

"So that's not true, then?"

"I'm sorry, Uncle, I really can't talk about it. However, I seriously doubt your daughter-in-law's liver is at risk."

"So you say. You police never tell us simple folk the truth."

Lu turns away, picks up his glass, and swallows the rest of his beer. "Let's change the subject. How is your father doing?"

Yanyan's expression darkens. "He's taken a bit of a downturn in the past week."

Lu knows Yanyan's father has been sick for some time—cancer—and his illness weighs heavily on her. It's just the two of them. No husband, no siblings, no other family, and no doubt she would rather be home caring for him, but as the sole breadwinner in the family, here she is slinging drinks at the Red Lotus.

"Let me know if I can do anything to help."

"Thank you," Yanyan says. "Another?"

"Always assume yes, unless otherwise directed."

Yanyan fetches Lu a second Harbin lager. Then she tends to the two old men, who continue with their furtive looks and hushed discussion. Lu studiously ignores them.

Lu is just about to order a third beer when the door to the Red Lotus opens and Dr. Ma enters. She looks at Lu in surprise.

"Inspector!"

"Dr. Ma! Fancy meeting you here."

"Yes, well, I need a drink, and I've been wandering around for the past thirty minutes trying to find a place that looked halfway decent."

"The Red Lotus is wholly decent," Lu says.

"Should I join you?"

"It would be my honor."

Dr. Ma takes a seat and sloughs off her coat. Her cheeks are freshly scrubbed, and she's applied a touch of lipstick and eyeliner. She's wearing Western jeans and boots and a black cashmere sweater with a deep V that reveals a generous amount of cleavage.

"You ate dinner?" Lu says.

"At the hotel. It was predictably terrible."

"Your colleagues are checked in?"

"Yes."

"They didn't want to join you for a drink?"

"I didn't ask. We are colleagues, not drinking friends."

"Right."

Yanyan appears. "Evening." She smiles at Dr. Ma and arches an eyebrow at Lu.

"Yanyan, this is Dr. Ma," Lu says. "Dr. Ma, this is Ms. Luo Yanyan, the owner of the Red Lotus."

"A pleasure to meet you," Yanyan says.

"Do you have whiskey?" Dr. Ma asks, somewhat brusquely.

"Johnnie Walker?"

"Eh, no," Dr. Ma says. "Yamazaki?"

"No. Sorry."

"What do you have that's single malt?"

"I have a bottle of Yoichi."

"I'll have that one. Neat."

"It's quite expensive, I'm afraid."

Dr. Ma's expression falls just short of a sneer. "I think I can manage it."

Yanyan understands that she's insulted Dr. Ma. She bows slightly. "Of course, sorry. I'll get it right away."

She retreats behind the counter. Dr. Ma rolls her eyes. "I hate coming to these backwater towns."

"Well . . . on behalf of Raven Valley Township, allow me to apologize for the primitive conditions you are being forced to endure."

Dr. Ma raises an eyebrow. "Are you scolding me, Inspector Lu?"

"Maybe."

Dr. Ma smiles. "You're right. I'm being grouchy. Sorry. I'm tired and cold, and even more than small towns, I hate performing autopsies on young women."

"Of course. I understand."

The two old men are staring openly at Dr. Ma. She turns in her chair. "Enjoying the view?" Abashed, they retreat to their huddle.

"Curious locals," Lu says in a low voice. "They rarely see a celebrity like yourself."

"I don't think it's my celebrity they're gawking at," Dr. Ma says, readjusting her neckline. "Anyway. This is your regular hangout?"

"Yes. I like it."

Yanyan arrives bearing a tumbler filled with amber liquid. "Enjoy."

"I'll have another beer when you have a chance," Lu says.

Yanyan nods silently, picks up Lu's empty bottle, and walks away.

Dr. Ma watches her go. "I can see *why* you like it."

"I'm strictly here for the drinks."

"Right." Dr. Ma sips her whiskey. "I hope I'm not making your girlfriend jealous."

"She's not my girlfriend."

"Are you married?"

"No. Are you?"

"Who has time for such nonsense? Do you *have* a girlfriend?"

"No."

"Are you gay?"

"*What?*"

"Don't be insulted. There's nothing wrong with being gay. Never mind the 'three nos.'"

The "three nos" are the government's unwritten policy regarding homosexuality: no official approval; no official disapproval; no official encouragement.

"That's just not a question you hear people ask very often," Lu says.

"I spent some time overseas. Perhaps a touch of foreign influence has rubbed off on me."

"Where overseas?"

"I did a residency program at Johns Hopkins. Baltimore. Do you know where that is?"

Yanyan drops off a fresh bottle of lager. "Thanks," Lu says.

"Sure thing." Yanyan leaves Lu to pour for himself.

Lu frowns at her retreating back. "Yes, I know. I also studied abroad."

"Oh? Where?"

"Michigan. A training program for police officers."

"So you speak English?"

"Moderately. I also took English courses when I was at university."

"Shall I test you?"

"Please don't."

"How do you say, 'I'll have a hamburger, fries, and a large Coca-Cola'?"

"That's easy." Lu translates into English.

"Very good. How about, 'Hands up, or I'll shoot'?"

"Er, let's see." Lu translates.

"Well done. How do you say, 'What's a nice guy like you doing in a place like this?'"

Lu doesn't fully apprehend the playful nature of this phrase, but he dutifully translates it into English.

"Not bad," Dr. Ma says. "And now I'm ready for another round."

It takes Lu a moment to catch Yanyan's eye. He points at Dr. Ma's empty tumbler. Yanyan nods curtly.

"Definitely jealous," Dr. Ma whispers.

"Nonsense."

"Have you and she ever . . . ?"

"No! Never."

"Why such a strong denial?"

"I don't know, I just . . . She's not like that."

"Like what? A living, breathing woman who enjoys giving and receiving pleasure?"

"You enjoy saying provocative things."

"I like to penetrate below the surface," Dr. Ma says, "and get to the heart of the matter."

"You and our perp are alike in that way."

Yanyan brings over a fresh tumbler of Yoichi and another beer for Lu. By now, Lu has a pleasant buzz. He and Dr. Ma chat freely about their experiences in America. The customs they found curious. How everyone seemed to have at least two guns, including children and old ladies. The American notion of food portions.

"When you go to a restaurant, they give you so much!" Dr. Ma says. "Enough to feed a small village."

"And Americans feel like they wasted their money if they don't eat it all," Lu agrees.

"That's why they are so huge and fat."

"And they drink ice-cold water even in dead of winter."

"So bad for your qi."

"You believe in qi?" Lu says. "Even though you were trained in Western medicine at the illustrious Johns Hopkins?"

"Why is that hard to believe? We Chinese were unlocking the mysteries of the nervous system when Westerners were still crediting illnesses to the presence of demons."

"Oh, I believe in qi also. That's why I usually drink wine instead of beer."

"A cup of wine is medicinal. A bottle of wine is poison."

"I only drink wine one cup at a time."

The discussion eventually circles around to the Yang case.

"How long for the toxicology reports and so on?" Lu asks.

"Two to three weeks."

"And now that you're done with her, what will happen to Yang's body?"

"I have no idea."

"Should we continue to store it?"

"Not on my account. I've got what I need. She can be returned to the family."

"I don't think there is a family. She was an only child, and both parents are dead."

"Surely she had an aunt or uncle or cousins?"

"I don't know. No one has inquired about her so far. Maybe, even if she has relatives, they don't want to pay for the funeral."

Dr. Ma nods. "All too common these days. Morgues are stuffed with unclaimed bodies."

"Sad when no one cares enough to lay the dead to rest."

"The dead are dead. It doesn't bother them any."

"It's just a shame when you cease to exist, even in a memory."

"When you're gone, Inspector, you cease to exist, whether or not someone burns paper money and feeds you incense and rice on your death day."

"I suppose." Still, Lu is troubled by the thought of it. To die and be forgotten, both in body and spirit.

He glances over at Yanyan. She is smiling and chatting with the two old men. A widow and childless, if she were to die tomorrow, her situation would be much the same as Yang Fenfang's.

As would Lu's, come to think of it.

"Anyway, it's getting late, and I'm drunk," Dr. Ma says. "I think it's time I made my way back to my rustic accommodations."

Lu asks for the bill, and then he and Dr. Ma argue over it. He is secretly relieved when she insists on paying for three of her four whiskeys. Each tumbler costs as much as a full meal at the most expensive restaurant in Raven Valley.

There is an awkward moment after the bill is settled. Both Lu and Dr. Ma put on their coats and prepare to leave—but he is concerned that walking out with Dr. Ma will give Yanyan the wrong impression. He hesitates for a moment.

"Everything all right?" Dr. Ma asks.

"Yes, sure. Let me, uh . . ." He raises his voice. "Let me get you a taxi."

"No need," Dr. Ma says. "I'll walk. The hotel is not far."

"Right. Okay." He looks over at Yanyan. "Good night!"

Yanyan bids them a subdued farewell. Outside, Dr. Ma adjusts her red scarf and winter hat. "This weather will be the death of me."

"You get used to it."

"Not without a warm body to curl up next to." They start walking, somewhat aimlessly but in the general direction of the Raven Valley Friendship Guesthouse. After a few minutes of silence, Dr. Ma looks sidelong at Lu. "How about it?"

"How about what?"

"Feel like keeping a southerner warm tonight?"

Lu stops in his tracks. He is shocked. Scandalized.

And flattered.

Dr. Ma is unlike any Chinese woman he has ever met. Confident, brash, openly sexual. He admires the courage it requires for any citizen of the People's Republic, especially a woman, to cast off the shackles of thousands of years of Confucian tradition.

And why shouldn't he accept? He has no wife, no girlfriend. No one to whom he owes an oath of fidelity.

He looks back toward the Red Lotus. To abstain because of some unspoken and perhaps completely imaginary bond with Yanyan would be ridiculous. There has never been the hint of anything between them outside the confines of their proprietor-customer relationship.

"I take it that's a no?" Dr. Ma asks.

"I don't know what to say," Lu answers. "I'm not used to . . . that kind of offer."

"Perhaps we should just say good night, then," Dr. Ma says.

"I don't . . . I didn't . . . I mean . . ."

"It's fine," Dr. Ma says. "If it's going to be a source of emotional distress, what's the point? Anyway, it's late. Thank you for the pleasant evening, Inspector."

"Can I at least walk you back to the hotel?" Lu asks.

"That's all right. I'm a big girl. See you tomorrow."

She crosses the street and heads off down the block.

Lu mentally kicks himself. How often does one get a come-on from a brilliant and beautiful quasi-celebrity?

He shuffles home in the bitter cold, a poem by Du Mu running through his thoughts:

> *Abundant feelings somehow become no feelings at all*
> *Over a farewell bottle, we can't even manage a smile*
> *Only the candle demonstrates a reluctance to part*
> *All night it weeps little wax tears for us*

MONDAY

Concrete analysis of concrete conditions, Lenin said, is "the most essential thing in Marxism, the living soul of Marxism." Lacking an analytical approach, many of our comrades do not want to go deeply into complex matters, to analyze and study them over and over again, but like to draw simple conclusions which are either absolutely affirmative or absolutely negative. . . . From now on we should remedy this state of affairs.

—*Quotations from Chairman Mao Zedong*

The morning briefing takes place in the *paichusuo*'s canteen, the only room large enough to hold such a large number of participants.

Present are Dr. Ma; Deputy Director Song; Technicians Jin and Hu; Lu Fei; Chief Liang; Sergeant Bing; Party Secretary Mao (no relation to his famous namesake); the Raven Valley Township magistrate, surnamed Lin; and Procurator Gao.

Tea is poured and cigarettes lit.

Smoking has recently been banned in most workplaces, but as this particular conclave has assembled the highest authorities in Raven Valley Township, its members are free to ignore onerous public health laws without fear of reprisal.

Song says a few words of welcome and then addresses his comments to Magistrate Lin and Party Secretary Mao. "Just a reminder, gentlemen, your presence here is a courtesy, and I must ask you to keep the contents of this discussion completely confidential. We don't want any information getting out that might alarm the populace."

Song touches here on the concept of *weiwen*—the directive to maintain social stability and order, which is, to some extent, the primary function of law enforcement in the People's Republic. It goes without saying that solving crimes and catching criminals is part of the job, but Chinese police are notoriously closemouthed when it comes to releasing information that might cause widespread fear or panic. Stability always—always—takes precedence over public safety.

The importance of *weiwen* also helps explain the nation's incredibly low crime rates. According to Chinese statistics, homicides in the People's Republic are one-fifth that of the United States, despite the country having a population four times greater.

Many China watchers believe these figures don't tell the whole story. They estimate only about 2.5 percent of all criminal activity nationwide is acknowledged by the government. Rumors abound that local police stations routinely keep two sets of records—one accurate and one, heavily doctored, used to compile official reports.

In any case, both Magistrate Lin and Party Secretary Mao understand how this works, and they quickly nod their assent.

Chief Liang opens with a quick review—prepared for him by Lu—of the case thus far: "The victim, Yang Fenfang, was twenty-three years old. A resident of Raven Valley, but she had been living and working in Harbin for the past three years. Her parents were deceased, the father eight years ago, her mother one week ago. The cause of her mother's death is listed as kidney disease."

He goes on to detail the circumstances of the body's discovery, the subsequent canvassing of the neighborhood, the evidence against the current suspect (surveillance photos of the victim on his phone, his work as a butcher, his general status as a pervert), and then he hands the baton over to Lu.

"Earlier this morning, we went to the pork processing plant and questioned Zhang's supervisor and some of his coworkers," Lu says. "They all basically said the same thing. Zhang is not very bright, but he's a hard worker and has never exhibited any signs of violent behavior. We did find a pair of plastic overalls at Zhang's house, which he denied having put there. Our colleagues from the CIB have tested blood residue on them."

"It was pigs' blood," says Technician Hu.

"You say the suspect denied having the overalls," Procurator Gao says. He is in his forties, dark suit, glasses, the only man at the table besides Lu who doesn't smoke. Lu has worked with him on more than a dozen cases and still doesn't know whether or not Gao is married, has kids, where he lives, what his educational and family background is.

"Correct," Lu says. "My guess is because he took them from work and was afraid of getting in trouble for doing so."

"So why did he take them in the first place?"

"I don't know. Maybe he wanted to wear them when doing something around the house to keep his clothes clean." *Such as emptying chamber pots?*

"Could he have worn them to commit the murder and then washed the human blood off?"

"Unlikely," Technician Hu says. "We would have found some trace of it mixed with the pig blood."

"In other words," Lu summarizes, "we don't believe the overalls are relevant to this case."

"Only insofar as they indicate that Zhang is something of a liar and thief," Gao says.

Good point, Lu silently concedes.

"What about fingerprints?" Gao wants to know.

Again, Technician Hu chimes in. "We compared latents found at the victim's house to the suspect's. No match."

Gao nods and motions for Lu to continue.

"One thing that bothered us when searching the victim's residence was the absence of a television," Lu says. "We did find a television set at the Zhang household, but it's ten years old, at least. This morning, a few constables asked around the neighborhood to see if anyone had heard of Zhang trying to sell a TV—none had. We'll continue this line of questioning during the coming week."

"Have you determined for certain if the victim actually owned a newer model?" Gao asks.

"We're in the process of obtaining her bank and WeChat financial transaction records," Lu says.

Gao jots this down in a notebook. "Anything else?"

"Not at the moment."

"Autopsy report?" Gao says.

Dr. Ma is likewise all business this morning. When Lu greeted her earlier, she responded politely enough, but with no hint that she had been prepared to share his bed the night before. He is confused and dismayed by her remoteness. He feels as if he's proven to be a disappointment.

"The victim was discovered in an unheated house in subzero weather," Dr. Ma says. "Making body temperature and the onset of rigor mortis an inaccurate means to pinpoint the time of death. There was very little decomposition—again, partially a factor of the subzero ambient room temperature. But judging from the victim's state of digestion, I'd estimate she was killed within four hours of her last meal, which I am assuming was dinner. The victim was found Saturday evening, and, as Chief Liang already mentioned, the neighbor said the victim's dog had been barking intermittently since Friday night. Given the evidence, my best guess is that the homicide took place somewhere between 10:00 p.m. Friday and 2:00 a.m. on Saturday. There is, of course, a large margin of error.

"The victim displayed extensive bruising and ligature marks around her neck and wrists. I believe she was strangled into unconsciousness— manually—by means of the perpetrator's hands. Then her wrists were bound by duct tape. Following that, she was either sexually assaulted and strangled again with a belt or strap until she was dead, or strangled to death and then sexually assaulted. It's difficult to be certain of the sequence of events, because there was vaginal tearing but not a great deal of bleeding."

Magistrate Lin sucks air through his teeth. He is in his late fifties, with thick glasses and a messy mop of graying hair. He wears a rumpled suit and tie and is so thin that his neck protrudes from the collar of his shirt like bamboo stalk in a round clay pot.

"How do you know she was manually strangled?" Procurator Gao asks.

"Her thyroid cartilage was contused and torn. The damage was more widespread than you would expect from a simple ligature strangulation."

Gao enters this into his notebook.

Dr. Ma continues, "The victim's right temporoparietal skull and cerebrum region displayed injury consistent with impact. I suspect a hammer was used."

"Impact sufficient to knock her unconscious?" Gao asks.

"Possibly," Dr. Ma says. "At least enough to daze her. I speculate the hammer or whatever the perpetrator hit her with was also used for the sexual assault."

Party Secretary Mao chimes in: "Do you suppose this ... er ... What was her name again?"

In contrast to Magistrate Lin, Mao is neat and polished in his Western suit, silk tie, and leather shoes.

He is by far the most powerful man in Raven Valley Township.

Local government in the People's Republic consists of four levels. In order of importance, they are: provincial, prefectural/municipality, county, and lastly, township. Each jurisdiction has authority over the level below it, and each level is run by a system of dual leadership consisting of an elected official *and* a representative of the Chinese Communist Party. In the case of Raven Valley Township, the elected official is Magistrate Lin, and the CCP representative is Mao. Magistrate Lin's job is to execute government policy, Party Secretary Mao's job to decide what that policy will be.

Mao is exactly the sort of odious government functionary that Lu abhors. He exudes a smarmy sense of entitlement and bulls through his interactions with other people like a battleship under full steam, leaving an oily slick in his wake.

"Yang," Lu says. "Yang Fenfang."

"Do you suppose this Ms. Yang knew the killer? She let him in, turned her back to him?"

"It's possible that she knew him or at least felt comfortable opening the door when he knocked," Lu says. "There was no sign of forced entry."

Gao jots down another note. "Please go on, Dr. Ma."

Dr. Ma nods. "After the victim was murdered, the perpetrator cut her open and removed her heart, lungs, and liver."

"*Tian ah!*" Magistrate Lin squeaks. "Who could be capable of such a thing?"

"A madman, clearly," Party Secretary Mao says.

"What kind of skill would that require?" Gao asks, ever the practical one.

"A decent knowledge of anatomy," Dr. Ma says. "The ability to locate and excise organs, some facility with a scalpel, and experience cutting a rib cage, which is not easy."

"This suspect you have in custody?" Party Secretary Mao says. "I understand he's a pig butcher?"

"He works at a pork processing plant," Lu says. "I'm not sure if he's ever done any of the things Dr. Ma just mentioned in the course of his job."

"Well, you can't really be sure of anything at this point," Song says. "Isn't that correct, Inspector?"

"Of course, Deputy Director."

Dr. Ma taps her pen on the table. "Also, after the removal of the organs, the perpetrator sutured the incision closed with nylon thread."

"Wouldn't that have taken a great deal of time?" Mao says. "Why bother?"

"Perhaps twenty minutes," Dr. Ma says. "And good question."

"Is that hard to come by?" Gao asks. "The nylon thread?"

"Not terribly. It's available in medical supply stores and the internet."

"Who might typically use it in the course of their employment?"

"Doctors. Veterinarians. Physician's assistants. All kinds of health care professionals. Pathologists such as myself."

"What about the instruments required?" Gao says. "For the cutting, excising, and suturing?"

"A good-quality scalpel, a needle and thread, scissors, forceps. A pair of shears."

"So does that rule out the pig butcher?" Party Secretary Mao asks.

"Not entirely," Song says. "Zhang is a big man, fully capable of over-powering and strangling the victim. His position at the pork processing plant has doubtless afforded him some familiarity with anatomy."

"Zhang butchered pigs, but stitching them up again was outside the scope of his duties," Lu says.

Song flashes Lu an annoyed look. "I understand pigs are commonly employed as a teaching tool in medical schools, are they not, Dr. Ma?"

"Correct," Dr. Ma says. "They share a number of anatomic and physiologic similarities with humans."

"So Zhang's work experience is relevant here," Song says.

Lu opens his mouth to answer, but Chief Liang, fearing what he might say, quickly interjects. "You mentioned sexual assault, Doctor. How do you know she was assaulted by, ah, a hammer? And not raped?"

"I don't know that, Chief. But as I said, tears in the vaginal tissue lead me to believe the instrument used was something other than a penis. In any case, we took swabs to rule out the presence of semen or condom lubricant, spermicide, or powder, so we'll know for sure soon."

Magistrate Lin blushes behind a cloud of cigarette smoke.

"The perpetrator also placed joss paper in the victim's mouth," Dr. Ma says. "A one-billion note."

"Can that be traced?" Gao asks.

"Common denomination and manufacture," Technician Hu says. "You can buy such notes in any large town or on the internet. Nearly impossible to track where it was purchased."

"The killer put this joss paper in the victim's mouth as what?" Party Secretary Mao asks. "An offering to her soul?"

"Perhaps as a way to keep the girl from haunting him," Magistrate Lin suggests.

"So our killer was depraved but also scared of ghosts?" Mao says.

"I don't think Magistrate Lin is far off the mark," Lu says. "I assume everyone here is familiar with the concept of the Five Elements?"

"Fire, water, earth, wood, and metal, and so on," Song says.

"Yes. As the theory goes, these elements are the basic building blocks of the universe, and they continuously interact in a productive or destructive cycle, giving rise to all the various natural phenomena."

"What's this got to do with the joss money?" Gao asks.

"Nothing. But each of the elements corresponds to a cardinal direction, a season, an emotion, a color—"

"We don't need a lecture on metaphysics," Song snaps. "Get to the point."

"The elements also correspond to a bodily organ—liver, heart, lung, kidney, spleen—and each organ, in turn, is associated with a spiritual or mental attribute. The spleen with intent. The kidneys with will. But the heart, lungs, and liver—these three are all imbued with some aspect of the soul or spirit. So—maybe by removing them, the suspect was either trying to 'steal the soul' of his victim or, as Magistrate Lin said, prevent her vengeful ghost from haunting him, and the joss money was part of that effort."

"Ah, now it's all very clear," Song announces. "We just need to focus our search on murderous Daoist priests and homicidal feng shui masters."

"Five Element theory is fairly common knowledge," Lu says. "The perpetrator doesn't have to be an expert on the classics."

Gao glances at his watch. "As fascinating as this discussion is, I have another appointment. So where does this leave us now?"

"Notwithstanding Inspector Lu's hypothesis, I think we can fairly confidently establish a profile of the perpetrator," Song says. "He is antisocial and reclusive. He's also patient and premeditated, given the fact that he, we conjecture, waited until a quiet hour of the night to commit the crime and brought along an extensive tool kit. I can say with complete confidence that he hates women. Perhaps he has felt the sting of repeated romantic rejection, which has built up a deep-seated resentment toward the female gender, or maybe his mother was cold and overbearing. He is most definitely a sexual pervert. And given Dr. Ma's conclusion that he used a foreign object to sexually assault the girl, I think it's extremely likely he's impotent."

"So what about the pig butcher?" Party Secretary Mao asks.

"We should proceed with our investigation of him," Song says.

"Fine," Gao says. "Send me an arrest request, and I'll write up the order."

According to legal procedure, once Procurator Gao has issued an arrest order, Zhang can be held for up to three months while the investigation takes place. If Gao then determines there is sufficient evidence to prosecute, Zhang will be indicted, and the case will go to trial.

The conviction rate in the People's Republic is north of 90 percent. If Zhang ends up in court, his fate is all but certain.

"Zhang has the mental capacity of a child," Lu says. Chief Liang tries to subtly wave him off, but Lu ignores him. "I don't think he's capable of this kind of premeditated crime, and he has no history of violence."

"Didn't he violently resist being taken into custody?" Song asks.

"Not *violently*."

"Did he not, according to your statement, throw one of your constables across the room and knock you off your chair?"

"He was scared. That's different from being willfully violent."

"I don't get the distinction."

"You don't need to be a genius to cut a woman open, remove her organs, and stick something up her . . ." Party Secretary Mao stops himself. "You just need to be sick."

Gao curtails further debate. "At this point, I believe there's sufficient cause to issue an arrest order."

"Thank you, Procurator," Song says.

"What are your next steps?" Gao asks.

"Well, to have a look at the victim's financial records," Song says. "Talk to her employer and any friends we can track down in Harbin. Have a look at her apartment there."

Gao closes his notebook. "Sounds good. Thank you, everyone."

The meeting breaks up. Lu catches up with Song. "Deputy Director? Do you have a moment?"

Song stops and turns. "What?"

"I'd like to go with you to Harbin," Lu says.

"Perhaps it's better if you focus on things here. Harbin is not in your jurisdiction."

"I know the city. I worked there for ten years."

Song stares coldly at Lu. "Somehow I feel like we're not on the same page here, Inspector."

"We're on the same page, Deputy Director—that is, if you want to catch the person who actually killed Yang Fenfang, not just railroad a convenient suspect in order to close the case as quickly as possible."

"You insult me."

"Not at all. You said yourself you're ambitious, but I trust you do have integrity."

"I've never put an innocent man behind bars."

"And I'd like to help you maintain a perfect record. Listen, Deputy Director—Yang Fenfang was murdered in my town. My only *angle,* as you called it, is to see the murderer brought to justice. But I need your help. That's why I called CIB. I'm not after commendations, a transfer, or a pat on the back—just justice for a young woman."

Song considers for a moment. "Do you agree to follow my lead?"

"Yes."

"You won't undermine my methods?"

Lu thinks of Song's interrogation of Zhang. He didn't like it, but this is what Song does for a living. Catches killers. "No, Deputy Director."

"Fine. Since you know the city, you drive."

Thirty minutes later, Lu, Song, and Technician Jin, who has brought along two cases of equipment, are doing 130 kilometers per hour on the Tongjiang Expressway. Song cracks a window and lights a cigarette. He opens a notebook where he has recorded the details of Yang Fenfang's city apartment, the Harbin Good Fortune Terrace. There is a phone number for the management office, which he calls. A young lady answers. She sounds petulant. Song is instantly annoyed.

"This is Deputy Director Song of the Ministry of Public Security. I'm looking for information about one of your residents."

"You'll have to speak to someone at Ruzhu," the lady says.

"What's Ruzhu?"

"You don't know Ruzhu?"

"If I knew, I wouldn't be asking, would I?"

"I suppose not."

"So? What is it?"

"A rental platform," she says. "All our property transactions are through Ruzhu."

He asks her to look up the phone number and name of the Ruzhu agent who has rented the apartment to Yang Fenfang.

"I'm sorry, you'll have to just call the company directly." She sounds less than sorry.

"What's your name?" Lu says.

"Ms. Hong," she answers warily.

"Ms. Hong. This is an official investigation. So quit wasting my time. Get that name and phone number for me immediately, or I'll arrest you for obstruction of justice. The regulars down at the detention center have a term for soft young girls like yourself. *Nen ji.*"

Tender chicken.

Ms. Hong produces the name and contact details for the agent listed on Yang's rental agreement without further delay. His name is Mr. Wang. Of course, another Wang.

Song calls the number. He explains that he's conducting an inquiry regarding Yang Fenfang and asks Mr. Wang to meet at the Good Fortune Terrace.

Before long, they arrive at the outskirts of Harbin. Once Lu knew the city well, but it's been nearly a decade since he lived here, and the landscape has changed dramatically.

As the capital of Heilongjiang, Harbin is the province's economic, cultural, and political nexus. Its humble origin as a small settlement on the banks of the Songhua River is reflected in the name—Harbin means "a place to dry fishing nets" in the Manchu language. Until 1898, it was just a sleepy frontier town—but then it was chosen to serve as the administrative base for the Chinese Eastern Railway, an extension of the famous Trans-Siberian Railway. It subsequently grew rapidly into an international city, with a large population of expats, especially Russians. The Russians built European-style buildings, boulevards, parks, theaters, and churches and established Russian-speaking schools and newspapers. Then came the Russo-Japanese War, the Russian Revolution, and the Japanese invasion, each leaving their mark. When civil war broke out between the Chinese nationalists and the Communists, Harbin was the first large Chinese city to come under governance by Mao's forces. Later, it suffered mightily under the depredations of the Red Guards and again due to rising tensions between the Soviet Union and China in the 1970s.

Harbin has survived all these challenges and more and has since developed into one of the PRC's most important industrial and agricultural centers.

Over its short history, the city has accumulated numerous nicknames. Poetically, "the pearl on the swan's neck," so called because when viewed from above, Heilongjiang resembles a swan with outstretched wings, with Harbin forming a dot just under its elegantly curved neck. Also, the "Oriental Moscow," due to the prevalence of Russian architecture.

But most locals just call Harbin "City of Ice." Winters here are excruciatingly long and cold, with average temperatures in excess of twenty degrees below zero Celsius. Harbin has cleverly turned a negative into a positive by hosting a variety of cold-weather activities during an annual winter festival, a highlight of which are incredibly elaborate ice sculptures dotting the city, including nearly full-size ice castles, palaces, and replicas of famous monuments emblazoned with colored lights.

The Harbin Good Fortune Terrace is located in one of the newer residential districts. When Lu and Song arrive, they find it to be a sprawling housing development consisting of several modern high-rises, each boasting thirty floors, arranged within a landscaped setting of winding walkways, neatly tended hedges, and young elm trees.

Lu parks. "What now?"

"We wait for Mr. Wang," Song says.

Lu's phone rings. It's Sergeant Bing.

"We had a look at Yang's purchasing history," Sergeant Bing says. "Two months ago, she bought a Xiaomi TV. A big one—140 centimeters."

"Aha!"

"She also bought an ASUS computer tablet."

"I don't remember seeing that in the inventory of the house."

"It's missing, too."

"Hold on." Lu covers the mouthpiece and tells Song and Technician Jin about the TV and tablet.

"Find those electronics, and maybe we find our killer," Song says.

"Right." Lu speaks into the phone. "Sergeant, see if you can get serial numbers for the TV and tablet and then check around electronics shops and on Taobao to determine if our suspect is trying to sell them."

Taobao is the biggest e-commerce website in the world, a potent combination of Amazon and eBay. You can find virtually anything for sale there. Rare books. Fresh soup dumplings. Nike Air Jordans. Not long ago, some enterprising salesman even advertised Vietnamese brides at a bargain price of 9,998 yuan (about $1,500 US dollars) apiece.

"Will do," Sergeant Bing says.

"And ask around Zhang's neighborhood again."

"We're on it."

"I know you are. Thanks." Lu hangs up.

"One other thing," Technician Jin says. "Is there a location feature on the tablet? Is it linked to an IP address? Maybe we can track its use."

"Can you work with Inspector Lu's guys on that when we get back?" Song says. "They probably have no idea how to go about it."

"Sure," Jin says.

Lu wants to defend the Raven Valley PSB against Song's disdain—but the truth is, he doesn't know how to trace the digital footprint of the tablet, and he suspects no one else at the *paichusuo* does, either.

Song pulls a pack of cigarettes out of his pocket. Before he can light one, a car pulls up beside the patrol vehicle. "This must be Mr. Wang." He opens the door and gets out.

Wang is young, dressed in a suit and heavy coat. He's visibly nervous. "Sorry to keep you waiting. Traffic."

Song perfunctorily introduces Lu and Technician Jin.

"You wanted to see Yang Fenfang's apartment?" Wang says.

"Yes."

"Right this way, please."

They start walking. Lu and Technician Jin fall in behind.

"What do you know about Ms. Yang?" Song asks.

"Nothing, really. I never met her personally."

"How's that?"

"All rental procedures are conducted online. The application, the payment."

"How about the key?"

"It's a key card, and we send it by courier. I almost never interact with my clients in person."

"Such is the way of the modern world."

"What about her rent?" Lu asks. "She's been living in Raven Valley for the past couple of months. Do you know if her payments are up to date?"

"Our rental platform automatically deducts payments at the first of the month," Wang says. "So as long as she has money in her account, she can be anywhere in the world and rent will still get paid. Which I assume it has been. Otherwise, I would have gotten an alert."

Wang leads them through the courtyard and past dormant topiary and naked trees to one of the high-rises. He uses a key card to open the front door. Inside is a small lobby. It is empty. There is no old PLA soldier here who keeps watch and sleeps on a cot in the utility closet like where Lu grew up. Just a row of mailboxes and a bank of elevators. They ride up to the nineteenth floor.

"Is there security footage we can access?" Lu nods at a camera attached to the ceiling of the elevator.

"Most of these new housing developments have cameras as crime deterrents but don't actually record footage."

"Typical," Song says. "Nothing but window dressing."

The elevator door opens, and Wang escorts them down the hall. He locates Yang Fenfang's apartment and unlocks the door.

Lu steps inside. His first impression is that the apartment is incredibly large and luxurious for a young girl from Raven Valley who works in a bar. How can she—*could* she—possibly afford such a place?

There is a living room and attached kitchen. A huge picture window overlooks the courtyard below. The walls are a pristine white, the floor polished wood. Furnishings include a leather couch, two matching chairs, a glass coffee table, and an entertainment console with a massive flat-screen TV.

"These apartments are rented furnished or unfurnished?" Lu asks.

"Unfurnished," Wang replies.

Technician Jin opens one of his equipment cases and takes out several pairs of latex gloves. He hands one each to Song and Lu. "Please don't move anything until I've taken photos and drawn up a grid."

The gloves snap as Lu slides his fingers into them. He walks over to the TV and checks the model—a Sony. He examines a messy collection of fashion and gossip magazines on top of the coffee table. He notes the presence of an ashtray. It's clean. He sniffs it. It still smells of cigarette ash.

There is a collection of Western and Chinese DVDs neatly lined up on the entertainment console. A couple of dying houseplants on the windowsill.

The kitchen is outfitted with the latest appliances. A glass table and modern chairs occupy a dining nook.

"All this stuff must have cost a small fortune," Lu says.

As Technician Jin starts documenting the apartment with photos, Lu and Song root through the kitchen cabinets. They find instant noodles, chocolate wafers, salty snacks. One of the cabinets appears to have been reserved exclusively for higher-end items. A bottle of cognac, two-thirds full, some Western gourmet crackers, tins of mackerel and cod liver, canned nuts, dried mushrooms, and the like.

"The girl had expensive tastes," Song remarks.

The fridge is bare apart from a carton of apple juice, some condiments, a moldy loaf of bread, a plastic takeout container of leftover soup, and two bottles of wine. Western wine, one red and one white. The apple juice is two months past its expiration date.

Lu enters the bathroom. Beneath the vanity is a large assortment of skin care and other beauty products in plastic caddies. A package of tampons, half-used. Extra toilet paper. A hair dryer and curling set. Soap, cotton balls, disposable razors, and all the other things you might expect to find in a young woman's boudoir.

Song pokes his head in. "Anything?"

"Nothing out of the ordinary."

There are two bedrooms. One is obviously Fenfang's. Whereas the living room, kitchen, and bathroom are minimalistic and spotless, here Fenfang has given full reign to her girlish sensibilities. She's plastered the walls with movie idol and boy band posters. Her bed is unmade, and discarded clothes are piled on the floor. A table groans under the weight of magazines, cosmetics, and tchotchkes. Lu opens a closet. He finds skirts, tops, dresses, more casual outfits. Lots of shoes.

Song opens the nightstand. "What have we here?"

Lu walks over. He sees, in the open drawer, a box of condoms, a small black vibrator, and several rubber phalluses in assorted shapes and sizes. One is impossibly long and thick. Lu can't imagine how Yang could have possibly inserted such a monster into any of her bodily orifices.

"Suddenly, I begin to understand how Yang could afford this apartment," Song remarks.

Lu is shocked by the contents of the drawer. Technician Jin comes into the bedroom and has a look. His assessment is remarkably blasé: "I'll get these tested for DNA." He snaps off a series of photographs.

Lu moves on to the second bedroom. In contrast to Fenfang's, this one appears to have never been occupied. There is a bed, but it's minus sheets. A chest of drawers, empty. A nightstand, empty.

It doesn't make sense. Why rent a two-bedroom apartment if you're just one person? And if you happen to have a second bedroom, why not use it? As a guest room, a storage space, anything at all?

Lu goes out to the living room. "What is the monthly rent here?" he asks Wang, who is still standing in the open doorway.

"About five thousand yuan."

"That's a lot."

"It's reasonable, given the location and amenities."

"I'm not a prospective client, Mr. Wang."

"No. Sorry. Force of habit. Is there something I should know about the, er . . . Ms. Yang?"

Song comes out of the bedroom. "She's dead."

Wang gasps. "Dead? How?"

"Murdered."

"How horrible!"

"Do you have any information, any at all, that might help us find out who killed her and why?" Song asks.

"I'm so sorry. Like I said, I didn't know her personally."

Song turns to Lu. "Let's knock on some doors."

"Everyone will be at work."

"It's worth a try."

Lu and Song go up and down the hall, but as predicted, only a handful of residents are home. Most of them are uncomfortable speaking to the police and have nothing of value to say, but one older lady is more than happy to gossip.

"Yes, I know the girl by sight, but I don't think we've exchanged more than two words the entire time she's lived here."

"All right, well, thanks for your time," Song says.

"But," the old lady continues, "I noticed she slept during the day and went out in the evening. And didn't return home until the wee hours of the morning."

"She worked nights," Lu says.

"And sometimes . . ."

"Yes?" Song says.

"Sometimes I saw men going into her apartment."

"Men?" Song asks.

"Yes."

"In the company of Ms. Yang?"

The old lady shrugs. "I don't know. It's not like I stood here with my eye to the peephole. Just, sometimes, I heard men's voices in the hallway, and I'm certain they went into that apartment."

"What can you tell us about the men?" Lu asks. "Old, young? How were they dressed?"

"Some were older, some were younger. Dressed normally. There was nothing weird about them, other than the fact that I know for sure they didn't live there."

"Could they have been friends of Ms. Yang?" Lu says.

"I suppose it depends on what you mean by 'friends.'"

"Are you suggesting that Ms. Yang was a prostitute?" Song says.

"I'm not suggesting anything. I'm just telling you what I saw."

Further questioning fails to elicit additional insights, so Song thanks the old lady, and they return to Yang Fenfang's apartment.

"Can I go now?" Wang asks. "I have other appointments."

"Yes, but call me if you think of anything," Song says.

After Wang has left, Song suggests leaving Technician Jin behind to process the apartment while they go interview Yang Fenfang's employer.

"Should we call first?" Lu says. "I doubt the bar is open yet."

"I prefer the element of surprise. Maybe we'll get lucky."

The Black Cat is in Daoli District, on the first floor of a five-story building. It's sandwiched between two hole-in-the-wall restaurants, one of which serves dumplings, and the other, traditional dishes made with donkey meat.

Lu is reminded of the old saying: "When in heaven, consume the flesh of dragons; while on earth, eat donkey meat."

While both restaurants are open for business, the Black Cat is not. Song knocks anyway. The door is answered by a bald man with a mustache and goatee. He opens his mouth, perhaps about to tell Lu and Song to get lost, but then sees Lu's hat with the PSB insignia on it.

"We're closed," he says carefully.

"Are you the owner?" Song says.

"Yes. Is there a problem?"

"No problem," Lu says. "May we come in?"

"I'm a little busy right now. Can you come back later?"

"It won't take long."

The man knows better than to say no. "All right."

Lu and Song step inside. The interior is more spacious than Lu had anticipated. The walls are painted black and hung with mirrors, posters, and photographs. Exposed air ducts and water pipes snake across the ceiling. There is a bar area in front, and at the back of the room, a dance floor with a mixture of tables and chairs and booths surrounding it on three sides.

"May I see your identity card?" Song says.

The man goes to the bar and takes his ID out of a leather clutch. "My name is Ji Yinxian. But everyone calls me *Monk*." He runs a hand over his hairless pate.

Song looks the ID card, then hands it to Lu. Monk has a refined yet hipster-artist look about him. He's wearing a black shirt and fashionable sweatpants. Earrings in both ears. Rings on multiple fingers.

"All my paperwork is up to date," Monk says.

"That's not why we're here," Song says. "Do you have an employee named Yang Fenfang?"

"Why?" Monk says.

"Do you or not?"

"Yes, she worked here, but then her mother got sick, and she went back home."

"When was that?"

"Several months ago. Is this going to take long? I'm short-staffed today, and I have a lot to do before I open."

"Feel free to work while we're talking," Lu says. He hands the ID card back to Monk.

Monk takes the card and goes behind the bar. He starts removing bottles of beer from a caddy and loading them into a chiller.

"Have you spoken to Yang since she left?" Song says.

"Maybe once. Why? Has something happened?"

"Once, when?"

"Four or five weeks ago. She called just to check in. That was the last time."

"What did she do here?"

"Mainly worked as a bartender."

"Anything else?"

"Whatever needed doing. Kept inventory. Cleaned the bathroom when necessary. Called taxis for drunk customers. Listened to guys complain about their love lives. The usual bar stuff."

"Was she popular?" Lu asks. "With your customers?"

"Popular? Yeah, sure. She's a nice kid. Gets along with everyone."

"Did she have a boyfriend?" Song says.

"I have no idea. I'm her boss, not her father."

"How much did Ms. Yang earn working for you?" Lu asks.

"About fifteen hundred yuan a month."

"That's all?"

"Plus tips. So maybe double that, when business was good."

Lu looks at Song. "That's not nearly enough to even cover her rent."

Monk shifts an empty caddy to the floor and starts unloading a fresh one. "I don't know anything about that. I pay what's fair, but this is a business. No iron rice bowl here."

Lu sees a poster on the wall. A shirtless Caucasian man. Lu can't quite determine what the poster is advertising.

"Let me be frank, then, since I don't want to waste your time or mine," Song says. "Did Ms. Yang perhaps use your bar as a way to meet men? Men who paid her for certain services?"

"You mean, is she a prostitute?"

"Yes, exactly."

"Uh, no. I don't think that's her thing, and she wouldn't have met any clients along those lines here at the Black Cat."

"How can you be so sure?"

"Because . . ." Monk stops what he's doing and looks at Lu and Song. "Because this is a gay bar."

"Ah," Lu says. He almost laughs.

Song is not amused. "A gay bar."

"That's right," Monk says. "It's not illegal."

"Illegal, no . . ." Song leaves the sentence dangling.

"Why are you asking about Fenfen, anyway?" Monk says.

"She's been murdered," Song answers, more harshly than necessary.

"What?" Monk's mouth drops open.

"I'm sorry," Lu says.

"Can you tell us anything that might help with our investigation?" Song says. "Perhaps she had a stalker? An enemy? An ex?"

Monk shakes his head. "God. No, no. You don't know who did it?"

Lu answers Monk's question with one of his own: "Is it only gay men who come into your bar?"

Monk picks up a cocktail napkin and dabs at his eyes. "No straight man wants to be seen in the Black Cat."

"How about your employees?" Song says. "Are they all . . ."

"Yes," Monk says. "I don't imagine they'd want to work here otherwise."

"So Yang Fenfang was a . . . ?" Song starts.

"Lesbian?" Monk says. "No. She was the exception."

"How can you be so sure?"

"She told me so."

"Why did you employ a heterosexual girl?" Song asks.

"Because I was short-staffed, and because when I met her, I thought she was charming. She had a . . . a nice energy about her."

"Why do you suppose she wanted to work *here*?" Song asks.

Monk's voice betrays a touch of irritation. "I guess because she needed a *job*."

"Ms. Yang never mentioned anything about who she might have been dating?" Lu says.

"We didn't really talk about it."

"She was living in a very expensive apartment," Song says. "Are you aware if she had another job or source of income or if someone was supporting her?"

"No. I'm sorry." Monk picks up a pack of cigarettes and shakes one out, puts it in his mouth, and lights it. "If I knew anything more, I'd tell you. I liked her. She was a great kid. Not a mean bone in her body."

Lu gives him one of his cards. "Please call me if you think of anything else."

"I will. I really hope you find whoever did this."

Lu thanks Monk for his time. Song simply turns and leaves. Out on the sidewalk, he lights a cigarette. "There's definitely something off about this Yang Fenfang. Working in a bunny bar."

In this context, "bunny"—*tu zi*—is a pejorative term for a male homosexual.

Lu pulls up the collar of his coat. "I imagine she was relieved to have a job where the men weren't constantly grabbing her ass."

If it is possible to smoke derisively, Song does so.

By now, it's late afternoon. Lu and Song circle back to the Good Fortune Terrace to collect Technician Jin. Jin tells them he was unable to find any fingerprints in the guest bedroom.

"What do you mean, no fingerprints?" Song says.

"I mean, none whatsoever," Jin says. "Someone wiped it clean."

When they arrive at the Raven Valley Township *paichusuo,* Lu sees a small crowd gathered out front. It consists of a dozen or so citizens and two television news teams.

"What's this?" Song says.

"Trouble," Lu mutters.

He parks around back. He checks to make sure the coast is clear. It is. He unlocks the back door to the station house and ushers Song and Jin inside. He is about to follow when he is waylaid.

"Inspector Lu! What can you tell us about the murder of Yang Fenfang and the suspect you currently have in custody, Zhang Zhaoxing?"

Lu turns. A young woman thrusts a microphone into his face. Behind her is a cameraman. The camera's spotlight shines directly into Lu's eyes—he imagines this must be what it's like to be tied to a chair in a dank cellar and interrogated by the American CIA.

Lu knows the woman, of course. Her name is Annie Ye, and she's a reporter for one of the TV news channels based in Harbin.

Up until the mid-'80s, all media in the People's Republic was state run and under strict government supervision. But as a by-product of the country's economic and social development, independent news outlets have recently begun to proliferate like wildflowers following a spring rain. In contrast to the heavily censored official news sources, such as Xinhua, CCTV, and the People's Daily, these upstart media companies are allowed a certain amount of leeway in the content of their reporting—although they remain careful to avoid taboo topics, such as religious freedom, pornography, criticism of the Chinese Communist Party, and unrest in Tibet and Gansu Province.

Lately, the competition for market share has become quite fierce, as has the struggle for advertising dollars, with the result that any story with a wide commercial appeal is hotly pursued. Entertainment, sports, business, and—most especially—true crime.

"No comment," Lu says. He turns away.

"What do you have to say to the people of Raven Valley Township who claim the Public Security Bureau is framing an innocent, mentally deficient boy?" Annie says.

"Framing? Don't be ridiculous." Lu is acutely conscious of the fact that he's being filmed. He adopts a more reasonable tone of voice. "We've only brought Mr. Zhang in for questioning, and he's being very well treated."

"Can I see him?"

"Certainly not."

"What evidence was there to justify his arrest?"

"I told you, he hasn't been arrested."

"So you plan to release him soon, is that what I'm hearing?"

"It's an ongoing investigation."

"Inspector, people want to know—is there a bloodthirsty madman roaming the streets of Raven Valley Township? One who is targeting young women?"

Lu smiles to convey calm. "I am quite sure that there is no bloodthirsty madman roaming the streets, and frankly, Ms. Ye, it's irresponsible of you to say such a thing. Think of the public good, why don't you?"

"I am," Annie says, unfazed. "If there's a killer on the loose, the people deserve to know."

"There is no killer on the loose."

"Then you've decided Zhang Zhaoxing is, in fact, guilty of murdering Yang Fenfang?"

"I didn't say that."

"Well, if he's innocent, then you have the wrong man in custody, and that means there *is* a killer on the loose."

He has to admit, she's got him there.

"The investigation is ongoing, and we've called in additional help from the Criminal Investigation Bureau in Beijing," Lu says. "We'll have this wrapped up very soon. Thank you for your time."

He escapes through the back door. As he closes it behind him, he can hear Annie Ye speaking into the camera.

"You heard it here first. Not only has the Raven Valley Township Public Security Bureau arrested an innocent, mentally challenged boy, there is a cold-blooded murderer stalking our women and children."

Chief Liang catches him as he's coming up the corridor.

"You saw the crowd outside?"

"Yes, Chief."

"They're making a stink. Saying our detainment of the Zhang kid is unjust. I mean, yesterday nobody even knew who the hell this kid was. Suddenly, he's got a fan club. And how the hell did the media catch wind of this so fast?"

Mrs. Chen, Lu thinks. From her mouth into someone's ear, and then to another, and so on down the line.

"It's a smaller town than we sometimes realize, Chief."

"Well, we've got to do something. If the provincial PSB sees this story is catching fire, it'll be my ass."

"Why don't you go out and make a statement? Tell them we just have Zhang in for questioning, we're making progress, and so on. The usual BS."

"I suppose I'll have to. Did you find out anything in Harbin?"

Lu gives Chief Liang a quick rundown regarding the apartment and the Black Cat.

"A drawerful of fake pricks? Unbelievable."

"Believe it."

Constable Huang appears with Dr. Ma and Technician Hu in tow, everyone dressed in coats and hats.

"Where are you going?" Lu asks.

"Airport," Huang says.

"We're heading back to Beijing," Dr. Ma says.

"What?" Lu says. "Already?"

"My work here is done. The rest is up to you."

"Oh. Well, if you go outside now, you'll find yourself surrounded by news cameras."

Dr. Ma smiles. "I'm no stranger to cameras, Inspector."

"No, I don't suppose you are."

"I'll get the car started," Constable Huang says. He heads for the door. Technician Hu follows, carrying equipment cases.

"Thank you for your help, Doctor," Liang says. "It was a pleasure to work with you."

"It's my duty." Dr. Ma looks at Lu. "Good luck, Inspector."

"Thank you. Safe journey."

Dr. Ma squeezes past him, then stops. "Inspector?"

"Yes?"

"If you ever happen to find yourself in Beijing, give me a ring. I'll show you around CIB headquarters. Maybe even give you a chance to redeem yourself." She turns and follows Technician Hu.

Liang waits until she's out of hearing range and then says, "What did she mean by that? 'Give you a chance to redeem yourself?'"

"I have absolutely no idea," Lu says.

Lu makes a thermos of tea and has just taken a seat behind his desk when Sergeant Bing comes in, holding a sheaf of papers.

"What do you have there?" Lu asks.

"Yang's bank and WeChat transactions. You didn't find the TV or the computer tablet in her Harbin apartment, right?"

"We did not. You asked around the neighborhood again?"

"Yes, both Zhang's and Yang's. Nothing."

Lu slurps tea. "What about Taobao?"

"We checked listings from Friday night onward. No matches. Anyway, there's something else here." Sergeant Bing lays several sheets of paper on the desk and points to highlighted entries. "Each month, like clockwork, Yang Fenfang deposited five thousand yuan, cash, into her bank account."

Lu scans the papers. He sees entries for that exact amount, deposited through an ATM on or about the first of each month. "Her boss said she made no more than three thousand yuan tops."

"And you can see those deposits, also," Sergeant Bing says. He points to other entries, which range from one thousand to three thousand yuan. "They stop around the time she came back to Raven Valley to take care of her mother, so it stands to reason they were for her work at the Black Cat. But the allotments of five thousand, they've continued even up until this month."

"So maybe Yang had herself a *gan die*." The literal meaning of *gan die* is "foster parent," but in this context, it is the equivalent of "sugar daddy."

"She definitely had an alternate source of income."

"Maybe a pimp." Lu tells Sergeant Bing about the condoms and sex toys in Yang's nightstand.

"If she was working as a prostitute, you'd think the income would rise and fall, depending on the number of customers she serviced in a particular month," Sergeant Bing points out. "But this amount, five thousand, it's the same each time."

Lu leans back in his chair. "Right. A *gan die* is more likely. He gave her money for rent, and in return, she did whatever she did. And the arrangement allowed him to stay completely anonymous."

"It's an old story," Sergeant Bing says.

"This *gan die* should be considered a primary suspect."

"But how do we find him? Are there any security cameras in the Harbin apartment building?"

"Cameras, but no recorded footage. There's a neighbor who said she saw a few men going in and out of Yang's apartment, but she couldn't give us a description."

"I can," Sergeant Bing says. "Chinese male, between the ages of fifty and sixty, dark hair, brown eyes, medium build, perhaps glasses, perhaps not, no distinguishing characteristics."

Lu laughs. "Yes. It would be so much easier if he were a redheaded foreign devil."

"Even better, a black foreign devil."

Ten minutes later, Deputy Director Song calls for a meeting in the canteen. He updates Chief Liang, Sergeant Bing, and Technician Jin on what he and Lu have learned in Harbin.

Chief Liang slurps a sports drink through a straw. "Someone purposely cleaned the apartment to remove evidence?"

"Looks that way," Song says.

"Who? And when?"

Lu chimes in with the theory regarding a *gan die*.

"That's not a bad thought," Liang says. "Maybe the Yang girl fell in love or just made various demands, threatened to tell the guy's wife. Blackmail, perhaps. So he killed her, but before that, he made sure there was nothing linking him to the apartment."

"There's only one problem," Lu says. "A simple stabbing or strangulation would have done the trick. Why remove her organs and so on?"

"Like you said," Liang responds. "He's superstitious."

"Or he's trying to throw us off the trail," Technician Jin says. "Make it look like one of those occult killings you always read about in Mexico and the United States."

"Or this really is a case of organ theft," Song says.

Everyone chews on these theories for a moment.

"You checked the girl's expenditures?" Song asks.

Sergeant Bing sits up a little straighter. "Uh . . . yes, sir. We saw automatic monthly payments to the apartment management company. Another monthly transfer to her mother's account. Utilities and so on. The purchases of the television and tablet. Nothing unusual."

Song nods wearily. "Okay. We can pick this up tomorrow."

"What about the media outside?" Chief Liang says.

"What about it?"

"We should probably make a statement."

"Go ahead."

"Well, I could. But I feel like the people of Raven Valley Township would rest more easily knowing the Deputy Director of the CIB is on the case. I mean, you're quite famous, after all."

"I'm hardly famous," Song demurs. "I'm just a simple policeman."

"Don't be so modest. Weren't you elected as a Public Security Model Worker a couple of years back?"

"As a matter of fact, I was."

"If *you* made the statement, I'm sure it would go a long way toward maintaining public order."

Many men in Chief Liang's position would be eager to step in front of the camera and attract a bit of attention to themselves. That kind of thing can be a boost to one's career.

But Liang lives by the adage "The nail that sticks up gets hammered down." There are many pitfalls to fame, and Liang is wise to all of them.

"Fine," Song says. "Give me a few minutes to gather my thoughts."

"Sergeant Bing," Chief Liang says. "Go out and let the crowd know the deputy director will be coming out to speak to them shortly."

Song makes a statement at the entrance of the *paichusuo,* flanked by Chief Liang and Lu. He strikes a subtle balance between candor and obfuscation, answering reporters' questions with little of substance. He insinuates there have been important developments in the case that will be revealed when the time is right. He responds to the angry shouts of those in the crowd who protest the detention of Zhang Zhaoxing with an effective blend of sincerity and officiousness.

In the end, he has revealed nothing but somehow has convinced the assembly that all is under control, the case is proceeding apace, and that everyone can sleep well in their beds tonight.

Afterward, the media and public slowly disperse with a slightly dejected air, as if they came for something and know they didn't get it but have forgotten what it was they were seeking in the first place.

The man watches the local evening news while he eats a late dinner. It features Annie Ye's coverage of the protest outside the *paichusuo*. Footage of Inspector Lu, squinting at the light shining in his eyes, cornered like a rat in a sewer tunnel.

Annie: "What do you have to say to the people of Raven Valley Township who claim the Public Security Bureau is framing an innocent, mentally deficient boy?"

Lu: "Framing? Don't be ridiculous. We've only brought Mr. Zhang in for questioning, and he's being very well treated."

At this, the man laughs, inadvertently inhaling grains of rice, which he then coughs out all over the table. "*Ta ma de,*" he mutters, wiping his hands on a paper napkin.

The interview continues. Inspector Lu is made to look like a stuttering fool. He finally manages to worm his way through the back door of the police station, and Annie Ye turns to face the camera.

"You heard it here first. Not only has the Raven Valley Township Public Security Bureau arrested an innocent, mentally challenged boy, there is a cold-blooded murderer stalking our women and children."

Hm. The man is not sure how he feels about *that*. It was a stroke of luck that the police turned up a suspect—and now here is Annie Ye telling the public that the cops have the wrong person.

The man switches off the TV and turns on the electric water kettle to make tea. He considers Annie Ye. She's pretty—of course she is; otherwise, who would hire her to be a TV news reporter? But with her short hair and glasses, she's a bit too butch for his taste. And, naturally, given her choice of profession, she's got a pushy personality. He prefers a more classic beauty, a softer demeanor.

As the man stands at the sink waiting for the water to boil, he thinks about the first girl who awakened in him certain . . . feelings.

You never forget your first.

Junior middle school, morality and ethics class. Late spring—the weather was growing hot, making it difficult to stay awake through the long afternoon lesson. Even now, all these years later, he vividly remembers sitting at his wooden desk as the teacher droned on and on, his unfocused gaze directed at the back of the girl sitting in front him. His eyelids clicking open and shut like a camera shutter, capturing images that barely registered through his stupor: the girl's neat white shirt collar, a glossy black ponytail neatly bisecting her slim brown neck, the curve of her jaw, a dainty sliver of earlobe.

The girl's name was Xiaoyan. She was beautiful and smart, top of her class. All the boys liked her, and she knew it.

She was a stuck-up bitch.

Whenever the man—then just an awkward twelve-year-old boy— tried to speak to Xiaoyan, she made a face like she'd just caught a whiff of something deeply unpleasant.

On this particular afternoon, as he lost his battle with consciousness and started to nod off, he experienced a strange and unsettling vision—a reverie that hovered at the intersection of a dream and a fantasy.

He pictured himself straddling the girl. Wrapping his hands around that supple neck. Squeezing. Watching her flat, prepubescent chest heave in panic. Her coral pink lips turning blue.

A sudden electric thrill jolted him upright in his chair. His heart beat wildly in his chest. His armpits grew damp with sweat. He felt himself stiffen beneath the desk.

What a delicious and addictive sensation!

The man never touched the girl. After that vision, he never even tried to converse with her again. But from this day forward, he spent the countless mind-numbing hours of morality and ethics class imagining different things he and Xiaoyan might do together. Things he might do *to* her.

He knew, even as a boy, to keep such thoughts to himself. Xiaoyan never had a clue.

And neither did anyone else.

TUESDAY

A revolution is not a dinner party, or writing an essay, or painting a picture, or doing embroidery; it cannot be so refined, so leisurely and gentle, so temperate, kind, courteous, restrained, and magnanimous. A revolution is an insurrection, an act of violence by which one class overthrows another.

—Quotations from Chairman Mao Zedong

At Tuesday morning's briefing, Song shares the results of a criminal database inquiry he has obtained from CIB headquarters.

"I had my analysts focus on female homicides with a similar MO," Song says. "They got dozens of hits involving some combination of strangulation, postmortem sexual assault, and organ removal."

"Dozens?" Chief Liang says. "That many?"

"We live in a country of 1.4 billion citizens," Song says. "Given the odds, a couple of dozen is not so surprising. But most of these homicide cases have already been closed. Soured love affairs, organ theft, criminal revenge plots, things like that."

"Might some of those closed cases also be the work of our perpetrator?" Lu says. "Just attributed to the wrong suspect?"

Song gives Lu one of his patented cold stares. "Our justice system doesn't wrongly convict innocent people."

Lu wonders how Song can say such a thing with a straight face.

"Anyway," Song continues, "there *are* two local cases that are a match. Slight variations—in one, the victim was stabbed to death, but otherwise, we have the missing organs, joss paper in the mouth, suturing. Both took place in Harbin, one in 2017 and the other last year."

"I don't recall hearing about those cases," Chief Liang says.

"They were kept confidential," Song says. "For reasons of public stability."

"Ah. Right."

"I've made a call to the Harbin metro headquarters and requested access to their files. I have an appointment with their chief of homicide division this afternoon."

"I'd like to join you, if possible?" Lu asks.

"Perhaps your time would be better spent investigating Zhang, since he is currently our only viable suspect."

"I'm not sure I'd agree with the word *viable*," Lu says.

"Inspector Lu, ever since Zhang was arrested," Song says, "you have made it clear you consider him to be innocent. Do you really think this demonstrates the lack of bias with which one should investigate a homicide?"

Chief Liang pauses in the process of lighting a cigarette and gives Lu a warning look.

Lu sighs. "You're right, Deputy Director. The evidence and my gut tell me that Zhang is not the killer. But I agree with you—it is wrong to summarily dismiss him as a suspect. We should collect all the facts before we make a determination."

"I'm so glad you agree," Song says.

"Perhaps the case files in Harbin will prove useful one way or the other. I would very much like the opportunity to view them with you."

"You mean to check up on me—make sure I don't, how did you put it? 'Railroad a convenient suspect'?"

Yes, Lu thinks. "No. Not at all."

Song taps his fingers on the table. "Just to lay my cards on the table, I also am not sure about Zhang. Especially now that we have two other murders in Harbin that fit the same MO. But until I have specific evidence implicating someone else, or exonerating Zhang, he will be detained and actively investigated."

"That is logical, Deputy Director. I totally agree."

There is a short and uneasy silence broken by Liang, who smiles and slaps his hands onto his legs. "There! All settled. I'll look forward to hearing more upon your return from Harbin."

Lu signs out one of the patrol cars, and he and Song once again find themselves speeding down the Tongjiang Expressway. They make a quick stop to buy takeout cups of tea. Then they present themselves at the front desk of the metro PSB headquarters—an older Russian-style building of yellow brick—and are ushered into a small conference room. Song seems perfectly at ease. Lu is nervous. It's been a long time since he worked in the city. He can't help but feel like the country cousin visiting his fancy relatives.

After a ten-minute wait, the door to the conference room opens. A man enters—he's in his late fifties, dressed in a suit, and has a jowly liver-spotted face with pendulous lips that have always reminded Lu of a flounder.

This man is surnamed Xu, and he was once Lu's supervisor—the very one responsible for Lu's transfer to Raven Valley Township seven years before.

Initially, Xu's face is plastered with an ingratiating smile, but his expression turns cold when he sees Lu. His jowls wobble a bit, then he quickly recovers. "I am Xu, chief of homicide division." He gives Song a slight bow and takes a business card out of his pocket. "I'm sorry to have kept you waiting."

Song gives Xu one of his own cards. "Deputy Director Song, CIB."

"Your reputation precedes you."

Ass-licker, Lu thinks.

"This is Inspector Lu, deputy chief of Raven Valley PSB," Song says.

"I know who he is."

"Oh?" Song raises an eyebrow.

"Chief Xu used to be my boss," Lu says.

"I'm not sure what Lu Fei has told you about me," Xu says, "but he is not a reliable source of information. That's why he's no longer in Harbin. Had I known he was attending this meeting, I might have made other arrangements."

"Well, he's here now," Song says, "so why don't we just get down to business?"

Xu reluctantly takes a seat at the table. Song sits across from him.

Xu clears his throat. "You said you wanted to look at some of our files."

"We have a homicide in Raven Valley that matches two of your cases. Very unusual MO. The victims, female, were murdered and some of their internal organs removed. Then they were sewed up, and joss paper was placed in their mouths."

Xu nods. "Yes, I remember the incident last year. We figured the husband for it, but the investigation was inconclusive. He went to prison anyway on unrelated charges. The other case was before my promotion to chief of homicide, so I don't know the details."

"But you never linked the two," Lu says.

"I just told you, the first case dates to before I was promoted."

"Right. And you're not responsible for any unsolved crimes that occurred previous to the exact moment you sat your ass in your shiny new chair."

"Perhaps you've forgotten how policing works while you've been off in the countryside investigating sexual crimes against livestock, but it's not generally procedure to assume a serial killer is at work every time a body turns up," Xu says. "And you'd better watch the way you speak to me!"

"Gentlemen, please," Song says. "Let's keep it professional. Chief Xu, we'd like to see everything you have on those homicides."

Xu doesn't immediately respond. Song's request puts him in a difficult position. If Song finds something in the case files the Harbin homicide division missed, it will reflect badly on him. At the very least, he will lose major face. At worst, he might get blamed for not linking the murders together earlier. For every mistake, someone must take the fall. He doesn't want to be that someone.

But at the same time, although he and Song share an equivalent rank, Song's position at the CIB is greatly elevated above his own, and Song is likely to keep rising up the Ministry of Public Security ladder. Xu would do well to cultivate a friendly relationship with him.

"Of course, Deputy Director. Anything I can do to help. I'll have a room reserved for you here and get the files transferred over."

"I appreciate that."

"Would you like me to assign any of my detectives to assist you?"

"Not at this time, though we may want to speak to whoever was involved in the investigations."

"No problem. In the meantime, now is a perhaps good time to have lunch—it will take an hour or so for the files to arrive. Unfortunately, I cannot join you, as I have other duties to attend to."

"I understand."

Xu shakes hands with Song and pointedly ignores Lu on the way out.

When he is gone, Song turns to Lu. "I understand you don't like the man, but antagonizing him when we need his help is not very strategic."

"Don't worry. Xu is a first-rate suck-up. He's not about to pass up an opportunity to curry favor with you."

"Even so, a little diplomacy goes a long way."

"You're absolutely correct, Deputy Director. I will strive to be more tactful from now on."

"Now you're just being a smart-ass."

They find a small restaurant a block away. It's early for lunch, so they are able to commandeer a table in the back, away from other patrons. They both order bowls of *niurou mian*—bits of questionably sourced red-braised beef in a spicy broth with thick egg noodles.

When the *laoban* brings over their bowls, Song adds a pinch of pickled mustard greens and stirs them into the broth. "So what happened between you and Xu?"

"Why?"

"Because you're both involved now in Yang's case—to varying de-grees. And because I'm curious."

"I'm not the most objective source."

"Consider it an opportunity to insult him behind his back."

Lu slurps noodles. "We had a missing girl case. She was sixteen. Signs pointed to her being a runaway, not a kidnapping victim. We quickly ruled out the usual possibilities—hiding at a friend's house, eloping with a boyfriend. We made the rounds of hostels, cheap hotels, flophouses. We checked to see if she'd booked a train ticket out of town, and so on. Then I decided to search the local brothels. Sometimes these young girls, un-happy at home, in trouble at school, they get roped into the sex trade, but I didn't clear my approach with Xu because, in our district, the brothels were off limits."

"You mean, because the owners were paying bribes."

"Bribes. Or they had *guanxi*."

Guanxi. Connections. Influence. Power. The grease that turns wheels at all levels of business and politics in the People's Republic. With the right *guanxi,* you can make a fortune in business. Flout laws. Ignore regulations.

Get away with murder.

Such has been the case for a thousand years. The revolution changed a lot of things, but it didn't change *that*.

"I get the picture," Song says. "So you bust into one of these joints looking for the girl, and the owner complains to someone who complains to someone else, who gives Xu an earful."

"Worse," Lu says. "I caught Xu. With an underage girl."

"What?" Song exclaims. "Seriously?"

"Seriously."

"What did you do?"

"Well, I considered beating the shit out of him. But in the end, I did nothing. What could I do, really?"

"You could have reported it."

"The report would have just gotten quashed, as would have my career."

"Such blatant corruption in this day and age. It's a disgrace."

"Yes, and it was my word against his."

"So then what happened?"

"After a couple of weeks of ignoring each other, I finally marched into his office and told him I could no longer work for him. He said that's fine, because he was giving me a promotion and arranging for my transfer to Raven Valley."

"Half carrot, half stick."

"Right."

Song wipes his mouth with a napkin. "And now you're exiled."

"At that point, I was ready to get out of Harbin anyway. At least in Raven Valley, I can make a difference in the lives of ordinary citizens."

"Inspector Lu, National Public Security Model Worker!"

"No, thanks. I don't need that kind of pressure."

"Yeah, you don't strike me as the type. You're probably not even a party member, am I right?"

Membership in the Communist Party of the People's Republic is by no means a given. One must apply, be interviewed, pass a background check, and endure a long process of ideological training, self-study, and self-criticism. Out of a population of 1.4 billion, only 88 million citizens belong to the CCP.

But nearly every important government post is under the control of the Communist Party. Anyone who wishes to rise in business or politics would be wise to join. It's like the VIP section in a popular nightclub. Only the coolest, best-looking, or richest kids are allowed past the velvet ropes.

"Correct," Lu says.

"Why not?"

"I never applied."

"Why?"

"During the Cultural Revolution, my grandparents lost everything. My grandfather starved to death. My father was torn from his family."

"You can't make an omelet without breaking an egg or two. Look at us now. We're kicking America's ass."

"True. But growing up, my feelings about the revolution were complicated. The ideology of it seemed to conflict with the reality. So instead of worrying about abstract ideals, I decided I'd focus on something concrete. Like being a cop. That way, I could protect people who are helpless. People like my grandparents."

"How's that worked out for you?"

"About as you'd expect."

"It's naive to think you can be a cop without facing political realities."

"I know."

"Hence the reason you're in the boondocks. Career-wise."

Lu shrugs. After seven years, he has grown accustomed to living in Raven Valley. The caseload is not very exciting. He spends more time mediating family squabbles and helping farmers search for missing chickens than he does solving serious crimes. But on the plus side, he is not faced with the same ethical quandaries as he was on an almost daily basis in Harbin. Sure, there is still corruption, favoritism, nepotism, and fraud, even in a modest township like Raven Valley, but he doesn't leave the office each night feeling like he needs a long, hot shower to wash off the filth.

After lunch, they return to the metro PSB headquarters. A room has been assigned to them, and a young constable shows them where the canteen is so they can buy snacks and drinks. Song requests an ashtray.

"I'm afraid there's no smoking inside the building," the constable says.

"No problem," Song says. He buys himself a cup of tea in the canteen. Back in the room, he drinks the tea, cracks a window, and lights a cigarette, using the cup as a makeshift ashtray.

It is another hour before the files arrive, packed in a series of boxes. Song and Lu each take a case and review the relevant materials. In due course, they share what they have discovered.

Lu goes first. "Tang Jinglei. Twenty-eight. Single. Employed in a beauty parlor. She lived alone. When she didn't show up for work or answer her phone for a couple of days, some of her coworkers grew worried and convinced her landlord to let them into the apartment. They found her in the bathroom. The ME determined the cause of death was a slashed throat, not strangulation. The rest is the same. Heart, lungs, liver. Joss money in mouth. Sexual assault, but no DNA present."

"Serial killers have been known to change their MO as they gain experience and confidence."

"Right. Maybe in this instance, the perp was nervous and rushed, so he used a knife."

"Any suspects?"

"One. Surname Wan. The suspect and the victim had dated, she dumped him, she was murdered two weeks later. Evidence was circumstantial. Mainly, he had no alibi, and the apartment was covered in his fingerprints."

"If they were previously dating, that would be expected."

"Yes. Unfortunately, he committed suicide in jail during the investigation. Case closed. At least as far as the Harbin cops were concerned."

"That's it?"

"The bare bones, yes."

Song lights his twentieth cigarette of the day. "My victim's name was Qin Liying. She was thirty-eight, worked as a bank manager, and was married. No kids. She was also part of a swinger group."

"A swinger group?"

"She and her husband had a chat room where they recruited couples and singles for orgies."

"Orgies? Like sex?"

"Yes. Like sex."

"Really? I didn't know such a thing existed."

"The chat room or the orgies?"

"Both."

Song blows smoke out the window. "The legal status is unclear. More on that later. As far as the homicide goes, the husband claims that he came home one evening and found her dead. Heart, lungs, and liver missing. Joss money in her mouth."

"Sexual assault?"

"Same as the Yang girl. The ME determined something was inserted into Mrs. Qin's vagina, but there was no trace of semen or condom use."

Song taps ashes into his teacup. "As Xu said, Harbin cops figured the husband was good for it. Their investigation revealed that the swinging was more the husband's cup of tea than the wife's, and she eventually tried to put a stop to it. He resisted, she got angry and threatened to make things difficult. So the theory went. Oh, by the way, he was a professor at the Harbin College of Technology. Computer science."

"I guess that explains the naughty chat room. So what happened?"

"Not enough evidence to prosecute for murder. Instead, he was arrested for public licentiousness, put on trial, and sent to prison for a year."

"He's out now?"

"Just recently. I have a current address. I think he's worth talking to."

"Agreed," Lu says. "I'm amazed the cops didn't pick up on the similarities between the two murders."

"Different districts, different investigators, poor communication. And like Xu said—no one ever assumes there's a serial killer at work."

As much as Lu would like to lay responsibility wholly at Xu's feet, he can't deny the fact that Chinese authorities prefer to downplay such crimes. But still, Lu can't help but think that if Xu had been better at his job, Yang Fenfang would still be alive.

He glances at his watch. The afternoon is fast slipping away. "Shall we go see the professor?"

Professor Qin lives in an ugly concrete residential building centered around a courtyard that is devoid of trees, grass, or any charm whatsoever. Nevertheless, it is filled with children at play when Lu and Song arrive. The children shriek and climb all over one another like wild animals.

"It was a mistake to get rid of the one-child policy," Song remarks as he and Lu zigzag hurtling bodies.

Song and Lu walk up the stairs to the third floor and traverse a narrow open-air walkway that fronts a long row of apartments. The walkway is crowded with laundry racks, cookstoves, stools and benches, discarded household items, winter shoes, toddlers, old people, and bicycles.

Song locates the proper apartment door and knocks.

A voice comes from inside. "Who is it?"

"Public Security," Song says.

"What do you want?"

"I want you to open up!"

Lu hears the sound of locks being twisted, then the door opens a crack. "Let me see your identification," a man says.

Both Song and Lu hold out their IDs.

"Why are you here?" Lu can see only a narrow sliver of the man's face—a single eye behind thick glasses. Dark and suspicious.

"Open the door, please, Professor Qin," Song says.

The professor hesitates, then steps aside. Song and Lu enter. Lu shuts the door behind him.

The apartment is tiny, cramped, cheaply furnished, and clogged with untidy stacks of books. It smells of cigarette smoke and boiled gizzards. Professor Qin is in his fifties, short graying hair, a bit of a paunch, dressed in shapeless pants and an old sweater. He holds a cigarette between his fingers.

Hardly the sexual athlete Lu had imagined.

Song introduces himself and Lu and says they want to talk about Mrs. Qin.

"Why can't you people just leave me alone?" Qin moans. "You've already ruined me. What more do you want?"

"Just a few questions, and then we'll be on our way," Song says. "May we sit down?"

"If you must." Qin waves at a broken-down couch. Lu moves a pile of books to make space. Song offers Qin one of his Chunghwas. Qin waves it away. Song takes one for himself and lights it. Qin slumps into an old recliner.

Song asks Qin to clarify some details regarding the discovery of his wife's body.

"Why?" Qin says. "Why now? I told the police everything. There was an extensive investigation. Every detail of the murder and of my personal life was put under a spotlight. What more do you want me to say?"

"Please just cooperate with us," Song says.

"Is this entertaining for you? A game of some sort?"

"Not at all. It's a very serious matter."

"Once upon a time, I was a highly respected professor of computer science. I've written four books and more than twenty research papers. I was devoted to my students, and they to me. Now I have nothing. No money. No teaching position. I make my living coding websites for take-out restaurants and bicycle repair shops."

"As I understand it, Professor Qin, you were engaged in behavior that was counter to socialist ideals."

"Is sexual pleasure against the principles of Marx and Lenin? I don't remember reading about that in *The Communist Manifesto*."

"You organized orgies," Song says.

"So I did. I never forced anyone to attend. They all came willingly. These were activities that took place behind closed doors, among consenting adults."

"How about your wife? Was she a consenting adult?"

"She was a willing participant. Initially. Then, over time, she changed her mind. That was her prerogative, as it was mine to continue what I did, openly and with her knowledge, from day one."

"Even though your wife wanted you to stop."

"If you and your wife enjoy eating meat and then one day she wakes up and decides she is going to become a strict vegetarian, does that require you to become a vegetarian also?" Qin looks back and forth between Song and Lu. "She knew who I was when she married me. If she no longer wanted to be with that person, she could have just divorced me."

"Social order is built upon the foundation of the family," Song says. "Parents, a husband and wife, children."

"That is a very conservative outlook and one that our own government has on many occasions subverted through forced sterilization, herding people into communes, smashing the 'four olds.' This is the twenty-first century. Why can't people have the freedom to determine what makes them happy? What affords them fulfillment and pleasure?"

"I'm not here to get into a philosophical discussion with you," Song says. "I'm here about the murder of your wife."

Qin leans forward. "So he's done it again?"

"Who?"

"The killer."

"Do you know who the killer is, Professor?"

"I told the police what I suspected when my wife was murdered."

"What was that?"

"Haven't you bothered to read the police report?"

"I want to hear it from you."

Qin stubs out his cigarette. He takes off his glasses and cleans them on his sweater, then sets them back onto the bridge of his nose.

"I suppose you know I moderated a chat group where like-minded people could discuss topics of sexuality and arrange for meetups. It was a closed group, but naturally, we had people who joined under false pretenses just to troll us. Of course, I banned these trolls immediately, but it was like shoring up a dam. You'd plug a leak here, and another one would spring up over there. One person, in particular, kept coming back under different aliases. He was easy to identify because of the content of his messages. Extremely violent language. Such as, he was going to rape all our female members, since they were whores anyway. Rip out their uteruses. Cut off their breasts. Stick a knife up their vaginas. Castrate the men. Things like that. He also peppered his invective with hard-line socialist jargon. He said we were bourgeois decadents. Running dogs. That we sucked Western cocks. And so on."

"And you suspected this person of murdering your wife?" Lu says.

"I thought he should be investigated, at the very least."

"Didn't you use an alias in your chat room? So people couldn't track you?" Song asks.

"Of course."

"Then how would he have known where you lived? Who your wife was?"

"I'm not sure. I thought perhaps one of the other participants talked about our little gatherings. Word got around and somehow this guy heard about it, but I don't really know for sure."

"If he was using an alias, how do you know who *he* was?" Lu asks.

"Through his IP address. I was a professor of computer science, remember?"

"So you used hacker skills?"

"I'm not sure what you're referring to," Qin says disingenuously. "In any case, I gave all this information to the Harbin police, but they weren't concerned with the murder of my wife. They just wanted to make an example of me."

"That's a serious accusation," Song says.

"And I'm serious about it. Besides, this bastard—he was protected."

"What do you mean?"

"Those turtle's eggs left all of this out of the official report, didn't they?" Qin shakes his head angrily.

"We just want to hear your perspective," Lu says carefully.

Qin snorts. He goes to his desk and roots among reams of paper. He finds what he's looking for, casts about for another piece of paper, writes on it, and brings it to Lu. "Here's his name and address."

Lu reads what Qin has written. "Mr. Peng Yuan. I don't recognize this district."

"It's on the outskirts of the city," Qin says. "An industrial no-man's-land."

"What else do you know about him?" Song asks.

"He's in his late sixties. An ex-sergeant in the PLA and a war hero."

"War hero?" Song says. "What war?"

"One of the border clashes with Vietnam in the early '80s," Qin says.

Lu coughs—the apartment atmosphere is thick with cigarette smoke. "Please explain what you meant when you said he was protected."

"He's chairman of something called PLA Veterans for Socialist Values. It's a radical far-left, anti-Western, anti-economic reform group."

"Never heard of it," Song says.

"You wouldn't have," Qin says. "It's a local Harbin organization, and I think it only consists of a handful of bitter old hard-liners. Mao worshippers. But for such a small group, they make a lot of noise, and I'm guessing someone in the Harbin government likes having them around to stir the pot, which is why the police did nothing when I showed them Peng's posts."

"We'll look into it," Song says. He rises from the couch.

"You're really going to talk to him?" Qin sounds surprised.

"We'll go straight to his apartment now."

Lu doesn't fancy driving out to the middle of nowhere to brace a potential hothead radical and then brave rush hour traffic on the way home, but Peng does sound like an intriguing lead.

"Then it's true," Qin says. "There's been another murder. Otherwise, you wouldn't bother."

"Thank you for your time, Professor," Song says. He looks around the disheveled state of the apartment. "Please try to be a productive member of society moving forward."

On the drive to Peng's apartment, Song calls Chief of Homicide Xu and demands to know why Peng Yuan was not included in the police report.

Xu breathes loudly into the receiver. "We spoke to him, of course. He's not the murderer."

"How can you be so sure?"

"Because he knows just enough about the internet to post on the professor's chat group but never in a million years could he figure out the professor's true identity or where he lives. And the professor is not the only one he's disparaged online. There are plenty of other liberal types he's threatened, most of whom are still alive. So yeah, he's an old dog who just barks really loudly."

"Even if that's the case, he should still have been referenced in the report."

"What good would that do?" Xu asks. "Other than shame him? The guy's a war hero."

"And perhaps someone in a high place has a certain soft spot for him?" Song suggests.

"That could well be the case," Xu says delicately. "There are still a few Communist hard-liners floating around the Harbin government."

"I see. I'm going to talk to him anyway."

"Please don't," Xu says. "That's just courting trouble."

"Too late. I'm almost at his apartment, and if I find out someone's called to warn him before I get there, I'll know who to blame."

"Deputy Director—"

Song hangs up without saying goodbye.

"Now you see who Xu is for yourself," Lu says.

"He's just a typical cop," Song says. "More worried about covering his ass and sucking up to superiors than catching criminals. But honestly, a guy like that, who's willing to carry water for powerful people, the sky's the limit. He might be chief of the entire metro PSB department in five years."

"Over my dead body," Lu says.

"Even that's not out of the question," Song says. "You'd best stick to Raven Valley and out of Xu's hair in the future."

"Glad to."

By the time they reach Peng Yuan's neighborhood, night has fallen, and they find themselves drifting through an eerily vacant landscape of small manufacturing plants illuminated by a sickly yellow halogen glow.

They locate Peng's residence with some difficulty. It's an old building, five stories, cheaply constructed of cement and brick, dirty and neglected.

Lu parks and they enter the lobby. There is no security guard. Song stabs the elevator button. Nothing happens. They take the stairs.

Peng lives on the third floor. As they walk down the hallway to his apartment, Lu hears music. He recognizes the song. It's "Nan Ni Wan"—an old revolutionary tune:

> Mountains full of flowers
> Mountains blossoming
> Know that in Nan Ni Wan
> Everywhere is like Jiangnan
> Yes, like Jiangnan
> Learning again how to cultivate

The 359th Brigade sets the example
Let us go forward
Let the example blossom

Song knocks on Peng's door. "Public Security! Sergeant Peng? Please open the door!"

The music switches off. The door opens. An old man stands looking out at them. He's short and looks every bit his age, but he's solidly built, barrel-chested, his forearms as thick as howitzer shells.

"What do you want?" Peng says.

Song and Lu flash their IDs. "May we come in and talk to you?" Song says.

"Why?"

"We have some questions. About Mrs. Qin from a few years back? Remember her?"

"Fuck off." Peng moves to close the door, but Lu reaches out and puts a hand on it.

"It will only take a moment, Sergeant Peng."

"This is ancient history. Why are you bothering me about it?"

"Because it's our job," Song growls. "Now let us in or we'll take you down to police headquarters and ask our questions there in less relaxed surroundings."

"Just you try," Peng says.

"Sergeant Peng," Lu says calmly. "Please. It will be easier if you give us five minutes of your time."

Peng glares for a moment. Lu can smell liquor on his breath. Finally, he waves them inside.

The apartment is a mess. The walls are decorated with old propaganda posters bearing slogans like "We Are Chairman Mao's Red Guard" and "Love Your Country Ardently!" The few pieces of furniture look to have been dragged in off the street. A box of printed broadsides sits in one corner. A coffee table is covered with Styrofoam takeout containers. The couch appears to do double duty as Peng's bed—it is heaped with old blankets. Peng sits there and picks a pack of cigarettes up off the table. Song immediately offers him a Chunghwa—his go-to means of establishing a rapport.

"Chunghwa, eh?" Peng takes one and puts it in his mouth. "You must be rich."

Song lights Peng's cigarette. "I just *smoke* rich."

Peng takes a drag, then pours liquor from a bottle on the table into a filthy glass and drinks.

Lu wanders over to look at the box of broadsides. They are cheaply printed on low-quality paper. Lu surmises the PLA Veterans for Socialist Values organization is not exactly swimming in cash. He reads the headline: WORKERS, PEASANTS, SOLDIERS, AND REVOLUTIONARIES, UNITE!

Song takes a seat in a wobbly chair across from Peng and lights his own Chunghwa. "You live here alone?"

"What's it to you?"

"Just answer the question, if you please."

"Yes, I live alone. No wife. No kids. I have spent my life serving my country, not myself."

"Admirable."

"Are you making fun of me?"

"Absolutely not. Thank you for your service. Now we are aware that you were previously questioned regarding the murder of Mrs. Qin."

"I told the cops last time. I didn't know either of them personally, just through the internet. I didn't even know the husband's real name. He used some ridiculous and filthy pseudonym. Iron Cock or Golden Rod or something." Peng drinks from his glass and pours another. "I'll tell you one thing, though—that whore got what she deserved."

"What makes you say that?"

"Because spreading your legs for every prick that happens by makes her a whore, that's why. And her disgusting pig of a husband. They are a perfect example of what happens when we allow liberal values to pollute our society."

Lu picks up one of the broadsides and scans the first paragraph:

More than seventy years since the great socialist revolution, bourgeoisie elements have slunk back to promote old ideas, culture, customs, and habits in order to exploit the working class and poison the minds of our younger generations.

"So you admit you disapproved of their lifestyle?" Song says.

"Hell yes! But I didn't kill her, although I wouldn't have minded doing it." Peng makes a chopping motion with his hand, laughs, and then refills his glass.

Lu continues reading: *We must oppose those who take the capitalist road—who abandon socialist values and seek to get rich off the backs of workers, peasants, and soldiers. Workers, peasants, soldiers, and revolutionaries, unite!*

"You cops should be out rounding up bourgeois scum like that," Peng tells Song, "instead of hassling old patriots."

"Professor Qin did go to jail," Song points out.

"Jail?" Peng says. "That fucker should have been executed. Maybe you don't understand what's going on around you, Mr. Policeman. You think we won the war in 1949? Not even close. Open your fucking eyes. Chiang Kai-shek and the Guomindang, the combined military might of the Americans, the Russians, the Koreans, the Japanese, the Vietnamese—they are nothing compared to the insidious influence of Coca-Cola and Zhushi Qiangsen."

Lu has to smile at that one. He is not much of a foreign movie fan, but everyone is familiar with Zhushi Qiangsen, the hugely muscled, brown-skinned American actor who was once a fake wrestler and now rules the Chinese box office with ridiculous films about furiously fast cars, King Kong–size apes, and burning skyscrapers.

"Movies and magazines, jeans and hamburgers, and decadent Western liberal attitudes," Peng continues. "It's a scourge. A plague. Remember what our Great Leader said: 'Liberalism is extremely harmful in a revolutionary collective. It is a corrosive which eats away unity, undermines cohesion, causes apathy, and creates dissension. It is an extremely bad tendency.'"

"Thank you for the lesson in socialist principles," Song says dryly. "But just for the sake of our investigation—since it wasn't noted in the police report—where were you the night of Mrs. Qin's murder?"

"*Ta ma de,*" Peng says. "I don't remember. That was years ago." He finishes the Chunghwa and drops it into an empty tea cup. "Give me another cigarette."

Song hesitates, then reaches into his pocket and fishes out the pack. He shakes out a cigarette and hands it over.

Peng puts it in his mouth and leans forward. Song extracts his lighter and holds the flame to Peng's cigarette.

Peng inhales and blows smoke in Song's face. "No need to be grudging about it. I'm sure you've got a warehouse full of these at home. Bribes, gifts, whatever you want to call it."

"I don't take bribes," Song says, his voice betraying a hint of anger.

Peng drinks from his glass, pours another, and smokes his cigarette. "Fucking cops. No different from criminals, apart from a shiny badge."

"Why be so antagonistic, Sergeant Peng?"

"I'm just honest. Unlike you college boys, I'm too stupid to use pretty words and twist my tongue in knots."

"The night Mrs. Qin was murdered."

"Good riddance. A shame the killer didn't cut up the husband and all those other whores, too."

Lu considers this is a waste of time. The old soldier is belligerent, bitter, and drunk. He may even prove violent, given sufficient reason, and Lu doesn't think he's Mrs. Qin's murderer. He's too crude and transparent for such a crime.

However, he's already interrupted Song once during the interrogation of a suspect. He's not about to do it again.

"Where were you?" Song says.

"I don't remember."

"Try."

Peng draws on his cigarette and then grins. "Ah, yes, I recall now. I was fucking your mother!"

Song springs up from his chair. Peng does the same. Lu rushes to get a hand between them. "Stop!"

Peng ignores Lu and taunts Song. "Come on, you shit egg!"

"Sergeant Peng!" Lu shouts. "That's enough!"

Peng looks at Lu. "Fuck your ancestors to the eighteenth generation!"

"Your war record won't dissuade us from running you in and letting you spend a few nights in a jail cell crammed with foreigners, homosexuals, and Muslims," Lu says.

"Ha!" Peng grunts. "I'd kick the shit out of all of them!"

"I guess there's one way to find out."

"Ass-licker," Peng growls, but he sits back down on the couch.

Song's fists remain clenched, his face white with fury.

"Deputy Director," Lu says softly.

"*Gan!*" Song turns and stomps over to the window.

Peng grins and pours another drink. "Pussies."

Lu gives it a moment, then continues, "I just have two more things to ask you, Sergeant, and then we'll be on our way. Do you have a car or motorcycle or other means of transport?"

"I told you, I'm not rich. I only have a bicycle."

"Have you traveled outside Harbin recently?"

"Like to your friend's mother's house, so I could fuck her again?"

Song whirls away from the window. "That's it. Time to beat some manners into this old bastard."

Peng responds by picking his glass up and hurling it across the room. Song ducks. The glass shatters, and alcohol sprays. Lu reaches for Peng's arm, but Peng lashes out and catches Lu with a surprise punch.

Lu lands on his butt. The old soldier packs a wallop.

Peng snatches the liquor bottle off the table and smashes it against the table. It breaks in half, leaving a jagged weapon in his hand. He leaps over the table and goes for Song.

Song crouches. He's cornered, and he's not much of a fighter. Peng comes at him, slashing and stabbing.

Lu shakes the cobwebs loose and scrabbles to his feet. Peng rakes Song's outstretched arm with the broken bottle, then jams it into his chest. Song shouts in pain.

Lu wraps his arms around Peng from behind. He struggles to pull Peng away. Peng frenziedly stabs and cuts at Song with the bottle. Lu jams the edge of his foot into the back of Peng's knee and pulls him backward onto the floor. He locks his legs around Peng's waist and sinks in a choke, but Peng is much stronger than he looks—he flails and bucks himself out of Lu's grasp.

Peng and Lu both roll to their feet. They face off. Song curls up into a bloody ball on the floor.

Peng thrusts at Lu with the bottle. Lu sidesteps and catches Peng's wrist. He twists with all his strength, turning Peng in a half circle, generating momentum, and flipping Peng's entire body into the apartment window. It shatters, and Peng disappears through the gaping hole.

Lu steps over to the windowsill and peeks out.

Peng lies in a broken heap on the sidewalk three stories below.

"*Ta ma de*," Lu says.

Lu drives as fast as he dares, lights flashing, siren wailing. Song lies in the back seat, silent, still. Lu isn't even sure if he's still alive.

He lifts a hand off the steering wheel, reaches into his pocket, and takes out his phone. He is approaching a four-way intersection. He sees the light is red and slows down, but there are no cars, so he doesn't stop.

He looks down at the phone and dials 110. Bad timing. Just as he finishes, he enters the intersection and is suddenly transfixed by the headlights of a truck hurtling toward him from the side. A horn blares.

There is no time to do anything but slam on the gas and wrench the wheel over. Lu avoids impact by a matter of centimeters.

"Can't you see I have my fucking lights and sirens on!" Lu screams at the retreating taillights of the truck.

In the chaos, he has lost his phone. He pats the floor by his feet, finds it, and puts it to his ear.

"Hello? Hello? Is anyone there?" the operator is saying.

Lu gives his name and ID and explains he has a badly wounded colleague in his car and is heading for the nearest hospital, which happens to be the same facility where Dr. Ma autopsied Yang Fenfang. He tells the operator to call ahead and have a trauma team standing by.

Then he tosses the phone onto the passenger seat and stomps on the gas pedal.

When he reaches the hospital, Lu is relieved to see a medical team waiting with a gurney by the emergency entrance. He pulls to a stop, jumps out, and yanks open the back door. The medical team rushes forward.

Lu buttonholes the lead doctor. "This man is a high-ranking official in the Ministry of Public Security. He's lost a lot of blood."

"What happened to him?" the doctor asks.

"He was attacked with a broken bottle."

"How long ago?" the doctor says.

"About twenty minutes."

"What else can you tell us?" the doctor asks.

"His name is Song, he's in his fifties, a smoker. That's it."

The orderlies push the gurney through a set of swinging doors. The doctor holds up a hand. "You can't go in there, but if you ask the front desk attendant, she'll find a place for you to wait." He looks Lu up and down. "You might want to get cleaned up." He turns and follows the gurney.

Lu returns to the patrol car. The interior is smeared with gore, as are his clothes. He finds his cell phone and calls Sergeant Bing, who is at home with his wife and son.

"Sorry to bother you, Sergeant."

"No problem, Inspector. What's up?"

"The answer to that question is more complicated than you can possibly imagine. For now, I need someone to bring me a change of clothes at the county hospital."

When he gets off the phone with Sergeant Bing, Lu calls the Harbin metro police to report what has happened with Peng Yuan. He expects there will be serious heat for throwing the old man out a window. Then he calls Chief Liang. As anticipated, Liang is apoplectic.

"*Cao ni de ma!*" Liang says. "How could you let Song get hurt like that?"

"I didn't let him do anything, Chief. We were attacked by a madman."

"What did the doctor say?"

"They took him into surgery just now."

"*Cao!* And this old man?"

"I don't think he killed Yang. We were just talking to him as due diligence, but it's pretty clear he didn't know the actual identity of the victim who was murdered in Harbin."

"*Cao ni de ma!*"

"I'm not injured, by the way. Thanks for asking."

Lu hears Liang exhale into the mouthpiece of his phone. "Sorry, kid. You're right. This is no time to point fingers. Do you need me to come down to the hospital?"

"I don't think that's necessary. I'll just wait here until I get an update."

"Right. I'll call the county chief and have him call someone in Harbin metro to make sure you're covered, okay?"

"Thanks, boss."

Lu hangs up. He gets a rag out of the trunk of the car and wipes down the front and back seats. Then he waits inside with the engine running.

He notices his hands are shaking. He closes his eyes and focuses on taking deep breaths, and by the time Sergeant Bing shows up, he is reasonably calm.

"*Cao!*" Sergeant Bing says. "Tell me that's not yours!"

"The blood? It's Deputy Director Song's."

"Is he dead?"

"I haven't heard from the doctor, so I guess not yet." Lu tells Sergeant Bing about the evening's events.

"What a mess," Sergeant Bing says.

"Yes. Anyway, I'll wait here. You head on back home. Thanks for the clothes. You didn't have to come yourself, you know. You could have sent one of the constables."

"I'll stay."

"No, Brother Bing. Go on home. Thanks."

Lu asks the front desk attendant where he can clean up. She summons an orderly to take him to a dormitory for unmarried male staff, and Lu showers and changes and puts his dirty, blood-encrusted clothes into a plastic bag. He tosses the bag into the back of the patrol car.

Lu buys hot tea from a vending machine. Now that he's back at the hospital, he can't help but think of Yang Fenfang's autopsy. He asks the front desk attendant if anyone is on duty in the morgue.

"Go see for yourself," she says, annoyed at his interruption of the program she's watching on her phone. "Basement level, last office on the left."

Lu descends the stairs to the green-tiled corridor and walks down to the office, where he finds a young attendant dressed in scrub pants and a sweater, sound asleep with his head on his desk. Lu wakes him up.

"I'm Inspector Lu, PSB. Can you look someone up for me?"

The attendant rubs his eyes. "Patient registration is upstairs."

"The person I'm looking for is dead."

"Oh. You're sure she's here?"

"I watched her autopsy take place just down the hall on Sunday. Her name is Yang Fenfang."

The attendant checks his records. "Yes, she's still here. No one's claimed the body."

"What will happen to her?"

"She'll be held until someone claims her or we get permission to cremate the remains."

"Who gives you the permission to cremate?"

"You do. Public Security Bureau."

"Oh, right." This is a level of administrative detail that Lu does not generally handle.

"But honestly speaking, the PSB is extremely slow to stamp the death certificates of homicide and accident victims, or unidentified bodies," the attendant says. "We have more than sixty such cases clogging up our morgue right now. Confidentially, Inspector, we've had to double up in some of the cold storage spaces."

"That's disgraceful."

"I agree. I burn incense for these pour souls every night." The attendant nods at an urn sitting on the windowsill. "But our hands are tied. Unless a family member comes to retrieve the body or we get permission from the PSB to cremate the remains, they just sit here year after year."

"It's kind of you to burn incense, at least."

The attendant looks around as if checking for eavesdroppers and speaks in a low voice. "This hospital is filled with hungry ghosts. I feed them as best I can, but working here makes me a nervous wreck."

"Maybe you should find another line of work."

"Like what? Planting wheat in the hot sun and bitter cold? Standing on an assembly line in a refrigerator factory? Here, at least I'm inside, out of the weather. I can drink tea and read books. If it weren't for the ghosts and smell of death, I'd be very happy."

"Every job has it pluses and minuses, I guess. Thanks for the information."

Lu goes back upstairs and buys himself a second cup of tea. A coterie of cops from Harbin metro arrive. Lu is glad to see Xu is not among them. They find an empty office and take Lu's statement. Afterward, the senior officer claps Lu on the shoulder and tells him not to sweat it.

"Peng had quite a laundry list of offenses," he tells Lu. "Harassment, public disorder, stuff like that. No family to speak of. I don't think this is going to cause you any problems."

"So he's dead?" Lu asks. "That's confirmed?"

"Dead as a doorpost."

Lu thanks the officer. He takes a long walk up and down the corridors of the hospital, processing the night's events. Then he packs them away in a secure mental compartment and returns to the waiting room.

Technician Jin eventually appears, bedraggled and sleepy eyed. He and Lu sit together, drinking vending machine tea. Jin listens to Lu's description of the night's events.

"Taking a life is a heavy burden, but in the process, you saved one," Jin says.

"If Song lives."

"He will. He's too self-important to die so young."

Lu laughs. It feels good to laugh.

Ten minutes later, the doctor, drawn out and blood spackled, provides an update.

"He's critical but stable," the doctor says. "For the time being, we've placed him in an induced coma to assist the healing process."

"For how long, approximately?" Jin asks.

"Twenty-four to forty-eight hours."

"I'm going to stick around," Jin tells Lu. "Why don't you go home? Get some rest?"

It is nearly 3:00 a.m. when Lu arrives back at his apartment. He takes a long, scalding shower and climbs into bed. He closes his eyes, but despite his exhaustion, he cannot quit picturing Peng's body sprawled unnaturally on the sidewalk. He finally gets up and drinks two beers from his fridge. Then he takes an aspirin and eventually falls into a fitful sleep.

WEDNESDAY

We must have faith in the masses and we must have faith in the Party. These are two cardinal principles. If we doubt these principles, we shall accomplish nothing.

—*Quotations from Chairman Mao Zedong*

The next morning, Lu checks the newspapers and internet for any stories regarding Peng's death. There are none.

It's situations like these when he recognizes the benefits of living in a country where the media is heavily censored.

When he arrives at the *paichusuo,* he stops into the detention area to check on Zhang Zhaoxing, but Zhang is gone. Lu walks down the corridor to Chief Liang's office and finds it closed. He knocks.

"Enter!" comes Liang's muffled shout.

Lu opens the door and nearly chokes on a cloud of cigarette smoke. He finds Party Secretary Mao sitting behind Liang's desk and Liang himself sitting in front of it.

Lu nods politely. "Party Secretary. Excuse me. I didn't realize you were having a meeting."

"It's the hero of Harbin!" Mao says.

Lu can't tell if Mao is flattering or mocking him. Perhaps a bit of both.

"What is it, Lu Fei?" Chief Liang says.

"Where is Zhang Zhaoxing?"

"His formal arrest order came through, and he's been transferred to the county detention center."

"What? They'll eat him alive in there, Chief."

Liang shrugs. "We don't have the facilities to hold suspects long-term, you know that."

"Why are you so worried about what will happen to a brutal murderer while he's locked up?" Mao asks.

"I'm not so sure Zhang is the murderer, Party Secretary."

"He's been arrested, hasn't he?"

"An arrest isn't a conviction."

Party Secretary Mao exhales smoke. "One usually follows the other."

"The investigation is ongoing."

"Yes," Mao says. "I heard about the girl's luxury apartment in Harbin." Lu looks sharply at Chief Liang. He really shouldn't be sharing such details. Mao continues, "Seems unrelated to this case. Don't you think it's unlikely someone from Harbin came all the way out to Raven Valley Township in the middle of the night to kill the Yang girl? The murderer must be a local. Such as the pig butcher."

"I prefer to collect the facts and make a judgment rather than the other way around, Party Secretary."

Mao taps his cigarette on the rim of a brass ashtray. "So far, your investigation has turned up one probable suspect and one near-dead Ministry of Public Security deputy director. Perhaps you might consider listening to your superiors when they give you some direction."

"Yes, Party Secretary."

Lu shuts the door and walks to his office, fuming. He is too angry to sit down, so he makes a detour to the canteen. After a cup of Iron Goddess tea, he has cooled off enough to return to his office and attempt to make a dent in his in-box.

Paperwork, for a Chinese cop, is like the Dao: limitless and everlasting.

But Lu finds it difficult to focus. Yang Fenfang keeps returning to his thoughts. He pictures her stacked into a morgue drawer with some random body like a side of beef in a meat locker.

He checks Yang's *hukou* records and those of her parents to see if there are any family members still living. After some digging, he locates a cousin in a nearby village and phones him.

"I'm calling about Yang Fenfang."

"Eh?"

"Yang Fenfang. She was your cousin, I believe?"

"On my mother's side."

"Right. Well, it seems like you are her closest still-living relative."

"Me? Can't be."

"It is."

"I hardly knew the girl."

Lu knows exactly where this is going. "That might be the case, but you are her closest relative, and she's still being kept in the county morgue here. Do you have any plans to give her a proper burial?"

The cousin hisses through his teeth. "I wish I could, I really do, but I don't have the money for that."

"Perhaps I can work something out with the local funeral parlor."

"I have my own immediate family to worry about. I'm sorry. I just can't afford to be a *fennu*." The term *fennu* means "grave slave." Funerals have become so expensive in China—keeping up with Wangs and so forth—that many families go deeply into debt in order to bury their loved ones.

"So you're going to just let her rot in the morgue."

"Don't they keep bodies in a refrigerator?"

"I was using a figure of speech."

"Right. But anyway, won't the county just have her cremated?"

"What about her ashes? A suitable ceremony?"

"Like I said, my hands are tied. I have to go. Goodbye!"

The cousin hangs up.

There is only one *binyiguan*—funeral parlor—in Raven Valley Township. It's on the outskirts of town, at the end of a long, lonely road, surrounded by empty fields, fittingly removed from the domain of the living. Previously under the management of an elderly undertaker, the facility has recently been taken over by a young man named Zeng, one of the new breed of professionals who has graduated from a college program specializing in mortuary and funeral services. Lu calls and arranges a meeting.

He has a quick meal of noodles from a food cart, then takes one of the patrol cars and drives twenty minutes until he sees a low, tree-covered hill rising in the distance with a pagoda-like structure at its top, and below, cemetery grounds and the *binyiguan* complex. He passes through a gate with a tasteful signboard that reads *Everlasting Peace Funeral Home*.

Lu parks in a lot and walks up a path toward a two-story house that serves as the mortuary and residence of the undertaker. Off to the side is a hall for funeral ceremonies and a squat cinder-block building with a concrete chimney. Lu has attended a handful of funerals during his time in Raven Valley, so he knows the cinder-block building is the crematorium—a relatively new addition to the Chinese cultural landscape.

For thousands of years, the Chinese have cared for their dead by burying them in the ground in accordance with the laws of feng shui and providing them with regular offerings of food, incense, and joss money.

These practices are meant to demonstrate love and respect but also to ensure their deceased relatives are happy with their final resting places. According to traditional beliefs, a happy ancestor can bestow blessings from beyond the veil; an angry one can dole out misfortune.

One of Mao's first moves after taking power was to proclaim burial a waste of money and land resources and to suggest cremation in its stead. In urban areas, there was less resistance to this idea, but in the countryside, where folks are more rooted to the land, government edicts have come into bitter conflict with the sentiments of the people.

As it stands, the Everlasting Peace Funeral Home maintains a moderately sized cemetery neatly lined with grave markers, but these days, nearly all citizens of Raven Valley are destined for the crematorium and an ash urn when they die.

Even now, the smell of crackled pork hangs over the grounds like a layer of swamp gas.

Lu presents himself at the door of the residence. Undertaker Zeng answers his knock and leads Lu into a formal parlor, where he serves tea.

Zeng is a tall, thin, serious-looking man. Lu estimates him to be in his late twenties. Lu notes that he has the hands of a scholar—long, elegant fingers, unblemished by manual labor.

"I won't take up much of your time," Lu says. "I'm here about Yang Fenfang—I'm sure you've heard about her in the local news."

Zeng nods solemnly. "Tragic. I held a service for her mother just a little over a week ago."

"Oh, the service was here?"

"Yes. We're the only funeral parlor in Raven Valley, so . . ."

"Right. Did you notice anyone acting strangely at the funeral?"

"People always act a bit strange at a funeral, Inspector."

"Yes, I suppose. Anyone who didn't seem to belong? Or who Yang Fenfang didn't know personally?"

"It was a very small gathering. I have a list of attendees if you want to see it. We always record who attends and how much money they gave as part of our service to the family of the deceased."

"I would like to see that list. But what I really wanted to talk about was Yang Fenfang herself. She's being kept at the county hospital morgue and doesn't have any relatives who are willing to pay for her cremation and funeral."

Zeng clucks his tongue. "That's unfortunate. I know it's frowned upon these days to observe traditional funeral rites—waste of good farmland and money and resources and so on—but for the living to not honor dead ancestors is neglectful. And for the dead to have no one to care for them in the afterlife is a tragedy."

"So you believe in an afterlife, then?"

"I believe humans have a soul and the soul continues on in some fashion after death."

"In a world that mirrors our own? House, streets, cities? Cell phones, TVs, gourmet meals? Karaoke parlors?"

Zeng smiles. "I haven't visited it as yet, so I can't say. But I am quite certain our dead ancestors remain linked to us in some manner, and although they are no longer what we might consider human, they do experience feelings. Joy, sadness. Anger. And as we owe our very existence to them, it is our responsibility to ensure their comfort after they pass on."

"Sounds like you are the right man for this job."

"My mother would have preferred me to become a doctor, but I told her this kind of work is important and our society had a serious need for it." Zeng leans forward and stares intently into Lu's eyes. "May I speak frankly?"

"Please."

"The funeral business in our country is just that—a business. When a person dies, their relatives are besieged at the hospital by packs of undertakers looking to sell their services. The hospital staff allows this to happen, because they receive kickbacks. The dead are passed around like pigs to market, everyone just looking to make a couple of hundred yuan off them. It's a disgrace. As you may know, Master Kong believed respect for one's elders and ancestors was the core value of our civilization. Stability, harmony, social order—all these things are based on filial piety. What better expression of filial piety is there than the proper burial of loved ones?"

"I quite agree, and it's refreshing to meet someone your age who has bothered to read what Master Kong had to say. Has your mother come around to your way of thinking?"

Zeng sits back. "Not exactly. She worries it will be difficult for me to find a wife, given my profession, and she complains about having to live so close to a cemetery."

"Oh, she's here with you?"

"Yes. She's a bit infirm, so most of her time is spent in her room upstairs."

"It must be difficult for you to do your job and care for her at the same time."

"Both are equally important, and I do the best I can."

"I'm sure you do. In any case . . . back to Yang Fenfang."

"Yes. What can I do to help?"

"How much would a basic package cost? A funeral, cremation, and putting her urn near her mother?"

"A full funeral with all the trappings costs eighty thousand yuan."

Lu sucks in a breath. "That much?"

"Yes, but we can streamline. Boil it down to the essentials. Without forgoing the proper attention and care, of course."

"Of course."

"Preparation of the body, cremation, an urn, a simple ceremony—I can do it for fifteen thousand."

"That's really kind of you, Mr. Zeng."

"Not at all. She was a member of the community, and it's only right that she be laid to rest beside her mother. Would you like a quick tour of the facilities?"

Lu wants to be on his way, but considering Zeng's generous pricing, he feels obligated to indulge the young man.

Zeng shows Lu a room at the back of the house where he prepares bodies for funeral services. There is a stainless steel table, a refrigerator unit, trays of equipment, and so on. Lu is relieved to find no corpses lying about.

"What's this?" Lu asks, pointing to a device that looks like a fancy water heater.

"Embalming machine."

"Embalming? You still do that even if you're just going to end up cremating the body?"

"No, but on rare occasions, we do have a family that has the ... resources ... to secure a burial plot. In that case, we do embalm."

They walk out to the foyer, and Zeng is about to open the front door when a voice comes from above: "Ah Zeng?"

"Yes, Mother?'

"Who's there?"

"It's Inspector Lu of the Public Security Bureau."

"What does he want?"

"He's here about a funeral."

"Bring him up."

Zeng turns to Lu. "Sorry, do you mind? My mother is a bit formal. She likes to be introduced to people who come into the house."

"Sure."

Zeng leads Lu upstairs, down a hall, and into a room overlooking the front yard. There is a narrow bed, nightstand, and chest of drawers on one side and a couch, two chairs, low table, and television on the other.

An older woman, perhaps in her sixties, sits on the couch. She's dressed in a long skirt and sweater. Her hair is coiled into a tight bun, and she's wearing full makeup. Powder and rouge. A slash of red lipstick. Two penciled arches in place of eyebrows.

She doesn't rise from her seat when Lu enters—he sees a folded-up wheelchair and a pair of walking braces leaning against the wall.

"Inspector Lu, this is my mother."

"Call me *Auntie*," Zeng's mother says.

Lu bows slightly. "Good afternoon, Auntie."

"I would stand to offer you a proper hello, but I'm not as mobile as I once was."

"My mother suffers from a neuromuscular ailment," Zeng says.

"Ah Zeng," Mrs. Zeng admonishes. "The inspector does not need to concern himself with our health issues."

"Yes, Mother."

"I'm sorry to hear that," Lu says. "Is there some treatment available?"

"Sadly, doctors can't do anything to stop us from getting old." Mrs. Zeng waves to a chair. "Why don't you sit down?"

"I'd love to, but—"

"Visit with a lonely old lady for a moment, Inspector. It's so boring to be cooped up in this dreary old house."

Lu doesn't want to be rude. He sits. He and Mrs. Zeng chat for a bit. He notices that her hands display a slight tremble. But her mind is as sharp as a tack. She inquires as to his business at the funeral home, and he tells her he's there to see about Yang Fenfang. She has heard about Yang's murder, of course, and wants to gossip about it, but Lu is not forthcoming. She then turns to his family background, his job, whether or not he is married.

"Not yet," he says.

"How old are you?"

"I'm turning thirty-nine."

"Oh, Inspector, it's time, don't you think? Your parents must be anxious for grandchildren. Don't disappoint them."

"Of course, you're right."

"Don't let them end up like me, without anyone to carry on the family line."

"Mother," Zeng chides.

"Soon I will be dead, and as no self-respecting woman would stoop to marry an undertaker, I'll have no grandchildren and, therefore, no one to see to *my* comfort in the afterlife. Ironic, no?"

"Mother!"

"I begged him to become a doctor. An ophthalmologist. A veterinarian. A pharmacist. Anything but *this*."

"I'm making an important contribution to society," Zeng says, "and death is always with us. I'll need never fear not having a job, and you need never fear not having a roof over your head and enough rice to eat!"

"That's all well and good, but when you're gone, where will that leave me?"

"I really have to be on my way," Lu says. "It was a pleasure, Mrs. Zeng."

She tilts her head and gives Lu a pleasant smile. "It was so nice to meet you, Inspector."

Zeng and Lu swaddle themselves in coats and hats and take a quick tour of the grounds. Just through the gates of the cemetery is a large, somewhat industrial-looking columbarium—a mausoleum where ash urns are stored in tiny niches. Zeng shows Lu Mother Yang's final resting place.

"I can free up this space next to Mrs. Yang and place Yang Fenfang right beside her," Zeng offers.

"That would be wonderful, Mr. Zeng."

They climb the hill to the pagoda-like building.

"This is our second columbarium," Zeng says. "As you can see, it sits on a rise, with a wide-open view and plenty of sunlight. In the summer and spring, a small grove at the rear of the columbarium provides a burst of green. This site has very good feng shui."

"Must be quite a bit more expensive than the columbarium below."

"Yes. Unfortunately, the price I quoted you for Yang Fenfang is not enough for her ashes to be placed here."

"That's all right. I think she'd prefer to be next to her mother."

Zeng takes Lu into a large eight-sided room. There is a table in the center with an arrangement of flowers, fruit, and incense. The walls are honeycombed with elegantly appointed niches trimmed in red lacquer and gold foil. A set of stairs set flush into a side wall leads upward.

"What's above?" Lu asks.

"Another two levels holding urns. From the outside, it looks as if the pagoda has seven floors, but floors four through seven are actually just for show."

Zeng escorts Lu down the hill and through the cemetery gates to the parking lot, where they part ways.

"Thanks for your time, Mr. Zeng," Lu says. "I'll transfer a down payment later today so you can collect the body as soon as possible."

Zeng gives Lu a formal bow. "Thank you for entrusting Yang Fenfang to me. I will take excellent care of her."

Lu drives back to the *paichusuo* and checks in with Sergeant Bing and Technician Jin. Jin has already obtained a warrant and thoroughly searched Zhang Zhaoxing's property.

"I didn't find anything," Jin tells Lu. "No murder weapon, suture, nothing like that."

"I'm not surprised. How's the old man, Zhang's grandfather?"

"Took no notice of us. There's a young cousin or some relation there watching over him, a real spitfire of a girl. She followed me around, demanding compensation for having to watch Grandpa Zhang and missing out on work. Said we illegally arrested Zhang Zhaoxing, blah blah blah. She claims she's going to sue us."

"Typical," Lu says. "No sign of Yang Fenfang's missing television or computer tablet?"

Jin shakes his head.

"How about the electronics stores, pawnshops, and internet?"

"Zip," Sergeant Bing says.

"What about the evidence you collected at the apartment in Harbin?" Lu asks Jin.

"Still being processed."

"Any luck tracing Yang's tablet?"

"Last ping was Yang's residence the night before the homicide. Nothing after that."

"Does that mean it hasn't been activated by whoever took it?"

"Probably."

"Why steal it, then?"

Technician Jin shrugs. "Criminal psychology is not my expertise."

Lu takes Sergeant Bing aside and explains about the arrangements he's made for Yang Fenfang. He asks the sergeant to take up a collection at the *paichusuo* and to send constables over to Kangjian Lane to see if any of the neighbors are willing to contribute. Then he goes to his office and, before tackling anew the paperwork piled on his desk, transfers an initial payment to the Everlasting Peace Funeral Home.

At the end of the workday, Lu collects Yang Fenfang's case file, puts on his hat and coat, and borrows one of the *paichusuo*'s bicycles. He rides home and changes out of his uniform. He eats a meal of frozen dumplings and a persimmon.

Then he tucks the case file under his arm and walks to the Red Lotus bar.

The place is empty when he arrives, apart from Yanyan.

"Evening, Yanyan."

"Inspector Lu. Three nights this week."

"A new record," Lu says. He looks for signs of lingering awkwardness over Sunday night's events, but Yanyan's expression gives nothing away.

"What are you drinking?" she says.

"Shaoxing, please. My blood is frozen solid."

"Sounds like a life-or-death situation."

"Only you have the power to save me."

While Yanyan warms his wine, Lu sits, opens the file, and begins to leaf through it. It is rather thin at this point, and there is nothing here he hasn't seen before. But he is hoping for a brainstorm. An epiphany, perhaps brought on by a state of inebriation.

Yanyan brings over the jar of wine and a rice bowl. "Should I dust off that bottle of Yoichi, also?"

"Dr. Ma has gone back to Beijing."

"A shame." Yanyan pours for Lu.

"Is it?"

"You two seemed to be getting along so well."

"I was just trying to be sociable."

"You did an excellent job."

"Um . . ." Lu isn't sure how to respond.

Yanyan laughs. "I'm teasing you."

"Oh. I thought maybe you were angry."

"Why would I be angry?"

Lu shrugs. "No reason."

"The funny thing is, in all the time you've been coming here, that's the first time I've ever seen you in the company of someone," Yanyan says. "Let alone a beautiful woman."

"Yes, I suppose that's true."

"It's not good to drink alone, you know."

"Also true. Will you join me?"

Yanyan glances around the empty bar. "Maybe for just one."

She collects a bowl and sits. He pours for her.

"*Gan bei*," he says.

"*Gan bei*."

They drink. Bad Chinese pop music plays over the sound system.

"Why is that?" Yanyan asks.

"Why is what?"

"Why do I never see you in the company of a young woman? Or do you take your dates somewhere else?"

"I don't really have dates."

"Why?"

"Hm. Well . . . I guess because I'm not interested in the usual."

Yanyan raises an eyebrow. "The usual, Inspector?"

"I've been drinking your wine for two years now. I think it's time you called me *Brother Lu*."

"Brother Lu. Okay. So?"

"You know, the usual. Get married. Have a kid. If the first one's a daughter, two kids. Buy an apartment. Work my ass off and force the children to study four hours every night so they can attend a decent university."

"Isn't that the 'Chinese dream'?"

"Not mine."

"What's yours, then?"

Lu pours for Yanyan and attempts to pour for himself, but Yanyan gently takes the jar from his hand and fills his bowl.

"Love," Lu says. "I want to marry someone I fall in love with."

"Inspector—I mean—Brother Lu! How very romantic of you."

"Who says a policeman can't be romantic?"

"You spend all day around bad people. Crooks. Thugs. Even murderers. Seems like that would leach the romanticism right out of you."

"I don't think about it like that." Lu drinks.

"How do you think about it?"

"You've heard of Mengzi, right?"

"I always get him and the other one confused."

"Xunzi."

"Yes."

"They were polar opposites. Xunzi believed that human nature is inherently selfish. People only care about their own well-being, and because of that, governments must impose a strict system of law and order to stop folks from indulging in their worst impulses. Mengzi, on the other hand—he believed people are inherently good. His famous example was of a child about to fall into a well. Have you heard that one?"

"I've heard of the 'frog in the well.'" This a Chinese idiom that refers to a narrow-minded person.

"Not quite the same thing. What Mengzi said was that if you see a child on the verge of falling into a well, you will automatically rush to help him. Not because you want to gain favor with the kid's parents or to be perceived as a benevolent person by your neighbors but because you naturally feel empathy for the pain and suffering of others."

"But isn't the whole point of the Public Security Bureau centered on the idea that human nature is selfish? Shouldn't you be on Xunzi's side? Rules and regulations. Crime and punishment."

"To some extent. But there's more to the job than just punishing lawbreakers. Sometimes, it's enough to just act as a symbolic deterrent. There's this passage in the Analects of Master Kong."

Yanyan closes her eyes and pretends to nod off.

Lu laughs. "No, listen. The Duke of She tells Master Kong, 'In my land, men are righteous. If a father steals a sheep, the son will testify against him.' And Master Kong replies, 'In my land, a father covers for a son, and a son for a father. That is what we call righteous.'"

"Sounds like Master Kong is saying it's okay to break the law."

"His point is that things are never as black and white as you make them out to be. Everything is relative. A law can't consider every nuance, every extenuating circumstance, and it can't anticipate the full range of human experience. Let's say the father stole a sheep because he was starving. You know what Master Kong considered to be the most important human virtue, right? Filial piety. Respect for one's elders. He said filial piety was the foundation of a harmonious society."

"So the kid doesn't rat on the father when he steals, because his father was hungry? And Master Kong calls that justice?"

"That's one interpretation. The other is that perhaps the son reasons with the father and convinces him to return the sheep before he gets caught. That way, the crime is rectified, and the authorities don't even need to get involved. In such a case, it's the son's filial duty to instruct his father on the right thing to do, rather than just going to the police and turning him in, which will end up badly for the father and waste the time and resources of the legal system."

Yanyan sips from her bowl. "If that's how folks handled things, you'd be out of a job."

"There will always be a need to make sure people don't run red lights."

Yanyan dabs her lips with the sleeve of her sweater. "This kind of philosophical discussion is over my head. I'm just a simple country girl."

"Nonsense. You may not have studied the classics, but after managing the Red Lotus for some years, seeing how people present themselves when they are sober and what they reveal of themselves when they are drunk, you probably have more practical experience with human nature than most cops who have been on the job for a decade."

Yanyan pours Lu another round. "Well, I told you I would make a good detective."

"I'm sure you would have. So now it's my turn to ask you. How come you have never remarried?"

Yanyan's expression darkens. She looks down and toys with the bracelet on her wrist.

"Sorry," Lu says. "I shouldn't have asked. It's really none of my business."

"No, it's just . . . I've never really spoken to anyone about it." Yanyan takes a sip of wine. "With my husband and me, it was as you said. We married for love. And when he died—it made me so unbearably sad. Honestly, I don't know if I could ever risk feeling like that again."

Lu reaches out and touches Yanyan's hand.

She immediately pulls away. "I have to . . . I should . . ." She abruptly rises and walks behind the counter and into the back room.

Lu has unwittingly crossed a line. He considers putting money on the table and leaving, but decides that would only make things worse.

Besides—the Shaoxing is heated to just the right temperature to bring out its complex melody of flavors. It would be a shame not to drink it.

Lu swallows what's left in his bowl and pours himself another round. He cracks open the case file and scans through the autopsy report. Examines the crime scene sketches. Leafs through a series of photos taken by Technician Hu. The living room. The empty TV stand. The bedroom. The bathroom.

He pulls out the photograph of Yang Fenfang standing in front of the Saint Sophia Cathedral. Lu looks into the face of the dead girl, trying to ascertain what part she may have played in her own murder. Did she threaten a rich lover? Ask him for more money? Demand he divorce his wife?

The twisted nature of the crime gnaws at him. Lu is certain it is not a simple matter of greed, or blackmail, or jealousy. The state of Yang Fenfang's body indicates that it was highly personal in nature. The work of a true psychopath.

Yanyan returns bearing a dish of candied haws as a peace offering. She sets the dish down and sees the photo in Lu's hand. "Pretty."

"You didn't know her, right?"

"May I?" Yanyan takes the photo and holds it up to the light. "No. Never met her. Are those real *Hong Di Xie*?"

"What are *Hong Di Xie*?" The term used by Yanyan, which Lu has never heard before, literally means "Red Bottomed Shoes."

"Shoes. High heels. Very expensive. They retail for something like four thousand yuan."

"For a pair of shoes? That's outrageous!"

Yanyan laughs. "That's fashion."

"How can you tell they are *Hong Di Xie*?"

"They have a red sole, see? Very distinctive. I mean, they could be fakes, but . . . I don't know, given the rest of her outfit, she seems like the kind of girl that would want the real deal."

"You know a lot about shoes."

"Just because I run a bar means I can't admire nice shoes?"

"No, no. Not at all."

"Anyway, if you want to confirm they're genuine, I'll be happy to try them on for you."

Now it is Lu's turn to laugh.

Then he remembers that the wardrobe at the Yang residence held several pairs of shoes, as did the closet in the Harbin apartment.

He's pretty sure the *Hong Di Xie* wasn't one of them.

At four thousand yuan, this single pair costs more than twice the average monthly rent in Harbin. Fenfang wouldn't have carelessly left them lying about.

"Hey, Yanyan. Do you think someone could sell a pair of shoes like this on Xianyu?" Xianyu, like Taobao, is an internet retailer, but a more popular site for second-hand goods.

"Oh, I'm sure. But are you thinking the person who . . . ? That would be kind of stupid, wouldn't it? So easy to trace them back to him."

"Yes. It would."

But Lu feels a rush of excitement nevertheless.

He closes the file and swallows the rest of his wine. He reaches over, takes Yanyan's nearly full cup, and drinks that, too. He gets up and slips into his coat and puts money on the table.

"Where are you off to in such a rush?" Yanyan says.

"You've given me a potential lead."

Lu flags down a taxi. He takes it to the *paichusuo,* where he borrows the key to the Yang residence from the evidence room. He drives one of the patrol cars to Kangjian Lane. He breaks the taped seal on the front door and lets himself inside. He searches everywhere for the shoes.

He does not find them.

THURSDAY

What is work? Work is struggle. There are difficulties and problems in those places for us to overcome and solve. We go there to work and struggle to overcome these difficulties. A good comrade is one who is more eager to go where the difficulties are greater.

—*Quotations from Chairman Mao Zedong*

On Thursday morning, Zeng presides over a wake at Yang Fenfang's house.

In times past, after a death in the family, the body was laid out at home for several days. Neighbors, friends, and relatives came to pay their respects and offer small gifts of money to help defray funeral expenses. Buddhist or Daoist monks performed rituals to guide the soul of the deceased into the afterlife and eventual rebirth. A funeral procession and burial were held on an auspicious date.

Nowadays, the dead go straight from the hospital to a mortuary and then shortly thereafter into a cremation unit. But the tradition of receiving guests at the deceased's home for a period of one to three days continues.

In Yang Fenfang's case, there are no close relatives to receive visitors, so Zeng acts as both greeter and undertaker. A handful of neighbors stop by (notably, not the Chens), but otherwise, it's just Zeng, Lu, Sergeant Bing, Chief Liang, and a couple of constables.

Zeng has procured the service of one Buddhist and one Daoist priest, each of whom carry out their own respective ceremonies in proximity to one another without apparent conflict or rivalry. Lu and the other mourners burn hell money and paper goods on Yang's behalf. Before he leaves, Lu hands Zeng an envelope of cash—donations from the *paichusuo* staff, supplemented from his own pocket.

"We can't join you for the funeral, I'm afraid," Lu says.

"Not to worry," Zeng answers. "Thank you for coming to pay your respects."

After their return to the *paichusuo,* Lu, Chief Liang, Sergeant Bing, and Technician Jin convene a brief meeting.

Lu tells Liang and Bing about the shoes. "When I didn't find them at Yang's house last night, I called Technician Jin and asked him to check the inventory for the apartment in Harbin."

"The shoes weren't there, either," Jin says.

"Might Yang have just lent them to a friend?" Sergeant Bing says. "Or lost them?"

"Anything's possible," Lu says, "but they were worth a lot of money. I have a feeling she would have been very protective of them."

"If what you say is true, did the perp take the shoes because of their value?" Liang asks. "Or as a trophy?"

"These *Hong Di Xie* are rare enough that for the suspect to try selling them openly would be a huge risk," Lu says, "but perhaps he knows of a place where he can market them to private collectors."

Liang curls his lips in disgust. "Maybe he has a foot fetish."

Technician Jin slurps from a cup of tea. "This morning, I called headquarters and asked one of our analysts to look up homicides featuring the theft of shoes as part of the MO. He came up empty."

"I'm not surprised," Liang says. "Panties, I can see. But shoes?"

"Remember Gao Chengyong?" Lu says.

There is a collective groan from around the table.

Gao Chengyong killed and mutilated at least eleven women and girls over a thirty-year period. He occasionally took body parts—sections of the scalp, ears, breasts. He was finally caught by chance when one of his cousins was arrested on corruption charges and administered a routine DNA test—the results of which proved to be a familial match for evidence left at some of Gao's crime scenes.

"There was a theory that Gao was attracted to young girls with long hair, dressed in red, and wearing high heels," Lu says.

"That was inconclusive," Technician Jin says. "Gao himself never gave any indication that he targeted his victims for any specific reason other than they were in the right place at the right time."

"Yes," Lu says, "but I think the shoes are still a viable lead. Keep in mind, it may not be about the shoes themselves but, instead, the color. Maybe red is the trigger mechanism. Red shoes, red shirt, red anything."

"Red is everywhere in this country," Liang says. "If the killer is triggered by red, he would be offing folks left and right every Lunar New Year."

"Obviously, it's something subtler than that," Lu says. "Perhaps the profile is a young woman wearing red shoes or red clothes. Signifying youth, fertility, good fortune. Something he resents. Wants to destroy."

"Or maybe it is the shoes, after all," Jin says. "High heels. Western shoes. Like the crazy old guy who tried to kill you and the deputy director. When he sees a young Chinese girl in high heels, he perceives it as an infection of traditional culture by the Western disease."

"Good thought," Lu says.

Liang grows impatient. "So what now?"

"I guess back to the internet to see if anyone is hawking a pair of *Hong Di Xie*," Lu says, "in case the killer really is that stupid. In the meantime, I'll check the Harbin case files to see if there's any mention of missing shoes or other items, specifically red ones."

"I don't think the killer is stupid," Jin says.

"Unfortunately," Lu says, "neither do I."

The Harbin files have been returned to the metro PSB records storage facility, and that is where Lu spends the early afternoon, sitting in a windowless room that smells of dust and mold and is almost as cold as the street outside. He scrutinizes crime reports and statements from the victims' circle of coworkers and friends through a cloud of his own condensed breath.

There is no mention of shoes, but he does find a notation about a missing piece of jewelry in the case of Tang Jinglei. The report reads: *Victim's coworker claims she lent victim a ring valued at 675 RMB that was not returned to her. Ring was not found on victim's person or in her apartment.*

Unfortunately, a description of the ring is not provided, but there is a phone number for the coworker. Lu can't get reception in the windowless room, so he goes out into the lobby and calls.

"*Wei?*" a female voice answers.

"Is this Ms. Liu?"

"Who's this?"

Lu explains who he is and what he wants.

"Ah. . . . Jingjing," Liu says. "Why are you asking about her?"

"I'm just looking into some things. I saw a statement you gave the police regarding a missing ring?"

"Did you find it?"

"No."

"Damn. That ring cost me more than six hundred yuan. I lent it to Jingjing several months before . . . before it happened."

"And then?"

"Well, I kept asking for her to return it, and she never did. The last time we spoke, we had a fight about it, and she promised she'd bring it to me. And just two nights later . . ." Her voice breaks.

"Sorry, I know it's difficult to talk about," Lu says gently.

"The police *said* they never found it. But cops in Harbin—they'll pick up anything that's not nailed down. One of them probably took it home and gave it to his girlfriend."

"Can you describe it, please?"

"It was a beautiful piece of coral in a fourteen-karat gold setting."

"Coral, you say?"

"Yes."

"What color was the coral, Ms. Liu?"

"Red."

"Thank you. You've been very helpful."

Lu selects what he feels are the most relevant entries in the case files—autopsy reports, crime scene sketches, background information on the victims—and stuffs them down the front of his shirt. He buttons up his coat and goes out to the lobby and tells the officer on duty that he's heading to lunch and will return in an hour.

Once outside, he searches on his phone for the nearest copy shop, finds one, goes there, and tells the proprietor he's on official police business and requires a copy machine and some privacy. He makes copies, pays the proprietor, has a quick bite at a street stall, and goes back to the storage facility. He replaces the originals in the case files and carries the copies he's made out with the duty officer none the wiser.

Lu drives back to Raven Valley Township. Chief Liang is out at some meeting or another—but Lu gathers Technician Jin and Sergeant Bing in his office.

"I think it's the color red, after all," Lu says. He explains about the ring.

"Nothing for the other Harbin victim?" Jin asks.

"No, but perhaps it was something as simple as a scarf or a hat. Nothing anyone would notice missing." He turns to Sergeant Bing. "I don't suppose you had any luck with the shoes?"

"Well, I can tell you there are a lot of websites out there selling footwear. Most of them are branded stores, though. So we tried narrowing it down to websites where private individuals are buying and selling shoes, especially Western high heels."

"And?"

"No *Hong Di Xie* were featured."

"As expected," Lu says. "Perhaps he *is* keeping them as a trophy. But if that's the case, I'm curious about the tablet and TV. This was a brutal, ritualistic murder. Seems strange for it to be paired with the theft of some mid-priced electronics, ones that the perp probably knows he can't sell. What size was the TV, anyway?"

"It was 140 centimeters."

Lu looks up 140-centimeter Xiaomi televisions on his computer. "About twenty kilos. Not heavy but not light. Awkward to carry. I don't think the perp could have carted it on a bicycle very easily. He must have parked a car within walking distance."

"Or he lives in the neighborhood," Jin says.

A notion suddenly occurs to Lu. He's not sure why it's taken him so long to think of it. He looks at Sergeant Bing. "Hot chestnuts," Lu says.

"Hot chestnuts?" Sergeant Bing asks, then remembers. "Oh, right!"

"Huh?" Technician Jin says.

"Better round up a couple of constables," Lu tells Sergeant Bing.

"What's going on?" Jin says.

"Why don't you come along?" Lu says. "And bring your equipment."

"Come along to where?"

"Kangjian Lane."

Lu, Sergeant Bing, Constable Sun and Technician Jin take one of the patrol cars. Big Wang, Yuehan Chu, and Li the Mute follow in the other.

Lu parks in front of the Chen residence. Everyone gets out and huddles up, hands in pockets, hunched over against the cold.

"We're looking for a Xiaomi 140-centimeter TV and an ASUS laptop."

"Here?" Big Wang says.

"Yes, here."

"You think the Chens are involved in the murder?" Technician Jin asks.

"Let's just look for the TV and laptop and go from there."

Lu sends Sergeant Bing and Big Wang around back. He and the others approach the front door, and Lu knocks. "Mrs. Chen! It's Inspector Lu."

Lu hears noises inside. Thumping. Scraping. Voices. He knocks again.

"Open up!" He tries the knob. It's locked. "Open this door immediately."

The door widens a crack, and Mrs. Chen looks out. "Yes? What do you want?"

"May we come in?"

"Why have you brought all those policemen?"

"May we come in and speak to you?"

"About what?"

"*Ta ma de.* Just let us in."

"Come back later. I'm busy now." Mrs. Chen tries to shut the door, but Lu blocks it with his foot.

"Move aside, Mrs. Chen." He pushes past her. She squawks angrily.

Inside, Mrs. Chen's mother sits on the *kang,* her rheumy eyes regarding Lu with open hostility.

The TV stand is empty.

"Where's your son?" Lu asks.

"At work," Mrs. Chen snaps. "This is my home. You can't just barge in—"

"Go open the back door for Sergeant Bing," Lu says. Li the Mute nods and walks into the kitchen.

Mrs. Chen pokes a finger into Lu's chest. "Tell me what you want, or get out."

Lu heads for the bedroom. Mrs. Chen moves quickly to block his way. "You can't go in there."

"Why?" Lu says.

"My grandson is sleeping."

Lu shunts Mrs. Chen aside and tries the door. It's locked. "Open up, or I'll kick the door in."

"I have rights!" Mrs. Chen shrills. "You can't treat me like this!"

Lu shouts through the door, "If anyone is in there, back up, because I'm coming in!" He kicks. The frame splinters. Mrs. Chen and her mother scream. Lu kicks again. The door pops open, and Lu steps through.

The daughter-in-law is huddled on the bed, her son wrapped in her arms. The boy begins to bawl. Lu jabs a thumb over his shoulder. "Out!"

He tosses the bedroom while Sergeant Bing tries to calm Mrs. Chen. She responds by slapping him across the face. Sergeant Bing loses his temper and shoves her roughly facedown on the *kang,* twisting an arm up behind her back.

The entire family, three generations, bleats like gutted sheep.

Lu finds the TV under the bed. It's a Xiaomi, and he estimates the size to be 140 centimeters. He goes back out into the living room.

"Run them all down to the station," he says. "Even the grandmother."

Li the Mute and Yuehan Chu are tasked with taking the family to the *paichusuo.* Big Wang is left to assist Technician Jin in searching the house for any relevant evidence and the missing computer tablet.

Mrs. Chen's son—given name Shiyi—works in the repair shop at one of the large agricultural concerns outside of Raven Valley Township. Lu, Sergeant Bing, and Constable Sun drive there and park in front of a huge corrugated steel building in the middle of a frost-limned wheat field. Inside, there are about twenty mechanics working on an array of tractors, combine harvesters, grain carts, planter units, sprayers, and various other vehicles, the purpose of which Lu doesn't recognize.

They locate the manager's office and explain that they are looking for Chen Shiyi. The manager is smoking a cigarette and reviewing reams of work orders. There's a space heater in the corner, but the office is cold enough that still he's wearing a sweater, jacket, knit cap, and cotton gloves.

"Chen Shiyi?" he says, confused. "Why?"

"Don't worry about that!" Lu barks. "Is he here?"

"Yes." The manager gestures at the office window with his cigarette. "But we're swamped today. Will this take long?"

Lu walks out of the office without responding. He goes looking for Chen, the manager dogging his heels.

"Officer! We have a quota to fulfill!"

Lu spies Chen tinkering with a tractor engine. He's wearing greasy overalls and holding a wrench. A cigarette dangles from his mouth. Perhaps smoking is not permitted, because when he sees the manager, he furtively drops the cigarette and grinds it out.

Then Chen catches sight of Lu. Panic registers on his face. He makes a break for the exit.

"Get him!" Lu shouts.

Chen is skinny and fast. He is halfway across the parking lot before Lu emerges from the building. Chen hops on a motorbike and furiously kick-starts the engine.

Lu doesn't bother trying to catch up with Chen on foot—he knows he won't. He makes a beeline for the patrol car. He unlocks it, yanks open the door, and scrambles behind the wheel. He starts the engine and throws the car into reverse. As he screeches backward, he sees a blur in the side window—Constable Sun and, five meters behind her, Sergeant Bing. Lu doesn't stop. There's no time. He shifts into drive and guns for the parking lot exit.

Chen is already fifty meters down the road. There's not much out here besides vast open grain fields, their flat, bland uniformity relieved only by the occasional farmhouse or water tank. Lu wonders where the hell Chen thinks he's going.

Chen is driving a 150 cc motorbike, with a top speed of about 95 kilometers per hour. It's no match for the patrol car. Lu comes up on Chen's taillight and hits the siren. Chen responds by leaning over the handlebars, as if reducing his wind drag will give him a newfound speed edge.

Lu doesn't want to get too aggressive and risk Chen wiping out, so he continues to ride on the motorbike's back tire for half a dozen kilometers. Chen stubbornly just keeps going.

"Dumb bastard," Lu growls.

Lu edges the patrol car along the shoulder of the road until it's about even with Chen's left hip, then slowly noses it over to force Chen off the road.

Chen first tries speeding up, but his bike is already maxed out. He then attempts to ride in the narrow space Lu has allotted him, which continues to shrink. Finally, he reduces speed and drops back behind the patrol car. Lu presses on the gas, gets some distance, pumps the brakes, and deftly turns the car sideways to block the road.

He gets out and waits for Chen.

Chen nears and, without slowing, veers around the patrol car onto the dirt shoulder of the road. But his bike is not made for off-roading. The front wheel whipsaws, and Chen loses control. The handlebars jerk out of his hands, the bike flips like a horse on a tripwire, and Chen tumbles in a cloud of dust.

Lu runs over and kneels to assess Chen's injuries. Chen is battered, scraped, and bleeding, whimpering and groaning, but when Lu asks him if he can wiggle his feet and hands, he can, so Lu assumes Chen does not have a broken neck.

Lu tries to gently help him to his feet, but Chen squirms like a bratty toddler. Lu cuffs him, drags him to the patrol car, and stuffs him in the back. He decides to take Chen to the Raven Valley Clinic, the closest medical facility.

Chen whines the entire way. Lu radios Sergeant Bing and apologizes for leaving him and Constable Sun stranded and suggests he get someone from the repair shop to drive them back into town.

He drives with lights and siren to the clinic. Chen is put on a gurney and wheeled into the treatment room. Lu uncuffs Chen and watches over the proceedings until Sergeant Bing and Constable Sun arrive, and then he leaves the supervision to them and goes out to buy a cup of tea and phone Chief Liang.

"Did the kid confess?" Liang asks.

"I haven't questioned him yet," Lu says. "He's being looked at by a medic now."

"If he's going to die, get a confession from him before he does."

"He's not going to die, Chief."

"Get a confession from him anyway."

When Lu returns to the treatment room, it's empty. He goes looking for the physician's assistant and finds him in the parking lot, smoking.

"Where's the patient I brought in?" Lu asks.

"Recovery ward."

"How is he?"

"Multiple abrasions, maybe a mild concussion, a jacked-up shoulder, but nothing's broken. I cleaned the wounds and gave him some painkillers. He's dozing now."

"Can I ask him some questions?" Lu says.

"I think it's better if you let him rest."

"I'm sure it's better for *him,* but it's not better for me."

"He's a little out of it."

"So much the better. Maybe he'll give me some honest answers."

The physician's assistant shrugs. "I don't have the authority to say yes or no."

"Can you wheel him into a private room?"

"I don't have time to deal with all that. Can't you just ask him what you want to know in the ward?"

"Some of these questions are of a sensitive nature," Lu says. "Never mind. I'll wheel him myself."

Lu goes to the recovery ward, where he finds Chen, Sergeant Bing, and Constable Sun and half a dozen other patients. Chen is hooked up to the pulsometer, which Lu detaches, setting off a piercing alarm. A nurse and the physician's assistant come running in. The physician's assistant huffs in annoyance, but then switches off the machinery and helps Lu wheel Chen's bed into an empty room.

"Don't beat him," the physician's assistant says.

"I would never," Lu says.

The physician's assistant leaves, closing the door behind him.

Lu pulls up a stool next to Chen. Chen's eyes are half-open. He looks like he's been stomped by a pack of mules. Lu records the subsequent interview on his cell phone.

> Lu: This is Inspector Lu Fei, deputy chief of Raven
>   Valley Township Public Security Bureau station. The
>   date is January 17. Location, Raven Valley Township
>   medical clinic. The subject is Mr. Chen Shiyi, resi-
>   dent of Kangjian Lane. Mr. Chen, do you know why
>   you are being questioned?
>
> Chen: (Unintelligible.)

Lu: Why did you run away when we came to your place of work?

Chen: (Groan.)

Lu: Mr. Chen, we found a television set belonging to Ms. Yang Fenfang hidden under the bed of your house. How did you come to have this television in your possession?

Chen: (Unintelligible.)

Lu: Speak up!

Chen: I didn't do it.

Lu: Do what?

Chen: Kill her.

Lu: Then why do you have her property?

Chen: (Unintelligible.)

Lu: You are in serious trouble, Mr. Chen. You'd better tell me everything.

Chen: I didn't kill her.

Lu: So what *did* you do?

Chen: I ... (weeping) ...

Lu: Pull yourself together.

Chen: My mother ... She told me to go to the house because the dog was barking.

Lu: So it was you and not her who went to the Yang residence on Saturday evening last?

Chen: Yes. I went and I saw ... *Tian*!

Lu: Hand him a tissue, would you, Constable Sun? Go on, Mr. Chen. I'm listening.

Chen: (Blows nose loudly.) I saw the dog in the yard. I knocked, and no one answered. I thought something must be wrong. I went inside. I ... It was horrible! I ran home and told my mother.

Lu: So you contend that Ms. Yang was dead when you got there?

Chen: Yes. At first, I wasn't sure. I . . . I touched her arm.
She was so cold.

Lu: And did you see anyone in the house?

Chen: No. I didn't stop to look. I ran.

Lu: Then what?

Chen: My head is killing me. Please call the doctor.

Lu: Answer the question first. What happened next?

Chen: (Unintelligible.)

Lu: What?

Chen: It was her.

Lu: What was?

Chen: The idea to take the TV.

Lu: Her who?

Chen: My mother. (Retching). I'm going to be sick.

Lu: Constable Sun, pull that wastebasket over next to
Mr. Chen's bed. Thank you. Now, Mr. Chen, you say
you went back home after discovering Yang
Fenfang's body, and your mother told you to steal
the TV. Mr. Chen?

Chen: Yes.

Lu: How did your mother know about the TV in the
first place?

Chen: She and Mrs. Yang were friends. She used to go over
there and watch programs.

Lu: I see. So you went back to the house and took it?

A break in the questioning while Chen vomits into the wastebasket.

Lu: Feel better?

Chen: I'm dying!

Lu: What about the computer tablet, Mr. Chen? Yang
Fenfang had a computer tablet, also.

Chen: Yes.

Lu: Yes, what?

Chen: That, too.

Lu: Your mother's idea?

Pause.

Lu: Mr. Chen?

Chen: I need water.

Lu: Constable, can you go out and find some water for Mr. Chen? Where did you find the computer tablet?

Chen: In the bedroom. On the bed.

Lu: So you went so far as to search the bedroom?

Chen: It was the first place I looked!

Lu: Just so I'm clear, what was your purpose in taking the TV and tablet?

Chen: My mother wanted the TV for my grandmother.

Lu: And the tablet?

Chen: I thought . . . I mean, my mother thought . . . we could use it.

Lu: Where is it now?

Chen: In the nightstand drawer, in the bedroom. We never even switched it on.

Lu: Why?

Chen: It was out of power. And I forgot to get the charger when I took it from the house.

Lu: You're certainly no criminal mastermind, are you, Mr. Chen? Now, let me ask you a very direct question. Did you or your mother have anything to do with Yang Fenfang's death?

Chen: Nothing, I swear. I just took the TV and the tablet. That's all.

Lu: Do you have any other information regarding the murder or who may have done it?

Chen: Nothing. I've told you everything.

Lu stops recording. Constable Sun returns, bearing a cup of water. Chen guzzles it.

Lu watches him with disgust. "Mr. Chen, if what you say is true, you may not be a murderer, but you and your mother are definitely guilty of being the absolute worst neighbors in Raven Valley Township."

Constable Sun remains at the clinic to watch over Chen Shiyi. Lu and Sergeant Bing return to the *paichusuo,* where Lu catches Chief Liang on his way out for an evening of karaoke.

"I'm already late," Liang says. "Just tell me the part where he said he killed the girl and stole her organs to sell to rich Thai people."

"Chen admits to stealing the TV and a computer tablet, but not to the murder."

"You think he's telling the truth?"

"Yes, I do."

"*Ta ma de.*"

"I'm going to question Mrs. Chen and the daughter-in-law to see if they corroborate what Chin Shiyi told me. If so, I'll submit an arrest request to Procurator Gao. For Chen and his mother."

"What charge?"

"For starters, theft. I'll see what else I can come up with."

"All right." Chief Liang looks at his watch. "Is that it for now?"

"Yes, Chief, enjoy your evening."

Lu and Sergeant Bing interview Mrs. Chen first. She refuses to say anything apart from: "I want a lawyer."

"Perhaps you don't understand how this works," Lu says. "You *have* to answer my questions regarding the case, and *then* you can have a lawyer."

"I want a lawyer. I want a lawyer. I want a lawyer."

Lu has Mrs. Chen sent back to the cell and the daughter-in-law brought in. She more or less confirms Chen Shiyi's account.

"Shiyi didn't want to do it, but his mother made him. She's an awful woman. Please have mercy on him!"

Lu goes to his office and writes up an arrest request for Procurator

Gao. As he sits at his computer, he can hear Mrs. Chen making a stink in the detention room from all the way down the corridor. He calls Fatty Wang into his office. "Go tell Mrs. Chen to pipe down or we will tape her mouth shut. And if she keeps shouting, go ahead and do it."

"By myself?" Fatty Wang says.

"Get Yuehan Chu to help you. He likes to beat up on old ladies."

It is nearly 8:00 p.m. when Technician Jin and Big Wang return from the Chen house.

"Did you find the computer tablet?" Lu asks.

"No," Jin says.

"Did you look in the bedroom nightstand?"

"Of course. It wasn't there."

"Where the hell could it be?"

"Maybe Chen sold it to a buddy or coworker."

"Maybe. You didn't happen to find any scalpels or suture thread lying around, did you?"

"Nope. Just a lot of pills for treating diarrhea and a lot of others for treating constipation."

"My shift was over two hours ago," Big Wang says. "Can I go?"

"Yes," Lu says.

He buys dinner from a street cart and eats at his desk. Sausages on skewers and a bowl of stinky *dofu*. Afterward, he drinks a cup of tea and ruminates.

Technician Jin has already left for the Raven Valley Friendship Guesthouse, but Lu calls his cell phone. Jin answers with a mouthful of food.

"Sorry to interrupt you at dinner, Technician Jin, but I have a question."

"Shoot."

"Was Constable Wang in your presence the whole time you were at the house?"

"Well . . . no. We weren't side by side the entire time."

"Was he ever alone in the bedroom by himself?"

"I suppose he might have been. Are you saying . . . ?"

"Not sure. Please keep this under your hat."

"Sure thing, Inspector."

Lu calls Big Wang's phone, but Wang doesn't answer. He drives to Wang's apartment, which he shares with Yuehan Chu. Neither of them are home. He makes a circuit of local restaurants and pubs. He quickly locates Wang and Chu at a hole-in-the-wall where food is served as an accompaniment to alcohol, rather than the other way around.

The restaurant is just a few square meters in size, with an open kitchen in the back. Two old men sit at one of the tables, eating grilled lamb skewers and drinking beer. Chu and Big Wang sit at another. They are still wearing their PSB uniforms and are flushed red from drinking.

Lu walks in and sits down. "Constables."

"What are you doing here?" Big Wang says rather rudely.

"You shouldn't be drinking while in uniform," Lu says.

"We're just having a couple," Wang says. "What do you want, Inspector? We're off duty."

"You and I have something to discuss," Lu says.

"What?" Wang pulls a pack of cigarettes out of his pocket and slips one into his mouth. He offers the pack to Chu.

"Constable Chu, would you excuse us?" Lu says.

"No," Chu says. "We're not at work now. You can't tell me what to do." He takes a cigarette and lights Wang's and then his own.

Lu sees at least four empty Harbin Pure Ice bottles on the table and a bottle of *bai jiu*. He is amazed that Wang and Chu have consumed so much alcohol in just the hour or so since they clocked out.

"Where is Yang Fenfang's computer tablet?" Lu asks.

"What?" Wang says.

"You heard me."

"How should I know?"

"Hey, Inspector," Chu says. "Why do you always pick on us?"

"Pick on you? Is that what you think?"

"You treat us like dog shit. And you dote on that stuck-up bitch Sun like she's a little empress."

"Don't speak about your colleague that way," Lu says. "I treat you two the way I do because you're ill-tempered, lazy slackers."

"*Cao!*" Big Wang snarls. "You think you're so far above us, with your fancy Beijing degree. Let me tell you something, Inspector, your shit smells just as bad as ours."

Lu squelches his rising anger. Perhaps the constable has a point to make. He will hear him out. Let him vent while alcohol has loosened his tongue.

"Go on," Lu says.

"Why?" Wang says. "What do you care what I have to say?"

"It's part of my job."

"Your job. Your job is to tell me and Ah Chu what to do. Our job is to do whatever the fuck we're told. Go here, go there, stand out in the cold, fill out paperwork, answer the phone, work ten-, twelve-, twenty-four-hour shifts with no break. For crap pay! My friend is a waiter, and he makes almost double what I do. Everyone treats us like we're a joke. Give someone an order, and they laugh in our faces."

Lu knows this is true, and the situation is not helped by the reputation the police have for taking bribes and engaging in illicit behavior.

"It's a difficult situation," Lu allows.

"The lack of respect," Chu grouses. "The defiance. The stupid things people expect of us. Do you know how many times a day old ladies call us asking for help in retrieving their lost QQ password?" QQ is a popular web application that offers instant messaging, games, music, and shopping services. "We're police, not some damn internet help desk!"

"It's our duty to serve the public," Lu says.

"Really?" Wang says. "I thought it was to enforce the law. Catch criminals. If I wanted to be a servant, I'd put on a skirt and let some rich man diddle me while I dusted his clocks!"

"Perhaps you are disappointed that the uniform does not command the fear and obedience you thought it would," Lu says. "Perhaps you are upset you are not allowed to carry a gun or beat people with your baton."

"Some people need to be beaten with a baton," Chu says.

"If you don't like being a cop," Lu says, "why don't you go buy yourself a skirt and a feather duster?"

Wang curses under his breath.

"Excuse me?" Lu snaps.

Wang downs his cup of *bai jiu* and pours himself and Chu another round.

Lu takes a deep breath. "All right. I've heard your complaints. Now, give me the computer tablet, Constable Wang."

Wang slams a fist on the table, knocking one of the empty beer bottles over. "*Cao ni niang,* I didn't take it!"

Lu stands up and slaps Wang off his stool.

Chu explodes out of his chair, knocking against the table, sending beer bottles and glasses flying. He draws his baton and swings it at Lu's head. Lu ducks, taking the brunt of the blow on his shoulder.

Chu raises his arm for another go, but Lu gets a hand on his biceps and wings an elbow into Chu's face.

Blood sprays down the front of Chu's shirt. He drops the baton and claps his hands to his nose. Lu knees him in the stomach.

Wang pops up to his feet. Lu can hear the restaurant's *laoban* yelling in the background. He's aware of the optics—three uniformed policemen brawling. Bad news. Can't be helped.

This fight has been brewing for a long time.

Lu slams the toe of his shoe into Wang's shin. Wang hops on one foot. Lu kicks the other leg out from under him.

Wang falls onto a bed of broken glass and spilled alcohol. Lu crouches over him and takes a fistful of Wang's shirt in one hand, curling the other into a fist.

"Where's the tablet, you bastard?"

Wang holds up his hands defensively. "I don't know. I didn't take it. I swear!"

Lu nearly punches Wang in the face, but holds back.

What, Lu thinks, *if he's telling the truth?*

In the aftermath of the dustup, nearly every constable assigned to the Raven Valley PSB station rushes to the restaurant, where they proceed to stand around and gawp at the carnage. Chief Liang arrives—three parts drunk from karaoke—and to his credit musters his considerable powers of persuasion to smooth matters over with the restaurant owner, promising to compensate him for any damages. He also offers the two old men cigarettes and tells them their meal will be paid for.

"And if I could ask a huge favor," he says, "please don't tell anyone about this. Quite frankly, it's an embarrassment for the Public Security Bureau."

"We won't breathe a word of it," one of the old men says.

"You'd better not, if you know what's good for you," Chief Liang says menacingly. Then he smiles broadly, claps the men on their backs, and ushers them out of the restaurant. "Have a good night, Uncles! Get home safe!"

Yuehan Chu and Big Wang are carted off to the Raven Valley Clinic for treatment, Chu with a broken nose, and Wang with a blanket of glass embedded in his back.

Chief Liang shoves Lu into the back of one of the patrol cars and leans in. "What the hell were you thinking, Lu Fei?"

"I suspected Wang of taking the computer tablet."

"So you decided it would be a good idea to beat the shit out of him?"

"No . . . he . . ." Lu is about to say that Wang started the fight, but that isn't strictly true. "It just got out of hand."

"We'll talk about this tomorrow." Liang slams the door and tells Sergeant Bing to take Lu home.

Sergeant Bing is silent on the drive back to Lu's apartment. When they arrive, he turns to look over the back of the seat. "Don't sweat it. It'll blow over. And guys like Wang and Chu, they need a good thumping every now and then."

"Thanks, Brother Bing."

"Get some sleep. You look like you could use it."

FRIDAY

We are Marxists, and Marxism teaches that in our approach to a problem we should start from objective facts, not from abstract definitions, and that we should derive our guiding principles, policies and measures from an analysis of these facts.

—*Quotations from Chairman Mao Zedong*

Lu sleeps late, then takes a long, hot shower and brews himself a cup of pu'er tea. He notices an unfamiliar call on his cell from last night, but there is no message. Probably spam. He dresses and takes a bus to work.

His first stop when he arrives is the detention room. The Chens are gone. He checks in with Constable Huang up front.

"Your arrest order was approved by the procurator, and Mrs. Chen was transferred to county," Huang says. "The daughter-in-law and grandmother were released."

"What about Chen Shiyi?"

"He was sent to the hospital ward in the county detention center."

Lu pokes his head into the squad room. Constables Sun, Fatty Wang, Li the Mute, and Sergeant Bing are at their desks, working.

"Morning," Lu says.

He receives a muted reply. Even Constable Sun seems reluctant to meet his eyes.

Sergeant Bing stands up. "Might I have a word?"

Sergeant Bing leads Lu upstairs. He unlocks the door to the evidence room. Inside are rows of floor-to-ceiling racks filled with cardboard boxes and plastic-wrapped odds and ends. Sergeant Bing takes Lu over to a shelf and shows him a computer tablet in a see-through ziplock bag.

"What's this?" Lu says.

"Yang Fenfang's tablet."

"Where'd you find it?"

"Buried in the Chens' backyard."

"How?"

"The daughter-in-law."

Lu looks blankly at Sergeant Bing.

"She struck me as the most sensible one of the bunch, so I spoke to her again this morning," Sergeant Bing says, "and I asked her about the tablet. After a bit of cajoling, she admitted that she warned her husband not to turn it on—she suspected its location could be traced if he did. She saw him put it in the nightstand in the bedroom, but because he and his mother are idiots, and she didn't trust them to not do something stupid, she took it a couple of days ago and buried it. She kept mum about it yesterday because she was worried she'd be implicated in the crime and we'd take her son away from her and toss her in jail."

"We could well do that."

"Do you really want to go down that road, Inspector?"

"No. Not really." Lu sighs. "I guess I jumped to conclusions regarding Constable Wang."

"I guess you did."

"It's not like him stealing a tablet is completely out of the question."

"Perhaps not."

"Even so."

"Even so," Sergeant Bing agrees.

"*Ta ma de.*"

"What you do not want done to yourself, do not do to others."

"Why, Brother Bing, are you quoting Master Kong?"

"No, I thought that was something the Christian god Yesu said."

"The one with long hair and a beard? Or his father?" Lu's understanding of Christianity is vague at best.

"The son."

"Hm. Perhaps Yesu was a Confucian?"

Lu takes a patrol car and drives to the Raven Valley Clinic. He finds Yue-han Chu in the main ward, staring up at the ceiling, his eyes swollen, his nose encased in plaster.

Lu draws the curtains around the bed, although they do nothing to block out the sound of the other patients and their families. Chu's eyes shift toward Lu, then back to the ceiling.

"I was wrong about the tablet," Lu says.

Chu doesn't answer.

"How is your nose?"

Chu says nothing.

"You shouldn't have swung your baton at me. I could have you fired. Even arrested."

"Go ahead."

"No. I'm not going to do that. Here's what I *will* do. I'll give you the weekend to consider your options. If you decide you still want to be a police officer, come back to work on Monday. If not, good luck on your next venture. Either way, I'll keep this incident out of your record."

"Do you expect me to thank you?"

"No. I expect you to decide whether or not you want to be a cop. Where's Wang Guangrong?"

"Sent home."

"All right." Lu pulls the curtains open. "Hope to see you Monday, Constable."

Lu drives to Wang's apartment. Wang is not happy to see him. He does not offer Lu any tea. Lu apologizes for accusing him of taking the tablet. He offers Wang the same deal. A few days to think and then a decision. "Is this really what you want to do with your life? You're still young. You can easily find another job."

Wang remains sullenly silent.

"If you come back, we will do things differently. I will work more closely with you."

"That's the last thing I want," Wang says.

Lu's phone rings. He answers. It's the county hospital. Deputy Director Song is awake.

When Lu arrives at the hospital, he is directed to the VIP ward, where Song occupies a private room. Song is covered in gauze and tape, hooked up to an IV, a pulsometer, and a blood pressure monitor.

Lu pulls up a chair. "How are you feeling?"

"Terrible. Where's the old man?"

"Dead."

Song winces in pain. "Are you in trouble?"

"I gave a statement to Harbin metro. Haven't heard anything since."

"If you get heat from them, let me know."

"Count on it. Thanks."

"Someone searched his apartment?"

"Harbin metro. No evidence connecting him to Yang Fenfang's murder. He's not the one. I'm sure of it."

Song closes his eyes and groans softly.

"Are you all right?"

"What else do you have?"

Lu tells Song about the TV and computer tablet and the Chens. He talks about the *Hong Di Xie* shoes and coral ring and his theory that the killer is triggered by the color red.

Song grunts. "So the killer sees these girls somewhere, wearing the red items, and develops a fixation. But where?"

"We can reliably place all three in Harbin, but not at the same time, and it's going to be impossible to track their daily movements and determine on which occasions they may have been wearing the red items in question. I mean, it could have been anywhere. A bar. A restaurant. A taxi. The street."

"Police work," Song says. "Methodical. Painstaking."

"I understand the concept of police work," Lu says.

"Comb through their transaction records and seeing if there's any intersection—as you said, a bar, restaurant, taxi. I'll call Beijing and ask them to run a violent crimes search filtered for anything having to do with the color red."

Lu's phone rings. It's the same unidentified number from last night. He ignores it. "I should probably let you get some rest."

Song nods, closes his eyes, and is almost immediately asleep.

Lu takes the elevator down to the lobby and wends his way through the crowded waiting room toward the exit. Then he spies a familiar face and stops in his tracks.

Yanyan.

She's sitting alone in a sea of human misery. Amid the din of crying babies, unruly toddlers, hacking, coughing, wheezing, ringing cell phones, and tense conversation.

Lu walks over to her. She stares at the dirty linoleum floor, taking no notice of him.

"Yanyan?"

She looks up. "Inspector? What are you doing here?"

"I was visiting someone. What are you doing you here? Is it your father?"

She nods.

"Oh, I'm sorry, Yanyan. What have the doctors said?"

Yanyan shakes her head. Tears roll down her cheeks.

The moment is excruciatingly awkward. Lu wants to put his arms around her, but he doesn't dare, not after her reaction when he touched her hand at the Red Lotus.

He crouches down to face her at eye level. "Do you want me to talk to someone, maybe impress upon the doctors the importance of giving your father the best possible care?"

"Please get up, Inspector." Yanyan stands and pulls Lu to his feet. Then she falls into his arms and presses her face into the lapel of his coat.

Lu holds her, his heart beating faster than even when the crazy old man, Peng, had attempted to stab him with the broken bottle.

They stay like that for perhaps ten seconds and then Yanyan pushes away and wipes her eyes and nose with the back of her hand. Lu digs into his pocket and pulls out what he hopes is a clean handkerchief and hands it to her.

"If there's anything I can do," Lu says.

She looks away, embarrassed. "Thank you."

Lu feels his phone vibrating in his pocket. He ignores it. "Can I get you anything? Something to eat?"

"No, no."

"Are you sure? How about some tea?"

"All right. Tea."

There is a hot water dispenser in the waiting area and a vending machine with assorted hot and cold drinks, but Lu skips those and goes outside to a food cart, where he buys tea and a container of soup. While he's waiting for the soup to be dished up, he checks his phone. It's that unidentified number again, but this time the caller has left a message. Lu listens.

"Inspector . . . This is Monk, from the Black Cat in Harbin. I need to talk to you. But I might be . . . maybe . . . I think maybe I'm being watched. Call me."

Lu does so immediately.

"*Wei?*" Monk answers.

"This is Inspector Lu."

"We need to talk."

"Just tell me when and where."

Monk gives Lu directions to an unfamiliar address, and they agree to meet in one hour.

That doesn't give Lu much time. He takes the soup and tea inside to Yanyan. "I have to go. Work. But can I call you later?"

"That's not necessary, Inspector."

"Brother Lu."

"Brother Lu. Please don't worry."

"I am worried. Here." He hands her his card. "This has my cell number. Call me."

"All right."

The address supplied by Monk turns out to be a café half a dozen blocks from the Black Cat. It's called Tongzhi, which means "comrade"—a non-gender-specific form of address in universal use during the Mao era, but now employed ironically as slang for "homosexual."

Monk is waiting at a table at the back. Lu doesn't see him at first—the interior is dark and womb-like—but then Monk stands and waves.

"Sorry about meeting you here," Monk says, "but this is the kind of place where everyone knows everyone. Any strangers will immediately be noticed."

"Is that why I'm getting suspicious looks?"

"That and the fact that you're in a cop's uniform. Most customers here haven't had pleasant experiences with the police."

A waiter comes over. "Everything all right, Monk?"

"Yes, Ah Q. This is a friend of mine."

The waiter looks to be in his midtwenties. He's thin and handsome, with dyed blond hair. He holds out a hand. "Any friend of Monk's is a friend of mine. You can call me *Ah Q*."

Lu shakes his hand briefly. "Like the story by Lu Xun?"

"A man of literature! How rare in these barbaric times. What's your name, handsome?"

"Inspector Lu. No relation to Lu Xun."

"Inspector, eh?" Ah Q looks at Monk. "It this some sort of cosplay thing you've cooked up, you saucy devil?"

"No. Inspector Lu is actually an inspector."

"Oh." Ah Q looks Lu up and down. "The uniform suits you."

"Thanks."

They order tea. As soon as Ah Q is out of earshot, Monk leans forward. "Two guys came to see me Monday night, not long after you and your colleague did."

"Two guys? Police?"

"No. Thuggish types. I mean, they weren't carrying meat cleavers, but they were thugs just the same. They asked about Fenfen. What I knew. If she'd told me anything that might shed light on who killed her. If the police had been to see me and what I told them."

"What did you say?"

"I told them the truth. I thought maybe they were from State Security."

The Ministry of State Security is a separate but parallel counterpart to the Ministry of Public Security. Whereas the MPS handles basic law enforcement, the MSS's directive is to protect "the security of the state through effective measures against enemy agents, spies, and counterrevolutionary activities designed to sabotage or overthrow China's socialist system."

In other words, it's a spy agency. Both foreign and domestic.

As a highly secretive government entity with the authority to basically "disappear" any citizen with little in the way of due process, the MSS is widely regarded with fear and suspicion. Lu cannot blame Monk for telling the men whatever they wanted to know.

"Anyway," Monk says, "they were very rude and threatening. They said if I spoke to anyone—even the police—about their visit or about Fenfen, I'd regret it."

"But you called me anyway."

"I liked Fenfen. I want you to catch whoever did that to her. And there's something else. I have another employee—he was probably Fenfen's closest friend at the bar. His name is Ruyi, but everyone calls him *Brando*."

"Brando?"

"Yeah, you know—like Marlon Brando. Young guys choose pretentious nicknames for themselves. Who are we to judge?"

"Such as your friend Ah Q."

"I'm sure you had a dumb nickname at some point."

Lu doesn't share the fact that, for a time in high school, given his fondness for martial arts, friends jokingly called him *Bruce Lu*.

"Brando was scheduled to work Wednesday, but he didn't show," Monk says. "Very unusual. I called him and left a message. No answer."

Ah Q brings their tea on a tray. He sets a cup down in front of Monk and another in front of Lu. "So, Inspector?"

"Yes?"

"Do you think I could borrow your handcuffs for half an hour?"

"Ah Q," Monk warns.

"Relax. I'm just playing. Enjoy your tea, boys."

Monk shakes his head as Ah Q walks away, then picks up his teacup and blows on it. "So I started to think—if those guys came to see me, maybe they also went to see Brando."

"The obvious connection between the three of you being the Black Cat."

"Right."

"What else can you tell me about these guys who threatened you? Distinguishing characteristics? Regional accents?"

"One was older, maybe forty, tall. The other one was younger. Short, but wide, like a weightlifter. Their accents were local Harbin. The older one had a mole, here." He points to a spot under his lip.

"Like the chairman?" Lu references the famous mole on Mao Zedong's chin.

Monk slurps tea. "Yes, very similar."

"Anything else?"

"Not really."

"What about this, uh . . . Brando? Can you give me his address and phone number?"

Monk slides over a slip of folded paper with a name, phone number, and address.

Lu takes out his phone and calls the number. It goes straight to voice mail.

"You didn't think it would be that easy, did you?" Monk says.

"Hope springs eternal," Lu says. "I'll see if I can track him down. In the meantime, just go about your business. If the thugs show up again or you hear from Brando, call me."

Monk's scrawled address leads Lu to one of the older apartment towers in the Wangzhao Residential District, about twelve kilometers from the Tongzhi café. With the afternoon traffic, it takes him nearly an hour to get there.

The building is nothing special. Perhaps twenty years old, it is beginning to show its age. The gold lettering that reads *Lilac Terrace* is chipped, the tiled floor is cracked, and the lobby smells of pickled vegetables.

When Lu enters, he finds an old doorman sitting behind a desk, watching Beijing opera on a knockoff tablet computer.

"Public Security Bureau," Lu announces. He doesn't bother to show the doorman his ID—the uniform is sufficient verification.

The old man stands up and nods deferentially. Lu leans over for a quick glance at the tablet screen and sees an actor dressed in red and yellow, his face painted to resemble a monkey, wielding a silver rod.

"*Pacifying Heaven!*" Lu says. It is his favorite opera, a retelling of the old folktale about a pious monk and a mischievous monkey with supernatural powers sent to India to retrieve Buddhist scriptures during the Tang dynasty.

The doorman smiles. His mouth is less than half full of teeth, and those that remain are in bad condition. "You like opera?"

"Well, to be honest, I can't say I love the singing—but the costumes, the acrobatics—incredible!"

"No other country in the world could have invented something like this," the doorman says. "Certainly not the Americans. Or the Japanese. Peking opera is the pride of our nation!"

"You may be right, Uncle," Lu says, "and while I'd love to sit and watch with you, I'm here on business. I'm looking for a young man . . ." He consults the full name given to him by Monk. "Cheng Ruyi. Apartment 16H."

The doorman sips tea from a metal thermos. "He must have done something pretty bad."

"What makes you say that?"

"You're not the first to come by looking for him."

"Let me guess. Two guys, one tall and thin, the other muscular."

"That's right."

"Did they show you any ID?"

"No, but I got the impression they were one of you lot. Police of some kind."

"So what happened?"

The doorman shrugs. "They went up, they came down. The next day, the kid left, carrying a couple of bags with him."

"You mean, he moved out?" Lu says.

"I guess. I didn't ask. I just watch the door."

"What day was this?"

"I think . . . Monday the men came? So Tuesday?"

"Can you let me up to the apartment?"

The doorman points to the elevator. "Help yourself."

"What about a key?"

"His roommate should be home, but let me see if I can find one." The doorman spends a good five minutes rooting around in a series of drawers. "Nope. You'll just have to knock."

Lu takes the elevator up to the sixteenth floor and walks down the narrow hallway to apartment 16H. He knocks. There is no answer. "Public Security!" he calls out. After a moment, he hears a muffled voice from inside.

"Show me your ID."

"I will after you open the door," Lu says. "Unless you have x-ray vision?"

"There's a peephole."

So there is. Lu takes out his ID and holds it up.

"Are you alone?" the man says.

"Yes."

The door opens. A young man looks out. "What do you want?"

"I'm looking for Brando."

"He's not here."

"So I heard. I also heard a couple of hoodlums came to see him. Were you here when that happened?"

The man doesn't answer.

"Listen," Lu says. "I'm investigating a case, and Brando might know something that can help. I'm not looking to cause him any trouble, but somebody doesn't want him to talk, so that means he's in danger. If I could just come in and speak to you for a minute."

"I don't know anything."

"May I come in, please?"

"Can't we just talk through the door?"

"No."

The young man reluctantly steps away, and Lu enters.

The apartment is small, cramped, and meticulously decorated. Modern furniture, colorful knickknacks, bizarre artwork, including some semipornographic illustrations depicting extremely muscular men with massive bulges in their leather trousers on the wall.

"What's your name?" Lu asks.

"You can call me *Daniel*."

Another English nickname. Lu pokes his head into the bathroom and bedroom.

"Do you mind?" Daniel says.

"Sorry. All right if we sit for a moment?"

"You've already made yourself right at home, haven't you?"

Lu lowers himself onto the couch. "Don't worry. I don't require any tea and biscuits."

"Good. I'm fresh out."

"So where did Brando go?"

"I don't know."

"These men who came calling," Lu says. "Perhaps they gave him the impression they worked for the Ministry of State Security, but I don't think that's the case."

"Who, then?"

"The case I'm pursuing is a murder—and I believe someone with money and perhaps connections is involved. He's trying to intimidate anyone who might have information that will reveal his identity. But I'm going to get to the truth."

"You must be new in town. Most cops don't care much about the truth."

"I take my job seriously."

"Then you are as rare as a *qilin*." A *qilin* is the Chinese version of a unicorn.

"I don't blame you for being cynical," Lu says, "but I'm not here to debate the state of justice in the People's Republic. I'm here to help Brando. I don't know what these men are capable of. If you care about what happens to him, you'd better tell me where he is."

"You don't care about Brando. You just care about your murder case."

"They are one and the same, Daniel. The only way Brando can be assured of safety is if I find out who those thugs are working for."

Daniel thinks for a moment, then goes into the kitchen and returns with a pack of cigarettes. He offers the pack to Lu.

"I don't smoke, but thanks."

Daniel perches on the edge of a chair and lights a cigarette. "Brando went home."

"Where's home?"

"The boondocks somewhere. A village I've never heard of. Where he's probably getting a lot of shit from the locals for having dyed hair."

"Were you and he . . . ?"

"Just because we're gay doesn't mean we were a couple."

"I didn't assume that—I saw that you only have one bed."

"This is my apartment. Brando and I became friends, and he needed a place to live, so I let him move in a year ago. He slept on the couch." Daniel points his cigarette to where Lu is sitting. "That's where he and the occasional boy he brought home had sex."

Lu knows he's being tested. "What did he tell you? About why he was leaving?"

"He said a friend of his at the Black Cat had been murdered. That's your case, right? He didn't even know his friend was dead until the two men showed up. They warned him not to talk to the police. Not to say anything about what the girl might have told him."

"Told him about what, specifically?"

"I don't know. They strongly suggested it would be advisable to leave the city for a while. They gave him some money."

"How much?"

"Not sure."

"So he split."

"Yes."

"Did he mention his friend's name? The dead girl?"

"No."

"Her name was Yang Fenfang. Have you ever met her, perhaps at some point through Brando?"

"No, sorry."

"Did he describe the men? Did they say or do anything that indicated who they were working for?"

"No. Sorry."

"Anything else you can tell me?"

"No. Sorry."

"These men haven't come to see you?"

"No."

Lu takes a card out of his pocket and sets it on the couch. "If they do, don't let them in. Call me immediately, and then call the local *paichusuo*."

"Should I be worried?"

"It doesn't hurt to be prudent."

"That's comforting."

"You'll be fine. China's last unicorn is on the case."

Lu drives back to Raven Valley and tracks down Chief Liang in the canteen, where he is eating an afternoon snack of instant noodles. Lu relates his conversations with Monk and Daniel.

Chief Liang talks with his mouth full. "This is getting rather complicated. Our sugar daddy is making sure nobody talks, and he's either got money or power. Or both. Does this mean we're back to the blackmail theory?"

"The link between Yang, Brando, and Monk is a gay bar. I'm not sure the sugar daddy thing works."

"Brando."

"It's a nickname. All the young guys have one these days."

"This country is doomed." Chief Liang slurps more noodles. "Then maybe it's not a sugar daddy. Maybe it's an old *tongzhi* who Yang saw at the Black Cat and she threatened to expose him."

"I don't really see Yang Fenfang doing that. She worked at the Black

Cat for a couple of years, at least, before her murder. I'm sure she had ample opportunity to pull a number like that earlier if she wanted to."

"Well, who knows? Maybe she waited until she hooked a big fish."

"Anyway," Lu says, "that theory doesn't jibe with the missing organs. The hell money."

"Perhaps meant to throw us off the scent."

"Seems extreme," Lu says.

"Killing a girl is extreme, no matter which way you slice it. Her. It. You know what I mean."

"What about the two previous murders in Harbin?"

"Not sure. Let me gaze into my magic bowl." Chief Liang swirls the broth, then tips the bowl to his mouth and loudly drinks. He sets the bowl down and wipes his mouth with a napkin. "The gods are silent today. I guess you'll just have to figure things out for yourself."

In his office, Lu runs a search for Cheng Ruyi—a.k.a. Brando—and determines his home village is indeed in the countryside, with the nearest city of consequence being Qitaihe in the far eastern part of Heilongjiang, a region known mainly for its coal mining.

Lu calls Brando's cell phone. It goes straight to voice mail. He cross-references Brando's *hukou* records, finds his mother's phone number, and calls that. No answer there, either.

He locates and phones the *paichusuo* nearest to Brando's village. The officer on duty is not helpful.

"Do you know the Cheng family?" Lu gives the officer their address.

"Am I expected to know every single citizen in the entire county by name?"

"No, but—"

"What abilities do you believe me to possess that I can instantly tell you everything you want to know about some potato farmers who live out in the middle of nowhere?"

"I don't—"

"Did you look up their *hukou* record?"

"Yes."

"Well, what more do you want?"

"You see, I'm trying to reach this person Cheng Ruyi—"

"Call his phone, then."

"I did. No answer."

"Perhaps I can go outside and shout really loudly. That might solve the problem, is that what you're thinking?"

"What's your name?" Lu asks.

"Mao Zedong!"

"I want to talk to your superior officer."

"He's busy. We're all busy!"

"Listen, you rude bastard, put your boss on the phone or I'll come down there and stick my foot up your ass!"

The response on the line is a dial tone. The insolent prick has hung up.

"*Ta ma de!*" Lu slams his phone back into the cradle. He fumes for a moment while considering his next step. In the end, he decides to go have a drink.

The Red Lotus is surprisingly busy tonight. Lu had half expected it to be closed, given the fact that Yanyan's father is in the hospital. But no, here she is, quite harried, running bottles of beer and liquor and snack dishes back and forth between the tables.

Lu takes a seat at the one empty table and waits patiently, not wanting to add to Yanyan's stress. She favors him with a tight smile and a nod and, when she has a free moment, comes over to the table.

"Evening, Inspector. I mean . . . Brother Lu."

"You're busy."

"It's Friday."

"How's your father?"

"They've admitted him to the hospital."

"You should be there, by his side."

"I have a business to run and no one to help. It's just me and him."

"Let me handle things here. Just for tonight."

Yanyan almost—but not quite—smiles. "What do you know about managing a bar, Brother Lu?"

"I understand the basic concept. You give people drinks, and they give you money."

"I can't have that. The deputy police chief waiting on tables. No, absolutely not."

"I'm not too proud to help a friend."

"It's out of the question. Now what can I get you?"

"Beer, please."

She brings him his beer and a glass and runs off to the next customer.

Lu decides he will have two beers and then usher everyone out and make Yanyan close up shop. The money she's making is important, but so is being with her father. Especially if his condition is truly that dire.

Halfway through his first beer, the door opens and Undertaker Zeng enters. He pauses in the doorway, his eyes scanning the crowded tables, until he sees Lu. Lu waves him over.

Zeng approaches tentatively. "Evening, Inspector."

"Evening, Mr. Zeng. Please, join me."

"Are you sure?"

"Of course."

Zeng sits. He takes off his hat and coat, looks around the room, then back at Lu. "The place is packed."

"Do you come to the Red Lotus often? I've never seen you here before."

"Once a month, at most, and only if I've got some business in town. Otherwise, I keep to myself. My presence tends to make people nervous."

"Is that right?"

"The negative perceptions of my work cling to me like a . . . a lingering odor. Certain shopkeepers even refuse to touch money I've handled. They regard death as a communicable disease."

"I didn't know."

Zeng shrugs. "I have no regrets. I provide an important service. Besides—you must experience something similar as a policeman. Folks see the uniform and automatically start acting . . . uneasy. Like they have a guilty conscience."

Lu nods. "True. It's as if they think I can peer into the very depths of their dark souls and know every bad thing they've ever done."

"I assume they generally go out of their way to avoid you, and when they do speak to you, they are guarded. Makes it hard to have a genuine conversation. A real friendship."

Lu stares into his glass of beer. Honestly, he hadn't thought of it that way, but Zeng is absolutely correct. Apart from Yanyan and the other officers in the *paichusuo,* he barely has any personal relationships at all, and certainly nothing he would classify as a close friendship.

"Sorry," Zeng says. "I didn't mean to cast a pall over the evening."

"Nonsense. Let's get you a drink, shall we?"

Zeng orders a sour plum cocktail. Lu requests another beer. He and Zeng drink and talk.

Lu notes the occasional dark look cast Zeng's way from one of the other tables. Or maybe the looks are directed at him.

Lu's intended two beers turns into three. At some point, he quietly asks if Yanyan has told Zeng her father is seriously ill.

"She hasn't," Zeng says, "but people generally don't make arrangements for the death of a loved one beforehand. It's bad luck."

"When the time comes, she'll need a good undertaker. One who will provide a fair price."

"I will be more than happy to help when the time comes. At a fair price."

After his fourth beer, Lu tells Zeng about the old man Peng Yuan. Why, he isn't sure. An attempted confessional? To exorcise his guilt? Because, as an undertaker, Zeng might have some unique insight into the murky mysteries of death?

"It sounds like you were defending yourself and your colleague," Zeng says.

"Yes, but . . . I don't suppose I *had* to throw him out the window."

"Did you consciously decide to kill him and then act accordingly?"

"No. It all happened so fast."

"This man, Peng, sounds like a person with a lot of hate and violence in his heart. And perhaps, a desire to go out swinging."

"Yes, maybe."

"It sounds callous, but perhaps you did him . . . and the world . . . a favor. Who knows what crime he might have committed as he fell deeper into a pit of grievance and alcohol? Stabbed schoolchildren at a bus stop? Killed a black foreigner on the streets of Harbin?"

"When you put it like that . . . You are wise beyond your years, Mr. Zeng."

"Not at all."

They finish their drinks, and then Lu suggests it is time to go home. He insists on paying Zeng's bill.

"I couldn't," Zeng says.

"Consider it payment for your pep talk." Lu settles up and then gently convinces the lone remaining holdouts—two inebriated young men—to be on their way. He ushers everyone out the door and, when they are gone, offers to help Yanyan clean up and then drive her to the hospital.

"I couldn't ask you to do that," Yanyan says.

"You didn't ask. It was my idea." He starts carrying empty bottles and cups over to the counter.

"Let's just leave it for now," Yanyan says. "I'll come back tomorrow and finish up."

"Very sensible."

Yanyan gathers her things, shuts off the lights, and locks up. Outside, the steam from their breath comingling, she gives him a tired smile. "Thank you so much, Brother Lu. You are very kind."

"Not at all. Let's take a taxi to the *paichusuo,* and I'll pick up a patrol car and drive you to the hospital."

"No. You go home. I'll call for a car on Didi Chuxing." This is China's version of Uber or Lyft.

"Let me drive you."

"Brother Lu, you've been drinking." She places a hand lightly on his shoulder. "Go home. Get some sleep. Thank you for everything."

Lu realizes Yanyan is right. "Call me if you need anything."

"I will."

He waits with her until the car arrives and then watches her drive off.

Lu considers calling for a taxi but figures the walk home in the cold will sober him up. It does, but by the time he arrives on his block, his toes and fingers are frozen, and he is in dire need of a cup of tea and a hot shower.

As he approaches the entrance to his apartment building, two men get out of a car parked across the street. They come directly toward him.

One of the men carries a club of some kind. He is tall. The other is short and wide, like a weight lifter or a wrestler.

The tall man takes the last few yards at a run and swings at Lu. Lu backpedals and narrowly avoids being struck. He finds himself with his back against a storefront. The two attackers fan out. Lu notices both are wearing dark caps and cotton face masks.

The tall man feints with the club. Lu reacts by throwing up his hands. The wrestler crouches and shoots forward, crashing into Lu's midsection. Lu doubles over. He and the wrestler fall to the ground, Lu on the bottom. Lu throws a couple of elbows. They bounce off the wrestler's thick skull with a muted thud. Lu tries to jam his thumb into the wrestler's eye socket, to no avail.

Lu has practiced martial arts for much of his life. Early on, it was one of the Shaolin five animal systems. Later, in college, a little judo and a lot of *san shou*—a style of Chinese sport fighting that incorporates kicks, strikes, elbows, knees, sweeps, and throws. As a police officer, he's learned an array of joint locks and wrestling techniques, and while living in Harbin, he was fortunate to train with one of the few last practitioners of authentic "dog boxing"—a traditional ground-fighting art.

But none of these are working at the moment. The wrestler is just too big and too strong.

Lu slips a hand between them. He seeks, finds, clutches the wrestler's genitals. He squeezes and twists. The wrestler screams. Lu shoves him to the side. He gets hit across his shoulder with the club by the tall man as he regains his feet. A sharp pain shoots down his arm. Lu kicks the wrestler in the face, then leaps over his body, out of range of the club.

The tall man cautiously advances. Lu shakes out his arm and sinks into a side stance. When the tall man is close enough, Lu feints with a backfist strike. Instinctively, the tall man raises the club for protection. Lu throws a sneaky side kick. The tall man flies backward, tripping over the wrestler.

Kickboxing 101. The oldest trick in the book. Lu is astounded it worked.

He turns and runs for the entrance to his building. He fumbles for his keys, gets them out of his pocket, locates the correct one, and slides it into the lock. He hears grunting and cursing behind him, the slap of shoes on the sidewalk. He twists the lock, wrenches open the door, jumps inside, slams the door shut.

Lu finds himself facing the tall man and the wrestler just on the other side of the glass door. He can see nothing of their facial features apart from their eyes, but he has no doubt that these are the two thugs who have visited Monk and Brando.

Lu shows them the back of his fist with a pinkie raised—a rude gesture.

The tall man brandishes the club, and for a brief moment, Lu is afraid he's going to smash the door. Instead, he points at Lu's face and waggles a finger, then puts it to his lips. He and the wrestler turn and walk back across the street, the wrestler pausing along the way to shake out his legs and adjust his crotch.

Lu waits until they are inside the car, then opens the door and runs after it. The car surges forward, speeds down the street, and screeches around a corner.

Lu can't be sure, but he thinks the car is a VW Jetta Night. Blue. Definitely blue. Or maybe gray? Possibly light green. It's hard to tell under the streetlights. As for the license plate, Lu could only read the initial character—*hei,* meaning "black," which indicates that the plate was issued in Heilongjiang Province.

Lu goes upstairs, takes a hot shower, brushes his teeth, and climbs into bed.

It is tradition, in countries where Buddhism is the predominant religion, to make a ritual offering every seven days after a loved one dies until forty-nine days have passed (seven times seven being a lucky number) and then again at one hundred days.

Today is Friday, the one-week anniversary of Yang Fenfang's passing. Of course, the People's Republic is officially atheist, and the man is not a devout Buddhist, but he is most definitely superstitious—and he likes to hedge his bets.

So here he is, once again in the oddly shaped, windowless room, kneeling before the altar, burning hell money and reciting a prayer cobbled together from Buddhist sutras, Daoist blessings, the Christian Bible, and the shadowy recesses of his own mind.

In addition to paper money and some other funerary goods, he has prepared a tray of fresh food. Steamed rice, cold chicken, fruit, tea, even a cold Harbin lager beer. He places the dishes one by one on the altar, then burns incense and invites Yang Fenfang to partake of this meal. After bowing three times, he sticks the incense upright in a cup filled with uncooked rice and shifts it to a prominent spot—beside a pair of high-heeled shoes.

SATURDAY

At no time and in no circumstances should a Communist place
his personal interests first; he should subordinate them to the
interests of the nation and of the masses. Hence, selfishness,
slacking, corruption, seeking the limelight, and so on, are most
contemptible, while selflessness, working with all one's energy,
whole-hearted devotion to public duty, and quiet hard work
will command respect.

—Quotations from Chairman Mao Zedong

Lu is off duty this weekend, but after breakfast, he goes into the *paichusuo*
anyway. He sits at his desk and dials the phone number for Brando again,
and again, it goes straight to voice mail. He tries the mother—and this
time, a woman answers.

She has a very thick northeast accent—similar to the Beijing dia-
lect, but as if spoken with a mouthful of sticky rice.

"I'm looking for Cheng Ruyi."

"Hah?"

"I'm with the Raven Valley Public Security Bureau, and I need to
speak to Cheng Ruyi right away."

"Hah?"

Patience, Lu thinks. Better to spend five minutes trying to get
this deaf old lady to produce Brando than drive four hours to Qitaihe.
"Cheng . . . Ru . . . Yi!"

"That's my son. What do you want with him?"

Lu decides to go the authoritarian route. "Put him on the phone. This is a police matter."

"Hah?"

Ta ma de. "Police matter! Put . . . him . . . on . . . the . . . phone."

"He's not here."

"Listen, madam—I'm sure you don't want me showing up on your doorstep, now do you? So go get Ruyi. Immediately!"

The woman grumbles. Lu doesn't fully understand the words, but he gets the gist. There is a long silence, and then a male voice with a more standard accent speaks: *"Wei?"*

"Cheng Ruyi? Also known as Brando?"

"Who is this?"

Lu explains, about Monk, Daniel, and Yang Fenfang. "I'm not interested in causing you any problems, Mr. Cheng. I simply want to catch whoever murdered Yang Fenfang, and if I understand correctly, you two were friends. So I'm sure you'd like to see justice done."

Silence on the line.

"I understand threats have been made," Lu continues. "You've been told not to talk to anyone about this."

"I don't know you," Brando says.

"I understand that. If it makes you feel better, you can call Daniel or Monk. They will vouch for me."

There is a pause. Then: "What about those men who visited me?"

"One tall and one broad?"

"Yes."

"The sooner I find out who they are working for, the sooner I can catch them and you can go back to your normal life."

"That would be . . . nice."

"So can you help me?"

"Wait a minute." Lu hears movement and voices, then a crackle of static. "Sorry. I had to come outside. My entire extended family is in there, and half the neighbors, trying to listen in."

"Right," Lu says. "What can you tell me about the two men?"

"Not much." Brando relates how they came to the apartment, told him not to talk to the police, gave him a few thousand yuan, and suggested he make himself scarce. "The message was clear. Take the money and go, or stay and get hurt."

"Can you provide any description or information about them that might help with identification?"

Unfortunately, Brando doesn't have much to add beyond what Daniel and Monk have already told Lu.

"All right," Lu says. "So I'm speculating that these guys work for someone Ms. Yang met at the Black Cat, and I'm assuming you met this person, too."

There is another long pause, and then Brando speaks in a low voice. "Yes."

"Elaborate, please."

"You know about the Black Cat, obviously. What kind of customers frequent it."

"Yes."

"Some are very open. Others aren't. It's not illegal to be gay, but it's definitely not an easy lifestyle."

"I understand."

"To protect privacy, we have a strict policy of no photographs in the bar. We accept cash payments. We don't want to hurt anyone who is in the closet because of their job or position, or because they're married. All right?"

"Yes."

"There was this guy who started coming in maybe two, three years ago. Early fifties. Not handsome, but he had the smell of success about him, you know? Even when a guy isn't wearing an expensive suit, you can see it in his shoes, his watch, his glasses. His haircut. His brand of cigarettes."

"What brand did he smoke?"

"Chunghwas."

"Of course."

"Anyway, he would come in once or twice a month, order some

expensive foreign wine, and take a seat in a dark corner. Rarely spoke to anyone. I got the sense that he was a bit new to this. Stepping out of his comfort zone. Probably married. Either owned a factory or was fairly high up in the municipal or provincial government."

"Right."

"After a few months, he began to loosen up, talk to the other customers. Once or twice, I saw him making out in a corner with some other guy like a randy teenager, but he was always cautious. Paid in cash. Called himself Mr. Wang, but I never saw a credit card or form of ID."

"I see."

"Around the time he started coming in, Monk hired Fenfen. Everybody loved Fenfen. She was just a happy-go-lucky, sweet kid, you know? A little ray of sunshine."

"Right."

"At first, Fenfen helped out behind the bar. When things were really hopping, she'd sometimes serve drinks. One night, she was carrying a tray of drinks, and somebody jostled her when she was walking past Mr. Wang's table, and she spilled a glass of punch all over his lap. There was a bit of a scene, of course, but she apologized up and down, and Mr. Wang finally just said forget it. The thing is, when I mentioned it to her later, she said that when she was trying to wipe punch off his pants, she realized she knew him."

"Knew him?"

"Not personally, but she'd seen him before. Said he was from her hometown. Some muckety-muck or other. She didn't want to say anything more. I thought maybe she was a bit scared."

"Of what?"

"Getting fired, for one thing. She never told Monk the part about recognizing Mr. Wang. But also, if he were a government official, there's plenty he could do to harm her if he so chose."

"True."

"The next time Mr. Wang came in, he asked for her."

"By name?"

"No, no. He just pointed and said, 'That girl.' What could I do but send her over?"

"And what happened?"

"Well, you'd better believe I kept an eye on them. She sat down, and they had a long talk, and everything seemed cool. When she came back, I asked her what happened, and she basically blew me off. Said he wanted to ask her advice about clothes or something and that was it."

"And after that?"

"He continued to come in once or twice a month. He didn't pay much attention to Fenfen, and she didn't pay much attention to him, other than saying hello."

"So that was it?"

"Well, then Fenfen's mom got sick, and she went back home."

"Did the man stop going to the Black Cat?"

"Nope, same as before. Every now and then."

"When was the last time you saw him?"

"I guess about three or four weeks ago. I can't remember exactly. We actually had a nice chat. He asked me my name, where I was from, stuff like that. I thought maybe he was trying to pick me up."

"You weren't interested?"

"I'm not into daddies."

"And you're sure he's the one who sent the two men to your apartment?"

"Had to be. They were there to warn me not to talk about Fenfen, and my connection to Fenfen was the Black Cat. Mr. Wang saw us together lots of times. I'm just putting two and two together."

"Do you think this man had her killed?"

"I don't know. Possibly. Guys like that might do anything to keep a potentially damaging secret under wraps."

"But if he's going to a gay bar, there's a risk of being recognized, isn't there?"

"Like I said, Fenfang told me he was from her hometown."

"Raven Valley Township."

"I don't remember where it was, but I got the impression it's a small place and not that close to Harbin."

"Forty minutes or so by car."

"Right. The point is, how likely is it that he would run into someone from Raven Valley in a gay bar in Harbin?"

"I suppose not very likely, unless the other person was gay, too."

"Exactly. In which case, neither of them would be tempted to say anything to anyone else."

"So, yes," Lu agrees, "seeing Yang Fenfang there and realizing she recognized him would be a shock."

"Yeah."

"Do you know any of the guys this Mr. Wang picked up at the bar?"

"No, sorry. None of them were regulars; otherwise, I might have gossiped with them about it."

"Would you recognize him if you saw him again?"

"Definitely."

"One last question. It's kind of a strange one."

"This whole situation is strange," Brando says.

"Do you remember Yang Fenfang ever wearing high-heeled shoes with red soles when this guy was in the bar?"

"Sorry to say, I didn't make a note of her daily fashion choices."

"It was a long shot. If I need to reach you in the future, what's the best way?"

"You can email me." He recites his email address, and Lu writes it down. "I hope you catch this guy soon." There is a note of desperation in Brando's voice. "I'm going out of my damn mind here."

Lu calls Monk and asks about Mr. Wang.

"I remember him vaguely," Monk said. "I don't think I ever exchanged more than a dozen words with him. He was a sporadic customer. I can check receipts to see if I have payment information on record, but that would take a long time, unless you know a specific date that he was at the bar."

"Brando said he always paid cash."

"Well, then, all I can do is ask the other employees or some of the regulars if they knew more about him."

"That would be helpful."

Lu makes instant coffee and puts his feet on his desk and sips the coffee slowly. Given that it is a Saturday, the *paichusuo* is quiet, and there isn't the usual stench of cigarette smoke drifting down from Chief Liang's office. The atmosphere is conducive to thinking.

A rich older *tongzhi*. From Raven Valley. Recognized by Yang Fenfang. Their relationship is not built upon sex. Her body is not what he's after.

But perhaps he sees in her an opportunity. A chance to indulge his private desires. He rents an apartment in her name and pays for it in cash. It cannot be traced back to him.

She occupies one room. He uses the other for his occasional trysts. It's a win-win situation.

Then something happens. He kills her or has her killed. Why?

Apart from the blackmail angle, Lu can't think of a reason.

In any case, once she's dead, or just before, he has the apartment wiped clean to remove any evidence of his presence. Then he sends hired thugs to ensure no one who can link him to Yang Fenfang through the Black Cat will speak to the authorities.

But what's the connection to the Harbin murders? The red shoes and ring?

Was the mutilation of Yang Fenfang's body and theft of her shoes meant as a diversion? That doesn't make much sense. Until Yang turned up dead and CIB got involved in the investigation, nobody seemed to even realize there was a potential serial killer at work in Harbin.

Unless—maybe someone knew, but just hadn't publicized the facts. Someone who, say, had access to the Harbin metro PSB's criminal files.

It seems like a long shot. Using the Harbin serial killer's MO to divert suspicion would presuppose that whoever investigated Yang's murder was going to make a connection between the three homicides.

Lu takes a sip of coffee.

There is one person who has access to the criminal files. Who might have concluded Tang Jinglei and Qin Liying were killed by the same person. Who could reasonably predict that Lu might call in the CIB.

Who is dirty as hell and would probably even go so far as to conceal the murder of an innocent girl for a large sum of money.

Please, oh please, oh please, let it be Xu, Lu thinks. How satisfying it would be to nail that bastard's balls to a concrete wall.

But first things first. Identify the man from the Black Cat.

Even in a small township like Raven Valley, there are many wealthy businessmen, mostly in the manufacturing and agricultural fields, and a large government bureaucracy consisting of the local Communist Party committee, the magistrate and his staff, the Raven Valley people's committee, and various township departments.

The businessmen will be difficult to winnow down—some are factory owners, Raven Valley born and raised, others are management types dispatched from the headquarters of agricultural conglomerates in Harbin or Beijing or Shanghai to oversee the production of grains and livestock.

Lu decides to start with the bureaucrats.

The majority of the Raven Valley government functionaries will be of quite low status—clerks and so on—with little in the way of wealth and status. Lu eliminates them from consideration. Others, like Magistrate Lin, are quite powerful but are too old to fit Mr. Wang's general description.

Lu combs through local government websites and Communist Party resources. He filters for age, financial and political standing, physical appearance. He comes up with a list of eleven possible suspects. Among them is Party Secretary Mao, which Lu finds amusing—although Mao is married and has children, he has a reputation as something of a lecher. If he's the man from the Black Cat, he has certainly taken pains to cover his tracks.

Lu compiles digital photos from various sources and zips them into a file. He finds the scrap of paper where he's written down Brando's email and sends the file along.

In the early afternoon, Lu receives a phone call from Undertaker Zeng.

"I thought you might like to know that Yanyan's father died last night."

"How awful!"

"Yes," Zeng says. "She will be receiving guests at her house tomorrow starting at ten."

"I'll spread the word."

Lu hangs up. He wants to call Yanyan but then remembers he doesn't have her cell phone number. He calls the Red Lotus, but of course, no one answers. He calls Zeng back and asks for her number, which Zeng provides. Lu phones Yanyan and leaves a message telling her he's sorry for her loss and to let him know if she needs anything.

He pictures her alone in her house, the mirrors covered with red cloth, perhaps a makeshift altar arranged with fruit and incense. Curled up on her bed. Her pillow wet with tears.

He looks up her *hukou* record and finds her address. It's not far from the Red Lotus, not far from his own apartment. He wants to go over there, knock on her door, have her fall into his comforting embrace.

Instead, he checks his email. No response from Brando.

Lu putters around with paperwork for an hour or so and then goes home. He changes into heavy sweats and jogs to a nearby park. Despite the cold, many local residents are out getting their afternoon exercise. A handful run on a path circling the park. A group of middle-aged couples dance to swing music from an old cassette player, bundled in coats, hats, and scarfs. Half a dozen women practice *tai ji* sword.

Lu warms up a bit and runs through some animal *gong fu* forms— tiger, crane, leopard. He throws some kicks and shadowboxes. It's no good. He can't focus today. He gives up, goes home, showers, and takes a long nap.

In the evening, Lu attends an annual banquet put on by the county Public Security Bureau. The county chief and his staff are present, along with all the chiefs and deputy chiefs of the various local *paichusuo*. A collection of VIPs—party secretaries, magistrates, prosecutors, and the like—have also joined the festivities, lured by free booze, a good meal, and a chance to rub shoulders with anyone possessing higher status than themselves.

The banquet is really just an excuse to get sloppy drunk, but it does provide a rare chance for someone like Lu to mingle with the local brass. He has barely entered the restaurant when Chief Liang pulls him over to a quiet corner for a quick chat with the county PSB chief.

The chief's name is Bao. He is a grizzled, gray-haired career cop with a deep scowl permanently etched on his face. Lu has heard various rumors about him. He has a wife and two girlfriends. He has two wives, and one girlfriend. He's killed three criminals in the line of duty. He once caught a man who raped a nine-year-old girl and beat him to death with a wooden stool leg. But most of all, that he is dirty.

It is no secret that the People's Republic has a corruption problem. Graft, bribery, embezzlement, even the illegal theft of personal property—anything and everything that can make a buck is fair game, from the lowest village committee all the way up to the national politburo.

Pundits lay the blame squarely on the market liberalization efforts initiated by Deng Xiaoping in the late 1970s—it's a fact that many socialist countries in the post-Soviet eastern bloc have faced increased levels of corruption as they attempt to reform their economies.

But corruption is as endemic to China as malaria is to a swamp.

In the dynastic era, government officials were dispatched throughout the country to enforce laws and maintain social order, a nearly impossible task for which they were ill suited and poorly equipped. They received a paltry salary, out of which they had to pay their attendants and expenses and buy gifts for social and political superiors to ingratiate themselves.

Although it was counter to Confucian principles, the collection of bribes was not only an economic necessity, it was tacitly approved. As the old saying went, "Money falls into the hands of officials like a lamb into the mouth of a tiger."

In any case, whether or not the rumors are true, Chief Bao has managed to navigate the uncertain waters of a highly visible and potentially perilous position, and thus is not a man to be trifled with. Lu is nervous speaking to him.

"Chief Liang says you are making rapid progress in the case," Bao says.

"Yes, sir. Rapid? Well . . . we're definitely making progress."

"What progress, exactly?"

This question puts Lu in a difficult position. He hasn't yet told Chief Liang he's looking into Raven Valley officials as possible suspects, and that is very dangerous ground to tread on. Perhaps Chief Bao has a personal or business relationship with some of the names on Lu's list. Even if he doesn't, the idea of a local cop investigating bureaucrats without the support of the Communist Party apparatus is unthinkable.

"We believe the girl had some kind of benefactor who paid for her apartment and, subsequent to her death, had it swept to remove any traces of his presence. Once we find this benefactor, we should be able to fill in some blanks. In the meantime, we think the perpetrator could be triggered by the color red. Or that he is aware of previous homicides in Harbin dating back to 2017 that featured the same MO. Or worst-case scenario, we have a serial killer on our hands."

Chief Bao squints at Lu through a haze of his and Liang's combined cigarette smoke. "It sounds to me like you don't have a fucking clue who did it."

"We are getting closer by the day," Liang says.

"What about this kid already in custody?"

"He remains a suspect," Liang says. "For the time being."

Bao grunts and draws deeply on his cigarette. "I spoke to Deputy Director Song yesterday. He said you saved his life."

"Did he?" Lu is pleasantly surprised to hear it.

"That was good work taking out the old man. He sounded like a powder keg just waiting for a spark."

"Yes, sir. Thank you, sir."

Bao jabs his cigarette at Liang. "We can't keep this under wraps from the public much longer. You'd better catch this fucker soon and pray to Buddha that no more murders take place."

"Yes, Chief," Liang says.

Bao spies someone across the room and waves. "Oh, look. It's the president of the People's Court. I'd better go over and kiss the ring before he has a temper tantrum." He takes a last drag of his cigarette and drops it into the dregs of his drink. "I want results, Liang. Fast."

"And you shall have them, Chief!"

At dinner, Lu is seated beside a woman surnamed Hong, the party secretary for another county township. She's in her late thirties, and the rumor has it that she has climbed her way into a leadership position on her back.

Lu doesn't give much credence to these rumors. That is the way men talk about a woman when they are jealous of her achievements.

Ms. Hong eats sparingly, drinks copiously, and deflects off-color comments directed her way with a sharp wit. Lu enjoys chatting with her. Naturally, she knows of the murder case and wants to gossip, but he declines to divulge details.

"You're no fun," she says, mock pouting.

"Occupational hazard," he says.

At some point in the evening, he crosses paths with Party Secretary Mao in the bathroom. Mao is flushed from drinking and in a boisterous mood.

"How goes the case?" Mao says, squeezing into the urinal next to Lu's.

"Hasn't Chief Liang kept you up to date?" Lu knows Liang feeds regular reports to Mao, which is against protocol, but again, as party secretary, Mao wields enormous power. If he were completely sober, though, Lu wouldn't dare make such a bold observation.

Mao just grunts. "How did you get lucky enough to get seated next to Party Secretary Hong?"

"No idea. Perhaps whoever did the seating chart figured I was harmless."

"I'm stuffed from dinner, but even so, I wouldn't mind sampling her fried rice." Mao cracks up at his sexual innuendo.

"Yes, well . . . enjoy the rest of your evening." Lu gives himself a few hasty shakes and makes his escape.

The banquet wraps up without further incident. Lu pours an inebriated Chief Liang into a car and drives him back to Raven Valley. Liang sleeps on the way, which relieves Lu of the burden of talking to him. When they arrive at Liang's apartment, Lu helps him upstairs. He doesn't relish the thought of digging through Liang's pockets to find his keys, so he knocks. Liang's wife answers in her pajamas. She doesn't look pleased to see Liang in this state, nor does she look surprised.

"Drunk again, you lout!" She takes one of Liang's arms. "Help me get this fat fool to the couch." The two of them ferry Liang over and lay him down. Liang lies splayed on his back, his mouth wide open, snoring.

"Should we roll him over onto his side?" Lu says.

"No. Let him swallow flies. Let him choke to death."

"How about taking off his coat and shoes?"

"What is he, the emperor of China?"

"No. Uh . . . all right, then." Lu goes to the door. "Sorry to wake you up."

"It's me who's sorry to trouble you with this disgraceful old goat."

"It's nothing," Lu says. "Don't worry."

Although it's not exactly on the way, and he can barely keep his eyes open, Lu stops by Yanyan's house. It's a small two-story structure with a modest yard. Old but well preserved. Lu sits there, engine idling, until he finds himself drifting off. Then he rolls down the window to get some cold air on his face and drives home.

SUNDAY

The Chinese Communist Party is the core of leadership of the whole Chinese people. Without this core, the cause of socialism cannot be victorious.

—Quotations from Chairman Mao Zedong

Lu wakes to a message from Brando.

The message reads: *Mao Zhanshu.*

Lu's mind is still fuzzy from alcohol consumption and lack of sleep. He rubs his eyes and reads the message again.

Mao Zhanshu.

There is no mistaking its meaning. Brando has identified Party Secretary Mao, he of the stated desire to eat Ms. Hong's rice, as the man from the Black Cat.

Yang Fenfang's friend—erstwhile benefactor—and perhaps killer.

Cao ni de ma!

This is a nasty can of worms. Accusing Mao of being homosexual, let alone of being a murderer, is career suicide.

Chief Liang will be beside himself.

Can't be helped. The trail leads to Mao; it must be followed, no matter the consequences.

Lu showers and eats what little his stomach can take and drives to Chief Liang's apartment.

He knocks on the door. When it opens, Lu is relieved to see that it is

Liang, not his wife, who answers. Liang is wearing a T-shirt and boxers. He looks hungover, but Lu suspects he's going to look much worse in a moment.

Liang runs a swollen tongue over cracked lips. His voice is a croak: "What are you doing here?"

"We need to talk."

"Why?"

"Can I come in?"

Liang belches. The sour stench of bile-flavored whiskey washes over Lu like a noxious cloud. He gags.

Liang turns around and walks away. Lu follows. Liang goes into the bathroom.

"Your wife is out?" Lu asks.

"Looks like."

Lu hears a trickle of urine splashing into the toilet bowl. Lu closes the front door. "I'm going to make tea."

He goes into the kitchen and plugs in the electric teakettle. He roots around the cupboards until he finds two cups and a tin of oolong.

Lu hears water running in the bathroom. The sound of Liang snorting and spitting. He eventually comes out, drying his face with a towel. He and Lu sit at the kitchen table, and Lu sets out the tea.

"Where are my cigarettes?" Liang says. He gets up and searches the pockets of his coat, finds a beaten-up pack. He sits back down, lights a cigarette, and slurps tea. "Let's have it."

"I tracked down the missing employee from the bar. Brando."

"He's not dead, I hope?"

"He's alive, and he confirmed that Yang Fenfang met a guy at the Black Cat. This would have been more than a year ago. An older guy, looked rich, looked connected."

"How does someone look connected?"

"They smoke Chunghwas."

"Ah."

"Brando says this guy was definitely a *tongzhi*, so he wasn't having an affair with Yang. But I'm still operating on the assumption that he was the source of the money for the apartment in Harbin. That way, he had a place to take his occasional conquests, and nobody could trace it back to him."

"Okay. So they had an arrangement. Then what?"

"Brando said Yang actually recognized the guy."

"What do you mean, recognized him? Is he famous?"

"She said he was from her hometown."

"Here?"

"Yes."

Liang taps cigarette ash into an old teacup. "Where are you going with this, Lu Fei?"

"I put together a list of possible suspects. Locals. I went on the assumption that the suspect had some money and status. It made sense to start with local officials. I sent a collection of photos to Brando, and he identified the man from the Black Cat."

Liang holds up his hand. "I don't want to know. Don't tell me."

"Brando says the man is Party Secretary Mao."

Liang laughs. "That horny old wolf! Absurd."

"Brando says it's him."

"It's dark in those *tongzhi* bars. How can he be sure?"

"Mao visited once or twice a month. Brando saw him more than a dozen times."

"No. I can't believe it. Mao's always talking about tits and asses."

"I'd do the same if I were putting up a smoke screen."

"He's married and has two kids!"

"Chief, don't be naive."

Liang shakes his head and slumps over the table.

"We have to question Mao," Lu says.

"Do you know what will happen to us if we accuse him of murder?"

"We aren't accusing him of murder. Not yet."

"Okay. Just of being an old *ji lao* and intimidating witnesses. For starters."

"Yes."

"He'll eat our souls for breakfast."

"Not if we're right."

"What proof do you have, other than the say-so of this ridiculously named Brando character? And who knows how reliable he is? Maybe someone paid him to frame Mao."

"If that were the case, I hardly think he'd do his best to disappear by running off to some small village near the ass end of the Russian border."

"We can't brace Mao without some solid evidence, Lu Fei."

"We have a witness. That's evidence. If we show Mao's picture around the Black Cat, maybe we can get corroboration. If we obtain access to his bank accounts, perhaps we'll find a withdrawal of five thousand yuan each month."

"All circumstantial."

"You're right. That's why we need to hit him and hit him hard. Make him think we have more than we do. Hopefully, he'll just cave."

"A party secretary? Cave? Do you know how many backs you have to stab to obtain such a position? How massive your balls have to be?"

"Chief. This is a major break. It could bust the case wide open."

Liang finishes his cigarette and lights another. He puffs furiously. Lu remains silent, giving Liang time to work the angles, calculate the odds, arrive at the inevitable conclusion. Liang sighs. "I'm going back to bed for a couple of hours. Come pick me up after lunch."

"Yes, Chief."

"I hope you're right, Lu Fei. Otherwise, we're going to spend the rest of our careers sweeping streets in Xinjiang."

Lu returns at 1:00 p.m., driving a patrol car, in uniform. He has taken the extra precaution of checking out a firearm from the *paichusuo*'s armory.

The gun is one of the recently issued 05 Chinese police revolvers, a six-shooter that fires 9mm rounds. The simplicity, capacity, and caliber of the 05 are designed to reduce the risks of introducing a weapon to a police force that has little training or experience with sidearms and to make it difficult for criminals to obtain the proper ammo should they get their hands on one.

Lu is relieved to find Chief Liang showered, dressed, shaved, and looking reasonably recuperated.

"Did you call Mao?" Lu asks.

"Yes."

"I'm surprised you reached him on a Sunday."

"Are you kidding? He's been on my ass since this thing began. Now I guess we know why."

"What did you tell him?"

"There have been some developments I don't want to go over on the phone."

"How did he sound?"

"Intrigued. Let's go."

"Where to?" Lu says once they are in the car. "Office or his house?"

"Neither. Someplace outside of town."

"Does that sound right to you?"

"Not really, but what's he going to do? Whack two cops?"

"Depends on how desperate he is."

"Lucky thing you brought a gun," Liang says.

"How'd you guess?"

"You don't get to be an old tiger just by having sharp teeth."

Following directions from Liang's GPS phone app, they drive out to the suburbs, where houses and factories give way to grain fields and pig farms. They turn down a dirt road and encounter an open gate and a sign that reads:

PROPERTY OF ABUNDANT HARVEST INDUSTRIES
NO TRESPASSING

"See that?" Lu says.

"I can read, same as you, college boy."

"I don't like this at all."

"No turning back now."

Ahead is a cluster of huge, conical grain storage bins constructed of steel, linked by a network of ladders and conveyer belts.

Lu slows the car to a crawl. He peers up through the windshield at the tops of the bins, looking for telltale flashes of sunlight reflecting off telescopic sights and rifle barrels.

Chief Liang notices and scoffs. "This isn't an American spy novel, Lu Fei. You don't need to look for snipers."

"Mao could have us murdered and fed to pigs and the car buried in a field, and no one would ever know."

Behind the bins is a small clump of buildings—equipment storage sheds, a sheltered parking area, a mobile office trailer. An SUV and a Mercedes sedan are parked outside the trailer.

"Two vehicles," Liang remarks.

Lu parks next to the SUV. They get out of the patrol car. Lu feels terribly exposed.

The door to the office opens, and Mao pokes his head out and waggles his fingers downward in a "come here" gesture. Lu looks at Liang. Liang shrugs. He stops to light a cigarette, then trudges across the frosted earth.

Lu reaches inside his coat to makes sure the police revolver is accessible before following along. They climb the few short steps to the doorway of the trailer and enter.

Inside is a jumble of desks and filing cabinets, a broken-down couch, an open door leading to a filthy bathroom, a stack of cardboard boxes, and a collection of orange safety vests and hard hats hung on a series of hooks.

Party Secretary Mao leans against one of the desks. Another man sits on the couch, smoking. He's around sixty, with short gray hair, thick glasses.

Lu recognizes this man, as does Chief Liang—his name is Deng Qiao. Deng is the local chairman for Abundant Harvest Industries. As such, he is the poster child for a major shift in the way the People's Republic aims to feed its massive populace in the years to come.

During Mao's era, collective farming was the mainstay of China's socialist agrarian revolution. Now, under the direction of professionals like Deng, who are businessmen, not farmers, corporate agriculture is the name of the game.

The average size of a family farm in China is just a few acres. The work is extremely labor intensive and makes inefficient use of water and fertilizer. Increasingly, rural residents, especially young ones, have fled to the greener economic pastures of the cities, leaving good fertile earth untended.

The government's solution has been to combine smaller plots into more midsize farms, and to transfer the exclusive right of rural residents to use farmland—a policy that emerged from Maoist era collectivization policies—over to commercial farming concerns.

The result is that companies like Abundant Harvest, and men like Deng Qiao, carry a lot of weight in the local economy and politics.

"Chairman Deng," Chief Liang says. "Fancy meeting you here."

Deng doesn't even bother to look up from his cigarette. He just nods imperiously.

"I asked the chairman to join us," Mao says.

"Why?" Liang says.

"What is it that you wanted to talk about, Chief?"

"That's a private police matter."

"If it concerns me, I authorize Chairman Deng to be present."

Lu is surprised to see Deng, but perhaps he shouldn't be. As Raven Valley Township party secretary, Mao would have been instrumental in helping Deng to secure contracts for land use in the surrounding villages. In return, Lu expects Mao has received kickbacks or some sort of remuneration. It's just how these things work.

The point is, Mao and Deng are in bed together, and given their combined political and economic influence, they are like two barrels of a large-bore shotgun.

Chief Liang, nothing if not politically astute, has come to the same conclusion. He sighs and drops his cigarette on the floor, then grinds it out. "Why don't you start by telling us about the apartment you rented for Yang Fenfang in Harbin."

"What apartment?" Mao says.

"Where were you a week ago Friday?"

"At home. With my family. You can ask my wife and kids. They'll confirm it. I arrived home at eight and didn't leave until the following morning."

"Where did you go the following morning?"

"Golfing."

"With?"

"Me," Deng says.

"But of course," Liang says. He forges on. "Do you deny that over the past several years you have frequented an establishment in Harbin called the Black Cat?"

"The Black Cat? It doesn't ring a bell. I've been to many establishments in Harbin. Not always my choice—I have various business associates who take me around."

"We have multiple witnesses who place you at the Black Cat on a regular basis," Lu says.

"What witnesses?"

"I think you know," Lu says. "Which brings up a question for Mr. Deng."

Deng brushes ash off his sleeve. "I'm not here to answer your questions."

"Where are your employees?" Lu says. "One tall with a mole on his chin? One short and built like a wrestler?"

"Right behind you," Deng says.

Lu and Chief Liang turn. The tall man and the wrestler are standing on the stairs, just outside the open doorway. They are not armed, so Lu doesn't draw his revolver. Not yet.

"Who the hell are these guys?" Liang says.

"The thugs who tried to intimidate the owner of the Black Cat and his employee."

"Ah," Liang says. "If they move, shoot them."

"Glad to, Chief."

Liang turns back to Mao. "Why did you murder Yang Fenfang?"

Mao laughs. "I didn't!"

"Was it because she blackmailed you? Threatened to reveal that you are a homosexual?"

Mao stops laughing. "Even if you could prove that, it is not a crime."

"Your wife might not take kindly to it."

"My wife? Please. How many people in this day and age—or ever, for that matter—marry for love? Marriage is a practical matter, based on convenience, economics, social status. I'd wager my wife and I have a solider relationship than ninety percent of couples. We respect one another. We work as a team to create a prosperous household and raise our children, and as long as it doesn't cause either of us any loss of face, we don't ask and don't care who the other sleeps with."

This is a remarkable confession, and to a large extent, Lu can't disagree with Mao's reasoning. Most of the married couples he knows exist in a state of low-grade vexation. The husband is always out drinking. The wife spends too much money. Whatever the specific complaint might be. At best, they learn to compromise, neither completely satisfied, but recognizing the mutual benefits of staying together.

"What about the provincial party apparatus?" Liang says.

"Do you think my colleagues don't have their own secrets?" Mao says. "They keep mine, and I keep theirs."

"So you admit it?" Liang says. "That you're homosexual?"

"I admit no such thing," Mao says.

"Party Secretary Mao," Liang says. "With all due respect, let's be honest. You're fucked. We have witnesses. I can legally detain you now. Once I explain the situation to Procurator Gao, I'm sure he'll be happy to approve an arrest request. The subsequent investigation will confirm our suspicions, and even if the evidence turns out to be circumstantial, your reputation and career will be ruined."

Mao reaches into his coat. Lu goes for his revolver. Mao holds up a hand. "I'm just getting a cigarette." He slowly takes out a pack. "What if I told you, Chief, that you're right. In part."

"I guess it depends on what part."

"Let's say—theoretically—I met Yang Fenfang in Harbin. Perhaps something in her reaction made me think that she recognized me. Perhaps I spoke to her about it. A man in my position can't be too careful. Maybe my original intent was to threaten, to intimidate, but I was immediately taken by her honest and open manner, and I believed her when she said she wouldn't betray my confidence." He lights his cigarette. "Then let's say I had an idea. An arrangement that would benefit us both. I give her money, she rents the apartment in her name and lives there for free, and once or twice a month, she clears out and I make use of it."

Lu glances at Deng. Is that a sneer on his face? Perhaps Mao's lifestyle disgusts him. But money is money.

"And then the poor girl is murdered," Mao continues. "Not by me. Not on my orders. I am as surprised as everyone else. The first time I hear about it is when you call me the day after her body is found. But I am concerned. I know the apartment in Harbin will be searched, so I turn to a friend." He points the tip of his cigarette at Deng. "And my friend, my close business associate, says he will take care of it. I don't ask questions. I just assume it will be done. And it is."

"So you sent your henchmen to clean the apartment and threaten potential witnesses," Liang says to Deng.

"Henchmen?" Deng laughs. "You read too many crime novels."

"But that is what you did."

"I have no knowledge of the events you describe. Party Secretary Mao is speaking hypothetically."

"Our witnesses can positively ID these two," Liang says, pointing at the tall man and the wrestler.

"I didn't kill that girl," Mao says. "I swear to heaven. I'm not the person you're looking for."

"Can you prove it?" Liang asks.

"According to my understanding of the law," Mao says, "the burden of proof lies with you."

"That's what an investigation is for."

Deng stands up and throws his cigarette butt at Lu's feet. "There will be no investigation. That's why you two were brought down here. To make that abundantly clear."

"Excuse me, but that's not your decision to make," Liang says.

Deng walks up to Liang—he's several inches taller—and stares down his nose at him. "Don't you get it? The county PSB chief isn't going to let you open an investigation. Procurator Mao isn't going to issue an arrest warrant. Don't be a damn fool."

Liang glowers. "Take a step back, Deng, or I'll slap those glasses through the back of your skull."

Deng's men start up the stairs. Lu draws his revolver and aims it at them. "Stay. Good dogs."

"Gentlemen!" Mao holds up his hands. "There's no need for this. Please!"

Deng and Liang glare at one another. The thugs quiver on the stairs. "You," Lu tells Deng. "Tell your mutts not to do anything stupid. And go sit your ass back down on the couch."

"How dare you—"

"Now, damn it!"

Deng sputters. Lu cocks the revolver. "Last chance."

Deng stomps over to the couch and sits down. "You motherless shit sticks are only hurting yourselves."

Lu lowers the hammer of the revolver but keeps the muzzle pointed at the open doorway.

"That's better," Mao says. "I'm sure we can work this out."

Liang laughs. "Ever the optimist, Party Secretary Mao." He takes a handkerchief out of his pocket and wipes his forehead. "Chairman Deng, was that the distinctive scent of a Chunghwa I smelled you smoking earlier?"

"What about it?"

"Might I trouble you for one?"

"You must be joking."

"No, I'm quite serious."

"Unbelievable." Deng takes out a pack and shakes out a cigarette. Liang walks over and takes one.

"Thank you." Liang puts the cigarette in his mouth, lights it, and takes a deep drag. He nods at Mao. "What do you suggest?"

"I will provide any resources or assistance available to me to help with your investigation. All I ask is that you keep the apartment in Harbin, the Black Cat, and my personal business confidential."

"What about the owner of the Black Cat and the employee Chairman Deng tried to intimidate?" Lu says.

"As long as they keep their mouths shut and go about their business," Mao says, "no one will bother them. The employee can return to Harbin and resume his old job, if he so chooses. He has already been compensated for his trouble, yes? So no harm done."

"He may not be of the same opinion," Lu says.

"Come off it," Deng says. "Mao didn't kill the girl. Aren't you listening? He's not innocent, by any means, but he's no murderer. So stop wasting your time. You want to catch the real killer, don't you? Then look elsewhere." He begins to rise from the couch, hesitates. "I'm getting up now, all right?" Deng stands and buttons up his coat. "This matter is at an end. Just do your job and keep out of our business, and we'll keep out of yours. Do we have a deal?"

Chief Liang and Lu exchange a look. Neither of them say anything.

"Good," Deng says. "I'm leaving. Get out of my way."

Lu doesn't. He and Deng stare each other down.

"It's okay, Lu Fei," Liang says. "Let him go."

Lu reluctantly lowers the revolver and moves aside. Deng shoulders past him. "Come on, you idiots!" he snarls at the thugs.

Lu watches from the doorway as Deng and his heavies walk to the Mercedes. The tall man reaches out to open the door for Deng, but Deng slaps his hand away. He opens the door for himself and climbs into the back. The tall man and the wrestler get in up front. The Mercedes pulls out and then circles around the grain bins and disappears from sight.

"May I go now?" Mao asks.

"Chief," Lu starts.

"I know," Liang says. He puffs on his cigarette. "This isn't over, Party Secretary. You're still a suspect until proven otherwise."

"I understand, Chief. I'm just asking you to keep this unofficial for the time being. I'm confident you'll find the real killer, and then this will all be moot."

"We'll see about that."

"I'm innocent, Chief," Mao says. "Now—may I go?"

"Go on. Get the fuck out of here."

Lu drives them into town and drops Chief Liang off at home. Liang gets out, then leans back in. "Go home, kid. Get some rest."

"You believe Mao?"

"He is a politician, and that means, for him, lying is as easy as drawing a breath. But actually, I do. My gut says he's an old *tongzhi* and a crook but not a killer."

"You are very trusting for a cop."

"Make no mistake, he's still on the hook. But for now, I think we're better off barking up a different tree."

"Fine."

"Maybe without the distraction of the mystery surrounding the apartment in Harbin, your cunning little mind will come up with a tantalizing new direction to pursue."

"Maybe. Tell your wife I said hello."

Liang grimaces. "Why be so cruel, Lu Fei?"

Instead of going home and getting some rest, Lu drives to Yanyan's house. He parks outside and makes two phone calls on his cell phone— one to Monk and the other to Brando. Neither answer, so he leaves messages and tells them that they will likely never see or hear from "Mr. Wang" again.

He gets out of the car and knocks on Yanyan's front door. Zeng answers.

"Inspector," Zeng says. "Good of you to come."

"Not too late, I hope?"

"Not at all." Zeng waves Lu inside.

Yanyan is sitting in the front room, visiting with an older couple. She's wearing somber clothes and a white flower in her hair. Lu extends his condolences. She thanks him for coming. He offers incense at a makeshift altar displaying a photograph of Yanyan's father. Zeng takes him outside to burn the paper items he has brought—hell money, paper clothes, some household appliances, a laptop, and a prepaid debit card, just on the off chance that there is an ATM in the underworld.

When Lu is finished, he hands a white envelope containing some cash to Zeng. He goes back inside and sits with Yanyan and the old couple for as long as it takes to drink a cup of tea. He'd rather be alone with her, but the couple doesn't seem inclined to leave, so finally he says goodbye and goes home in a funk.

MONDAY

New things always have to experience difficulties and setbacks as they grow. It is sheer fantasy to imagine that the cause of socialism is all plain sailing and easy success, without difficulties and setbacks or the exertion of tremendous efforts.

—Quotations from Chairman Mao Zedong

On Monday, Deputy Director Song is discharged from the hospital. A flight is scheduled to take him and Technician Jin back to Beijing.

"Already?" Lu says when Song reaches him by phone that morning.

"We've processed the crime scene and collected evidence. So for now, it's just a matter of good old detective work. I don't have time to run down every avenue of inquiry with you." Lu hears the *snick* of a lighter on the phone. Song inhales deeply. "There are always more victims, more crimes, more murderers that require my attention."

Lu hears a raised voice in the background of Song's call.

"*Ta ma de,*" Song says. "They are yelling at me to put out my cigarette. Can you ask Jin to get my belongings and the two of you come get me? We can head directly to the airport from here."

Lu instructs Constable Huang to drive Jin to the Raven Valley Friendship Guesthouse to pick up his and Song's luggage. When Huang and Jin return, Lu takes over driving duties, leaving Huang behind at the *paichusuo*. They arrive at the hospital, and Lu waits in the lobby while Jin takes a change of clothes up to Song.

Song finally appears, thin and unshaven, walking like a man thirty years his senior, and they climb into the patrol car for the trip to the airport.

"How do you feel?" Lu asks when they are on the expressway.

Song cracks a window and lights a cigarette. "Like a slaughtered pig."

"Is it safe for you to fly?"

"Who cares? I can't wait to get out of here. No offense."

Lu is, in fact, slightly offended, but he just shrugs. He hasn't had a chance to fully brief Song and Jin on yesterday's developments regarding Mao, so he does so now.

"Dirty pervert," Song says.

"For now, please keep what I just told you confidential."

Song blows smoke out the window. "This is a murder case. Whether or not Mao likes to play with rubber dicks is irrelevant, but at the very least, it sounds like he's in bed with Deng. There's definitely money changing hands in return for land concessions."

"Yes," Lu agrees, "but we're not working a corruption angle."

"Well, now that our Harbin apartment connection has been blown out of the water, what are we left with?"

"There's Zhang Zhaoxing, pig butcher, Yang stalker, simpleton."

"Next."

"Three victims, connection unknown."

"With widely varying profiles," Song says. "Two single, one married. No kids. Different socioeconomic status. Different sectors of employment. Two murdered in Harbin, one in Raven Valley. I guess no luck on finding a link in their purchasing records, taxi receipts, restaurant bills, and so on?"

"We don't have Qin's records yet, but I have constables looking into Yang's and Tang's transactions. Nothing so far. It's slow going."

"It generally is."

"If the perp did meet Yang Fenfang in Harbin, I'm not sure how he would even know how to find her in Raven Valley."

"Perhaps he gained her confidence in some way," Song says. "Maybe they were friends. Coworkers. Maybe it was Mr. Wang, the rental agent for the Good Fortune Terrace." He sighs. "The possibilities are endless."

"Then there's the red ring and red shoes. And the hell money and organ removal, indicating a knowledge of anatomy and Five Element theory and a belief in the supernatural."

Song scratches at one of his bandages. "Hard to get a handle on this guy." He tosses his cigarette butt through the window and rolls it up. "Unless the lab report comes back with some DNA, there's nothing for it but to keep digging through those purchasing records and looking for a physical point of intersection between the three victims."

"No hits on homicides with a connection to the color red in the crime database?"

"Nothing solid, I'm afraid."

Lu drops Song and Jin off at the departure terminal. He offers to help them with their luggage, but Song declines and waves a porter over. "Stay in touch, Inspector."

"I will. Thanks to you and your team for the assistance."

"Remember, we're still on the case. If you catch a lead, we're just a flight away."

"All right. Safe journey."

Lu watches them disappear into the terminal. Although his relationship with Song has been an uneasy one, he can't help but feel bereft, as if Song is leaving him after a brief but intense love affair. He is reminded of a poem by the famous Tang dynasty renaissance man Wang Wei:

> *We bid each other adieu at the hill*
> *As day turns to dusk, I shut the wicker gate. The spring grasses*
> *will be green again next year*
> *But will my friend return?*

TUESDAY

A man in China is usually subjected to the domination of three systems of authority [political authority, family authority, and religious authority]. . . . As for women, in addition to being dominated by these three systems of authority, they are also dominated by the men . . . These four authorities— political, family, religious and masculine—are the embodiment of the whole feudal-patriarchal ideology and system . . . As to the authority of the husband, this has always been weaker among the poor peasants because, out of economic necessity, their womenfolk have to do more manual labor than the women of the richer classes and therefore have more say and greater power of decision in family matters . . . With the rise of the peasant movement, the women in many places have now begun to organize rural women's associations; the opportunity has come for them to lift up their heads, and the authority of the husband is getting shakier every day.

—Quotations from Chairman Mao Zedong

The funeral for Yanyan's father is held at the Everlasting Peace Funeral Home on Tuesday morning. There is a surprisingly large turnout: a dozen or so elderly folks—doubtless friends of the deceased—and twice that many other attendees, some of whom Lu recognizes as regulars at the Red Lotus.

Yanyan looks exquisitely, achingly sad, her skin as pale and translucent as rice paper apart from purplish semicircles under each eye. She's dressed in drab colors—the cinnabar bracelet is the only variation in her otherwise monochromatic appearance.

Zeng runs the proceedings efficiently. He makes a short but touching speech. He assists Yanyan in burning various paper funeral goods. Then he calls up mourners to pay their respects by lighting incense and bowing three times in the direction of the father's casket.

The whole thing takes barely twenty minutes. As Yanyan's father will be cremated, she and a few of the old man's more intimate friends will return the following day to witness the placement of his urn in the columbarium, but for now, most of the attendees slowly disperse to the parking lot for the trip home.

Lu wanders the grounds a bit while he waits for an opportunity to have a private moment with Yanyan. Morbid curiosity takes him in the direction of the crematorium. He glances around to make sure no one is looking, then tries the door. It's locked. Just as well. He probably doesn't want to see what's in there.

Lu makes his way over the cemetery and into the columbarium, where Yang Fenfang's mother's urn is kept. Sure enough, as promised, a new urn is in the niche beside it, along with a photograph of Yang Fenfang and a small plaque bearing the Chinese characters for her name.

Zeng has even arranged a bouquet of fresh flowers.

Lu walks back to the main compound and finds Yanyan bidding farewell to the last of the guests. He waits until she is done and then approaches.

"Can I give you a ride home?" Lu asks.

"Auntie and Uncle are going to drive me." Yanyan nods at an old couple laboriously descending the path toward the parking lot.

By *Auntie* and *Uncle,* Lu understands they are not blood relatives, just old friends of her father's.

"Okay. Can I stop by later to check on you?"

"It's not necessary, Inspector. I mean . . ." She smiles faintly. "Brother Lu."

"I don't mind."

"It's fine."

"I'd be happy to bring something to eat. Chicken-and-mushroom stew?"

Yanyan relents. "I don't have much of an appetite, but that's very kind. Thank you."

"I'll see you tonight, then."

Lu spends the rest of the day with mundane tasks, happily anticipating his upcoming visit with Yanyan, despite the sad circumstances.

He puts in a call to the county detention center and inquires about the welfare of Zhang Zhaoxing, Mrs. Chen, and Chen Shiyi. Zhang, he is told, has been transferred to the medical ward. He's refusing to eat. As for the Chens, their appetites are healthy, and Mrs. Chen has threatened to sue every staff member she's encountered.

At 5:30 p.m., Lu leaves the *paichusuo* and buys a large serving of chicken-and-mushroom stew at a nearby restaurant, then drives over to Yanyan's house. She answers the door wearing baggy sweatpants and an old sweater. She looks like she's been crying, or sleeping, or perhaps alternating between the two.

"Hungry?" Lu says, holding up the bag of food.

"Not really."

In the kitchen, Yanyan sets out bowls, chopsticks, and spoons and offers to heat up some Shaoxing wine.

"Only if you're having some," he says.

"Sure."

She heats the wine. They sit at the table. She barely eats a bite of stew. She keeps pouring wine for Lu and he keeps drinking it, but he can't return the favor, because she hardly drinks a drop.

He tries to keep the conversation light. She smiles at his jokes, but mostly just stares into her bowl of slowly cooling stew, her thoughts a thousand miles away.

When the meal is finished, Lu offers to clean up, but Yanyan tells him to just leave it. "I'll take care of it tomorrow," she says.

"All right," Lu says. "I should probably let you get some rest. Thanks for the wine. If there's anything you need, don't hesitate to call me."

"I won't."

She walks him to the door. He says good night. She thanks him again for coming.

Then the door shuts, and Lu is out in the cold. Shaoxing wine, on this occasion, has failed miserably to warm his qi.

The man sits in his car, watching Yanyan's house. He is very cold, despite his heavy coat, gloves, and hat, but is loath to turn on the engine and crank up the heater, lest a nosy neighbor see the car exhaust and come out to inquire what he's doing there.

In truth, he's not sure himself of the answer to that question. There is a roll of duct tape in the glove compartment. A squat silver hammer with a heavy cylindrical head rests on the floor under his seat.

But he knows now is not the time. It is much too soon after Yang Fenfang.

As dusk falls, a patrol car pulls to a stop in front of the house. Inspector Lu Fei gets out, carrying a plastic bag of takeout food. He goes to the front door, knocks. And is admitted.

The man clenches the steering wheel. He gnashes his teeth. He mutters scathing curses under his breath.

He considers picking up the silver hammer, going to the front door, kicking it in. He imagines himself swinging the hammer at Lu Fei's head. Crushing bone. Splattering blood. Scattering brains across the floor like bits of scrambled egg.

But the man is not confident that he can overcome the inspector, who is reputed to be proficient in the martial arts. And despite his past actions, the man is not a savage or indiscriminate killer. When he takes a life, it is for a higher purpose.

Lu Fei presents a problem, however, and not just because he is the lead investigator on the death of Yang Fenfang.

Equally as concerning is his rapidly escalating relationship with Luo Yanyan.

She is not meant for you, the man thinks.

He watches the house, his toes and fingers numb, his blood boiling, furious and impotent, until Lu Fei emerges twenty minutes later, a dejected air about him, and drives off.

The man lets out a breath. *Rejected you, did she, you bastard?*

He is relieved but still anxious. Lu Fei possesses both good looks and status. Luo Yanyan is beautiful, yes, but a widow who runs a bar. She could do much worse than the inspector. It is perhaps just a matter of time until he wears her down.

It is risky, it is dangerous, it is foolhardy. But the man cannot afford to wait.

First, he will create a diversion. Throw Inspector Lu off the scent.

And then he will take Luo Yanyan.

WEDNESDAY

We must thoroughly clear away all ideas among our cadres of winning easy victories through good luck, without hard and bitter struggle, without sweat and blood.

—Quotations from Chairman Mao Zedong

Lu is up early, after a sleepless night. He's the first person on the day shift to arrive at the *paichusuo*. He checks the night's incident reports. A farmer called to report a stolen pig. There was a car accident downtown. Fortunately, only minor injuries. A fire broke out in a restaurant kitchen but was quickly extinguished. An old lady called for help with her internet service.

The usual.

Lu pulls out the case files from the Tang and Qin homicides—purloined from Harbin—and also collects Yang Fenfang's file. He makes himself coffee—coffee today, not tea. The bitterness will keep his mind sharp.

He begins pulling together information and drawing it out in a diagram—boxes, arrows, bits of text, a visual and annotated list of dates, addresses, places of employment, Harbin transportation hubs—which he privately dubs a "murder chart."

The Black Cat is in Daoli District, near the center of the city's urban core. The beauty parlor where Tang worked is one district over. Mrs. Qin's bank branch was all the way on the other side of town. The residences of the three were scattered. There is no clear indication of where their paths might have crossed.

The records of Mrs. Qin's purchases have finally arrived, and when Constables Big Wang and Yuehan Chu clock in (both have returned to work without another word about the events of last Thursday, Chu still bearing a bandage across his nose and dark circles under each eyes), Lu enlists their help to comb through them. It is painstaking work, and after an hour or so, Lu can no longer see straight. Rank has its privileges, though. He leaves it to Wang and Chu and returns to his office to try another tack.

The murder chart continues to expand. Marital status. Two single victims, one married. Children—none. Mrs. Qin was a college graduate. Neither Tang nor Yang had any education after high school. From what he can tell, the trio did not subscribe to any of the same hobby groups, associations, fan clubs. They did not frequent the same restaurants or bars. They did not, as far as Lu knows, have any friends in common.

None of them had siblings. Tang's parents were both deceased. Yang Fenfang's parents were both deceased. Mrs. Qin's father is still alive, but her mother is dead.

There is a phone call on Lu's extension. He answers. It's Fatty Wang, who is manning the front desk today.

"Inspector Lu—we just got a report that an organ has been discovered on Zhang Zhaoxing's property."

Lu isn't sure he heard that correctly. "What?"

"An organ. A lung."

"Where?"

"Zhang's house."

"Yes, I got that part. *Where* at Zhang's house?"

"Apparently, one of the neighbors' dogs dug it up."

Lu, Sergeant Bing, Big Wang, and Yuehan Chu drive out to Yongzheng Road. A small crowd has gathered in the front yard of Zhang's house. Mostly women in their sixties and up, and a couple of old men, a few toddlers. Lu hears shouts and a dog barking. He pushes his way through and finds an adolescent girl screaming at an older lady who is holding a dog by its collar.

"What's going on here?" Lu says. No one hears him. The faces of the crowd are lit up with excitement. This is high entertainment.

"*Quiet!*" Sergeant Bing roars.

The shouting quickly subsides.

"Thank you, Sergeant," Lu says. "Now what's going on here?"

The adolescent girl starts screaming again, and the lady holding the dog screams back.

"*Quiet!*" Sergeant Bing yells.

In the brief moment of silence that ensues, Lu points at the girl. "Who are you?"

"Zhaoxing's cousin, Zhang Mei. Who are you?"

Lu is taken aback by her question. It's obvious who he is from the uniform. "Inspector Lu Fei, deputy chief of Raven Valley Public Security Bureau."

"Ah! So *you* are the one who arrested my cousin and threw him in jail!"

"I—"

"Because of you, I have to stay here to watch Grand-Uncle when I should be at work. Who's going to compensate me for my missed salary? How do you expect me to feed my family? Huh?"

This one is *lihai,* Lu thinks. *Fierce.* "Zhang Zhaoxing is a suspect in a homicide."

"That dumb ox couldn't kill a cockroach if it crawled under his shoe!" the girl says. "How dare you arrest him. He's innocent."

"Then why is there a lung buried in your front yard?" the woman holding the dog snaps.

"Your filthy mutt dragged that over here from somewhere else," the girl snaps back.

"There's the hole right there!" Dog-woman points to a shallow pit in the earth. "We live on the same street as a murderer!" she says to the crowd. "Beware Zhang Zhaoxing doesn't slaughter your children!"

The young girl slaps dog-woman across the face.

It takes Lu, Sergeant Bing, Chu, and Big Wang several chaotic minutes to sort out the resulting fracas. In the process, Wang sustains a minor dog bite and somebody—Lu can't be sure who—kicks him in the ass.

Finally, the young girl is dragged into Zhang's house and made to sit on the *kang* with Zhang's grandfather, who, as usual, is watching TV with no apparent awareness or interest in what is going on just outside his front door. The other woman, who as it turns out is the next-door neighbor, is escorted with her furiously barking dog back to her residence.

Lu sets about questioning the girl.

"How old are you?"

"Sixteen."

"Shouldn't you be in school?"

"Some of us have to work to eat."

"I want you to tell me what happened here."

"I want you to tell me who's going to compensate me for the work I'm missing because I have to take care of this senile old fool."

"Listen, Miss . . . Mei, you said your name was?"

She folds her arms, looks up at the ceiling.

Lu takes a deep breath. "If you want to help your cousin, you'd better talk to me."

"Aren't you the one who arrested him in the first place?"

"No. I detained him. He was arrested later."

"What's the difference?"

"Just tell me what happened here."

"That old bitch next door said her dog dug up a lung in our front yard. Why don't you *detain* her for letting her dog trespass on our property?"

"Then what?"

"I don't care what happens to her after that."

"I mean, what happened after her dog dug up the lung?"

"Oh. Then she started to scream and fuss and run around telling all the neighbors Zhaoxing has body parts buried everywhere. Her stupid mutt probably dug it up at her house and she's just trying to put the blame on us. Maybe she's the one who murdered that girl!"

Lu asks more questions, but the girl sticks to her account. He goes next door to talk to the neighbor, whose surname is Yuan.

"It was horrible! Disgusting!"

"Please start at the beginning," Lu says.

"I let Xiao Li outside—"

"Xiao Li is your dog?"

"Yes."

"Go on."

"Well, I'm in my garden, working, minding my own business when Xiao Li comes back with something in his mouth. Something that smelled awful and looked rotten. I made him spit it out and immediately saw that it was a lung."

"How did you know it was a lung?"

"How? How? How do you think? I'm not a rich city girl who only buys her food in shiny, air-conditioned supermarkets where everything is in cans and plastic packages! I've seen every kind of animal part there is."

"All right. So it was a lung. How did you know it was a human lung?"

"Didn't I just tell you I've seen every kind of animal part there is?"

"I suppose you did."

"So I asked Xiao Li, 'Where did you get this dirty thing?' He led me over to the Zhangs' yard, and I saw the hole in the ground, and of course I know Zhaoxing was arrested for butchering that poor girl."

"So then you called us?"

"That's right! It's proof of the murder, isn't it? Maybe he's got lots more cut-up limbs and body parts over there. *Tian ah!* I'll have to burn incense and make offerings to ward off all the hungry ghosts."

The object in question is still lying in the dirt near Mrs. Yuan's vegetable garden, and it is indeed a lung. Lu gets on his hands and knees and gives it a close-up examination. It lets off a pungent odor, one Lu knows well from his college biology and anatomy courses.

Formaldehyde.

Lu and Sergeant Bing return to the Zhang residence. Lu finds an old hoe leaning against the chicken shed and tentatively digs around the hole in the ground. He doesn't find any more wayward organs, just a sheet of plastic that he assumes the lung was wrapped up in.

"I wish Technician Jin hadn't gone home already," Lu says.

"I'll cordon off the yard and get some more constables over here to search the property," Sergeant Bing says.

"Make sure they don't contaminate any evidence. If they find something, leave it in place so we can photograph it before it's moved."

"What about the Zhangs and the Yuans?"

"I'll talk to them."

Lu collects an evidence bag out of the trunk of the patrol car and slips the lung into it. He speaks to Zhang Mei and tells her that constables will be conducting a search. She rails at him. Old Man Zhang says nothing, but he nods at Lu and jerks his chin toward the chamber pot.

"Oh, no, Uncle," Lu says. "I've done my duty on that score."

When Lu is finished with Zhang Mei, he goes next door and tells Mrs. Yuan to keep her dog on her property and to quit inciting the neighbors against the Zhangs. "We don't know if Zhang Zhaoxing is guilty," Lu tells her. "The investigation remains open."

"What about the lung?"

"As I said, the investigation remains open. For now, leave the Zhang family alone. And if I find you've been gossiping around town, I'll have you detained for disturbing the public order."

"The Zhangs are a family of cannibal murderers and *I'm* the one you threaten with arrest?"

"Don't be ridiculous, Mrs. Yuan. And stop spreading rumors."

Lu takes the lung back to the *paichusuo* and asks Fatty Wang to mail it to CIB headquarters in Beijing.

"How am I supposed to send it?" Wang asks. "In an express envelope?"

"Figure it out."

Lu informs Chief Liang of the new development and then calls Deputy Director Song.

"I'll overnight it," Lu says. "Can you have Technician Hu or Dr. Ma determine if it's Yang Fenfang's?"

"Yes," Song says. "This doesn't look good for Zhang."

"It's a plant," Lu says. "This perp knows we're making progress, and he's trying to throw us off."

"You can't be sure of that."

"The lung smelled of formaldehyde."

"Ah. Hm. Maybe he thought pickling it in formaldehyde and aging it in the dirt would improve the flavor. Like a thousand-year-old egg."

"You're joking, right, Deputy Director?"

"If the perp did plant the lung, it means two things. One, you're right—he fears we're getting closer. And two, he's probably local, as we surmised. Oh, and something else."

"What's that?"

"He's getting a bit desperate, and that makes him even more dangerous."

Lu hangs up and returns to his murder chart, but the smell of formaldehyde lingers in his nostrils, and this gives him an idea. Could the intersection of the three victims have been a medical facility? A hospital or clinic? Perhaps the killer was a physician, an orderly, or even a security guard.

Unfortunately, there is no easy way to find out. The People's Republic lacks a unified IT system for tracking patients as they circumnavigate the country's byzantine health care system. Individual hospitals and clinics generally maintain separate records and are not required to share them with one another. Often, it falls to the patient to track all their doctors' visits, medications, and procedures in a homemade cut-and-paste book or a bag filled with old receipts and handwritten notes.

It will be a daunting amount of legwork to ferret out the medical histories of Yang, Qin, and Tang. But, as the old saying goes, "a journey of a thousand *li* begins with a single step."

Lu asks Sergeant Bing to go over to Yang Fenfang's residence and see if he can find Yang's medical records. Then he calls Harbin metro and asks for another round with Tang's and Qin's case files. He is told his request will have to be approved by Chief Xu. This sends Lu into a rage, and he yells into the phone. The person on the other end of the line abruptly hangs up. Lu calls Deputy Director Song and asks for help.

"Don't worry," Song says. "I'll take care of it."

Fifteen minutes later, Lu receives a call from the Harbin metro records department letting him know the files will be waiting for him.

Lu drives to Harbin and is directed to the same windowless, dank room as before. File boxes are arranged on the table. Lu digs through Tang Jinglei's personal papers and locates her medical records. He makes a note of doctors, clinics and hospitals, lab facilities, everything that seems relevant.

He does not find a similar record book for Qin Liying. Perhaps her ex-husband still has it. He goes out into the lobby and calls. The professor doesn't answer, so Lu leaves a message.

Lu returns to the room and packs up. He is just about to leave when the door opens and Xu comes in. Two men whom Lu suspects have been selected for their large size and low moral fiber slope in behind him. Lu knows one of the men—surnamed Han. They used to work together as detectives under Xu. They were not fond of each other back then, and Lu is not surprised to see Han attached to Xu's teat now.

"Well, well," Xu says. "If it isn't Pigfucker Lu. It must be quite a shock to be back in the city. All the tall buildings and bright lights."

"What do you want, Xu?"

"That's Chief Xu to you."

"I'm in a hurry. Get out of the way."

Xu plants himself in front of the door with folded arms. Han sidles around to one end of the table. The other cop, whose name Lu doesn't know, flanks Lu on the opposite side.

"This is *my* city," Xu says. "You're not welcome here. I thought I made that clear seven years ago. If I didn't, I'm going to make it clear now."

"You brought along these two melon heads to beat me up? Right here, in the records department of the Harbin metro police department?"

"Don't worry," Xu says. "They'll avoid your face so the damage won't show."

Lu looks at Han. "I see you've been growing fat off the droppings coming out of Xu's ass."

Han smiles. "I've been wanting to beat the shit out of you for ten years. Today, I get my chance."

"Fine. But first, give me a minute." Lu takes off his coat and drapes it over the table. Then his uniform jacket. He pats his pockets to make sure they're empty. He puts his left foot against the side of the table and carefully ties a fresh knot in his shoe. Followed by the right foot.

Han rolls his eyes. "Ready?" He takes a step forward.

"Hold on!" Lu holds up a hand. "You're not carrying any weapons, are you? It's already two against one—give me a fighting chance, at least."

Han glances over at Xu. Xu gestures impatiently. Han reaches into his back pocket and removes a leather sap weighted with lead shot. It lands on the table with a dull thud.

Lu turns to the other cop, who spreads his hands and shrugs.

"All right," Lu says. He begins removing his tie. "Almost ready."

"*Cao ni ma!*" Xu says. "Get him!"

Lu snatches the sap off the table. He swings it, two quick strikes, backhand and forehand, into Han's face. He immediately pivots, catches the other cop with a kick, ducks an incoming punch, and whips the sap across the cop's nose.

Han has fallen against the wall, but he gets to his feet, blood streaming down his face. He throws an overhand right. Lu deflects it with a forearm, sidesteps, and pops Han behind the ear with the sap. Han drops, out cold.

The other cop crawls under the table, cradling his ruined nose.

Lu drops the sap. He puts on his uniform jacket, coat, and hat. He collects his notebook. He steps over Han's limp body. Xu is struggling with the door, trying to escape. Lu clutches Xu's shoulder, jerks him around, and slams him up against the wall.

"If you hit me, I'll have you arrested for assault!" Xu whines.

"You're pathetic," Lu says, "but evil is repaid with evil. You'll get yours. And if I find out you have anything to do with these murders, there will be a government-issued bullet with your name on it."

"Murders?" Xu sputters. "Don't be ridiculous! Don't talk nonsense. You've gone insane!"

"Remember the old saying," Lu says. "A man made of mud fears the rain."

"How dare you threaten me!" Xu shouts. "I'll have your job for this!"

Lu opens the door and walks out. He congratulates himself on not kneeing Xu in the balls.

But Xu can't contain himself: "You're nothing! You're an insect. A turd. Don't show your face in Harbin again, you hear me?"

Lu keeps walking.

"And don't forget, idiot, while you're out in the middle of nowhere rounding up some illiterate farmer's wayward chickens," Xu snarls, "I'll be right here, chasing a few tender chickens myself!"

Lu stops. He slowly turns.

Xu is laughing, but when he sees the look on Lu's face, his laughter dies in his throat. He retreats back into the room, but Lu rushes forward and catches the door and wrenches it open.

"I should have done this seven years ago," Lu says. He feints high and then slams his hand into Xu's crotch. Xu squeals. Lu gives him a brutal squeeze and a wrenching twist, then another for good measure. When he releases his grip, Xu folds like a cheap card table.

Lu watches Xu retch on the floor for a moment, then closes the door behind him when he leaves. He nods politely to the attendant in the lobby on his way out.

"Did you get what you needed, Inspector?" the attendant asks.

"More or less," Lu says.

Lu drives back to Raven Valley, where he and Sergeant Bing review the medical histories for Tang and Yang. They can find no overlap of doctors or facilities. In the late afternoon, Professor Qin returns Lu's call. He informs Lu that he threw out Qin Liying's records some time ago.

Another dead end.

Then Sergeant Bing has an idea.

"What if it wasn't the victims themselves," Sergeant Bing says, "but a family member?"

"Hmm." Lu refers to his murder chart. "None of the three had any siblings. Only Qin had a husband, but they all had parents, of course."

A search of *hukou* records reveals that Tang Jinglei's mother died when she was very young, but her father, not long before her murder—only three and a half months.

Qin Liying's father is still alive, but her mother died just five weeks before Qin's homicide.

"And Yang Fenfang's mother died only a week before she did," Lu says. "Maybe we're onto something."

"The death certificates will list the facility where the parents passed away," Sergeant Bing says.

"We already know Yang's mother died at the county hospital, and I assume Tang's father and Qin's mother both died in Harbin."

"Do hospital staff typically move around from place to place?"

"I doubt it. But maybe—given the fact that they have special training. Let's check all the death certificates and then get a listing of employees at each facility for the periods in question."

"That's going to be a hassle."

"It sure is."

It requires two hours of phone calls to obtain copies of the death certificates. They discover that Tang's father died at the Harbin Number One hospital in Shengli District; Qin's mother, at the Harbin Medical University Cancer Hospital.

Sergeant Bing looks at his watch. "The administrative offices will be closed for the day. We can call first thing tomorrow to request employment records."

"Fine," Lu says. "It's getting late. Why don't you go on home?"

Lu considers calling Yanyan to see how she's doing, but he doesn't want it to seem like he's stalking her. Besides, she has shown zero interest in his attempts to reach out. Perhaps now is just not the time.

Or he is just not the *one*.

Lu goes home, showers, eats dinner, drinks a couple of beers, and then stares up at the cracks in his ceiling until he falls asleep.

THURSDAY

Investigation may be likened to the long months of pregnancy, and solving a problem to the day of birth. To investigate a problem is, indeed, to solve it.

—Quotations from Chairman Mao Zedong

As the country's premier criminal investigation agency, the Ministry of Public Security's forensics lab in Beijing possesses equipment that can process DNA samples in as little as two hours. The lung from Zhang's yard arrives from an overnight courier at ten in the morning on Thursday, and by noon, Technician Hu calls Lu with the results.

"It's Yang Fenfang's."

"I suppose I should be relieved it's not somebody else's," Lu says.

"Deputy Director Song wants to know if you found any additional body parts or evidence."

"No, but you smelled the formaldehyde on the tissue, right?"

"Couldn't miss it. I'd say, given the lack of decomposition, the lung has been sitting in a solution of formaldehyde since shortly after it was removed from the victim."

"Right. And while we did find the lung on Zhang's property, what we didn't find is any formaldehyde. I'm not even sure where he—or anyone else who isn't a biology professor or a medical examiner—might have gotten a supply."

"Taobao, like everything else."

"You don't need a license or anything to buy it?"

"It's not a controlled substance, but few professionals use it these days. By professionals, I mean scientists and forensics specialists. There are other, less smelly alternatives. You can still find it floating around, though. It's a cheap alternative for amateur specimen collectors and the like, and formaldehyde is also used to manufacture building materials and tons of household items. Pressed-wood products, particleboard, glues and adhesives, insulation materials."

"There are maybe two dozen factories making those kinds of products here in Raven Valley."

"Yes—I feel your pain, Inspector."

After lunch, Lu hashes out theories with Chief Liang and Sergeant Bing.

"Tracking down every business in Raven Valley that uses formaldehyde is like fishing a needle from the sea," Chief Liang says. "We don't have the manpower. And I think we still need to follow up with Zhang."

"I'll drive out to the county detention center and speak to him, but I think we can agree he's not the perp and the lung just proves it. We picked him up the Saturday following the homicide. That means he would have had to kill Yang Fenfang, pickle her lung, bury it, and get rid of the other organs and evidence within twenty-four hours. And Technician Jin searched the property Wednesday and found nothing. And what's the point in burying a single lung? And another thing—"

"Yes, I get the idea," Liang says. He sucks on his cigarette. "Which leads us back at square one. Almost. We know our perp gets turned on by the color red, has access to formaldehyde, has a vehicle, knows anatomy, maybe can't get his dick hard, is afraid of ghosts, on and on and on. We know a million things about him, but we're still getting nowhere!"

"We should probably give up," Lu says.

"Don't be a smart-ass." Liang slurps tea from his cup. "Keep working

the hospital angle. Let's not waste time chasing down every pint of formaldehyde sold in Heilongjiang Province."

Lu drives to the county detention center, an olive-green, multistory
building constructed of cinder block and steel, with a concertina-wire
fence surrounding it. He passes through a checkpoint, parks, goes inside,
and requests to see Zhang Zhaoxing. He fills out paperwork, is questioned as to his business by a clerk, and waits for thirty minutes until a
guard comes to collect him.

The guard leads him through series of locked doors to the medical
wing. The wing is meant for perhaps twenty patients, but there are easily
twice that many in the room, some lying in temporary cots lined up in
the center aisle.

Zhang Zhaoxing is at the far end, facing a wall. He wears a blue
prison uniform with stripes on the breast pockets and shoulders. An IV
tube trails from a bag hung on a stand into his arm.

"Zhang Zhaoxing," Lu says.

No response.

Lu moves around to the foot of the bed. He is shocked by what he
sees.

Zhang's skin is sallow and riddled with acne. His eyes, devoid of
intelligence in the best of times, are sunken and lifeless.

Lu tells the guard to fetch a doctor, then reaches out and puts a
hand on Zhang's leg. "Zhang Zhaoxing. Look at me."

Zhang does so, mechanically, without an ounce of interest.

"Are you sick?" Lu asks.

"No."

"Why are you in the medical ward?"

Zhang turns back to the wall.

A doctor arrives. He is short, thin, young, and prematurely balding.
"Yes?"

"What happened to this man?"

"He refuses to eat."

"Is he ill?"

"Not in the sense that he has a disease. He just won't eat."

"So what are you doing about it?"

"You can see for yourself he's on an IV drip. Short of putting a tube down his throat, I can't do much, can I?"

"He obviously needs some sort of psychiatric help."

The doctor snorts. "This is a detention center, not a hospital for rich foreigners."

Lu is not surprised by the doctor's response. Mental health remains a touchy subject in the People's Republic. Cultural and religious stigmas discourage the diagnosis and treatment of psychological disorders. Many citizens still believe such conditions are the product of an immoral life or bad karma. Meanwhile, the country has a serious lack of qualified mental health practitioners—there are just 20,000 certified psychiatrists and 400,000 therapists serving a population of 1.4 billion.

Lu knows this and doesn't care. "I am Inspector Lu Fei, deputy chief of the Raven Valley Township Public Security Bureau. This man is important to my case. If he dies under your watch, I'll hold you directly responsible."

"Look around you, Inspector. This facility is set up for twenty patients. I'm currently dealing with nearly three times that many. There's just me, one other doctor, and a few orderlies with rudimentary medical skills. I'm here twelve hours a day, seven days a week. So give me a break, will you?"

Lu sees his point. "I didn't realize the situation was that dire. Well . . . as a personal favor, can you do your best for him? I expect him to be released, but it might take another week or so. It would be a great tragedy if he were to die in the interim."

"I'll do my best, but I can't make him eat. He has to want to live."

"Understood."

After the doctor has gone, Lu leans over the bed. "Zhang Zhaoxing, listen to me."

Zhang ignores him.

"I'm trying my best to get you out of here," Lu says, "but if you are dead, what's the point? You must start eating again. Do you hear me,

Zhaoxing? Stay strong a little while longer, and hopefully you'll be able to go home soon."

Zhang's eyes show a faint spark of life. "Home?"

"Yes, home."

Zhang starts to cry.

"All right, don't do that," Lu says. He looks around and doesn't see any facial tissue, so he takes a handkerchief out of his pocket. "Wipe your nose."

Zhang wipes and hands the handkerchief back.

"That's all right, you keep it," Lu says. "Now I need to ask you a couple of questions."

"I didn't do it. I already told you."

"That's not one of the questions. I want to know if your pork processing plant uses formaldehyde?"

"I don't know what that is."

"So you don't have any at your house?"

"I don't know what it is."

"Right. You are familiar with your neighbor—Mrs. Yuan—and her dog?"

Zhang briefly smiles. "Xiao Li."

"That's right."

"He comes to visit me sometimes."

"Xiao Li dug up a lung in your yard."

"A lung? What lung?"

"You don't know anything about it?"

"A lung? In my yard? I don't understand what you're talking about."

Lu is inclined to believe him. He urges Zhang again to resume eating and then summons the guard to escort him back to the parking lot.

On the drive back to Raven Valley, Lu calls Procurator Gao's office. As expected, Gao is in a meeting, but to Lu's surprise, he calls back fifteen minutes later.

Lu lays out his case regarding why Zhang should be released.

"Once an arrest warrant is issued, it's difficult to reverse without incontrovertible proof of the suspect's innocence," Gao says. "You know that, Inspector."

"Zhang didn't do it, and he's going to die in detention if we don't free him soon."

"Then you'd better find me the person who *did* do it."

By the time Lu reaches the *paichusuo,* night has fallen. Lu calls Sergeant Bing into his office for a quick update.

"I spoke to administrators at all three hospitals," Bing says, "and got something of a runaround. I won't bore you with the details, but I think we're going to have to visit each in person. Otherwise, they'll just stall, the lazy bastards."

"Fine, starting tomorrow," Lu says. "Divide and conquer."

"Okay. What else?"

"Nothing turned up on Qin's financial records, right? Some connection to the other two?"

"Nothing obvious."

"I guess that's all for today."

After Sergeant Bing leaves, Lu makes tea and sits alone in his office. He twists and turns the murders in his mind, seeking a solution as to how the pieces fit together.

It's times like these when he believes a good buzz is beneficial as a means to allow his mind free and easy wandering. To think outside the box, come up with creative avenues of inquiry. Through inebriation, insight.

He wonders if the Red Lotus is open and how Yanyan is doing. He considers calling her—but doesn't.

Instead, Lu wanders restlessly through the *paichusuo.* Constable Sun is on duty at the reception desk. He sees that she is reading a Chinese translation of Sherlock Holmes stories. "How is it?" he asks her.

"Good, but not like actual police work."

"I wish every crime had all the clues necessary for solving it neatly laid out."

"How goes the case, if you don't mind me asking?"

"Glacially."

Lu stops into the squad room. He finds Big Wang alone there, filling out paperwork.

"Never ends, eh?" Lu says.

Wang gives Lu a curt nod.

So much for that.

Lu returns to his office and sits at his desk, but after fifteen minutes, he decides he's done for the evening. He puts on his hat and coat and walks up front to say good night to Constable Sun just in time to watch her take a call on the emergency line.

"Reports of a fire on Jianshe Road!" Sun tells him breathlessly. "A big one."

"Alert the fire department, and call Chief Liang and Sergeant Bing," Lu says. "I'll take Constable Wang and drive out there now."

Lu rushes into the squad room and rouses Big Wang from his paperwork. They climb into one of the patrol cars and race out to Jianshe Road.

When they reach the scene, they find a storefront burning brightly, glass from its blown-out window littering the sidewalk, flames licking their way up the façade of the building. A fire crew is already on-site attacking the blaze with water hoses. Lu parks the patrol car sidewise to block the street, tracks down the fire chief, and yells over the noise of the commotion.

"What do we have?"

"You can see for yourself!" the chief yells back. "The building is probably a goner, but we'll try to keep it from spreading."

"Anyone inside?"

"Don't know. Guess we'll find out when the fire's extinguished."

Lu hears a siren approaching. "Any idea how it started?"

"Arson," the chief says.

"How can you be sure?"

"It stinks of gasoline. I think somebody broke through the front door there, drenched the interior, came out here onto the sidewalk, and tossed a match."

Chief Liang and Sergeant Bing arrive in the other patrol car, accompanied by a handful of constables in the riot van. They cordon off the street and then watch as the fire crew struggles to keep the conflagration contained. Lu tells them about the fire chief's suspicion regarding arson. Now that he has been standing here for a bit, he can also smell the strong odor of gasoline.

"Great," Liang says. "First a serial killer, now a firebug."

"Don't they say serial killers like to start fires?" Sergeant Bing says.

"Yes, and kick puppies and piss the bed," Liang says.

Liang is being sarcastic, but he isn't completely off the mark. There is an old theory in law enforcement circles known as the *homicidal triad,* which predicts that children who exhibit some combination of three telltale behaviors—wetting the bed, setting fires, and cruelty to animals—grow up to commit violent serial crimes.

Assuming the person who killed Yang Fenfang is the culprit who lit the storefront on fire is a bit of a stretch, but the scent of gasoline does remind Lu of the stench of formaldehyde. And that conjures up the memory of Yang's disembodied lung and her autopsy at the county hospital.

Formaldehyde. Death. Autopsies.

Funerals.

Lu turns and walks away. He hears Chief Liang ask him where he's going, but he doesn't answer. He pulls out his cell phone and types a query into the internet browser:

Do undertakers use formaldehyde?

It turns out they do, or some variant known as formalin, when embalming the dead.

Lu recalls visiting the Everlasting Peace Funeral Home and asking Zeng about the apparatus that resembled a water heater in the mortuary room:

"What's this?"

"Embalming machine."

"Embalming? You still do that even if you're just going to end up cremating the body?"

"No, but on rare occasions, we do have a family that has the . . . resources . . . to secure a burial plot. In that case, we do embalm."

Lu knows Zeng handled Mother Yang's funeral arrangements, so he was acquainted with Yang Fenfang, at least in a professional capacity.

Lu has no idea where Zeng worked before the Everlasting Peace Funeral Home, but it might well have been in Harbin.

As an undertaker, he has at least a basic understanding of anatomy, and his duties include restoring bodies to a presentable condition. Sewing up their wounds. Dressing them. Applying cosmetics.

What's more, by his own admission, Zeng believes in an afterlife. How did he put it?

"I am quite certain our dead ancestors remain linked to us in some manner, and although they are no longer what we might consider human, they do experience feelings. Joy, sadness. Anger."

Anger.

That would explain the effort to ply the victims with joss money and assert control over their otherworldly powers.

Still, Lu is hesitant. Zeng appears to be a kindhearted and conscientious young man. Could he be capable of such monstrous crimes?

Then Lu remembers something else.

Zeng has just handled the funeral arrangements for Yanyan's father.

Lu calls Yanyan's cell phone. It rings and rings, and then goes to voice mail.

He runs to the patrol car.

Lu stops by the Red Lotus first. It is dark and shuttered. He tries the front door—locked. He runs around to the back entrance. Likewise locked. He peers through a window but can see nothing inside.

He drives to Yanyan's house. He feels a wave of relief at the sight of a light in the upstairs window. He parks and knocks on the front door. Yanyan doesn't answer. Lu has a sudden vision of Yanyan in the bathroom, nude, her makeup just so, her torso stitched up like an old rag doll. He tries the door—it's unlocked. He steps inside and calls out, "Yanyan? It's me. Lu Fei!"

No answer.

He rushes to the bathroom, throws open the door, and flicks on the light.

Empty.

Lu searches the house. He looks in the backyard. Yanyan is gone.

There is a brief moment where he wonders if she's met someone and run off to take solace in his arms.

He quickly dismisses the idea as irrational jealousy. In any case, he has no claim to her. If she is lying in the arms of another man right this moment, that's her prerogative.

Lu goes back into the house and calls Yanyan's cell phone. He hears ringing. He follows the sound into the bedroom, finds her phone on the nightstand. Along with her keys and her money purse.

Now he's absolutely positive she's with another man.

Zeng.

Lu sees several missed calls on his cell phone from Chief Liang and Sergeant Bing. As he drives out of town, with lights and sirens, he calls Liang.

"I don't have time to explain, Chief. I think Undertaker Zeng is our murderer."

"What? Zeng?"

"I'm heading to the funeral home now. Send backup."

"Zeng?"

"I don't have time to lay it all out for you now. Just send backup, please."

There is a brief pause. Lu is afraid Liang is going to either laugh at him or ask for a long-winded explanation. Liang does neither.

"Should we come armed?"

"Yes. But hurry." Lu wants to focus on his driving. "I'm going to hang up now."

He speeds through the center of town, into the suburbs, and then enters a vast stretch of empty, unlit farmland. He tries not to think about how long ago Zeng took Yanyan. What he might be doing to her now.

If she's even still alive.

Eventually, Lu sees a faint blue glow up ahead—lights from the funeral home.

He reaches the front gate—closed at this hour. Lu swings it open and drives through. He pulls to a stop, gets out, and races up the hill to Zeng's residence. He tries the front door. Locked. He pounds on it.

Lu waits, thirty seconds, a minute. Too long. He is about to go around to the back of the house when the door opens and Zeng looks out.

"Inspector?"

Lu rudely pushes past Zeng into the foyer. Zeng's face registers confusion, alarm.

"Where is she?" Lu asks.

"Who?"

"Yanyan."

"Ms. Luo? I have no idea."

Lu marches into the parlor.

Zeng follows. "Is she missing? What's happened to her?"

Lu doesn't reply. He pokes his head into the kitchen—there is a tray of food laid out on the dining table.

"I was just about to take dinner up to my mother," Zeng says. "Inspector, please tell me what's going on."

Lu opens the door leading to the mortuary room. He switches on the light. He sees the gleaming stainless steel table. Old, peeling countertops. He opens the refrigerator unit. It smells of frozen meat inside, but it's empty.

"Inspector?" Zeng says.

Lu runs back out to the foyer and up the stairs. Down to Mrs. Zeng's room. He opens the door.

Mrs. Zeng sits on the couch, watching TV. She's dressed in pajama bottoms and an old green sweater. She gasps and clutches her chest. "Heavens! Inspector Lu? You frightened me, bursting in like that!"

"Forgive me, Mrs. Zeng."

"What are you doing here at this hour?"

"Sorry for disturbing you."

"Is everything all right?"

"Yes, I—are *you* all right, Mrs. Zeng?"

"Why wouldn't I be?"

Zeng stands at the end of the hall by the stairs, quietly watching Lu. Lu suddenly feels embarrassed. Maybe he's way off mark.

"Inspector?" Mrs. Zeng says.

"I'll explain later, Mrs. Zeng," Lu says. "Sorry for intruding."

He shuts the door. He hears Mrs. Zeng calling for him. He ignores her. He walks down the hall.

"Would you mind telling me what's going on?" Zeng says, this time with an undercurrent of irritation.

"I told you. I'm looking for Yanyan."

"Well, she's not here. Look all you want. In the meantime, mind if I bring my mother's dinner up to her?"

Lu thinks about whether or not it's wise to let Zeng out of his sight. "Go ahead."

Zeng turns and goes back downstairs. Lu searches the rest of the second floor. A home office, a bathroom, a second bedroom that he assumes is Zeng's. As he's coming out of the bedroom, he sees Zeng enter his mother's room with a dinner tray. The door shuts, and he hears the muffled sounds of animated conversation. Then, in the distance, the sound of an approaching siren.

Lu waits in the foyer. Chief Liang, Sergeant Bing, and Constables Fatty Wang and Li the Mute run up the path at varying speeds. Lu opens the door. Liang is breathless when he arrives.

"Well?" Liang puffs.

"I don't know," Lu says.

"Don't know what?"

Zeng comes downstairs, carrying the empty dinner tray. "I'm waiting for an explanation. What is all this fuss about?"

Liang looks at Lu. Lu clears his throat. "Can you tell us your whereabouts today and this evening, Mr. Zeng?"

"Am I suspected of having done something?"

"Answer the question."

Zeng tucks the tray under his arm. "Would you gentlemen like to come in for some tea?"

"No," Lu says. "Answer the question."

"I was here. You can ask my mother."

"You have a car?" Lu asks.

"Out back."

"I want to see it. And the grounds, too."

"Whatever you want."

Zeng leads them through the mortuary room and into the backyard. Lu inspects the car. Nothing seems out of place. He touches the hood. Does he detect some lingering warmth there? Hard to tell. With the outside temperature as low as it is, it wouldn't take long for a car engine to cool off.

Zeng puts on a coat and hat. He escorts Lu and the others across the front yard to the crematorium. He unlocks it and shows them the cremation unit, the cremulator, where fragments of unburned bones are pulverized, stacks of storage container for ashes, and so on.

They walk down the path and enter the cemetery. They file in and out of the first columbarium, walk past neat rows of grave markers, up the hill, enter the second columbarium. They climb to the third floor. There is no sign of Yanyan.

They return to the house. Lu sends Zeng inside while he huddles in the yard with Chief Liang and Sergeant Bing.

"Looks like you dragged us out here for nothing," Liang says. "If the media gets wind of the fact that we ditched a major fire for this bullshit, guess whose ass is getting hung out to dry?"

"Let me explain, Chief." Lu tells them his theory.

"That's wild conjecture," Liang says.

"Yes, but—"

Liang holds up a hand. "However, it's not the worst theory I've ever heard."

"We need to see where the services for Tang's father and Qin's mother were held," Sergeant Bing says. "Maybe Zeng worked at those funeral homes. He's only been here in Raven Valley for, what, a little over a year?"

Liang lights a cigarette and puffs away in the darkness. "Sounds about right."

"I can dig into Zeng's work history when we get back to town," Sergeant Bing says. "Should we take Zeng into custody?"

"I think we need more to go on before we do that," Liang says. "For now, we'd best get back to the scene of the fire."

Lu doesn't force the issue of Yanyan's disappearance. He really has no evidence to speak of—just suspicion and intuition—and he fears that Liang and Bing will laugh at him for his silly infatuation.

"I'm going to apologize to Zeng and try to smooth things over," Lu says. "Why don't you head out first?"

"We're not going to leave you here alone with a possible serial killer," Liang says.

"Quite right," Sergeant Bing agrees.

"I'll just be a minute, then," Lu says.

He knocks on the door, and when Zeng answers, he extends what he hopes sounds like a sincere apology.

"I thought we were friends, Inspector," Zeng says.

"I am ashamed of my actions." Lu gives Zeng a bow.

Zeng relents. "You were just doing your job."

"We're going to leave now," Lu says. "If you don't mind, please convey apologies to your mother on my behalf."

"Of course. Good night, Inspector, and don't worry. I'm sure Ms. Luo will turn up soon."

"I'm sure."

Lu walks with Chief Liang and Sergeant Bing down to the parking lot. Fatty Wang and Li the Mute are already in one of the patrol cars with the engine running.

"Why don't you take Wang and Li and return to the scene of the fire?" Liang suggests. "Make sure the other constables aren't making a hash of it?"

"Who's there now?" Lu asks.

"Huang, Chu, and Wang Guangrong."

"I'll be happy to go, but I don't think we need all the constables on-site. Perhaps it's better if you all ride back to the *paichusuo* and Li and Wang sign out for the night. I'm sure the other three and I can handle things."

Liang takes one last drag of his cigarette and tosses it onto the ground. "All right. Radio if you need additional personnel."

The two patrol cars exit the lot and turn onto the road leading to Raven Valley. Lu drives slowly and allows the other car to gain distance. When its taillights fade into the darkness, he switches off his headlights and executes a U-turn.

Zeng stands in the foyer and watches as the patrol cars drive away. He waits for a long while to make sure they don't come back.

He goes into the kitchen and brews himself a cup of tea. He climbs the stairs to the second floor and enters his bedroom and watches the grounds below through his window. He drinks the tea slowly and broods.

Lu knows something. But what? Enough to come looking for Yanyan. But not enough to put Zeng in handcuffs. Not yet.

Best-case scenario, Zeng figures he has a day or two. Worst case, until tomorrow morning.

Zeng sets his cup down and walks down the hall to his mother's room. She's asleep on the couch, the TV on, the remnants of her dinner littering the front of her sweater. He gently lifts her and carries her to bed. She weighs next to nothing. He undresses her carefully. Her body is thin and white, her skin wrinkled and discolored, her breasts like deflated balloons.

Zen smooths a strand of hair from his mother's cheek. He kisses her forehead, her open mouth. Her breath smells of decay. Her body is slowly rotting. The cruel arrow of time. He's doing her a favor.

He unbuckles his belt and loops it around her neck. He climbs on top of her. He wraps a length of belt around each hand. He pulls.

His mother's eyelids spring open. She makes a horrible gurgling sound in her throat. She raises an arm, claws the front of Zeng's shirt. He is surprised she can still manage this, given the drugs in her system.

"It's all right, Mother," Zeng says. "Everything is arranged. Just let go."

She struggles, her face purpling. Zeng pulls tighter. Strangulation takes much longer than one might expect. Zeng knows from experience. He hears a ripping sound as his mother evacuates her bowels.

Zeng keeps the tension on until his arms can no longer bear it. Then he unwinds his hands from the belt and shakes them out. His palms are streaked white.

Zeng rolls off his mother's body. He goes into the bathroom and fills a plastic tub with hot water and collects a supply of towels from the closet. He wipes her down and strips the bed of its soiled sheets. He bundles the sheets together and tosses them into the bathroom. He dresses her in new undergarments and silk pants and a yellow blouse. He combs her hair and retouches her makeup.

He retrieves the belt and buckles it around his waist. He stands at the foot of the bed and bows.

"See you soon, Mother."

Tang Jinglei was the first woman he ever killed, and by then, he was already twenty-five and a college graduate.

It happened like this:

Zeng is newly graduated and working as a junior undertaker in a huge Harbin corporate funeral home when Tang catches his eye. It is her father's funeral, and the first thing he notices is Tang's lack of tears.

Family and friends always cry at a funeral. Even if the tears are contrived, it demonstrates sincerity. But Tang's eyes are as dry as desert hardpan.

Disrespectful, Zeng thinks. *Unfilial.*

Then, as Tang approaches the coffin, incense held high, and bows three times, Zeng notices something else.

A ring on her finger. A ring with a red stone.

Everyone knows red is the color of youth. Celebration. Weddings. Good fortune. Life. The red ring stands out like a peacock feather in a chicken coop.

Weeks pass, but Zeng cannot get the image of the ring out of his mind. It vexes him, like a bit of grit in his shoe, a grain of rice stuck in his teeth. He thinks of Tang often, and when he does, it's with a measure of contempt . . . and desire.

One night, Zeng has a dream. Tang Jinglei, dressed as a bride. Zeng is the groom. When he lifts her veil, he discovers her lips are painted a deep crimson. He kisses them.

Red wedding dress, red lips. Red ring.

He obtains Tang Jinglei's address from the *binyiguan* database. He visits her apartment building. He follows her through the streets on the way to the beauty parlor where she works. She is dressed provocatively. Long legs and large breasts, for a Chinese girl. He cannot deny her attractiveness.

Zeng has never been with a woman. He's never even had a girlfriend. His mother blames this on his choice of profession. There will be no marriage, no grandchildren, no future generations, she complains. But long before he elected to become an undertaker, girls seemed to recoil from him. Perhaps it is because they are frivolous and he is serious. They are rebellious and he is conservative.

Perhaps it is because they sense who he is despite his best efforts to conceal it.

He dreams of Tang again one night after he sees a report on the evening news about a man who has been arrested for murdering two women with mental disabilities and selling their corpses as ghost brides. It's not the first time Zeng has heard of such a case, but this time, it resonates.

Ghost marriage is an old custom, dating back thousands of years.

Tradition holds that the dead, in addition to houses, cars, money, cell phones, and all the rest, require companionship. To die unmarried is to be damned to eternal loneliness.

And an unhappy spirit is a dangerous one. Ancestors possess the power to reach out from beyond the grave to manifest their displeasure through illness or misfortune. Woe is the family that neglects the welfare of its dead.

A ghost marriage provides a solution. If a man and woman die unwed, they can be posthumously married and thereafter enjoy the company of a spouse in the underworld. If a man dies prematurely, a living woman might agree to marry him to join her husband's lineage—thus ensuring she will have descendants to provide for her spirit when *she* dies.

It is much less common for a living man to marry a dead woman, but this is the route Zeng contemplates. By taking Tang as his bride, he will enjoy the pleasures of a young and beautiful wife when he dies, and his mother will gain a dutiful daughter-in-law.

It starts out as a fanciful notion—but quickly spirals into an obsession.

He visits a doctor and complains of insomnia. He is given a prescription of sleeping pills. He begins mixing these pills in with his mother's evening meal, and then, when she is asleep, leaving the apartment and tailing Tang after work, watching where she goes, who she knows, determining her routine.

Zeng pores over true crime accounts in newspapers and books, studying strategies and methodologies. He peruses bookstores for old tomes on feng shui, burial rituals, Daoist rites, esoteric Buddhism.

His research provides some of the answers he is seeking, but not all of them. He decides he needs some expert advice.

The People's Republic is officially atheist, but it allows for, with varying degrees of harassment, the practice of five religions—Daoism, Islam, Buddhism, Catholicism, and Protestantism. All five fared poorly during the Cultural Revolution, and Muslims continue to face serious repression. But Daoism has lately been making something of a comeback. Perhaps it is because many of the foundations of Chinese culture—the concept of yin and yang, feng shui, traditional medicine, fortune-telling—originated from Daoist beliefs.

Zeng arranges to meet a Daoist priest who lives on the outskirts of Harbin. Zeng has chosen him based on the priest's internet advertisements claiming that he is an expert in the black magic rituals of the Shen Xiao sect. When Zeng arrives at the priest's place of business—a tiny shop messily stocked with an array of charms, talismans, coins, pendants, and amulets—he is reassured by the seedy character of the operation. He prefers someone who is not overly scrupulous.

The priest, who stinks of liniment and liquor, collects Zeng's consultation fee up front. "How can I be of service?"

Zeng has come prepared: "I am being haunted."

"Sorry to hear."

"I'm at the end of my rope."

"Tell me about it."

"I was previously engaged to a young lady, but I broke it off with her."

"You're young," the priest says. "Such is your prerogative."

"She committed suicide while wearing a red dress."

The priest sucks air through his teeth. "Oh. I *see*."

Everyone knows committing suicide while wearing a red dress is a surefire way to return from the dead as a vengeful ghost.

"This happened just five days ago," Zeng says. "Each night since, she has haunted my sleep—the first night, I dreamed she was outside my apartment building. The next night, in the lobby. The night after, down the hall from my apartment. Last night, she was outside my bedroom door."

The priest steeples his fingers. "You are in grave danger."

"That's why I'm here."

"I can perform a spell of protection for you and give you some charms that are efficacious for warding off ghosts. At a reasonable price."

"There's more. You see, I work in a funeral home, and it so happens, the young lady's body is there now, awaiting her funeral."

"Hmm . . . that *is* a strange turn of events."

"So . . . I'm wondering if there's anything I can do—with the body, I mean. To put a stop to this."

"That would possibly be . . . illegal?"

"I'm not talking about anything radical. Just . . . a charm I can put on it? Some other remedy? A sure way to stop her before she gets to me."

The priest tells Zeng he will need to consult some texts. He retreats into a back room. Zeng hears the sound of tapping on computer keys. The priest returns ten minutes later and gives Zeng a long soliloquy about the Five Elements and their relationship to the soul and various bodily organs.

"I'm not advising you do this," the priest says, "but if you were to remove the heart, liver, and lungs and keep them, perhaps on an altar where you can provide incense and offerings—you might thereby gain control over the young lady's spirit."

"Rather more extreme than just putting a talisman on the corpse."

"Well, as I said, I'd be happy to perform a spell of protection."

"That's probably the better option."

The priest conducts a long and boring ritual, which costs Zeng several hundred yuan. Then he loads him down with various paper charms and amulets—for which Zeng shells out more money.

Secretly, Zeng is taken with the priest's Five Element solution. It sounds logistically complicated, but also foolproof.

Zeng chooses a blustery Sunday night when Tang is not working. He rides his scooter to her apartment building, wearing a cap and cotton face mask. He buzzes and tells her he is from the Tianfu *binyiguan* and has some residual paperwork she is required to sign. Even though she must be curious at this odd excuse, she is the trusting sort.

Once upstairs, he hits her with a hammer purchased at a hardware store and chokes her until she is unconscious. He drags her into the bathroom and tapes her wrists. He stuffs a cloth into her mouth. She revives and spits out the gag and tries to scream. He stuffs the gag back into her mouth and wraps tape around her head to keep it in place.

Zeng takes off his clothes and neatly folds them on the floor outside the bathroom. He fully intends to consummate this marriage in the here and now, but he's dismayed to find that he is not erect. He has seen many pornographic movies, and this never seems to be an issue. Should he put himself into her mouth? That would require him to remove her gag, and he fears what she might do with her teeth.

Perhaps once she is nude, his body will cooperate. He kneels on the bathroom floor and tugs at Tang's pants. She flails wildly. He captures her ankles and sits on them. He pulls her pants and underwear down.

Zeng is momentarily transfixed by the sight of Tang's sex. He has viewed a woman's private parts before, of course, and not just in movies, but those women were all dead and generally old. This one is young and very much alive.

Zeng fully strips away Tang's pants and underwear. He tosses them through the open door. He pulls her legs apart. Tang rears back and kicks him in the face.

The kick carries enough force to momentarily stun Zeng. Tang kicks him again and squirms on the floor like a bug on a hot sidewalk. Zeng is consumed by fury. He snatches the scalpel he brought as part of his tool kit, pushes her down onto the tile, and cuts her throat.

He watches her bleed out, the gash in her neck respiring like a fish on a sandbank.

When she is dead, Zeng considers having sex with her anyway. Her body is warm and pliable, but there is too much blood. On her neck, her chest, her face. It's repellent. In a fit of pique, he takes the hammer and violates Tang with the handle.

Afterward, he pulls off her shirt and hoses her down. There is a rack outside the bathroom with towels and linens. Zeng dries himself with a towel and puts on his underwear, pants, shirt, socks, shoes. He zips himself into a set of plastic overalls he's taken from the *binyiguan*. Booties go over his shoes. He slips his hands into latex gloves.

Zeng uses the scalpel to cut Tang open. He carves through skin and muscle and uses shears to remove a portion of her ribs and sternum. He excises her heart, lungs, and liver.

This all takes close to an hour.

He encloses Tang's organs in ziplock bags. He sets her rib cage back in place and sews up the cuts he has made. He washes Tang's body again with hot water, black blood swirling down the drain. He pats her dry with a towel.

Zeng changes into a fresh pair of latex gloves and searches Tang's wardrobe for something suitable to dress her in. He finds a lovely silk dress and tugs it over her slack body.

Applying makeup was part of his coursework at the Changsha funeral services program, one he enjoyed. He uses Tang's cosmetics and does his best for her. Powder and rouge, eye shadow, lipstick. He styles her hair.

Now for the ring.

He searches Tang's jewelry box and is alarmed to not find it. He looks through her nightstand, then tosses the remainder of the apartment. On the verge of full-scale panic, he returns to the bathroom and finally finds the ring in a plastic caddy under the sink.

One final detail. Zeng folds a Hell Bank note and places it in Tang's mouth. He has borrowed this idea from the coins the Greeks put on the eyelids of their dead to pay for the voyage across the River Styx.

Zeng packs up his bag, taking the towel he used to dry himself, and puts everything in the apartment back the way he found it. Then, still wearing his latex gloves, he stands in the doorway of the bathroom and bows.

"Tang Jinglei—I promise to take good care of you from now on."

Zeng rides his scooter back to the apartment building where he lives with his mother. He checks to make sure that his mother is still asleep, then carries his bag into his bedroom and places a chair against the door.

Zeng has a cheap wardrobe constructed of particleboard into which he has fashioned a false bottom. He pries it open and removes several sealable plastic containers filled with formaldehyde. The formaldehyde was smuggled out of the *binyiguan* in Zeng's thermos over the course of several weeks. That was easy. The difficult part was finding food bins large enough to hold a human liver and lungs.

Zeng slides the organs into the bins and seals them and then sets the bins and the coral ring inside the wardrobe and replaces the false bottom.

Under his bed is a crude human effigy Zeng has cobbled together out of bamboo, paper, and magazine photographs.

Zeng lights incense. He slips a paper spirit tablet inscribed with Tang's name into the chest of the effigy. He kowtows three times, knocking his forehead on the floor. He mumbles prayers to the Jade Emperor, Buddha, Yan Wang, the ruler of the underworld, Tang Jinglei's ancestors, and finally Tang herself.

Later, he will buy and burn various paper funerary goods, but he doesn't want these lying around the house for his mother to find.

He offers the effigy a taste of glutinous rice and a sip of sweet tea. He swears his everlasting devotion to Tang. Then he carries the effigy down to the courtyard and burns it. The hour is late, and apart from the few curious stares from drunken passersby, no one pays him any mind.

That night, he dreams of Tang Jinglei, naked and beautiful, and when he wakes, he discovers he has climaxed in his sleep.

His marriage to Qin Liying follows much the same pattern.

Again, the occasion of their meeting is a funeral, but this time, he attends as a mourner, not an officiant. The deceased is Qin's mother, who was an acquaintance of his own mother. As a consequence, he has previously crossed paths with Qin on one or two unmemorable occasions.

She is there with her husband, and they make a rather dowdy pair. The husband is bookish and slovenly. Qin Liying is dressed in dark, conservative clothes, as befits the occasion, but the outfit does nothing to flatter her figure, nor does her short, unfashionable hairstyle.

It is the hairstyle that draws his attention to a hint of red in her earlobes.

Zeng contrives to get closer to Qin as the ceremony comes to an end. He sees that she is wearing ruby earrings.

He thinks long and hard about whether or not the earrings are a sign. He is not attracted to Qin, as he was to Tang. But perhaps that is the point. Two brides. One young and pretty. The other mature and dependable.

He follows the same pattern as before. He lingers outside Qin's residence. She lives with her husband, which complicates matters. But Zeng discovers that the husband is out every Thursday until past midnight.

Thursday it is.

This time, Zeng rings the buzzer and claims he is from a courier service, delivering a package. Qin lets him up. He's replaced a hammer with a bone mallet stolen from the *binyiguan,* but otherwise, events transpire very much in the same manner as with Tang, although he strangles Qin to avoid the excessive mess of cutting her throat.

In this instance, Zeng does not even attempt to fulfill his conjugal duties. He will cross that bridge in the next life. In the meantime, the handle of the bone mallet serves as his proxy.

For a time, Zeng is content with his two spiritual wives, although his mother continues to complain incessantly about his lack of earthly marriage prospects. He wishes he could tell her the truth, but she would not understand. He takes to dosing her each night with sleeping pills, just to get an hour of peace before he goes to bed.

The following year, when the undertaker of the Everlasting Peace Funeral Home in Raven Valley Township retires, Zeng applies for his job. Few young professionals in his field wish to leave a bustling metropolis like Harbin for a backwater like Raven Valley, so Zeng lands the position. His mother is not happy with the move, but Zeng will not even consider letting her live alone in Harbin.

He takes his filial responsibilities seriously.

Ensconced in their new home, Zeng and his mother settle into a tense routine. She stays in her room, watching television, and he sees to her needs and silently licks the wounds she inflicts with her razor-sharp tongue. He grinds sleeping pills into powder and adds them to her dinner each night. She has begun to suffer from physical ailments, whether as a result of the pills or some actual neurological issue, Zeng can't be sure, and he is reluctant to take her to a physician. In any case, he is not worried—the worst that can happen is that she will die and will finally recognize how dutiful a son he has proven to be.

Zeng has no intention of taking further brides, but then Yang Hong dies, and Yang Fenfang calls the Everlasting Peace Funeral Home to come collect the body. When Zeng arrives at the county hospital, he sees that she is wearing high-heeled shoes with red soles.

This causes Zeng some consternation. The occasion is not a funeral. Should the red shoes be considered a signal or not?

In the end, perhaps Yang Fenfang's good looks tip the balance. Zeng has lately begun to acknowledge inwardly that his mother might be right. He is destined to remain single on the earthly plane. The feelings of rejection he experienced in Changsha and Harbin have worsened in the more claustrophobic setting of Raven Valley Township. He finds himself all but shunned here.

The actual marriage, he can do without. There are already two brides waiting for him.

But he is tired of slaking his desires with pirated pornography. He wants to experience the real thing.

One week after the funeral of Yang Hong, he knocks on Yang Fenfang's door. Her dog barks and growls when she answers. As if the little beast can smell his intentions. Zeng is carrying a sheaf of papers. He apologizes for the hour. Some final documents to sign and so forth, *bu hao yisi. Sorry to disturb you.*

He's getting quite smooth with practice.

Yang lets him in. He apologizes—he's forgotten to bring a pen. She turns to fetch one, and he hits her with the bone mallet. She falls against the cabinet in the living room. Zeng locks the dog in the bedroom and drags Yang to the bathroom. When she is naked and her wrists taped, he shucks his clothes and pulls and tugs at himself. To no avail. His frustration is boundless. He strangles Yang and violates her with the handle of the bone mallet. Then he searches through her closet for the red shoes.

On the way out, he rearranges the knickknacks in the cabinet and puts the dog outside. He hopes it will freeze to death.

Finally, there is Luo Yanyan.

She is somehow different from the others. For one thing, although he does not know her well, neither is she a complete stranger. And she is one of the few people in Raven Valley who does not habitually treat him like a leper. He feels more of a connection with her than with any of his previous conquests.

He remembers the first time he saw her. A warm summer evening. He'd spent the afternoon running errands in town—shopping for food, picking up his mother's pills from the pharmacy, fueling up his car.

He'd attempted small talk with the checkout girl at the market. She was pretty in a cheap sort of way—dyed hair, heavy eyeliner, earlobes pincushioned with tacky jewelry. He'd made some innocuous comment about the heat. Her response had been a cold, indifferent stare.

She made him feel so small. Inconsequential.

At the gas station, the attendant—a skeletal old man dressed in filthy rags, grease under his ragged fingernails—refused to handle Zeng's money. He made Zeng place it on the counter and then stared at it as if it were a poisonous snake.

Zeng is accustomed to the stares. Whispered comments. The aversion to physical contact. But sometimes the ostracism is too heavy a load to bear. He finds himself desperate for a kind word, a gentle touch. A sign that he has not been completely exiled from the human race.

On this particular evening, Zeng stops into the Red Lotus, lured by the promise of air-conditioning. The need for a drink. The prospect of a normal conversation. Yanyan's welcoming smile is like a cup of cool water to a man who has been wandering in a desert. When she sets his drink down on the table, he immediately notices the cinnabar bracelet. He can see it's nothing special. Worth a hundred or so yuan, if even that much.

But the bracelet reminds him of the coral ring. The ruby earrings. The old lore about Yue Lao, the god of marriage and romance, who uses an invisible string to bind those who are fated at birth to become lovers.

It becomes Zeng's habit to visit the Red Lotus every third or fourth time he comes to town. He notes that Yanyan is never without the cinnabar bracelet. He assumes it has a sentimental value. He overhears customers at a neighboring table gossiping that Yanyan is a widow. He deduces the bracelet was a gift from her dead husband.

Zeng has also seen Inspector Lu at the Red Lotus on two occasions—but the inspector was drunk and took no notice of him. It helps that Zeng is a man who naturally blends into his surroundings. Watching quietly from his corner, he has seen the way the inspector stares at Yanyan. The way many of the men in the bar stare at her.

It is not originally his plan to take Yanyan as his bride. Especially so soon after his marriage to Yang Fenfang. Two women in one small town is too heavy a risk. But then Yanyan's father dies, and she wears the bracelet at the funeral.

What can he do? It is fate. The invisible string of Yue Lao.

The funeral for Yanyan's father is on Tuesday. That night, Zeng watches from his car parked down the street as Lu Fei pays her a visit.

He knows he should delay until the investigation into Yang Fenfang's murder cools off, but he is afraid. Afraid that, despite his best efforts, he might somehow be implicated. Afraid the inspector's obvious intentions toward Yanyan might bear fruit. He has no choice but to act quickly.

On Wednesday, he purchases several five-gallon gas cans and fills them up at a service station. This invites comment by the station attendant. A joke about cremating bodies. Zeng smiles and laughs but offers no explanation.

He knows the police will launch an investigation in the wake of the fire, make inquiries around town, and, if they are competent, will quickly determine that he is a culprit.

Zeng doesn't care. It will be all over by then.

The fire is meant to be a diversion, to draw the inspector away in case he continues to linger around Yanyan. Whether it works or the inspector has different business to attend to, Zeng doesn't know, but when he arrives at Yanyan's house on Thursday evening, she is alone. No sign of a patrol car parked out front.

Zeng knocks on the door. It is some time before Yanyan answers. She is dressed in sweatpants, a sweater, slippers. Her face is creased from lying on her sheets. *Poor girl,* Zeng thinks. *She is barely able to rouse herself from bed.*

He plasters his face with an ingratiating smile. "I'm so sorry to disturb you, Ms. Luo."

"What is it?" Yanyan says, too tired to be polite.

"There is a form I forgot to have you sign. It's required by the government, and the deadline is tomorrow. I wouldn't have bothered you otherwise. Can I please trouble you? It will only take a minute. Again, my apologies."

Yanyan sighs. "Come in."

He steps inside the doorway, and she shuts it. She sniffs the air. "Do you smell gas?"

"I just fueled up my car, and I'm afraid I spilled some on my shoes. Let me take them off." Zeng unties his shoes and places them on a wooden stand by the door. Yanyan turns and says, "Why don't we go into the living room," but then Zeng hits her with a bone mallet, and she goes down. He tapes her wrists together and carries her out to the car. He puts her in the back seat and climbs behind the wheel. He heads out of town.

Yanyan lies still for perhaps five minutes, then she sits up, dazed, confused. She looks out the window. "Where am I?"

"Lie down," Zeng says, his eyes on the road ahead.

"What happened?" Yanyan realizes she is in the back of a car and her wrists are taped together. "Why are my wrists . . . What's going on?" She has a headache, a tinge of nausea, and a wet, sticky feeling on her neck.

Zeng switches on the radio.

Yanyan suddenly understands. She screams. Zeng turns up the volume. Yanyan slams her feet against the door.

"Stop that!" Zeng barks.

Yanyan aims for the window. She's wearing slippers, so her kicks are ineffective, but she tries anyway. The glass rattles.

Zeng abruptly pulls over. He turns down the radio and shows her the bone mallet. "Be still or I'll smash your face!"

"Why are you doing this?"

"I won't hurt you if you just do as you're told."

"Mr. Zeng . . . *Please.*"

"Just be still." He brandishes the mallet. Yanyan shrinks back against the seat.

Zeng resumes driving. He regrets threatening to smash her face. He would never do such an awful thing.

Yanyan tries reasoning with Zeng. Followed by begging. He ignores her. She reverts to panic and flails around in the back seat. Zeng finally pulls over, gets out, and retrieves a rag from the trunk, the one he uses to wipe down his windshield when it fogs. He opens the door and shoves the rag into Yanyan's mouth. He straps her down with seat belts. She bawls through the rag.

Zeng climbs back behind the wheel. He drives as fast as he dares. Soon, he sees familiar lights up ahead. The Everlasting Peace Funeral Home.

Lu parks on the shoulder of the road and switches off the car engine. There is a small flashlight in the glove compartment, which he takes. He opens the trunk and searches for something that can be used as a weapon. He considers the tire iron but decides against it. He walks up the unlit road leading to the *binyiguan* empty-handed.

He skulks his way through the parking lot and into the front yard. He crouches in the shadows and watches the house. He sees lights through the windows, but no sign of movement.

He waits the better part of five minutes. Then it grows too cold to sit still. He moves toward the house. He goes around back and tries the door leading to the mortuary room.

It's unlocked.

He opens it and slips into the darkness inside. He closes the door and stands perfectly still. Listening. He switches on the flashlight. The room is as before. An empty table. Counters. Cupboards. He crosses the room, listens at the door, opens it. Steps through. He switches off the flashlight and puts it into his pocket.

He walks through the kitchen. The parlor. The foyer. He frequently stops and listens. The house is silent.

He walks up the stairs. The floorboards creak. He stands on the landing and pricks his ears. The door to Zeng's room is open. He goes inside. Doesn't spend much time there, just opens some drawers, looks under the bed. He searches the second-floor bathroom, the home office.

The last room is Mrs. Zeng's. The door is shut. He puts his ear against it. He hears the sound of the TV. He sees a light bleeding through the crack at the bottom of the door. He grasps the knob, slowly turns, pushes.

The couch is empty. The TV plays to an audience of no one. Lu catches a foul scent.

He sees Mrs. Zeng on the bed. He doesn't even have to walk over and place his fingers against her carotid to know she's dead. He does so anyway. Confirmed.

He takes his phone out of his pocket and calls Chief Liang. "Come back," Lu says. "Zeng is the one." He hangs up before Liang can begin asking questions. He's sure that Zeng has Yanyan here, somewhere. She might already be dead.

Lu's phone buzzes. Liang calling him back. He ignores the call, takes a picture of Mrs. Zeng, and sends it by text. That should be sufficient explanation for the time being.

Lu goes downstairs and exits the front door of the house. He has searched the property thoroughly not twenty minutes ago.

What has Zeng done with Yanyan?

Yanyan sits in darkness, in the freezing cold. She wonders if this is what it is like to be dead.

She expects she will know the answer to that question very soon.

Earlier, after arriving at the funeral home, Zeng leads her on a forced march into the cemetery. The temperature outside is minus twenty-five Celsius. By the time they reach the columbarium on top of the hill, Yanyan can no longer feel her toes, her fingers. She can't stop shivering.

Not just from the cold.

There is a secret room in the columbarium, above the third floor, accessed by a staircase hidden behind a false wall. It is meant to be used as an unobtrusive storage area and a temporary repository for urns while their appointed niches are prepared or refurbished.

Zeng has converted it into something else altogether.

Zeng takes her into this room and tosses her onto the floor. He turns on a light, sits on her legs, and wraps tape around her ankles.

Yanyan looks fearfully at her surroundings and sees the following: a homemade altar constructed of wood scraps and painted cinnabar red, like her bracelet; a pair of five-gallon gas cans set by the door; a collection of paper funeral goods arrayed against the walls—a miniature house and car, servants, furniture, hell money, paper clothes, and most unnervingly, a life-size bride and groom built out of papier-mâché and bamboo.

Atop the altar is a row of big-bellied glass jars holding chunks of gray matter suspended in liquid. Incense urns. Bowls of fruit. Three wooden spirit tablets.

Yanyan cannot read the names on the tablets, but resting beside one of them is a pair of high-heeled shoes.

Hong Di Xie.

Yanyan begins to cry.

After trussing Yanyan securely, Zeng gets up, walks out, reaches back in to turn off the light, and shuts the door.

Time passes. Thirty or forty minutes. Yanyan struggles to free herself from the tape and fails. She worms across the floor, seeking a chip of wood, a discarded piece of metal, anything she might use as a tool. She brushes up against one of the paper funeral goods and recoils at its touch.

At length, the door opens. Zeng enters and turns on the light. He's carrying a bag. He sets the bag down on the floor and closes the door. He takes off his hat and coat.

"I'm going to take that rag out of your mouth and give you something to drink," Zeng says. "You can scream, but no one will hear you." He removes a water bottle from the bag and shows it to her. He crouches down and pulls the rag from her mouth. "Open up," Zeng says. He tips the bottle to her lips. She drinks and coughs. "Better?" Zeng says.

"Please," Yanyan begs.

"No," Zeng says. "Don't. This is a joyous occasion." He gestures at the paper goods. "I've prepared all this for us."

"No," Yanyan says, shaking her head. "Please, Mr. Zeng."

"Call me *Brother Zeng.* No need to be formal."

"Brother Zeng. Let me go. I won't tell anyone."

"I understand you are afraid. Don't be. You won't be alone. I'm going with you. We shall make the journey together."

Yanyan takes a breath and then screams, "*Help!*"

Zeng is not insulted by her reluctance. It's perfectly normal to fear the unknown.

He walks over to his bag and begins to lay out his equipment. A set of scalpels with green plastic handles and disposable blades. Rib shears.

Needle and thread. He has no need of gloves or protective clothing. There will be no evidence left behind. It will be consumed in the fire. And besides, he'll be dead, so who cares?

He picks up one of the scalpels and removes its protective cover. He walks over to Yanyan. She shrinks away.

Zeng grabs her arm and flips her over onto her stomach. She shrieks, her voice echoing off the walls of the room. Zeng sits on her back, facing her feet, and cuts the tape from her ankles. She kicks wildly—like a child in the throes of a tantrum. Zeng has to toss the scalpel aside to avoid accidentally cutting himself.

He sticks his hand into the waistband of her sweats and tugs them down. Beneath them, Yanyan is wearing cotton panties. Their fabric is as clean and white as freshly poured milk. Zeng pulls off Yanyan's slippers and sweatpants and tosses them aside. She struggles furiously. He considers hitting her with the bone mallet but decides against it. He wants her conscious.

He flips Yanyan onto her back and steps away.

She lies on the floor, wrists beneath her, back arched, her sweater riding up to reveal the flat, pale plane of her stomach. Zeng can see a faint shadow of dark hair beneath the panties.

He grips himself through his pants. He feels a stirring. A growing heat.

"I'm glad it's you, Yanyan," he whispers.

She shrieks and rolls away across the floor.

Zeng closes his eyes and kneads his crotch. When he imagined this moment, he pictured himself on top of her; watching her mouth as it voiced unspeakably dirty things, goaded him on. But Yanyan's caterwauling is proving to be a distraction.

He sighs and walks over to his coat, takes the bone mallet out of his pocket. He turns. Yanyan is now sitting with her back against the wall, by chance, right beside the effigy of the bride.

Zeng looks at the pair of them. Papier-mâché. Flesh and blood.

The bride's face is flat and expressionless. Two blank circles of paint for eyes, an uneven slash of red for a mouth.

In contrast, Yanyan's eyes burn with fury. Her mouth is set with grim determination. Her hands twist and turn behind her back as she struggles against the tape binding her wrists.

Zeng shakes his head. "Quit fighting. Just accept your fate."

"*Qu si!*" Yanyan screams. *Fuck off and die!*

Zeng crosses the room. He grips a fistful of Yanyan's long black hair and raises the mallet.

He feels a hard jolt in his leg. He looks down and sees the green handle of a scalpel sticking out from the side of his knee.

At first, there is no pain. Just a moment of confusion. *Where did that come from?* Then it hits him like a truck. A sharp, searing agony.

Zeng raises the mallet. He will smash her face, after all.

Yanyan shoves Zeng. He falls backward, roaring as his knee flexes. She scuttles away on all fours, reaches the door, wrenches it open. Zeng feels a rush of cold air and hears the slap of Yanyan's bare feet on the stairs.

Lu crosses the front yard and opens the door to the crematorium. It stinks of burned hair and cooked pork. No Zeng. No Yanyan.

He inspects the funeral hall. Dark and deserted. He trots up the path leading to the cemetery grounds. He doesn't use his flashlight. If Zeng is hiding out here somewhere, Lu doesn't want to warn him he's coming.

He arrives at the first columbarium. He searches inside. His labored breath echoes off stone walls. He glances at the niche holding Yang Fenfang's urn. He wonders where Zeng has hidden her heart, liver, and the remaining half of her lung.

And those damn shoes.

Lu climbs the hill, winding his way through tomb markers, miniature stone shrines, dead topiary.

He approaches the second columbarium and listens at the entrance. He hears a distant sound. He steps into the main hall. It's clear. He walks up to the second floor. Likewise clear. The third floor.

He sees a narrow opening in the wall, one that was not there before. Beyond it, darkness. He pokes his head in. There is a set of narrow stairs leading to an open door above. A rectangle of light. The sound of metallic rattling.

Lu wishes he had a firearm, but he couldn't very well have asked to borrow Liang's or Bing's without tipping his hand.

He walks softly up the stairs. Stops at the entrance to the room.

He sees Zeng standing in front of an altar, his back to Lu. He sees the paper funeral goods. Clothes on the floor.

He coughs, and his eyes water. Gasoline fumes.

Zeng turns. "Inspector. Back so soon?"

"Where is she?"

"Who?"

"Don't play games, you sick bastard."

"Don't hover there in the doorway. Come in."

"No, thanks."

Zeng holds out his wrists. "Have you come to arrest me? I won't resist."

"Walk over here."

"I can't." Zeng gestures at the blood splatter trailing from his leg. "I'm injured. I need help."

Lu sees that Zeng's hair is plastered to his head. The floor is wet. The walls are stained with dark splotches. The paper groom and bride droop as if they've been left out in the rain. "Crawl."

"Don't be cruel. If you don't help me, I might bleed out."

"That would be a shame."

"Then it'll be too late."

"Too late for what?"

"To save Luo Yanyan."

Lu resists the urge to run at Zeng, commence breaking bones. "Where is she, Zeng?"

"Come closer," Zeng says, "and I'll whisper in your ear."

Lu clenches his fists, but otherwise remains motionless.

"Tick tock," Zeng says.

Lu decides he will make this quick—grab Zeng by the scruff and drag him outside. He steps over the threshold, moves briskly.

Zeng immediately drops to his knees. He places his hands on the floor. He touches his forehead down between them. "Forgive me!"

"Get up," Lu says.

Zeng lifts his head, then bows again. "I deserve a thousand agonizing deaths!"

"Get up, damn you!"

Zeng kowtows a third time. "Please punish me for my bad deeds!"

Lu curses, steps forward, and grabs Zeng by the collar. Zeng lurches up and wraps his arms in a tight embrace around Lu's waist. Lu tries to peel him off, but Zeng clings like a leech. They dance awkwardly in a circle until Zeng finally lets go and slides across the floor.

"*Ta ma de!*" Lu wipes his hands on this coat. They are slick and oily. His coat is wet.

Zeng gets to his feet, shuffles quickly to the door, and shuts it. He turns and holds out a hand. It's not until Zeng flicks the wheel and a lick of flame appears that Lu realizes he's holding a cigarette lighter.

"*Wo kao!*" Lu says.

"Come, Inspector," Zeng says. "Let's die as friends."

"Move away from the door!" Lu barks.

Zeng's eyes stay focused on Lu as he raises the lighter and touches the flame to his sleeve. The sleeve ignites; fire shoots up his arm, across his chest, down his shirt.

Zeng doesn't make a sound. Not even as the flames lick his chin, curl and blacken his hair. He lurches Frankenstein-style toward Lu.

Lu backpedals.

Zeng drops the lighter; flames shoot across the gasoline-soaked wooden floorboards. The funeral goods, the altar, the walls—everything burns.

Lu hops and skips over patches of fire. He knocks up against the altar. One of the glass jars tips over, falls and shatters on the floor, the pungent stench of formaldehyde briefly mingling with the odor of gasoline. A gray lump of flesh lies among the shards.

A heart. It sizzles and smokes.

Zeng, a human bonfire now, pursues Lu like a heat-seeking missile.

Lu evades Zeng's outstretched hands, leaps to the closed door. Zeng spins and follows, but then collapses. He shrieks. It is a sound straight out of the depths of hell. Lu can't help but look. He sees Zeng on his knees, his clothes melted into his charred flesh, his facial features dripping like wax. The smell of cooked flesh makes Lu gag.

Lu turns back to the door, grasps the door latch. Zeng improbably rises, takes a few final steps, tackles Lu.

Lu feels a sudden rush of heat. He flings Zeng off, only to find his coat and sleeves aflame. He beats at the fabric. The gasoline residue on his hands lights on fire. He frantically waves his arms in the air, slaps his hands against his pants. The fire spreads.

Lu wrestles with his coat, rips it off, kicks it away. He coughs. Smoke blinds him. He can't see the door. He reaches out with hands that are already curled into claws.

His fingertips touch wood. He finds the latch, opens the door. Stumbles down the stairs. His uniform jacket smolders, and he strips that off, too. He reaches the third floor. The second. The first. He staggers out of the columbarium, into the freezing cold, wiping tears from his eyes with the backs of his wrists. He reels down the path leading through the cemetery grounds.

Lu is in agony. The unbearable cold, the scorching heat. Torn between excruciating extremes.

He makes it to the cemetery gates, finally collapses in the front yard outside the house. Frost hisses against his blistered skin.

He lies there for a long while, melting into the earth, racked with pain. Wondering if it will be the fire or the cold that kills him.

Then he hears a voice: "Brother Lu? Merciful Buddha!" Hands touch him, roll him over. Lu screams. "*Tian!*" the voice cries. "Can you hear me?"

Lu opens his smoke-swollen eyes. "Yanyan?"

"Yes."

"Am I dead?" Lu asks.

"No."

"Are you?"

"No!"

"What happened?" Pain muddles his thoughts.

"Stay with me, Brother Lu. I hear a siren coming."

Lu listens. "I hear it, too. Help me sit up."

"You should lie still."

"Up!"

Yanyan doesn't know where to touch Lu without hurting him. She settles for placing a hand under his head and gently levering him into an upright position.

Lu blinks, looks at Yanyan. She is trembling, tears frozen on her cheeks, lips blue. "Did he hurt you?" Lu whispers.

Yanyan hesitates, then shakes her head.

The siren grows louder.

Lu coughs. Something deep in his chest rips loose. "Yanyan?"

"Yes, Brother Lu?"

"Where the hell are your pants?"

EPILOGUE

The world is yours, as well as ours, but in the last analysis, it is yours. You young people, full of vigor and vitality, are in the bloom of life, like the sun at eight or nine in the morning. Our hope is placed on you. The world belongs to you. China's future belongs to you.

—Quotations from Chairman Mao Zedong

Chief Liang stays behind with Fatty Wang and Li the Mute while Sergeant Bing rushes Lu and Yanyan to the Raven Valley Clinic. The physician's assistant there determines Lu's injuries exceed his skill set, so Lu is taken to the county hospital, where he is treated for second- and third-degree burns and smoke inhalation.

Yanyan is treated for a head wound and exposure and then released.

It takes two days to retrieve Zeng's blackened corpse from the remains of the columbarium. CIB claims the body, and it subsequently disappears into thin air. Lu assumes Zeng has been ignominiously dumped into an unmarked grave. Ironic, given his obsession with proper burials and so forth.

Deputy Director Song flies to Raven Valley to tie up loose ends and manages to get himself featured in a flurry of news stories. Chief Liang grouses about this when he visits Lu at the hospital a week after the deadly events at the Everlasting Peace Funeral Home.

"Remember," Lu tells him, "the nail that sticks up . . ."

"Yes, kid, you're right. Better to be obscure and happy than famous and miserable. By the way, I should mention I'm pissed at you for that stunt you pulled at the *binyiguan*. Why didn't you trust me to have your back?"

"I'm sorry. It *was* stupid. But I wasn't sure if . . ." Lu clears his throat and looks up at the ceiling.

"If what? The girl you're in love with had actually been kidnapped by Zeng?"

"Huh? What? I don't know what you're talking about."

"Good thing you're a cop, kid, because you're a terrible liar."

"Don't you have some jaywalking tickets to write up?"

"Nope. I'm the boss around these parts. That means I can pretty much spend all day interrogating you if I want." Liang leans back in his chair and folds his hands behind his head. "Now, about this girl—"

The door pops open, and Song enters. He's carrying a fruit basket he's scrounged up from somewhere. "Inspector! How are you feeling?"

"Deputy Director!" Lu says. "How kind of you to stop by."

Chief Liang abruptly gets to his feet. He gives Song a polite, if unenthusiastic, nod. "Deputy Director."

"Chief," Song says. "Am I interrupting something?"

"No, I was just leaving," Liang says. He reaches down and lightly pats Lu's arm. "Sorry, kid, gotta run. I'm busy as hell."

"I can imagine," Lu says.

Liang says his farewells and departs. Song sets down the fruit basket and takes a seat.

"Well," Song says. "You don't look too bad."

"You, either."

"I'm recovering, thank you. Congrats on cracking the case."

"I couldn't have done it without CIB."

"True." Song takes a pack of Chunghwas out of his pocket.

"Sorry, no smoking in here," Lu says.

"You won't tattle, will you?" Song gets up and cracks a window. He lights his cigarette and takes a drag. "I thought you might like to know that your old pal, Chief of Homicide Xu, filed a report against you. Something about you assaulting him and a couple of other cops."

"That miserable turtle's egg."

"Yes, well, the report made it all the way up to the Ministry of Public Security personnel department, but I know the director there—our wives play mah-jongg together every Sunday afternoon—and naturally, he asked me for my input, seeing as how you and I have been working together of late. I told him you saved my life *and* caught a bona fide serial killer. You're practically a national hero! And I might have let it slip that Xu likes underage prostitutes. Needless to say, the report is going directly into the shredder."

"I appreciate that, Deputy Director. I really do."

Song waves his cigarette. "Think nothing of it." He takes a last puff and tosses the butt out through the crack in the window. "You know, if you play your cards right, there might be a spot for you at CIB one of these days."

"That's very flattering," Lu says, "but . . . I'm pretty content where I am."

Song shrugs. "If want to spend your golden years eating instant ramen, that's your prerogative." He looks at his watch. "Anyway, my work here is done, and I have a plane to catch. I'll see you around, Inspector."

"Safe journey," Lu says.

Song walks to the door, stops, turns around. "Oh, I almost forgot. Dr. Ma sends her regards." He smiles enigmatically, and then he's gone.

Later that afternoon, Yanyan stops by, as she has on an almost daily basis. She always brings Lu something to eat, but today, she has a special treat—a bit of Shaoxing wine in a thermos.

"Better not let the nurses catch you with that," she tells Lu as he sips from a plastic cup.

"Who cares?" Lu says. "I'm getting out of here soon anyway."

"Really?"

"The burns are healing nicely. I'll have some scars, but only on the bits that don't show. Otherwise, I'm in perfect shape."

"Have they checked your liver?"

"*Ha ha*. Speaking of my liver, how's business?"

"The Red Lotus is jam-packed every night. Curiosity seekers wanting to hear all about the Mad Undertaker of Raven Valley."

"Is that what the press is calling him? You could probably sell your life story to a movie production company for a pretty sum. Quit running a bar."

"I like running a bar."

"Good. I like drinking there."

"There," Yanyan says. "Here. Your apartment. A broom closet. Basically, you like drinking anywhere."

"You've got jokes today. Lots of jokes."

Yanyan laughs, and Lu's heart swells. He wants to open his mouth wide and shout his feelings for her at the top of his lungs.

But then Yanyan stops laughing and looks down at the red cinnabar bracelet on her wrist, and her face takes on an expression of profound sadness.

They sit and talk until Lu is finished with the wine, and it's time for Yanyan to go open the Red Lotus. After she's gone, Lu lies alone in his bed, a bit drunk, and thinks of a poem by Li Yu, the last emperor of the Southern Tang dynasty, who met his untimely end by poisoning:

> *How many teardrops*
> *Run down your face and across your cheeks?*
> *Don't speak when troubles make you weep*
> *Or try to play the phoenix flute through your tears*
> *Because then your heart will just break all the more*

ACKNOWLEDGMENTS

A tremendous debt of gratitude to: my editor, Keith Kahla—I hope this is the beginning of a beautiful friendship; my agent, Bob Diforio, for not giving up on me; my writing brothers-in-arms, Chris Alexander and Nicholas Sigman, for their encouragement, notes, suggestions, and, when warranted, brutal honesty; to Chris, additionally, for the priceless cop details and Nick for the blues licks; my old friends Ace St. George and Graham Sanders, gentlemen and scholars, for poetry advice and corrections; my parents, as always, for everything; and Sophie and Sylvie, for reminding me of what's really important in life.

While this is a work of fiction, I have endeavored to provide honest and respectful insights into a rapidly evolving modern Chinese society. In addition to my personal experiences, I've drawn heavily on a variety of sources—literary, academic, and journalistic. I am eternally grateful to the poets and philosophers, the scholars, the reporters, the satirists, the activists, and the social commentators who have provided a window into such a complex place and people.

Any shortcomings, inaccuracies, or mistakes in this manuscript are entirely my own.

"ENGROSSING AND ATMOSPHERIC...AN UNMISSABLE JOURNEY."
—CARA BLACK

WILD PREY

AN
INSPECTOR
LU FEI
MYSTERY

BRIAN KLINGBORG

AUTHOR OF THIEF OF SOULS

Available Spring 2022

PROLOGUE

MYANMAR

The man and the boy wait until dark—then they go in search of something to kill.

They hide their motorbikes in the thick underbrush and enter the forest by foot. The bikes are Frankenstein machines—chimeras cobbled together from Chinese, Thai, and local Burmese parts, whatever keeps their motors running and wheels turning.

The man's gun is no different. It's an ancient AK-47, weathered and battered and held together by scrounged hardware and a silent prayer. Threaded to the muzzle is a jury-rigged sound suppressor the man has cleverly manufactured from an old oil filter.

Aung is the man's name, and he is thirty-five, but looks fifty. He wears a ragged shirt, a traditional Burmese sarong known as a *longyi*, a hat, flip-flops, and carries a canvas bag slung over his shoulder. He smokes a thick cheroot and as he trudges through the brush, clouds of sweet-smelling smoke waft into the verdant canopy overhead.

Aung was once a soldier, fighting in the endless conflicts between the central government and separatist groups. Sometimes he fought on the side of the *Tatmadaw*—the government's armed forces. Sometimes on the side of the separatists. Whoever paid more. He had a family, and they had empty bellies to fill.

Given his past, Aung figures he has accumulated enough bad karma for ten lifetimes and will be reborn as a snake, or perhaps a fish. But he wants to avoid making things worse and coming back as a grub or a cockroach, so more recently, Aung has turned to hunting animals instead of people. In doing so he continues to incur a karmic debt, but that can't be helped. He still has a wife and children, and they still have bellies to fill.

He could, of course, return to the *Tatmadaw* and earn a paycheck killing teenagers and university students who have taken to the streets to protest the latest coup—but there are some levels to which Aung will not stoop for money.

Besides, there is plenty of gold in the forest if you know where to look. Turtles. Marbled cats. Lorises. Hornbills. Pangolins, but those are increasingly rare. For a python, Aung might earn 50,000 kyat. For a moon bear, 500,000 kyat. A leopard will bring in upward of 700,000 kyat. That's more than five times as much as he can earn in a month doing honest work, even if there was honest work to be had—which, in these increasingly desperate times, is severely lacking.

Often, Aung returns home empty-handed or only with enough bushmeat to feed his immediate family. But when he is successful in making a valuable kill, Aung gives money to others in the village who are in need and donates to the nearby monastery. His motives are not entirely altruistic—he hopes his generosity will earn him merit to partially offset his bad karma. Still, he enjoys great status in the village, and if not for him, the local monks would lack a decent television for viewing football matches.

As night blankets the forest, Aung navigates through the brush using an old flashlight with a cracked lens. He stops every so often to shine the light upward, looking for a telltale twin glow that indicates the presence of something worth expending a bullet.

The boy follows along dutifully. His name is Zaw, and he is Aung's nephew. He's just turned thirteen and this is his first time on a hunt. Aung did not want to take him along, but family is family, and after the boy's father begged him incessantly for months, Aung finally gave in.

"Just keep your eyes open and your mouth shut," Aung told Zaw before they left the village. "Don't make a move unless I say so. Don't cough, don't sneeze. Don't even fart loud enough to scare the animals away, or I'll skin you alive and sell your hide in the market."

Zaw knows that Aung's bark is worse than his bite. But he also knows what's at stake here—a great deal of money. More money than Zaw has ever seen in his brief life. So, he has followed his uncle's directive to the letter and not uttered a single sound since they left the road.

They walk for more than an hour before Aung stops to rest. Zaw lowers himself to the ground with a sigh of relief. His shirt is drenched with sweat. The trees are alive with the sound of insects and nocturnal birdcalls.

Aung tosses the remains of his cheroot into the dirt. "Very close now."

Zaw opens his mouth, then shuts it again, unsure if this means he has permission to speak. Finally, curiosity outweighs caution. "Close to what, Uncle?"

Zaw can't see Aung's face in the night, but he can hear the mischief in his voice. "You'll see."

They continue on.

Twenty minutes later, they come to a fence made of chicken wire. Zaw suddenly realizes what his uncle intends.

And that realization terrifies him.

"Hold this," Aung says, handing Zaw the AK-47. Zaw takes the rifle. Aung produces a pair of ancient bolt cutters from his bag and snips at the wire. He makes a hole just big enough for a skinny thirty-five-year-old and an even skinnier thirteen-year-old to slip through. He takes the rifle back before he enters. Zaw follows nervously.

They are greeted by a piercing sound: *wak-wak-wak-wak-wak!*

Zaw nearly jumps out of his flip-flops. Aung shines the flashlight—Zaw sees a peacock boldly confronting them, its eyes glittering. The peacock spreads its tail feathers, displaying a pattern of iridescent eyelike orbs. Aung hisses at it. The peacock turns and trundles away haughtily.

A few meters ahead they come upon a second fence made of thick steel mesh. Zaw knows this one isn't intended to hold peacocks. As they approach, he hears a low rumbling growl that shrinks his testicles deep into the cavity of his belly.

"Uncle!" Zaw starts.

"Shh!" Aung clicks off the flashlight. He pulls Zaw close and breathes in his ear, "Listen carefully. The rifle will make a loud noise, so we will have to move quickly. You hold the light. I'll do the rest. We'll take what we can sell for the most money. Whiskers. Paws. Skin. And most of all, the *lee*."

"Uncle, these animals must belong to the Lady. It's too dangerous!"

"The greater the danger, the bigger the prize."

"If we're caught—"

"Do as I say and we won't be." Aung can feel Zaw's shoulder trembling beneath his palm. "Be strong. Think of what you will buy with your share." He leans the rifle against the mesh and hands Zaw the flashlight. "Hold it up so I can see what I'm doing." He grunts as he cuts through the mesh with his bolt cutters.

Something coughs in the darkness. Zaw points the flashlight into the enclosure. He sees a pair of glowing orbs staring back at him. "Uncle!"

"Give me light!" Aung hisses. He finishes making a hole and returns the bolt cutters to his bag.

Another growl raises the hairs on the back of Zaw's neck. The glowing orbs are nearer now. Zaw starts to shake in fear.

Aung takes a package wrapped in newspaper from his bag. He unfolds it to reveal a hunk of pig liver. He tosses it into the enclosure. Then he sticks the barrel of the rifle through the hole in the fence.

"What if it ignores the meat and attacks?" Zaw whispers, his voice cracking.

"Then you'd better hope the rifle doesn't jam."

The beast slinks from the underbrush. It bares its teeth. Bloodred gums, yellow daggerlike canines.

"Steady," Aung says. He knows he'll only have time for one shot, maybe two. And the sound suppressor will greatly reduce the accuracy of the rifle. He needs his prey to be close. Close enough to smell its rancid breath.

The greater the danger, the bigger the prize.

The tiger roars. Zaw nearly drops the flashlight and runs. But he's never been this far from the village before. He wouldn't even know in which direction to flee. His fate is intertwined with his uncle's. They will either get rich together—or die horribly.

The tiger sniffs at the chunk of liver, blowing motes of dust into the air. Keeping a baleful eye on the two humans, it pads forward, opens its mouth to take the bait.

Aung fires. He fires again.

The tiger mewls, scrabbles in the dirt, then lies still.

"Come on!" Aung says. He slips through the hole in the mesh and yanks Zaw in after him.

"Light!" Aung orders. Zaw sees one of the tiger's eyes is now an empty hole, leaking gore. Blood stains its teeth. Aung draws a knife from a sheath on his belt. He works quickly, severing the tiger's four paws and wrapping them in twists of newspaper. He plucks out a handful of whiskers, valued as good luck charms and a remedy for toothaches. He amputates the penis and proudly shows it to Zaw. "Look at this beauty!" Aung wraps the member in newspaper and slips all the body parts into his bag. "Lift the leg for me."

"We have enough, Uncle," Zaw says. "Let's go. Before someone comes."

"But the skin!"

"Please, Uncle. Please."

Aung considers. The hide will fetch an astronomical sum. But the boy is right. Every moment that passes increases the risk of being caught. He sheaths his knife and picks up the AK-47. "Give me the flashlight."

They slip through the hole in the mesh and make their way out through the bird enclosure, then into the open forest. Zaw breathes more easily with each step. Before long, his fear turns to exultation. He and his uncle will be legends! And the money earned will be enough to feed the extended family for months. To buy a new motorbike. Ten new motorbikes! Zaw battles an urge to giggle deliriously by stuffing his knuckles into his mouth. He nearly bumps into Aung, who has abruptly stopped walking. "Uncle?"

Aung doesn't answer. He sweeps the darkness ahead with his flashlight.

"Uncle?" Zaw whispers.

"Shh!" Aung unslings the AK-47 from his shoulder.

A shrill whistle comes from the rear. Zaw and Aung turn. Aung's flashlight reveals a man standing five yards distant, a rifle raised and point-ing at them. "Drop it!" the man says.

Aung hesitates.

"There are many of us," the man says. "Drop it or we'll shoot."

The darkness is immediately transfixed with multiple beams of light. Men, holding flashlights under the stocks of their rifles, converge on Aung and Zaw from all directions.

Aung knows they will kill him for sure, regardless of whether he chooses to fight. But the boy . . . perhaps they will allow him to go free if he doesn't resist. He sets the AK-47 down and raises his hands. "The boy is only thirteen. Take me but let him go."

One of the men steps forward. "That's for the Lady to decide." He smashes the butt of his rifle into Aung's face.

Dawn finds Zaw and Aung kneeling in the dirt of a narrow path that cuts through the forest. Their hands are bound behind their backs. Dried blood from his ruined nose stains Aung's shirt.

Half a dozen soldiers in green fatigues lounge in the shade of a broad-leaf evergreen tree, smoking cigarettes and talking idly about the things that such men do—the quantity of alcohol they have consumed, the women they've slept with, the men they've killed.

A jeep approaches along the path and pulls to a stop a few meters from Zaw and Aung. The soldiers toss their cigarettes down and stand at attention.

A man hops out of the jeep. He's short and stocky and wears a pair of aviator sunglasses and a holstered .45 automatic at his hip. The soldiers salute him. He returns the salute, scowls disdainfully at Zaw and Aung, and lights a cigarette.

A young woman climbs out of the jeep. She wears a dark blouse and knee-length *longyi*. Her hair is cut boyishly short, and her face is creased with a lattice of tiny scars across the bridge of her nose, her eyebrows, her cheekbones. She unfurls a parasol and holds it up to shield the third pas-senger from the morning sun.

This passenger is an older woman, dressed in loose, flowing clothing, her face obscured by a wide hat and enormous sunglasses, her fingers, wrists, and earlobes sparkling with precious gemstones. Red earth crunches beneath her boots as she approaches Aung and Zaw, the younger woman shadowing her with the parasol. "So," she says, a hand propped on her hip. "You shits killed one of my tigers."

"Mercy," Aung says, his voice hoarse with thirst and fear. "I beg your mercy, Lady."

"I'll show you the same mercy you showed my tiger. How would that suit you?"

"If I'd known it belonged to you—"

"Enough. You will only make things worse by lying."

Aung hangs his head. "I'm sorry, Lady."

"You are now." The woman lights a sizable cheroot and blows smoke from the corner of her mouth. "Since you are fond of tigers, I will introduce you to my favorite. Contrary to their fearsome reputation, tigers are intimidated by humans. They will rarely attack unless they are absolutely starving, or they mistake a person for some other kind of prey. But this one is different. He has killed at least eleven people. We call him 'Throat-Ripper.'" She motions to the soldiers.

The soldiers set their rifles down, march over to Aung and Zaw, and haul them to their feet.

"Please!" Aung shouts. "Please, Lady! Mercy!"

There is a mesh-lined enclosure set half a dozen yards inside the forest. The soldiers drag Aung, kicking and screaming, toward it. Zaw allows himself to be conveyed along limply, unresisting, like an empty sack.

"The boy is only thirteen!" Aung shouts desperately. "It was all my idea! He didn't even know what I was planning to do!"

One of the soldiers unlocks a gate in the fence. He swings it open, and the others toss Aung inside, then Zaw. The first soldier closes and locks the gate.

Aung lurches to his feet and presses his face against mesh. "He's only thirteen!"

The woman watches as the tiger slinks from a tangle of underbrush in the corner of the enclosure. It pads back and forth warily. Aung tries to frighten it off with kicks and shouts. The tiger retreats, and then circles back around a few moments later. Aung curses at it. The tiger snarls.

Zaw remains curled up on his side, face buried in the dirt.

The tiger pounces. It drags Aung down to the ground. It savages his body, tearing skin and cracking bone. After swallowing a few chunks of flesh, its hunger appears satiated. It licks its chops and saunters over to Zaw, sniffs him curiously, and then, seemingly bored, walks off in search of shade.

The woman smokes her cheroot and waits for the tiger to return and kill Zaw, but when it does not, she grows impatient. "Just shoot the boy and deliver both heads to their village in a basket," she orders.

The matter settled, she, the young woman, and the man with the holstered .45 return to the jeep and head back the way they came, leaving a cloud of red dust in their wake.

ONE

Four thousand kilometers to the north, Inspector Lu Fei is hunting a beast of a different stripe.

Hunting is perhaps the wrong word—conjuring, as it does, the image of a man in camouflage, toting a high-powered rifle, pursuing his prey with a single-minded determination, undeterred by bad weather, rough terrain, hunger, thirst.

Lu, on the other hand, is sitting idly on a cement bench in a tiny plaza outside the entrance to an open-air market in Raven Valley, a modestly sized township seventy kilometers from Harbin, the capital city of Heilongjiang Province. The July sun beats mercilessly down upon on his shoulders like droplets of molten lava. His armpits are soaked with sweat. His toes are swimming in his shoes.

He badly—desperately—needs a beer.

On the edge of the plaza is a food cart selling cold sesame noodles and tofu pudding. The vendor is—a tad gratuitously in Lu's opinion—flaunting a cooler filled with Harbin lager. Row after row of emerald-green bottles, beaded with condensation. What joy it would be to place one of those glass angels against his feverish brow. To sip that crisp golden nectar!

But no. Duty calls.

Duty, in this case, being a fugitive named Chen, wanted for peddling black market animal products—meat, bones, teeth, skin, scales, genitals; anything that can be eaten or processed as a medicinal remedy—to various restaurants and apothecaries in the area. Marketing exotic wildlife to gastronomes and men who suffer from erectile dysfunction is an old story in the People's Republic, but in the wake of the coronavirus and intensifying international pressure by conservationists, the government has finally gotten serious about cracking down on the trade.

Chen has thus far managed to keep his center of operations secret, no small feat in a country where two hundred million surveillance cameras monitor its citizenry, but he was recently spotted on CCTV cameras buying groceries at Raven Valley's Ding Hao market.

Hence, the vigil under the blazing sun. The sweaty armpits. The unrequited desire for a beer.

As deputy chief of the township's Public Security Bureau, this kind of grunt work is below Lu's pay grade. However, in the interests of egalitarianism, and because the *paichusuo* only has so many constables to position at strategic spots around the market, Lu volunteered to take an afternoon shift.

Lesson learned. Next time outdoor surveillance is required in July, Lu will pencil himself in for a four-to-midnight shift.

The phone in Lu's pocket vibrates. It's a text message from Chief Liang: *What's the latest?*

Lu pictures Liang, sitting in his office, air-conditioning unit on full blast, smoking a *Zhongnanhai* cigarette. Relaxed and drowsy after having enjoyed a lunch of grilled lamb and Johnnie Walker over ice.

He texts back: *Avocados are on sale, three for the price of two.*

Liang's response: *What's an avocado?*

Lu shakes his head silently and puts the phone back in his pocket. He stands and massages some feeling back into his right buttock.

Where the hell is this turtle's egg?

He needs a spot of shade and something refreshing to drink, so he heads into the market. Three thousand square meters of food stalls, open on all four sides, with a corrugated roof overhead in case of rain, offering a bewildering variety of fresh produce, seafood, cuts of meat, sweets, drinks, snacks, and sundries. Post-epidemic, it's as packed as ever, but live animals are no longer permitted to be sold, much to the dismay of grannies who prefer to watch their dinner get slaughtered, bled out, gutted, skinned, and chopped into bite-sized pieces before their own eyes.

Lu pauses at one of the stalls to admire the brightly colored skewers of candied hawberries, bloodred, cheerfully delicious. If it wasn't for the buzzing gnats, he might be tempted to buy one. He moves along and rummages through a bin of *longyan*—"dragon eye" fruit. Sweet white flesh, a wonderful treat on a summer's day. But he doesn't want to bother with peels and pits. Another two aisles over is a smoothie stand. Perfect. Lu gets in line. There are two women working the stall, one of whom is Constable Sun. She's wearing civilian clothes, plastic gloves, and a dirty apron.

"Watermelon, please," Lu says.

Sun hesitates. She generally addresses Lu as Deputy Chief, but as they are both working undercover, that would be inappropriate. And yet, she doesn't want to be disrespectful. She comes up with a workable compromise. "Sure thing, *shuai ge*."

Lu nearly laughs. This term literally means "handsome brother," and it is a polite, yet casual way to address a stranger. Given his hierarchical relationship with Sun, and the fact that it's been a very long time since anyone called him handsome, Lu can't help but be amused.

When Sun returns with Lu's smoothie, he hands over his money and leans in: "You're supposed to be keeping your eyes peeled, not peeling oranges."

"It's been really busy, and I felt guilty just standing around, so I decided to help out."

"Don't get distracted."

"I won't. Promise."

Lu returns to the plaza, only to find that two middle-aged men, their shirts pulled up to their nipples to expose their ample bellies—a budget version of air-conditioning that some wag has dubbed the "Beijing bikini"—are lounging on his bench.

Fair enough. Lu goes over to lean in the shade against a wall. He sips his smoothie and scans the market.

The small portable two-way radio attached to his belt chirps. Lu pulls it out: "Leader One, go ahead."

"This is Red Two." Red Two is Constable Huang's designation. He's stationed on the west side, opposite Lu's position. "I see him. At least, I think it's him!"

"Red Two, what code?" Lu says.

Huang is good-natured and honest, but as dumb as a petrified tree stump. For his benefit, Lu has kept the radio transmission codes as simple as possible. Code One means the suspect has been sighted, alone, entering the market. Code Two—in the company of others. Code Three—he's in the process of departing the market.

"Code One!" Huang says.

"Copy," Lu says. "What's he wearing?"

"White shirt. Green shorts. Black hat."

"Copy," Lu says again. "All units, observe, but keep your distance. Remember, we want to see where the suspect goes. Over."

Lu watches the market, but the crowds make it impossible to spot Chen. He speaks into the radio: "Leader One to Red Four."

Constable Sun answers. "Red Four, over."

"Do you have a visual?" Lu says.

"Not yet, over."

"Go look. But be careful. Over."

Lu waits. A moment passes and then the radio crackles.

Sun: "He's buying vegetables."

"Copy," Lu says. "Keep watching and keep your distance, over."

Two minutes later, Sun reports: "He's buying a load of fruit . . . now sliced beef . . . some liver . . . *feichang.*" *Feichang* is the large intestine of a pig, a common addition to soups and stir-fries, infamous for its foul odor.

One of the other constables chimes in: "Is he making hot pot? In July?"

"Keep unnecessary chatter off the channel!" Lu hisses.

While he waits for further updates, Lu texts Chief Liang. He receives no reply. *Perhaps he's taking a nice afternoon siesta at his desk.*

Sun is back: "Now he's moving toward the exit. The south exit."

"Red Three, coming your way," Lu says. Red Three is Fatty Wang. "Wait for him to pass by, then follow. Don't lose him!"

"Copy," Wang says.

Lu hustles across the plaza and into the market: "All units, be advised, target is moving south." He spies Constable Sun several aisles over and zigzags between stalls to fall in line behind her. They emerge from the market onto a side street that is chockablock with food carts and sidewalk vendors. Lu doesn't see Chen. "Red Three, do you have eyes on the target, over?"

"He's turned left," Wang says, breathless. "Er, west. No, east! On Renai Road."

"Stay with him."

Lu takes a quick backward glance—constables Huang and "Yuehan" Chu are bringing up the rear. That's everyone on the team accounted for.

Lu and Sun turn left on Renai Road. Lu figures Chen is just taking the long way around as a precaution and will eventually circle back to his point of origin. He sees Fatty Wang weaving through pedestrians up ahead and jogs to catch up, Sun at his heels. Fatty Wang makes a sudden right turn before Lu can reach him.

"Suspect turned right on Xinsheng Road," comes Wang's report. "Suspect entering residential building."

By the time Lu rounds the corner, Chen is already safely inside. He huddles with Sun and Fatty Wang against the side of the building. Wang is sweating heavily, whether from exertion or nerves, it's hard to say. "I wasn't sure if I should follow him in," he says, sheepishly.

Lu glances up—the building is six stories of gray cinder block. He counts windows—ten per floor. That's twenty apartments per floor, or one hundred and twenty apartments altogether. *"Ta ma de."*

"I'm sorry," Wang says. "I thought he'd get suspicious if I just walked in right behind him."

Lu nods tersely. Wang is right, of course. But now what?

Constables Huang and Chu arrive. "Which apartment?" Chu asks.

"We don't know," Wang says.

"Great," Chu grouses. "Are we supposed to knock on every door in the building?"

"Why don't you go around and watch the back entrance," Lu tells him.

"Why me?"

"Because you're big and tough," Lu says.

Chu snorts and stalks off. Constable Sun looks up at the building and runs the same calculations as Lu. "*Are* we going to knock on every door?"

"Should we call for backup?" Constable Huang asks.

"I already alerted the chief." Lu checks his phone. Liang has responded. "He's on the way."

"Oh, good," Fatty Wang says, with obvious relief.

Lu adjusts the revolver stuffed into the back of his pants. He is the only member of the team carrying a gun. Given the paucity of weapons training among police in the People's Republic, he is concerned that issuing firearms to the constables is a recipe for disaster. They are as liable to shoot a bystander, or each other, as hit the suspect.

Chief Liang, Sergeant Bing, and Constable Wang Guangrong arrive ten minutes later. All three are in uniform and both Liang and Bing carry holstered revolvers.

Lu sends Wang Guangrong around back to wait with Constable Chu. He prepares to enter the building but Chief Liang motions for him to wait. Liang is smoking a cigarette and he takes a few last puffs, then tosses it onto the street.

"That was a *Chunghwa*," Liang says, by way of explanation. *Chunghwa* cigarettes are a luxury brand that cost five times as much as the *Zhongnanhais* Liang usually consumes by the truckload. "If I get my ticket punched today, at least I got to enjoy one last good smoke."

"You sure that's sufficient?" Lu says. "We'd be happy to wait while you finish the pack."

"Don't be impertinent," Liang says. "Which apartment is he in?"

"We're not sure," Lu says. "But he's making hot pot. We should be able to smell it."

Chief Liang is incredulous. "That's your plan? To stick your nose under every door until we find him?"

"He bought *feichang*. If you detect the odor of spicy broth and pig shit, you've probably got the right place."

"Unbelievable!"

"If you have a better idea, Chief, I'm all ears."

Liang doesn't.

The front door is locked. Lu randomly chooses an apartment on the first floor—he hopes this isn't where Chen is hiding out—and presses the call button. When the resident answers, Lu says: "Health Department! Buzz us in!"

After a brief pause, there is a click, and the electronic lock disengages. Lu opens the door and enters. The others file in behind him. Constables Sun and Fatty Wang stay downstairs to guard the entrance. Lu, Chief Liang, and Sergeant Bing work their way up, floor by floor.

There are a couple of false alarms—turns out, the building is a potpourri of smells, some pleasant, many not—but they finally converge outside an apartment on the fourth floor that betrays the telltale scent of red-pepper hot pot broth and the stench of *feichang*, overlaid with the cloyingly sweet odor of incense. Lu knocks while Liang and Bing flank the door.

"Health Department!" Lu says. "Temperature check." There is no response, but Lu is not surprised. Loud music blares inside the apartment. Lu could probably operate a jackhammer in the hallway without the occupant hearing. He tries again anyway, shouting this time: "Open up or we'll have to call the Public Security Bureau!"

The volume of music suddenly decreases. Lu hears a click as the door is unlocked from within. He reaches under his shirt for the revolver.

The door opens, just a crack. A man peers out at Lu. It's Chen, all right. Lu recognizes him from CCTV surveillance footage. Chen is shirtless and shiny with sweat.

Lu smiles disarmingly. "Good afternoon, Uncle. We have to come in and take your temperature." In the wake of the virus, this type of intrusion is unwelcome, but not uncommon.

Chen stares at Lu. Dressed in plain clothes, Lu doesn't look like a cop, but he doesn't look like he works for the Health Department, either. "Where's your uniform?" Chen asks.

"Don't give me a hard time, okay, Uncle? I have to check every resident in every single apartment on this entire block. Let me in and I'll be out of your hair in thirty seconds."

"Go ahead," Chen says. "Hold up your thermometer."

"I need to come in."

"No, you don't."

Lu pushes on the door. Chen tries to shut it. There is a struggle. Sergeant Bing adds his bulk and, together, he and Lu pop the door open. Chen sprawls onto the floor. When he sees Bing's uniform, he scrambles into the kitchen and snatches up a cleaver from the counter.

Lu draws his revolver, but then freezes, his mouth open in shock.

The cramped interior of the apartment has been converted to half animal market and half slaughterhouse.

A dozen wire cages placed against the wall hold a mini zoo's worth of animals. Lu sees cats, bamboo rats, birds, snakes, lizards, bats, and a pair of wolf pups. Meanwhile, the remains of some unfortunate creature are spread across the kitchen counter—bits of meat, bone, and a fuzzy pelt. Other animal skins dry on a rack near the window. The kitchen table is covered with bins holding dried animal parts, bones, and teeth. Four large pots boil on the stove, sending up huge clouds of greasy vapor. Lu assumes only one of them holds Chen's lunch.

Now that he's inside, he nearly gags at the combined stench of incense, hot pot broth, boiled meat, animal musk, and feces. He covers his mouth with his free hand and brandishes his revolver. "Easy, Chen. There's nowhere to go. You're outnumbered and we have sidearms. Put the cleaver down. Come quietly."

"*Qu ni de ma!*" Chen snarls. He hurls the cleaver at Lu's face. Lu ducks. The cleaver sails over his head and *thunks* into the wall above the doorway.

Chen turns to the stove and picks up a pot of boiling broth. Lu, who has recently recovered from serious burns sustained on a previous case, shouts, "Watch out!" and dives for cover. Chen flings soup across the room. Sergeant Bing hits the floor but takes a spray across his back. He cries out in pain. Chief Liang is a few paces behind Bing—Bing's body shields him from the worst of it, but the scalding liquid splatters all over his shoes.

The shoes are the nicest footwear Liang has ever owned, a gift he purchased for himself to celebrate his fifty-fifth birthday. Each night after work, he meticulously and lovingly polishes them to a high sheen.

Now he looks down at the precious Ethiopian leather, befouled with hot pot broth and bits of greasy meat. A thick white gelatinous ring of sliced pig's intestine lies directly on his right toe.

Liang roars. He draws his sidearm and aims at Chen. Chen holds the empty soup pot out in front of his body, then realizes it is no match for a bullet and ducks below the kitchen counter.

"Chief, no!" Lu yells.

Too late.

D. J. Klingborg, DVM

BRIAN KLINGBORG has both a BA (University of California, Davis) and an MA (Harvard) in East Asian studies, and has spent years living and working in Asia. He currently works in early childhood educational publishing and lives in New York City. *Thief of Souls* is the first Inspector Lu Fei novel.